P9-AGA-425

Hearts Aglow

STRIKING A MATCH, BOOK 2

HEARTS AGLOW

TRACIE PETERSON

BETHANY HOUSE PUBLISHERS

Minneapolis, Minnesota

Cover design by Jennifer Parker
Cover photography by Kevin White Photography, Minneapolis

Published by Bethany House Publishers
11400 Hampshire Avenue South
Bloomington, Minnesota 55438

Bethany House Publishers is a division of
Baker Publishing Group, Grand Rapids, Michigan.

ISBN 978-1-61129-353-1

Printed in the United States of America

To Jonathan Gerlund and the folks
at the Diboll History Center,
Diboll, Texas,
with gratitude for your help
with this project.

A special thanks to Emily
for reading the story for accuracy.

Books by Tracie Peterson

www.traciepeterson.com

A Slender Thread • *What She Left for Me* • *Where My Heart Belongs*

STRIKING A MATCH
Embers of Love • *Hearts Aglow*

SONG OF ALASKA
Dawn's Prelude • *Morning's Refrain* • *Twilight's Serenade*

ALASKAN QUEST
Summer of the Midnight Sun
Under the Northern Lights • *Whispers of Winter*
Alaskan Quest (3 in 1)

BRIDES OF GALLATIN COUNTY
A Promise to Believe In • *A Love to Last Forever*
A Dream to Call My Own

THE BROADMOOR LEGACY*
A Daughter's Inheritance • *An Unexpected Love*
A Surrendered Heart

BELLS OF LOWELL*
Daughter of the Loom • *A Fragile Design* • *These Tangled Threads*

LIGHTS OF LOWELL*
A Tapestry of Hope • *A Love Woven True* • *The Pattern of Her Heart*

DESERT ROSES
Shadows of the Canyon • *Across the Years* • *Beneath a Harvest Sky*

HEIRS OF MONTANA
Land of My Heart • *The Coming Storm*
To Dream Anew • *The Hope Within*

LADIES OF LIBERTY
A Lady of High Regard • *A Lady of Hidden Intent*
A Lady of Secret Devotion

RIBBONS OF STEEL**
Distant Dreams • *A Hope Beyond* • *A Promise for Tomorrow*

WESTWARD CHRONICLES
A Shelter of Hope • *Hidden in a Whisper* • *A Veiled Reflection*

YUKON QUEST
Treasures of the North • *Ashes and Ice* • *Rivers of Gold*

*with Judith Miller **with Judith Pella

TRACIE PETERSON is the author of over eighty novels, both historical and contemporary. Her avid research resonates in her stories, as seen in her bestselling HEIRS OF MONTANA and ALASKAN QUEST series. Tracie and her family make their home in Montana.

Visit Tracie's Web site at
www.traciepeterson.com.

Visit Tracie's blog at
www.writespassage.blogspot.com.

Chapter 1

Angelina County, Texas
February 1886

"Deborah, wake up! Deborah, hurry!"

At the sound of her mother's frantic voice, Deborah instantly awoke, bolting up from her bed as if the quilt itself were on fire. Her mother crossed the room—a lamp in one hand, Deborah's robe in the other.

"Sissy needs you."

"Sissy? But why? What's wrong?" Deborah pulled on the old dressing gown and tightened the sash.

A moment of silence hung heavily between the two women. "She's . . . been attacked."

Deborah met her mother's worried

expression, illuminated by the lamp she held. The single light gave Euphanel's face an eerie, unnatural glow. "Attacked? By animals?" Deborah felt her heart pick up its pace; dread pulsated through her veins. "What time is it? When did this happen?"

"Two, or thereabouts. Just come with me and you'll see for yourself. She's been wounded, and since you've been studying with Dr. Clayton, I thought you could help."

Deborah nodded and followed her mother. Downstairs she could hear Sissy wailing and the voices of Lizzie and G.W. trying to calm her. What in the world had happened? Deborah saw her brother's form heading out the back door just as she arrived in the kitchen.

Sissy sat on a ladder-backed kitchen chair. Her normally rich brown skin was now a sickly sort of gray, and blood streaked her skin and clothes. Deborah rushed to her side and assessed her wounds. The worst was a deep gash on the side of her head.

"What happened, Sissy?"

The woman rocked back and forth while Deborah carefully examined her. She noted a swollen eye, cut lip, and numerous scratches. But it was the nasty head wound that held Deborah's attention.

Her sister-in-law brought a basin of warm water and several towels. "Best as we've been able to understand, some men came to the house threatening David and George. I sent G.W. for the doctor. They're going to stop by the Jackson cabin first and then come here," Lizzie said.

"They said . . . blacks had to be taught their place . . . that they was . . . the White Hand of God," Sissy choked out the words. "Said they . . . was sent to do . . . God's will."

"The White Hand of God?" Deborah asked, looking to her mother.

"G.W. said it's a group of white men who go about with their faces covered so no one knows who they are. They cause trouble for folks of color, but of late it's gotten more violent."

Deborah shook her head and took up a towel. Dipping it in the water, she began to clean the head wound. "How did they do this to you, Sissy?"

"A big fella done hit me with the butt of his rifle," Sissy said. She looked to Deborah's mother. "You s'pose Mr. Arjan and Mr. Rob will get there in time to he'p my boys?"

"I'm sure they'll do what they can," Mother replied. She looked over Sissy's head to Deborah. "For now, let us tend to your wounds and get you safely in bed."

Deborah nodded and rinsed the bloody towel in the basin. "Mother, please get me the scissors. I need to trim back some of Sissy's hair from the wound site." She looked at the older woman and bent close to her face. "I'll not cut away too much of your covering glory." She gave the woman a sad smile. Sissy had helped Deborah dress her hair many times, always reminding her that Brother Paul in the Bible called a woman's hair her covering—her glory. Sissy didn't so much as try to respond.

Mother handed her the scissors and shook her head. "I just don't know what kind of men would do such a thing."

"Hate-filled ones," Lizzie replied. "Only bitter and hateful people could even consider hurting another human being in such a way."

"Right after the War Between the States, there were such heinous groups—men who would kill Negroes just for the right to say they'd done it," Mother replied. "The government had to step in and make laws to keep such things from happening—not that it was very effective in some areas. I have often prayed that such things would come to an end, but I suppose they never will—at least not in my lifetime."

"It is hard to rid the world of hate," Deborah said, carefully trimming the wooly hair. The wound was deep and splayed out in jagged tears. Sissy had lost a lot of blood; no doubt the woman was in shock. "I think it would be best if we could put Sissy to bed and get her feet up. I can tend her there." Deborah stepped back and seriously considered whether the older woman could even walk.

"No, I don' wanna go. I need to be here for George."

"Sissy, you can't do anything down here that you can't do upstairs in bed. Prayer is the best thing any of us can do." Euphanel gave the woman a tender smile. "Your husband wouldn't want you refusing treatment on his account."

"Mother is right," Deborah replied in a soothing fashion. She gave Sissy's head a gentle stroke as she looked for any wounds she might have missed.

"Let's put her upstairs in my bed," Mother declared. She reached for her friend's left arm while Deborah put the scissors aside and put her arm around Sissy from the right. A moan escaped the injured woman's lips.

"I'm feelin' a mite poorly," Sissy murmured. Her knees seemed to buckle with every step. "They kicked me pretty good."

"Oh, Sissy! What a horrible way to treat such a gentle soul," Mother said, tears running down her cheeks.

"They weren't thinkin' of me as havin' a soul, Miz Euphanel—they said I was no better than an old cur. An old cur . . . what had turned on his master."

She staggered and fell against Deborah, exhausted. She'd walked the entire way from her cabin to the Vandermarks', in the deep of night, injured. The poor woman likely struggled through the woods to reach them, for she would have been too afraid of her attackers to take the easier roadway.

Lizzie led the way with a lighted lamp, while Deborah and Mother mostly carried Sissy up the stairs. Lizzie opened the door to Mother's bedroom and they guided Sissy to the recently vacated bed. Mother left to light another lamp. "It's cold in here," she said with a backward glance. "I'd best stoke up the fire."

"I wish you wouldn't fuss so," Sissy said, looking to Deborah. "It's George and David I's worried 'bout. These old scratches ain't gonna hurt me none."

"Your wounds are more than mere scratches," Deborah told the older woman.

"I'm sure the men will help them," Mother said in confidence. But Deborah could see her mother's concern for the men's safety. Trouble had been brewing for months in their little community, and stories from surrounding counties didn't sound much better. It was hard to imagine where it was all headed.

"The boys are in God's hands," Mother

added, but Sissy never heard. She had mercifully surrendered to unconsciousness.

ꙮ

By the time Arjan and Rob arrived at the Jackson cabin, the attackers were long gone and the house was on fire—clearly too far gone to save. Rob immediately caught sight of the ghostly apparitions hanging from the front oak tree.

“They hanged ’em,” he said, urging his horse forward. He came to where David’s body swayed ever so slightly from a hastily fashioned noose. Flames from the burning cabin gave enough light to show that the man had been badly beaten before being strung up. David’s arms hung at awkward angles, leaving little doubt they’d been broken. Just beyond David was his father. The place where his face once had been was now nothing more than a mass of blood and mangled flesh.

Rob looked away as his stomach tightened. His uncle said nothing, but it was clear he was equally disturbed. There was no shame in being sickened over such a sight. He was glad supper had been some hours before, or he’d certainly have lost it at this scene. Surely only the monsters who’d done this evil could look upon it and not feel the effects.

“Let’s get them down. We can’t save the

house," Arjan said, coming alongside Rob. He handed Rob the reins to his horse and climbed down. "Thankfully the cabin is in the clearing and there isn't any wind. I'm thinkin' it won't catch to the trees."

"I ain't never seen anything like this," Rob admitted.

Uncle Arjan took his horse and tied him to the hitching post in front of the house. Rob dismounted and asked, "Why would a fella want to hurt George and David? They were good people."

"Good people with the wrong color skin," Arjan replied. "At least wrong in the eyes of those that done this."

Rob secured his horse and followed his uncle back to the oak tree. The older man reached for the rope that held George. It had been tied off at the base of the tree—knotted in such a fashion to allow quick release. He gently lowered the former slave to the ground while Rob guided George's body into a position on his back.

"Look, there's some kind of note," Rob declared, reaching for the bloodstained paper. The scrawling was poor, but legible.

"What's it say?"

"Ephesians 6:5."

Arjan nodded. "I heard it used often during the war."

Rob shook his head. "Do you remember what it says?"

" 'Fraid so. 'Servants, be obedient to them that are your masters according to the flesh, with fear and trembling, in singleness of your heart, as unto Christ.' "

The verse chilled Rob to the bone. "It's signed, 'The White Hand of God.' "

They said nothing more, but instead went to where David's body swayed. Working together as they had for George, they lowered David to the ground. Another note had been tacked onto David's bloody shirt.

" 'Let others be warned.' " Rob shook his head and reached out to remove the paper, only to realize that it had been affixed with a nail—a nail driven into David's chest.

He covered his eyes with his hand. "They were good men—good workers, willing to help anyone who needed it. This oughtn't have happened," Rob said.

"It's gonna keep happenin' as long as decent folks let it," Arjan replied.

They heard a wagon approaching and turned to see two men seated on the buckboard. G.W. had finally arrived with Dr. Clayton. Another man approached on horseback. As he drew closer, Rob could see that it was Ralph Nichols, the town constable.

Arjan stepped forward. "They're dead."

Dr. Clayton jumped down from the wagon and went to the bodies as if to confirm the statement. Rob went to where G.W. stopped the wagon. He couldn't contain his sorrow.

His voice broke. "We were too late. Too late." He shook his head. "Just ain't right."

"Who did this? Did you see them?" G.W. questioned.

"They were long gone when we got here. The cabin was burning and the men were . . . were . . . " He fell silent and regained his composure. "They were hangin' from the oak."

G.W. glanced past his brother but said nothing. The constable walked up to the brothers and pointed over his shoulder. "Doc confirmed they're dead."

Anger coursed through Rob at the matter-of-fact statement. He turned and glared at the man. "Of course they're dead. The question is, what are you gonna do about it?"

ဢ

The minutes ticked by ever so slowly, worry and fear taking each moment captive. Though Deborah was relieved to see that the bleeding had stopped, she still worried about the degree of damage done to Sissy's head. The swelling in her face had increased, making her nearly unrecognizable. She'd balanced precariously between wakeful moanings and unconscious peace ever since being placed in the bed.

When they finally heard the wagon pull into the yard, Deborah breathed a sigh of relief. Mother hurried to the door. "That will be G.W. with Dr. Clayton!"

Sissy stirred but didn't open her eyes. "Mebbe my men, too."

"I'll bring them right upstairs." Mother left Deborah with Sissy.

Deborah patted the woman's leathery scratched and scarred hand. She pressed a kiss on her cold fingers, pleading silently with God for good news. The older woman struggled to open her eyes. "Sissy, stay awake. Look at me—it's important you not sleep. We need Dr. Clayton to examine you first."

"I's tryin', Miss Deborah."

Soon she heard the sound of boots in the hallway and Dr. Clayton strode into the room. "How is she?" Christopher asked, meeting Deborah's gaze. He put his bag aside and began to take off his coat.

She raised a brow. "Very weak. I've cleaned the head wound and managed to stop the bleeding, though she's not able to stay conscious. There's fresh water in the basin by the bed."

He nodded and rolled up his sleeves. Next he took up the bag and drew out a brown bottle of carbolic acid. She waited as he washed his hands, then handed him a clean towel. His handsome face contorted in worry.

"Bring me more light."

Deborah did as he instructed. Shining the lamp just right, the wound was quickly revealed. Seeing that Sissy had once again passed out, she asked softly, "What about George and David?"

He said nothing as he studied the wound. Finally he glanced up momentarily, but his look told her everything. Deborah felt a sob catch in her throat and bit her lip to keep from crying out. She fought back tears and forced her mind to focus on the matters at hand. Steadying her voice, she pointed out the obvious.

"She has a swollen eye and . . . and . . . lacerations. She . . . well . . . they hit her with the butt of a rifle."

Christopher nodded and threw her a brief but compassionate look before retrieving several things from his black bag. "You did a good job here. The wound is extensive, but the skull appears intact. A miracle, to be sure."

"Sissy would tell you that she's hardheaded," Mother announced from behind Deborah.

Christopher looked up. "Sometimes that benefits a person, eh?"

Deborah saw her mother nod, but the look on her face revealed that she, too, was overwhelmed with grief. Straightening, Deborah took hold of her mother's hand. "We have to be strong for Sissy."

Her mother nodded. "I know."

Sissy remained unconscious for most of the doctor's ministrations. As Christopher and Deborah worked together to close the gaping wound, Euphanel maintained a hold on her friend's hand.

Deborah couldn't help but think of the years the two women shared. Sissy had once been the property of Deborah's grandparents. Mother, however, had been happy to see the slaves set free and had welcomed Sissy into her own home as a paid worker. But more important—as a friend.

They had gone through so much together. Sissy had been there for the delivery of each of the Vandermark babies. Mother, in turn, had helped Sissy deliver David. They had doctored and cooked, cleaned and gardened together for so long that each woman could very nearly guess the next move of the other. The color of their skin had never been important. Mother always said she'd never had a friend so dear as Sissy.

Moaning softly, Sissy opened her eyes as the doctor moved to exam her ribs. "Doc Clayton?" she asked. She struggled to focus.

"I'm here, Sissy. Rest easy now."

"My men. Where's my George? My David?"

Euphanel interceded. "Now, Sissy, you know we can't be worrying about that just now. You're hurt mighty bad and we have to get you mended first. Arjan and Rob are taking care of George and David."

This seemed to calm the woman. Both eyes were now swelling, making it difficult for her to keep them open. When Christopher touched a particularly tender area on her side, Sissy couldn't help but cry out.

"I would say you have some broken ribs," he told her.

"They was kickin' me and kickin' me. I . . . liked to . . . never got away."

Deborah frowned. "We will see to it that they pay for this, Sissy. It's hate, pure and simple—and it cannot be tolerated. Not by good Christian folk."

But Sissy never heard the words as she slipped back into sleep. Christopher straightened. "I'll keep watch. The next few hours will be critical. We'll pray there's no brain swelling, but it seems likely there will be. We may have to drill a hole through the bone to release the pressure."

"Now then, Dr. Clayton," Mother said with an edge of reprimand to her voice, "you either believe the Good Lord is faithful to answer the prayers of His children or you don't. We'll pray His will and trust that it includes Sissy's healing. I can see death being a more perfect way of meeting that, but I would be sorely distressed to lose my friend." Mother squeezed Sissy's hand one more time, then slowly released it. "I'm going to go start some breakfast. I'll bring you both a plate when it's ready."

"Thank you, Miz Vandermark," Christopher replied. He went to wash the blood from his hands as she exited the room.

Deborah stared down at Sissy's damaged body. The older woman had been a part of their family as long as Deborah had been alive. She had taught Deborah to weave baskets from reeds, to can her first batch of grape jam, to catch catfish in the river. The woman could truly do almost anything. At least she *had* been able to do those things. What would happen if she was unable to function normally?

Tears fell hot on her cheeks, and Deborah couldn't help but speak her thoughts aloud. "She's always been there for me . . . for all of us. I can't imagine losing her." Her voice cracked. "Sissy has always been family. She will always be family."

Christopher crossed the room and took Deborah in his arms as she began to sob. For several minutes, she found it impossible to compose herself. She shook from the intensity of her emotions. She could feel Christopher's hands on her head stroking her haphazardly fashioned hair. The ribbon that tied back the bulk of her tresses easily gave way under the new attention and Deborah's ebony locks fell about her like a veil.

"Life is hard, my dear. Injustice and misery will always be dreaded companions."

She tried to speak, but words would not come. Burying her face against his shirt, Deborah let out all of the fear and frustration she'd been feeling. How would she ever manage to help comfort Mother if Sissy died? She needed to bolster her strength, but Deborah felt as though she had none.

For a long while Christopher held her and let her cry. Deborah had never been so long in another person's arms—especially not a man. There had been times when her father had consoled her after a fall from a horse or the death of a beloved pet, but those times were never so lengthy. Aunt Wilhelmina had held her while she cried after learning about her father's death, and Mother had comforted her several times since. But this was different.

"You have the most beautiful hair," he whispered against her ear. "I've so often wanted to see it down like this—to touch it."

Deborah stilled in his arms. She allowed

her mind to clear and her body to relax in his embrace. It wasn't in keeping with propriety that she should be here in her nightclothes with the man she hoped to one day marry, but at such a time as this, there was surely no condemnation. Or was there? Didn't the Bible speak about weak-willed women? Was this one of those moments?

Her conscience got the better of her, and Deborah straightened and pulled away. Here the worst thing possible had happened—good men had been murdered, Sissy had been beaten—and Deborah was thinking of romance. "I'm sorry. I didn't mean to fall to pieces. Maybe I won't make a good doctor after all."

Christopher shook his head and glanced back to where Sissy remained asleep. "You did all that was required. Do you suppose I never break down after dealing with folks? That's why doctors are better off not tending their own family members. It's often hard to be objective when the broken body before you is that of a loved one."

"It seems you would be most competent in dealing with those folks," Deborah countered. "Because you care more for them than anyone else."

"True, but emotions can blind you, paralyze you. I once saw a doctor back East unable to amputate the mangled arm of his son. The young man had caught it in a thresher, and in order to save his life, the arm had to be completely severed. The father knew it would cost his son's life to do nothing, but he couldn't bring himself to do the job."

"And so *you* did?" Deborah asked.

"Yes. I was but a student, with a great deal to learn. But under the circumstances, I had to do what I could." Christopher looked away. "Sometimes life is like that. The choices we must make are made of necessity—to do nothing would be far worse."

"Some would say otherwise. They would tell you that you acted above your station or your training. In my case, it's a matter of acting in an unladylike manner or interest. Doing nothing is often expected—especially of women."

He looked at her with great consideration. "I suppose you're right. I hadn't thought of it that way. It seems that sometimes doing nothing at all is the lesser of two evils, but it isn't. I have often heard people complain of having no choices, but I believe there is always some sort of opportunity we can take hold of."

"I hope choices are made to put an end to this injustice. I can't believe anyone could be so cruel." Deborah went back to Sissy's side. "Her family . . . George and David . . .

they were both good people. Sissy would have taken in a complete stranger if there was need. She would feed any hungry soul, no matter the color of his skin or whether he was Christian or not."

"Hate grows where fear and misunderstanding thrive," Christopher replied.

Deborah looked at him and nodded. "That's it, isn't it? That's the reason behind this hatred of blacks. Fear—misunderstanding—a lack of knowledge. People are terrified of anything that seems different than what they're familiar with—anyone who threatens their beliefs and way of living."

"And knowing that should be the beginning of understanding." Christopher met her gaze. "But it seldom is."

Chapter 2

Shortly before breakfast, Deborah slipped back upstairs to dress. She donned a simple brown calico gown and pinned her hair back in a serviceable knot, then tied an apron around her waist. She smiled, remembering that in Philadelphia she had never once worn an apron. It wasn't acceptable for women of society. Aprons were worn by servants.

"Well, I'm a servant now," she said aloud. With a quick upward glance she offered a silent prayer that she would be a useful one.

She rejoined Christopher in her mother's room and noted that Sissy's coloring looked a bit better. "Perhaps it's wishful thinking, but she doesn't seem so pale."

He nodded. "There's some improvement.

Her pulse is stronger. Your mother brought some ice for the swelling. It should continue to help."

Deborah took a seat beside the bed. "I'm sorry for the way I acted earlier. Falling apart and all."

Christopher squeezed her shoulder. "Don't be so hard on yourself," he said, his voice soft and warm.

Deborah felt almost lulled to a rest by his smooth, comforting tone, then realized she was letting herself get carried away again. *Why am I being such a ninny?* She stood in an attempt to shake off the emotion of the moment.

"I tried to speak with the constable about what happened. He's out there investigating right now, but he says little can be done. The White Hand of God is comprised of men from several counties. They wear masks and cannot be identified. They claim they are doing God's work—righting a wrong done by the emancipation of slaves. They use the Bible as a basis of support for slavery, declaring that anyone who would go against such a thing is going against God himself."

Christopher shook his head. "It's ignorant."

"But the Bible does approve slavery," she

replied. "The very verse that was left behind on George speaks to that issue."

"I wouldn't exactly say it's an approval of all slavery," Christopher said thoughtfully. "The Bible does speak to the attitudes and issues of slaves and masters, but does that really suggest an approval? I hardly see slavery as God's institution. Doesn't the Bible speak about Jesus coming to set us free? That we are all slaves to sin?"

Deborah considered his words for a moment. "That's really the first sensible thing I've heard yet in regard to slavery."

"Not only that," Christopher continued, "but while the Bible does give guidelines to slaves and owners, it also quite readily speaks out against one man stealing and selling another. It says that such a man should be put to death."

Her eyes widened. "Truly? I never read that verse."

"It's in Exodus. Of course, we also have to remember that slavery was not the same in the Bible as what we saw here in America. On occasion, people in the time of the Bible put themselves into slavery to pay a debt. Some even chose to be slaves, for if they had a master, that person would clothe and feed them and keep them housed. It left the untrained and those without kin or other means of support with hope for a future. Some servitudes were only for a set number of years—rather like some apprenticeships or indenturements here in America."

"I never knew that," Deborah replied. "But given what you've just said, most slavery here in America was wrong."

"Absolutely." He felt Sissy's brow. "Much of the slavery here was born of man-stealing. People were torn from their families and homes, often stolen by enemy tribesmen to be sold. There was corruption at every level and from every society."

Deborah shook her head. "But to commit such heinous crimes and further that corruption . . . " She sighed. "It's beyond anything I can understand."

Sissy stirred and opened her eyes as best she could. "Miss Deborah?"

"I'm here, Sissy. Dr. Clayton is here, too. We've stayed with you—Mama, too."

"My head's 'bout to burst. What happened?"

Deborah looked at Christopher and then back to the older woman. "What do you remember?"

Sissy closed her eyes, and for a moment, Deborah thought maybe she'd fainted again. But the woman's eyes opened once more. "I know there was trouble. Some men comed to the house." She shook her head. "I don't 'member much more. Where's George?"

Deborah bit her lip and looked to Christopher for help. He seemed resigned to the job of telling Sissy the bad news. "I'm sorry, Miz Jackson."

"What are you sayin'?" The woman struggled to rise but had no strength and flattened back against the pillow.

Christopher put his hand on her shoulder. "You have a severe head injury. You must remain still. We can talk about everything when you are feeling better."

She gripped his hand with surprising strength. "No. Tell me now. Tell me everythin'."

Just then Deborah's mother stepped into the room. Rob and Arjan were with her. It was as if the trio had been summoned. Mother crossed quickly to Sissy's side.

"I see you're awake."

"Doc won't tell me 'bout George. You tell me."

"George and David have crossed over Jordan," Mother said softly. "Arjan and Rob tried to save them, but they were too late."

"No. No," Sissy moaned and shook her head ever so slightly. "Ain't true. Not my David. Not my George. Oh, Lord . . . oh, Father, he'p me."

Mother took hold of Sissy's hand and gave

her forearm a gentle rubbing. "I know how terrible it is to lose your man, Sissy. I will stand by you through this pain. You will stay here with us, and I will see to your wounds."

"Can't be so," the woman sobbed. Tears oozed out from her swollen eyes. "Oh, Jesus, say it ain't to be this way."

Deborah turned away; it hurt too much to watch Sissy bear the news. She walked from the room without another word, only to find Zed Perkins waiting at the front door. The sight of the town's founder gave her new determination.

"I heard about the trouble at the Jacksons' last night," he said as Deborah let him into the house.

She nodded. "George and David are dead. They were hanged, and the house burned to the ground. Sissy was badly beaten but managed to run away. She made it here before collapsing."

"I am sorry." Zed took off his hat and bowed his head. "Will she live?"

Deborah shrugged. "God alone knows. She's suffered a tremendous blow to the head."

Zed nodded. "Seems our sorrows continue to grow."

"Sissy just learned the truth about George

and David. Mother and the others are with her. You can imagine the horror of it all."

"Yes." Zed looked beyond Deborah. "Dr. Clayton . . . will she live?"

Deborah turned to find Christopher behind her. She felt a sense of relief at the sight of him.

"It's hard to say, but I have done all I can. I will remain here until I'm certain she is out of danger. If anyone needs me—you can direct them here or have Miz Foster see to them."

Zed gave a slow nod before adding another comment. "Ralph said murder was done."

"Two men were beaten and hanged," Christopher replied. "Mrs. Jackson is fighting for her life, but her husband and son are dead."

Mr. Perkins nodded. "I am sorry to hear that. Is there anything I can do?"

"You could catch the killers," Deborah said matter-of-factly.

Mr. Perkins met her stern expression. "I'd like to do just that. Seems hard to figure who's to blame, though."

"They claim to be part of the White Hand of God." Deborah put her hands on her hips. "Surely someone knows something about this if there are members in the area."

"You don't figure folks will just offer up such information, do you?" Zed Perkins questioned.

"What information?" Rob asked as he and G.W. joined the trio.

"Your sister suggested that we could nose around—ask folks to betray their loved ones and reveal who might have been involved in this mess."

Rob looked at Deborah and nodded. "And why not? Not everyone is going to agree with such actions. Laws were broken—lives were taken."

"But they were . . . " Mr. Perkins fell silent, but Deborah refused to let him off that easily.

"But they were black? Is that what you were going to say?"

Mr. Perkins looked uneasy. "You know how folks think."

"I do," she replied, "but that doesn't make it right. Surely if it is put to the people around here that this isn't a matter of skin color but of murder, then maybe we could catch those responsible."

G.W. seemed less convinced. "I think you would be hard-pressed to get folks around here to talk. There's a code of silence when it comes to such things. Remember a few years back, when all that thieving took place? A lot of folks knew who was responsible, but nobody was talkin'."

"Maybe we should offer a reward," Deborah

suggested. She looked to her brothers. "Perhaps that would loosen tongues."

"Don't be so sure," Christopher said, surprising her. "My guess is that more people will stand in support of last night's activities than against them."

Deborah turned in disbelief. "How can you say such a thing?"

"Because this isn't the first time I've seen such things," he replied, turning away. "I'm going to check on Sissy."

Deborah wanted to question him further, but let him go. Instead, she turned to Mr. Perkins. "Couldn't you hire additional men to help keep order?"

"I've already mentioned that to Ralph. I can put additional men around town, but that won't help the folks who live away from the area, like Sissy's family."

Deborah glanced at G.W. "At least an additional show of force might quell the next act of violence. What if we hired some men to act as guards?"

"Guards for each of our black workers?" G.W. asked. "We can hardly afford that. We don't even have a guard on the campsite—we rely on the workers to keep order and watch over the equipment."

"I cannot accept that nothing can be done. Surely good people will rise up against such matters." At least she prayed it might be so. "I still think we should offer a reward for information revealing who was responsible."

"Let's see what Ralph can find out with his investigation." Mr. Perkins gave Deborah a weak smile. "Seems reasonable that we should let the law take charge to resolve the matter." He tipped his hat. "Please give my best to your mother. I'll be heading back to town now."

The threesome followed the older man outside. G.W. and Rob exchanged a few inaudible words with Zed while Deborah waited on the porch. She hoped they were stressing the need for action. If the good people of the area didn't take a stand, this kind of behavior would continue.

ജ

Euphanel sat beside Sissy long after Dr. Clayton had gone. There was little anyone could do but watch and wait. Only time would reveal whether the injuries would take her friend's life.

Euphanel lifted Sissy's hand and held it tight. It was hard to see the once-vital woman so lifeless. Euphanel pushed down her anger. Why had God allowed such a horrible thing to happen? Why were good, God-fearing folks victims of such evil?

"I'm so sorry, Sissy," she murmured.

"Sorry?" The woman's barely audible voice caused Euphanel to open her eyes.

"I thought you were sleeping. I didn't mean to wake you."

"What you sorry for, Nellie?"

Euphanel smiled at her friend's use of her childhood nickname. "That this happened. That you have to endure such a thing."

"You ain't done nothin' to be sorry about," Sissy said, moving her head slowly from side to side. "Ain't fittin' for you to be sorry."

"You're my dear friend," Euphanel replied. "We've been through so many things together. When Rutger was killed, you never left my side. I wouldn't have made it through those awful days without you. I want to help you—like you helped me."

Sissy closed her eyes. "Ain't sure I wanna live in such a world."

Euphanel leaned closer. "Oh, my dear friend. I can't bear to think of my life without you in it. I know your pain is great, but God has kept you here. Surely there's a reason. We have to trust that He will show us that purpose."

"Ain't gonna be easy. I . . . " Sissy's voice faded into silence.

Clutching Sissy's hand to her breast,

Euphanel began to weep anew. It wouldn't be easy. Loss never was.

Someone touched her shoulders and Euphanel looked up. Arjan gave her a sympathetic smile. "You need to get some rest."

"I can't leave her, even to just go next door to Deborah's room. I don't want her to be alone."

Arjan nodded. "I kind of figured you'd say something like that. I've brought one of the camp cots. I'll set it up on the other side of the bed."

Euphanel tucked Sissy's hand under the covers and got to her feet. "Thank you. You were good to think of such a thing."

"No problem." He paused, as if trying to figure something else to say, then nodded and walked from the room.

Euphanel glanced back at Sissy and felt a helplessness she'd not known since the logging accident had taken Rutger. God seemed so far away—so silent.

Chapter 3

Sissy remained too ill to attend the funeral services for her husband and son. Dr. Clayton was encouraged by her strength and signs of recovery, but he forbade her to move from bed. Mother decided to remain at the house and care for Sissy, while the rest of the family attended the burial.

Deborah looked at the plain wooden coffins. They were simple and sturdy—much like the men who filled them. These had been good men—dependable, trustworthy—and now they were gone.

She felt great comfort that Pastor Artemus Shattuck had offered to lead the services. The black church was currently without a minister and relied on the elders to take charge of the services. It was a bold statement to the community that a white minister would think this a serious and important enough matter to officiate.

The black community stood to one side, while the whites were on the other. The two groups seemed in opposition to each other—just as the world would have it be. There were looks of accusation and anger on the faces of some of the blacks. Others bore tear-stained expressions.

Deborah had learned that some of the former slave women had dressed the bodies, and the men had put together coffins with wood supplied by Mr. Perkins. Thankfully, the coffins had been closed to hide the hideous damage done to the men. Deborah had no desire to remember George and David as the nightmarish image she'd overheard her brothers describe. Instead, she forced herself to remember the men as they had been in life.

A group of women began to sing. Deborah recognized most as former slaves who had been good friends to the Jackson family. The women had strong voices and the words of the song rang out, demanding her attention.

> *"Steal away, steal away, steal away to*
> *Jesus!*
> *Steal away, steal away home, I hain't got*
> *long to stay here."*

A chorus of "amens" and "glory be's" rippled through the congregated blacks. But it was only when the verse was sung in the powerful, mournful wail of the women that the crowd was really stirred up.

"My Lord, He calls me, He calls me by the thunder;
The trumpet sounds within my soul, I hain't got long to stay here."

Deborah felt deeply moved by the emotion of the song and its singers. These were people who had seen so much oppression, had endured great pain and misery. Their freedom had come at a high price—a price that left many bitter and angry. George and David had died because of such animosity.

The haunting melody and lyrics reached deep into Deborah's heart. She closed her eyes as voices from the congregation joined the singers. The music bound them together in a way that nothing else could.

"Green trees are bendin', Poor sinners stand a-tremblin';
The trumpet sounds within my soul, I ain't got long to stay here.
Steal away, steal away, steal away to Jesus!
Steal away, steal away home, I hain't got long to stay here."

The voices faded and muffled sobs took their place. Deborah opened her eyes and swayed ever so slightly. The moment—the deep spiritual intensity—overwhelmed her. Uncle Arjan put his arm around her shoulders as if to steady her. She glanced up to meet his concerned face, but said nothing.

"There is great sorrow in our community," Pastor Shattuck began. "Great sorrow in the death of good men—good men who were undeserving of such punishment."

Deborah looked around at the handful of whites in attendance. She was rather surprised to see Margaret Foster and some of her family. The Fosters had never been overly friendly with the former slave population, and in fact had spoken out against the blacks being given jobs that should go to whites first. Perhaps it signaled a change of heart. Deborah hoped so.

Christopher was there, along with her brothers, Uncle Arjan, and some of the men who had worked alongside George and David at the logging camp. Other than that, only Mr. and Mrs. Perkins represented the town officially. Constable Nichols was nowhere to be seen, and neither were the Huebners or Greeleys. Deborah frowned and lowered her head.

God, are you here?

The prayerful question nearly brought her to tears. How could God allow such pain? Surely He loved His dark-skinned children as much as He loved those with fair complexions.

You do love them, as you love me—don't you?

She glanced skyward as if expecting a booming reply, but God was silent.

"So often we are faced with adversity and conflict. We are left to wonder where God is when such things happen to the innocent."

Deborah started and raised her face to stare hard at Pastor Shattuck. It was as if he had read her mind. Could he possibly understand her feelings of confusion?

"Evil reaches out to quell the happiness of good people—God-fearing people who would do acts of generosity in the name of Jesus. Where is God when that evil overcomes as it did with George and David Jackson?"

The gathering was strangely quiet. It seemed as though everyone was silent with anticipation, awaiting the pastor's words.

"In the Psalms, David cries out to the Lord." He lifted up his well-worn Bible. "The thirteenth psalm speaks thus, 'How long wilt thou forget me, O Lord? for ever? how long wilt thou hide thy face from me? How long shall I take counsel in my soul, having sorrow in my heart daily? How long shall mine enemy be exalted over me? Consider and hear me, O Lord my God: lighten mine eyes, lest I sleep the sleep of death; Lest mine enemy say, I have prevailed against him; and those that trouble me rejoice when I am moved.' "

Pastor Shattuck paused to look across the sea of faces. " 'But I have trusted in thy mercy; my heart shall rejoice in thy salvation. I will sing unto the Lord, because he hath dealt bountifully with me.' " He lowered the Bible and closed it gently.

"We have trusted in God's mercy. We rejoice in His salvation. He has dealt us great bounty—great love. We do not face this sorrow alone. We do not put our eyes on the enemy at the door, but instead keep our vision fixed on God alone. This world will pass away and with it will go the sadness and injustices that Satan has imposed. God will not be mocked—nor will He be ignored. David and George will have justice—the Lord will avenge their blood and comfort our hearts. We have only to trust in His mercy. Let us pray."

Deborah bowed her head but heard very little of the pastor's prayer. Instead, God's presence surrounded her like a comforting breeze on a stifling day, like a glass of iced lemonade to quench her thirst. Uncle Arjan's embrace supported her, but it was

God's powerful presence that engulfed and strengthened her spirit.

You're all we truly have—the only constant in a troubled world. Yet the pain she felt seemed to smother that small flicker of peace. *Why did you let this happen, God? Why?*

Deborah took a deep breath and wrestled with her thoughts. God had not left them as orphans—He was here—He would always offer his comfort and strength. There was still a world of evil with which to contend, but they would not face it alone. She knew this somewhere deep in her soul . . . so why did it feel so hopeless?

ꕤ

After the service concluded, Deborah longed to get away. She had thought to start walking home but found that her brothers and even Christopher objected to the idea.

"You can't walk home alone," Christopher stated firmly. "After what happened to George and David, it would be too great a risk."

"Why in the world would you say that, Doc?" one of the Shaw brothers questioned.

G.W. answered before Christopher could speak. "Klem, it's not just the people of color who have to worry about the deeds of evil men."

"Seems to me, this was just a matter of dealin' with some old slaves."

Deborah's expression changed from peaceful to angry. "They weren't slaves anymore. They were free—just as we are."

"Besides," Christopher said, eyeing the man, "Miss Vandermark has dark hair and eyes. Her skin is tanned from the sun. Someone from the White Hand of God might mistakenly think her to be of mixed-blood or Mexican descent."

Christopher's words took Deborah by surprise. She'd never once considered that someone might think of her as anything but white.

"That's downright foolish," Klem's brother Kale declared. "Ever'one knows Miss Deborah. Ain't nobody gonna think her a Negro or Mexican."

"People make mistakes," G.W. said, drawing Lizzie close to his side. "Not every white woman sports blond hair and pale skin as my wife does. Seems to me, Doc makes a good point. In the heat of a moment—in the fading light of the forest—someone just might make such a mistake."

By this time, the few other white men had gathered around them. There was a general cry of disapproval at G.W.'s statement.

"Ain't no one gonna lay a hand on a white

woman," Matthew Foster declared. "That ain't the way things are done around here."

"I wouldn't think that a woman, black or white, would have to fear for her life in these parts," Rob threw in, "but we got proof that ain't the case."

Several of the men muttered curses under their breath. Their attitude took Deborah off guard. "I can't believe that you could be so callous. A woman lies near death in my home. A loving woman—a dear friend to my mother." Deborah pulled away from her uncle's side.

"I thought the men of this community to be honorable—to look beyond a person's skin color—but I see I was wrong. Perhaps some of you even participated with the White Hand of God to kill George and David." Her statement took everyone by surprise and seemed to momentarily stifle their ability to reply.

G.W. looked at her and then to Lizzie. Deborah read fear in her brother's expression. Did he also think there were people here capable of doing such heinous acts?

"I believe it does little good to speak in anger," Pastor Shattuck said, coming to intervene. "We are all disturbed and wounded by what has happened. The attack on one family from our community is an attack on all. No matter the color or gender." He offered Deborah a smile, then turned back to the men who seemed none too happy with her comments.

"Let us retire to our homes and pray for wisdom. Our town has suffered enough. It's time for forgiveness and peace."

For a moment, no one uttered a sound or moved to go. Then the crowd dispersed in an eerie solemnity.

Christopher watched the Vandermarks depart the funeral service and felt an immediate sense of loss. He longed to follow them back to their house, knowing he'd be welcome to do so, but he fought the urge. He would call on them later and check on Sissy. Otherwise, it seemed only right to allow them some privacy in their mourning.

He crossed the railroad tracks and walked slowly back to the white side of town. There was an unusual stillness in the air; Mr. Perkins had actually closed down the sawmill for the afternoon funeral, a rare occurrence. A dozen or so men were gathered on the porch of the still-open commissary, while a great many others milled around the hardware store.

At home again, Christopher poured a cup of lukewarm coffee and served himself the last slice of pecan cake. Mrs. Perkins had sent the cake as a gift, by way of her two silly daughters. It was clear that the girls thought him a good catch, and it didn't seem to discourage them that he was paying court to Deborah. Of course, he hadn't exactly gone out of his way to make his intentions clear. He supposed they might, in fact, question the validity of the courtship since Christopher had done nothing overtly public to inform the community. Perhaps the girls thought him only casually interested in Deborah. Maybe they thought if they were coy and flirtatious, he might well change his mind and court one of them instead.

He settled down to the table and picked rather absentmindedly at the cake. He supposed he had no one but himself to blame. Even though he and Deborah had agreed to court with an intent to one day marry, they had agreed to keep their courtship rather casual. The townsfolk were used to seeing them together, but then, too, they knew of Deborah's interest in medicine.

Not that this interest had been well received. It was one thing for a middle-aged healer to be a woman, but for a young, vibrant, unmarried lady to take up doctoring met with some discomfort in the little town of Perkinsville.

Christopher had said nothing to Deborah about the comments, but he was somewhat concerned. He'd had more than one family tell him that they did not wish to have Deborah involved in their medical needs. As the only doctor in the town, he felt he had to honor their desires, but it grieved him. Deborah was a quick learner and her passion for science knew no bounds. He hated to stifle her interests.

"Maybe I was wrong to come here," he said, pushing the cake aside. He gave a heavy sigh and abandoned the coffee, as well. Getting to his feet, he decided the best thing he could do was head on out to the Vandermarks' after all. He wouldn't have any peace of mind until he did. Whether that stemmed from his concern for Sissy or his desire to be close to Deborah, he couldn't be exactly sure.

He thought of his family as he crossed the road to the livery. He hadn't seen his mother in some time. Her last letter had been full of worries and woes. She wrote of his younger brothers, fearing friends were leading them astray. His father remained distant and withdrawn. He'd never been the same after the accident that had left him paralyzed.

Despite his turmoil he forced a smile and motioned to a young boy who worked at the stable. "I need my horse. I have to make rounds." He tossed a coin to the child.

"Yes, sir." The boy easily caught the money and smiled. "I'll be real quick."

Christopher waited patiently while the boy

went to the back of the livery to collect the doctor's mount. The heady smell of horses, manure, and straw mingled in the air, which today was strangely lacking the normal smoke and dust from the mills. The air wasn't of good quality on most days, and Christopher was glad to see that prevailing winds took most of the fumes away from the town.

"Here ya go, Doc," the boy announced, leading a sturdy sorrel gelding. "He's all ready for a run."

Christopher thought the boy reminded him a bit of his youngest brother, Thomas. "How old are you, Robby?"

"Thirteen. Be fourteen next month."

Smiling, Christopher nodded. "I have a brother just your age."

"Truly? Does he have a job?" The boy pushed back his shoulders and eyed Christopher quite seriously. "Pa says by my age a boy needs to be workin'."

"I haven't seen him in a while," Christopher replied, "but last I knew he was in school."

Robby spit and shook his head. "Pa says there ain't nothin' I can learn in books what will beat life itself."

Christopher knew that was the attitude of half the men in the county. There was no use demeaning the boy's father and suggesting he was wrong. "Say, it's been kind of chilly out—where are your shoes?"

The boy laughed. "Don't wear shoes, lessen I have to. Ain't no shoes I like."

"Well, you don't want to catch cold or worse."

"Ma says I'm too ornery. My sisters both had scarlet fever and measles, but I ain't been a bit sick."

Christopher climbed atop the back of the horse and took up the reins. Without waiting for the boy to reply, Christopher urged the horse out of the livery and onto the road. The boy's zest for life again reminded him of his siblings.

Memories of his family washed over him and the image of his petite mother, standing over a steaming pot of dirty clothes, immediately came to mind. She was aged beyond her years and would no doubt die young, as most overworked women did. The very thought caused him great sorrow. Never once in her life had she had it easy. Never once had she known a carefree day of rest. Even on the Lord's Day, there were children to care for and meals to put on the table. He knew the money he sent home helped, but it wasn't enough. Nothing would please him more than to hire a nurse or housekeeper to help his mother with the workload, but there wasn't any extra cash for such things. Not that his mother would ever allow for the frivolity.

He smiled and pressed on toward the Vandermarks'. Deborah reminded him of his mother. In fact, she reminded him of her a great deal. They were both hardworking and more than a little ambitious, and both had a special place in his heart.

Chapter 4

Pastor Shattuck called a community meeting at the church to discuss the Texas Independence Day celebration. The yearly event in March was anticipated very nearly as much as Christmas. Just thinking about the roasted meats and wonderful music put a tremor of excitement in Deborah's stomach. She hadn't been to an Independence Day celebration in some years and only now realized just how much she missed it.

"Before we finalize our plans for the Independence Day festivities," the pastor began, "I feel it's important we speak on the tragedy that has befallen our county."

There were murmurings and a barely audible curse. Stunned, Deborah turned to throw a disapproving glare in the direction of whoever might have said such a thing in God's house. Her mother did likewise, along with several of the other older women.

Artemus Shattuck let the matter go, however. He tucked his thumbs into his waistcoat pockets and rocked back on his heels. "I have a grave concern for this community. It seems to me that folks have closed their eyes to bad behavior in hopes that it will simply depart. I have rarely seen such a thing happen. It is important that we take a stand—together as a town—against the prejudices and injustices we've seen of late."

"I thought we were figuring out where to set up the judging booths for the quilts," an older woman declared.

"Yeah, I figured you were going to let us know what time the fiddlers and pickers were to commence playin'," a man in front of Deborah called out.

"All of that in due time. I hoped while I had your attention, it would be fitting to remind you of our recent tragedies so that we might prevent such things from happening again. After all, we wouldn't want such things to interfere with our preparations. I'm sure everyone here would agree that this is a community celebration. We wouldn't want anyone to feel left out or slighted. Given the problems we've seen of late, I fear that some of our black brothers and sisters might feel intimidated or fearful of attending."

"Long as they stay in their place, it won't be a problem." This came from Zed Perkins's eldest son, Todd. "We've always had a place where they could celebrate, as well."

"I had rather thought it might do us all well to include the black community in our own celebration. Unite the two parts of our town and get to know one another better," Pastor Shattuck declared.

A hush fell over the room. Folks grew uneasy. It was evident that they felt the pastor had lost his mind.

"We are all of different ancestry here. I'm of German and English descent. The Vandermarks are Dutch. The Huebners are German. The Fosters have Scottish and English ancestors. Doc Clayton sports an English name, and the founder of our town told me not long ago that his family has roots not only in England, as the name Perkins suggests, but also he shares a connection with the French. We have our differences, but we all have one thing in common. We are Texans. Before we are Americans or anything else—we proudly bear the name Texan."

Deborah saw several people nod in approval. At least that much was well received. She met

Christopher's gaze and smiled. She'd never thought of his name being English. The fact was, there was still a great deal she didn't know about the man. He spoke very little of his family except to say they needed his help. She would have to make a special point to get him to tell her more.

"Folks, what I'm trying to say here is that we're in a sorry state of existence when we focus on a man's skin color rather than his actions. The Good Book says God doesn't even see the outward appearance of man, but looks at his heart. Oughten we do the same?"

Pastor Shattuck came down from the pulpit and stood directly in front of the congregated people. "We want to celebrate our independence, but I don't see how we can do that by trying to restrict others. I'd like to suggest we start a new tradition. Let's have a black and white baseball game on our Texas Independence Day."

Deborah heard some grumbling, but then Zed Perkins stood and raised his hands. "Look, I think we need to get back to planning our festivities. I'm not opposed to a black and white baseball game. Seems likely they won't be very good, considering they don't get to play much, but I don't object." He looked to the gathered crowd.

Deborah thought his gaze lingered a little longer on some of the men. Perhaps he knew their hearts and wondered just as she did whether or not they had been involved. It was most disturbing to imagine that killers could lurk in their own little town. What if her friends and neighbors were amongst those who had killed George and David?

"Most of you know that I have my own issues with Injuns and Mexicans. Ain't necessarily somethin' I'm proud of, but it's just the way things are. I hire blacks, same as whites. I pay a fair salary for a fair day's work. I don't want to see any more killings in our town. I'd just as soon the White Hand of God not show itself around these parts anymore." He turned back to Pastor Shattuck. "But you ain't gonna change the way folks think overnight."

Pastor Shattuck smiled. "I didn't figure I could, but I do know that God is able to change the heart of any man or woman, and that is my prayer."

The discussion moved quickly after that to the original reason they'd gathered. When the plans were finally agreed upon an hour later, Deborah was more than ready to stand and stretch her legs. She looked at her mother and offered her a hand up.

"Seems like these issues should get a little easier to discuss each time they're brought up," Mother said, sounding bitter. "But they don't. Folks just seem unwilling to forget about the past and about our differences. Maybe it will never change. Maybe the color of a person's skin will always be the only thing people can see."

Deborah pondered her mother's words as Christopher came to join them. He appeared to have heard the latter part of the conversation.

"Introducing change is never easy," he said, nodding his head toward the two women. He then turned to Deborah's mother. "If it won't delay your departure, I have some medical journals your daughter should read."

"How soon do you plan to head home, Mother?" Deborah asked.

"Not for a little while. I have shopping to do, and G.W. and Rob were headed to the hardware store to pick up new saw blades. You go along. We'll come fetch you at the doctor's office when we're fixin' to go."

Turning to Christopher, Deborah smiled. "It seems I can manage a little time."

He nodded but didn't offer her his arm. Deborah walked easily at Christopher's side, keeping pace with his long strides. She liked the way he carried himself—so sure and confident.

"Before we talk medicine, I wondered if we might talk about you," Deborah said, smiling.

"It seems you know so much about me and my kin. When Pastor mentioned you were of English ancestry, I realized that I knew very little about you. You have family in Kansas City, and you're the eldest of fifteen children, but what else?"

Christopher shrugged. "There's not all that much to tell. You know that my father is crippled and my mother does what she can to keep the family together. There are still five children at home."

"Tell me about them," she insisted. They walked to the doctor's office and house, and Deborah pointed to the porch. "Let's sit out here to avoid all suspicion."

Christopher chuckled. "You think that will reduce concern, do you?" He allowed her to step onto the porch first.

Deborah quickly took a seat and waited for him to join her. "I think it will help. Folks seem uncertain as to what our relationship constitutes. With me seeking to learn about medicine and our courtship arrangement . . . well, I believe we have quite baffled most of the community."

"How so?"

"Well, women do not seek out jobs, especially ones that require them to train with men. And we had no formal announcement of our courtship, so most folks believe us to merely be in the early stages of trying to decide if we want to court." She shrugged. "But let them guess. I've never been conventional."

"I'm sure you speak the truth." He grinned.

She leaned back and smiled. "So tell me about the children who are at home. How old are they and what are their names?"

He looked rather hesitant as he settled back against the wooden chair and rubbed his bearded chin for a moment. "Well, I suppose it's just as easy to start with the youngest. Jonah is five and a rascal. Emma is eight and a very serious young woman. There would have been a ten-year-old, but Daniel died at birth.

"Darcy is twelve. She's a feisty young lady who grew up with too many older, ornery brothers. She's a bit of a wild one at times."

"I know how that can be. I had only brothers," Deborah replied. "Go on."

"All right . . . next is Thomas—he's thirteen. I think I told you that. James is next. We call him Jimmy. He's fifteen and quite the scholar. He loves school and has fought hard to continue his education. He works selling newspapers at the crack of dawn and then again in the evening and attends school during the day. My da—father thinks it a waste of time, but I've encouraged Jimmy to continue."

Deborah couldn't help but wonder at his stumbled words, but said nothing. "Surely your father can see the good you made of your education," she offered.

Christopher frowned momentarily. "He thought I should have come to work with him on the railroad. He's never had much regard for doctors. He thinks us all nothing but killers who act with society's blessing."

"I'm sorry. That seems such a shame."

He shrugged. "He's known so many bad ones, I can't really blame him. Anyway, John would be next. He died when he was seven. Next come the 'the swing-gate boys' as my father nicknamed them. Calvin is nearly twenty, Andrew is twenty-one, and Benjamin is twenty-three."

"Why does your father call them 'the swing-gate boys'?"

"Because they used to leave home and return so much that my father says they should have a swinging gate on the front of the house instead of a door. They're always getting into trouble. They don't have much schooling between the lot of them—spent more time using their brawn than their brains. Andrew made money for a time in boxing, but Benjamin and Cal looked for easier means to make a living. They haven't been heard from in a while." He quickly moved on.

"Samuel would have been twenty-four—almost twenty-five had he lived. He died at the age of three after falling off a swing. The wooden seat hit him in the head and knocked him to the ground. That would have been bad enough, but he impacted his head on a rock. He lingered for several days but never regained consciousness. My mother was inconsolable."

"Goodness . . . that would be so very hard." Deborah shook her head. "Poor woman."

"It was a sad time for all of us. My father had been especially fond of Samuel. I think some of his love of life went into the grave with my brother. He was never quite the same after that. I tried hard to offer solace, but my father chose other means of comfort."

"Such as?" Deborah braved the question.

Christopher stiffened and looked toward the road. "It's not important now." He drew a deep breath. "Last of all are three more sisters. Mary and Martha are twins. They married and moved west with their husbands. We seldom hear from them, but last I'd heard, they each had a couple of children. Then there's Abigail. She's twenty-eight. She's married and lives back East with her husband. She has three children."

"That's an amazing brood," Deborah said, smiling. "I can't imagine how noisy your house must have been. Did you have a really large home when you were growing up?"

He shook his head and his gaze took on a faraway look. "No. We didn't have much money. The house was quite small until we moved to Kansas City. It was a little larger then because my father finally got steady work with the railroad. I remember that move well because we finally had enough bedrooms that the girls and boys could be separated. The more children came along, the more crowded it got. But about the time we found it unbearable, some of us started leaving home."

Deborah tried to imagine the little house and all its children. Would Christopher expect her to have as large a family, should they marry? Never one to keep her thoughts to herself, Deborah posed the question. "And do you want a large family?"

He gave her a wicked grin that left her rather breathless. "Why, Miss Vandermark, what a forward question."

She shrugged and hid her discomfort. "You know I speak my mind."

"Indeed, I do." He shifted in his seat; it was his turn to look uncomfortable. "I suppose I've never really thought the number mattered, so long as the father and mother loved each other and took good care of their offspring."

She nodded, still unable to look at him. "Sounds reasonable and wise."

"What of you? Have you given thoughts to such matters?"

Deborah shook her head. "No, not really. I always figured I'd be taking care of my mother and father and hadn't considered a family of my own. You have to remember, for most of my life, I thought that was my purpose."

"And now?"

"I have to admit, I'm still rather confused about that . . . in fact, I'm confused about a lot of things." She finally lifted her gaze to meet his eyes. "Even though you've said nothing, I know there are a great many people in this area who aren't fond of my getting involved with medicine. Sometimes . . . sometimes I think I should forget about it."

"Is that what you want?" His voice was soft and gentle.

"No. At least not yet. The truth is, I still remain confused about where God wants me and how He plans to use me."

Christopher looked at her oddly. "And does that extend to your relationship with me?"

She shook her head. "I don't think so. I enjoy my time with you." Her breath caught and she bit her lower lip hard to keep from saying more. Christopher seemed to realize her feelings and moved the conversation away from the topic.

"As I mentioned, I have some medical journals you may take back with you. *The Boston Medical and Surgical Journal* has several very interesting articles. You are, of course, familiar with the Gemrig bone forceps. One of the articles details information about the new Helmond bone forceps. I'm considering ordering a set, if they aren't too expensive."

"That's fascinating. I'll be sure to read the article."

Despite the conversation's turn to a comfortable topic, Deborah couldn't help but think Christopher seemed uneasy—as though he needed to say something else, but was trying to figure out how.

"Oh, there's also an article about a new medical concern—it seems a mania has overtaken our young people in America."

She looked at him oddly and found Christopher smiling. "Roller skating," he said without making her ask.

"Roller skating is a mania? I tried it myself in Philadelphia and found it quite delightful." Deborah couldn't help but smile. "Why does the medical world believe this is a mania?"

"They believe it to be a 'psychological contagium' and that the vibrating brain cells of the skater have something to do with it all. You'll have to read the article."

"I promise you, I shall." She started to ask him what people were saying to him about her interest in doctoring, but spied her mother coming from the commissary with G.W. They were heading for the wagon with an armful of goods. "It seems my family is packing to return home. I suppose I should take my leave."

"Let me retrieve the journals," he said, getting to his feet. "I wouldn't want you to miss learning about what you may or may not have done to your brain while roller skating."

Deborah couldn't suppress a giggle as she waited for him to bring the journals from the house. She felt as if his uneasiness had passed and he was more like his old self. Her mother started walking toward them as Christopher reappeared with his offering. She waved, and Deborah stepped down from the porch with the magazines in hand.

"Dr. Clayton, please feel free to join us for supper. I know you probably planned to look in on Sissy later, and we'd love to have you at our table."

"Oh, do come," Deborah agreed. "I'll try to get the articles read by then and we can discuss them."

He smiled. "I would find that very . . .

um . . . worthwhile." He turned to her mother. "Might I bring something?"

"Not at all. Lizzie is already baking pies, and by the time I get home, Deborah and I will be able to handle the rest. We'll see you around five."

"I'll be there."

Deborah hugged the journals to her breast as she and Mother made their way back to the wagon, as if to contain the giddy sensations roiling in her stomach. She'd see Christopher again! She was losing her heart to him in a way she'd not expected, and if she were honest with herself, she was starting to regret their agreement to take their courtship very slowly.

"You look as though you have stars dancing in your head," her mother said as Deborah settled in the seat beside her.

Deborah smiled. "Sometimes Dr. Clayton has that effect."

Her mother laughed heartily. "So did your father."

Chapter 5

I've been speaking to Arjan," Euphanel announced some days later. She'd asked her family to assemble in the living room and fixed each one with a gentle look before continuing. "I'd like to offer Sissy a permanent home with us. There's no way of knowing whether she'll make a full recovery or if she'll be left debilitated. I hope you won't have any objections to this."

"Not at all," G.W. replied.

Rob and Deborah nodded eagerly. "I think it's a wonderful idea," Deborah replied. "Sissy deserves the best of care."

"Dr. Clayton and I spoke about Sissy's recovery, and he believes she may continue to have difficulties for some time. She doesn't remember things like she used to and often gets frustrated by that. She's spent her entire life taking care of others, and now I want to assure her that someone will see to her needs."

"I think we all feel that way," Deborah said. "Sissy is like family."

Euphanel gathered her thoughts and continued. "I think, in keeping with that, I want to expand the house. Arjan and I have discussed some ideas and I want your opinion."

"Tell us what you're thinking, Ma," said Rob.

She smiled. "Well, I'd like to change the office into Sissy's room and take back my old bedroom—the one G.W. and Lizzie are currently using. I'd like to add on to the front of the house, as it seems the most likely place to build. We could expand the living room, make a larger dining room and kitchen—oh, and add an office that could sit just off the house so that it can be more private. We can turn the old kitchen and dining room into bedrooms for G.W. and Lizzie, as well as a nursery. The old living room can be a sitting room for just the family."

"Sounds like you've given this a lot of thought," G.W. said, exchanging a look with Lizzie. "What do you think of this?"

Lizzie smiled. "I think the extra space would be very nice."

"I figure that one day, this will be your house," Euphanel said to G.W. Her husband, Rutger, had always planned to hand it down to G.W. He had intended to build Rob a house of his own elsewhere on their acreage, but the first son was entitled to inherit his father's place.

"It's gonna be a long time before we need to go worryin' over who owns what," G.W. replied. "But if we're gonna do this, we should do it right. If there's any other additions you want, we might as well include it all at the same time."

"Your ma gave it a pretty good piece of thought," Arjan explained. "I might have contributed an idea or two, but she pretty well figured out what she thought would work."

"What about expanding the second floor, as well?" Rob asked. "Seems like it would make it easier to keep the roof one level. That way we wouldn't have to worry about makin' places where the water'll gather."

"I think that makes sense," Mother replied. "It would give the house additional bedrooms."

"And what about a proper bathing room downstairs?" G.W. suggested. "Those of us on the first floor would appreciate that."

It wasn't long before everyone was chiming

in their ideas. Euphanel was glad they were of one accord. She hadn't been sure how the comment would be received, but Arjan had figured her children would go along with most anything she suggested. Euphanel was pleased to know her family enjoyed her company and considered this her home to do with as she pleased. No one ever said a word about it not being her place since her husband was dead. However, she had known plenty of widows who had suffered such attitudes and was thankful for the love of her family.

G.W. fetched a piece of paper and began sketching out the planned addition. It would be quite an undertaking, Euphanel knew, as it would nearly double the size of the house. Arjan said they could afford it, but she couldn't help but worry.

"If it's going to be too costly, we could wait a spell."

Her sons looked up and then to Arjan. "No, I think we can afford to move forward. It will take the bulk of our savings, but I feel confident we can make it back in a matter of months," G.W. declared. "Our accounts are in good order."

Deborah fixed him with a smile. "You've certainly picked up the bookkeeping quickly. Father would be proud of you."

G.W. rubbed his injured leg. The wound

he'd received last December bothered him from time to time; a fall from near the top of a tall pine had nearly cost him his life. He still walked with a limp and at times complained of a dull aching, but he was healing nicely. She knew he tended to rub the spot, however, when he began to feel embarrassed.

Euphanel got to her feet. "I'm going to go check on Sissy now. You boys can figure it all out with the help of Deborah and Lizzie." She slipped from the room.

I'm blessed, she told herself. *So very blessed.* The deaths of Sissy's husband and son had only served to bring back memories of her own loss. But how different life might have been had her husband been less generous in his attitude toward women and training of his sons. Her boys valued her opinion—Deborah did, as well. Where the fate of a widow was often tenuous, Euphanel's family had always made her feel useful and cared for.

She made her way upstairs and found Sissy awake, staring silently at the ceiling. She didn't bother to speak when Euphanel sat down beside her. Her pain and sorrow ran so deep that Euphanel couldn't help but take on a portion of it for herself.

"Some days, it feels as though this is nothing more than a bad dream," she whispered to Sissy. "But even in this, God has not left you nor forsaken you."

The woman nodded her head ever so slightly. "I never hoped to live this long—long 'nuf to bury my son—my man."

Euphanel nodded. "I know. I never thought to bury Rutger, either."

"I's sure sorry to be such a burden. Wish I were in the ground with 'em."

"Please don't say such things." Euphanel clutched Sissy's hand tight. "I can't bear the thought. I know this is painful, but our family loves you dearly. We want you to consider this your home now. We plan to make it larger so that everyone can live here comfortably for as long as they like."

Sissy finally turned to look at Euphanel. "Don't be doin' such things on my account. Ain't fittin'."

"What's not fitting is leaving you to fend for yourself when we have plenty and can aid you in your time of need. I don't want to make you feel that you have no choice, but I do want you to know how much we want you to be with us now."

Tears began to flow from Sissy's eyes. They slid back to her ears and wooly hair before Euphanel reached up to blot them with her handkerchief. "I ain't deservin' of such mercies," Sissy said, closing her eyes. "I's been layin' here, questionin' the Almighty. I don't deserve nuthin'."

"Oh, my dearest friend, you are deserving of this and more. The wrong done to you and your family should never have happened. It's only natural that you would have questions for God. I've been asking Him plenty myself—not because I don't trust Him, but rather because I just don't understand."

"Don't reckon we ever will."

Euphanel wiped again at Sissy's tears. "What's important now is that we figure out ways to keep it from happening again."

Sissy's head moved from side to side. "Ain't never gonna stop. Never so long as hateful folk live."

Euphanel knew Sissy was right, but she couldn't bring herself to admit such things. If she had anything to do with it—anything to say about such things—there would be a change. She would fight to keep anyone else from experiencing what her friend had been forced to endure.

ꕥ

The congregation took their seats after singing the last of their Sunday hymns and waited as Pastor Shattuck took the pulpit. He looked rather grim this morning. There was no casual greeting or comment about the weather; instead, he set his Bible in place and lifted his hands in prayer.

"Oh, Father, we ask for your wisdom. Teach us to be merciful and forgiving, and help us to understand your precious Scriptures. Amen."

"Amen," the congregation murmured in unison.

Deborah wasn't sure what to expect from the minister, but she felt confident he would address the concerns of the community. When he opened the Bible and began to speak instead of Joseph and his brothers, she felt rather disappointed.

"The thirty-seventh chapter of Genesis introduces us to Joseph," began the sermon. "I will read to you now. 'Now Israel loved Joseph more than all his children, because he was the son of his old age: and he made him a coat of many colours. And when his brethren saw that their father loved him more than all his brethren, they hated him, and could not speak peaceably unto him.' "

He continued, but Deborah gave it less than her full attention. She had so hoped that Pastor Shattuck would make the people listen to reason—help them see that something had to be done about the recent murders.

" 'Come, and let us sell him to the Ishmeelites, and let not our hand be upon him;

for he is our brother and our flesh. And his brethren were content. Then there passed by Midianites merchantmen; and they drew and lifted up Joseph out of the pit, and sold Joseph to the Ishmeelites for twenty pieces of silver: and they brought Joseph into Egypt.' "

The pastor looked up. "For twenty pieces of silver—only ten pieces shy of the price they gave Judas for our Lord. Jealousy led good men to make bad choices in this situation. Envy, jealousy, greed—all powerful influences when it comes to decision making."

There were a smattering of "amens" from amongst the listeners, but Deborah sensed the tension that ran through the entire gathering.

Pastor Shattuck stepped away from the Bible. "Evil wears many faces. Anger and bitterness—presumed wrongs, as well as those things I've mentioned—they all work together to send good men down bad roads.

"Not long ago, Mr. Perkins shared the story of his family's life in Texas. Having lived in the area for longer than I, it was fascinating to learn the experiences of others. Through his stories I came to understand him a little better. Stories are like that. We share information and learn the sorrows and woes of those around us, and it gives us insight into their hearts."

Deborah smoothed the skirt of her pale blue gown with her gloved hands and considered the pastor's words. She had heard the stories of Mr. Perkins's family but had no idea how it could possibly relate to Joseph and his brothers.

"I don't know if all of you are familiar, but Mr. Perkins has a past of great sorrows. It seems that members of his family—his grandparents and some of their children—were set upon by hostile Indians. The older folks were wounded or killed, while the children were stolen away. It was later learned that the Indians sold the children to wealthy Mexicans, but by the time those buyers were located—the children had been traded off and lost to the family."

Several people shook their heads. Some murmured derogatory remarks about the kidnappers.

"It is an awful thing to imagine, isn't it? Stealing a child and selling him. Just like Joseph's brothers. They sold their brother into slavery, just as Mr. Perkins's family members were sold. His own father only escaped the same treatment because he happened to have been in town with an older brother during the raid. Imagine his horror to return home and discover the truth."

There were additional comments and

agreements. The atmosphere seemed to change from one of reverence and a routine Sunday sermon to an interactive discussion on the injustices put upon the white man by the Indians and Mexicans.

"Mr. Perkins tells me that the neighbors and townsfolk did what they could to find the children, but they were never recovered. It was years later that one of the boys managed to get away and return to the family. He told the story of what had happened, but he had no idea where his sisters and brother had ended up. He only knew that they had been sold along with him and sent to various places. Can you imagine such injustice? Such a horrible thing. Children snatched from the bosom of their family and taken against their will to work in a place where they couldn't even speak the language."

"Should have killed ever' last Injun and Mexican," a gravelly voice declared from somewhere behind Deborah.

She considered the comment for a moment, knowing that most everyone there felt the same way. Pastor Shattuck seemed to nod in agreement. His action surprised her.

"Would seem a just punishment. Kill those who killed and stole away the family members of innocent bystanders. Who among us would say such a thing was unjust?"

"The Good Book says, 'An eye for an eye,'" another man called out.

"It also says that stealing a man and selling him is punishable by death. Exodus 21:16 speaks to just such a thing, so it would only be fitting that those who stole the children and sold them should be put to death."

There ran a wave of agreements from the congregation that increased in volume until the pastor finally held up his hands to continue.

"Joseph's brothers, by all rights, should have been put to death, but Joseph was full of mercy. He loved his family and he didn't want to cause them harm. He showed them mercy, even when they didn't deserve it."

Deborah felt a chill run through her body. Could it be possible that Pastor Shattuck would take his message even further? She leaned forward in anticipation.

"So I offer to you a question this day: Do you suppose the Negro came willingly to this continent? Or were they stolen by their enemies for whatever evil reason and sold to be slaves to those who needed workers—just as the Indians did with Mr. Perkins's family?"

The church went completely silent. There wasn't so much as a squirm from anyone in the pews. Deborah all but held her breath. The looks on the faces of the congregation conveyed stunned disbelief. They had been led where they did not want to go.

"We are so very quick to suggest that the Indian be killed for having stolen and sold slaves, but when it comes to people of our own skin color doing likewise, we are less inclined to see the wrongdoing."

He stepped down from the raised platform and gazed across the congregation. "We've witnessed many tragedies because of folks stealing other folks and selling them off. We've endured a war in this great nation because of such things. We've borne the agony of such injustice being done to people of our own skin color, and we stand up and cry out in anger at such wrongdoings. We raise a pleading hand to God to beg justice for our own, while pointing a finger of condemnation on the other hand at those whose skin is darker."

The congregation remained silent and fixed on Pastor Shattuck's every word. The man seemed to realize he had finally hit upon a chord they could all recognize. He tucked his hands in his pockets and stepped back to the pulpit and picked up his Bible. "I'll now close in prayer."

Deborah closed her eyes and felt a sense of elation. She had a new respect for Pastor Shattuck. He was much wiser than she'd given him credit for. He had found a way to get the people to listen to his heart and to the Word, even knowing they would never agree with what he had to share. He had addressed not the murders themselves, but the very origin of the problem.

Folks filed from the church in silence. Hardly a word was spoken as they departed. Pastor Shattuck extended his hand as he always did, and some folks took it while others passed by without even glancing up. A few, she was happy to see, thanked the preacher for his words. Her family was among those, as was Dr. Clayton.

But would the pastor's words only serve to put up walls of silence between those who agreed and those who disagreed?

Chapter 6

Word quickly spread that the Vandermarks were adding on to their house, and on the last Saturday in February, nearly half the town turned out to help. A palpable tension was evident, however. The ladies seemed to choose their words with great care as they shared the latest news, while the men spoke even less than usual. Deborah overheard several ladies ask her mother about Sissy. They approached her cautiously, whispering their questions. It was unfortunate that a community should be divided by something as heinous as the murders that had taken place; Deborah would have thought everyone could agree at least on the fact that the killings had been unjust. But apparently even that was too much to expect. There appeared to be an unspoken agreement to pretend that all was well, in order to accomplish what needed to be done.

Watching from the porch, Deborah marveled at how her mother moved among the crowd, making each person feel welcome. Mother was the consummate Southern hostess. She easily engaged their friends and neighbors, sharing a comment or asking a question. The tensions began to visibly ease, and finally people conversed, if not comfortably, then at least amiably. When Mother had finally made the rounds, she stepped to the porch.

"Friends, we're so glad to have ya'll here today," her mother told everyone. The crowd quieted down immediately. "Thank you so much for sharing your time and energy to help a neighbor. Arjan and my boys will direct you in what we're hoping to accomplish." She stepped aside to let Arjan take over, then held up her hand. "Oh, and of course the ladies and I will put together a wonderful lunch for you."

The men gave affirming comments and some even smiled. Perhaps they could put aside their troubled thoughts and disagreements for this one day. Deborah joined her mother to the side of the porch while her uncle took charge.

"We're thankful for the good weather and

hopeful that we can raise the entire addition and roof it in one day. It's a big task, but I believe we Texans have always been up to big tasks."

This time the men raised an affirming cheer. In the distance, Deborah heard the logging train whistle. It would bring the last of the needed lumber and building supplies.

"Uncle Arjan seems to have a good way with organizing these kind of things," Lizzie whispered to Deborah.

She smiled and nodded. "Father used to say his brother could have been President of the United States with his ability to coordinate efforts."

Lizzie put her hand to her growing abdomen. "I'm sure the men in this family could be anything they set their minds to. G.W. has taken to reading to me at night. Sometimes I have to help him, but he isn't letting his pride keep him from the task. I have you to thank for that, Deborah. It's given him something to live for since being injured."

Deborah considered her friend for a moment. "It always saddened me that my brothers held little value in book learning. Now it seems that both of them have a new interest, for Rob has actually begun to spend time reading, as well. I'd love to see the town's attitude toward schooling change . . . so many of the people are illiterate."

The men were beginning to break into teams as the logging train came to a stop. Arjan directed one of the teams to unload the new supplies, while the others immediately went to work framing up the walls.

"I suppose we'd better head to the kitchen," Mother said, joining them.

Mrs. Perkins approached and offered a basket. "I've brought three pies and five dozen cookies. I know they won't last long, but I figured it was a start."

Mother laughed. "We've been hard at it for days. We knew we'd have our loggers helping, and they can eat like an army. But what a pleasant surprise to have so many of our friends and neighbors join us."

"Your family is one of the most admired in the county." Mrs. Perkins lowered the basket. "Despite the recent troubles, I'm hopeful that perhaps this will afford us a coming together of hearts."

"That would be wonderful," Mother agreed. "Perhaps if there were more positive things to dwell on, folks would be less likely to cause harm."

"You know, I've been thinking that very thing," Mrs. Perkins replied.

"Oh, who's that with Pastor Shattuck?"

Lizzie said, leaning toward Deborah. “She looks like she could be your relation.”

Deborah followed Lizzie’s gaze and saw the young woman at the preacher’s side. She was nearly the same size and had dark black hair like Deborah, but unlike her, the stranger had arranged her tresses in a bevy of curls that gently draped her neck and shoulders. The young stranger carried herself in a very elegant manner, appearing to float across the yard on the pastor’s arm, a sort of teasing smile upon her lips.

Looking back at Lizzie, Deborah leaned in to whisper. “I’m guessing it might be the pastor’s daughter. He has two children who, as I heard it, lived elsewhere with their grandmother.”

“Mrs. Vandermark, Miss Vandermark,” Pastor Shattuck said as he approached and tipped his hat. He looked beyond them. “Mrs. Perkins, Mrs. Vandermark.”

Mother stepped from the porch and extended her hand. “How are you, Pastor?”

He shook her hand, then stepped aside. “This is my daughter, Mara. Mara, these are the Vandermark women.” He paused and smiled. “Of course, you’ve already met Mrs. Perkins.”

“I’m delighted to make your acquaintances,”

Mara Shattuck said, offering a brilliant smile. "My father has spoken so highly of you."

Mother took charge. "Well, we are quite pleased to finally meet you. I understand you've been living in New Orleans with your grandmother."

She nodded. "But now it's time to help Father with God's work."

The comment surprised Deborah. She had thought Pastor Shattuck rather negative when it came to women. He never wished to discuss the Bible with her, at least, always making some excuse when Deborah asked him about certain Bible verses.

"I'm certain you will be an asset to him," Deborah's mother declared. "You must excuse us just now. We need to start putting together the noon meal."

"Truly? It's only just past dawn," Mara said, looking surprised.

Mother laughed. "True enough, but we will need to ready the food, nevertheless. The men will work hard and need coffee and doughnuts to sustain them until lunch. If you'd like to help, we'd be glad for the extra hands."

Mara looked to her father, who nodded. She looked down at her stylish suit. "Do you suppose I could borrow an apron?"

"Of course," Mother assured. "We have plenty. In fact, if you're worried about your clothes, Deborah would surely be able to loan you something."

Mara met Deborah's gaze and smiled. "I'm sure an apron will be sufficient. I wouldn't want to put anyone out."

"You wouldn't," Deborah replied.

The dark-haired woman smiled. "Then perhaps I will take you up on the offer. This suit isn't all that comfortable. Grandmother told me it was the height of fashion, but I find it less than serviceable for everyday."

Deborah's mother chuckled. "We'll fix you right up. Thank you for coming today, Pastor Shattuck. Perhaps you will offer grace at dinner?"

He nodded. "For now, though, I'll set aside my coat and roll up my sleeves. I'm quite good with a hammer."

Mother reached out to Mara. "Come along, ladies. We shall find something suitable for Miss Shattuck to wear."

"Oh, please call me Mara. I should like very much to be a good friend to each of you."

Deborah liked her immediately. She appeared so stylish and refined, but at the same time, Mara Shattuck held no pretense of airs.

"Mother!" Rob crossed the yard carrying a large lidded pot. "Miz Huebner asked me to fetch in this pot of chicken and dumplings." He stopped at the sight of Mara. His eyes widened slightly as a grin spread across his face. "I don't reckon we've met."

"This is Mara Shattuck, the pastor's daughter," his mother introduced. "Mara, this is my youngest son, Rob."

She smiled and nodded. "I'm pleased to meet you, Mr. Vandermark."

"Not nearly as pleased as I am." He stood fixed in place and might have remained there had Mother not broken the spell.

"Rob, Arjan is going to need you, so just go ahead and deliver the food to the kitchen."

"Maybe Mara could help me," Rob said in his smooth, practiced manner. His blue-eyed gaze was fixed on the younger woman.

"Help you carry the pot?" Deborah teased.

Rob looked almost confused for a moment. "No, silly," he finally managed. "I only figured maybe she could hold the door for me."

"I'd be happy to help, Mr. Vandermark." Mara climbed the steps and cast a quick glance over her shoulder. "Is this the door of which you were speaking?"

He quickly bounded onto the porch as if the heavy load weighed nothing at all. "That's the one, and please . . . call me Rob."

Deborah rolled her eyes and looked to Lizzie. "My brother can move fast when he needs to."

"To be sure," Lizzie whispered in reply.

They followed after the others, smiling at their exchange. Deborah knew her brother could be quite charming when he wanted to be. He'd paid visits to most of the eligible young women in the area, checking the potential of each with the same thoroughness he might use to select a tool with which to work. It wasn't surprising that he'd noticed Mara, although Deborah found the timing quite incredible—even for her brother.

ꙮ

The lunch hour approached and the men were signaled to stop work. Deborah was amazed at how much they'd already accomplished. The main framework of the first floor was completed and a good portion of the second floor was in place, as well. An entire team of men even worked on setting the interior walls in place.

Pastor Shattuck shared a blessing for the food and for the safety of the workers. So far the worst of the injuries had been when one of the children had fallen off the scaffolding. He looked to be sporting some bruises and a few scrapes but otherwise had been unharmed. Still, Deborah was glad to see Dr. Clayton show up just as the eating commenced.

Deborah went to where he secured his

horse under the shade of a hickory tree. "Just in time for dinner."

He grinned. "That was the plan. Have you ever known me to pass up a meal cooked by the Vandermark women?"

She laughed. "Well, this meal happens to have been cooked by the entire community. We Vandermarks did plenty, but the ladies of Perkinsville have been most generous."

"I'm glad," he said, looking toward the new structure. "Looks like the men have been, as well."

Deborah followed his gaze. "It's amazing, isn't it? I remember when we raised the church in a day. . . . Of course, back then the entire town turned out. Here, not so much. We have a good number, don't get me wrong—but the tension at first was thick enough to cut with a knife. I figure there are still a good number of people here who don't agree with our thoughts on racial matters and stayed away."

Christopher looked back to her and nodded. "I just made the rounds in town, and believe me, there were plenty of folks more than happy to speak their minds." His expression darkened. "I've witnessed the damage that occurs when hatred and prejudice grows."

"Was it between blacks and whites?"

For a moment he said nothing, and Deborah

thought perhaps he would refuse to continue their conversation.

"I'm sorry," she whispered, putting her hand on his arm. "You don't have to tell me."

He shook his head. "It's not that. It's just sad to remember. And I see it all happening here again. There were battles in Kansas City between the black and whites, of course. And there were white folks during the war who were proslavery, as well as against it. They fought amongst themselves almost more than they fought in the war."

"We had a lot of that here, as well," Deborah admitted. "Father called them guerillas. They were forever causing problems."

"Well, the same was true up north. They didn't call Kansas 'Bleeding' without due cause. Kansas and Missouri very nearly had their own little war within the war. But there were other problems, as well."

"Such as?"

He looked at her for a moment. "There were great prejudices among the whites toward other whites. For instance . . . the Irish. A great many folks take strong stands against the Irish. They dislike them for their fighting and drinking, not to mention their religious views. They dislike them for their culture—the way they speak—the things they love to eat. It doesn't seem to matter. They feel that the

Irish take jobs away from others who were there first."

"But aren't the same problems true for the Italians and Polish?" Deborah questioned. "I know in Philadelphia, there were problems also with those of Jewish descent. It was sometimes quite ugly."

He nodded, then looked up at the canopy of trees toward the cloudless sky.

"Well, are you going to let the doctor come and eat?" Deborah's mother interrupted.

Deborah hadn't even heard her mother approach. "I'm sorry, Christopher. I didn't mean to keep you from dinner."

He laughed and gave a brief bow to Mrs. Vandermark. "I don't miss too many meals, as you can see." He patted his stomach.

"Nonsense," Mother declared. "You are the very image of health. Fit as a fiddle, my mother would say. Can you stay for long?"

"I can. I finished my rounds, and now I'm yours for the day. I figured that a house raising would be the perfect place for a doctor. One can never tell what might happen."

"Truer words were never spoken," Mother replied. She entwined her arm with Dr. Clayton's. "Come. I'll show you where everything is."

Deborah followed behind as Christopher and her mother made their way to the luncheon table. Seeing that many of the men were out of coffee, she diverted to where Lizzie was already filling several pitchers.

"Let me take those," Deborah said, reaching for the full containers. "How are you feeling? Did you eat something?"

Earlier, Lizzie had suffered some nausea, but now she looked quite well. "I feel much better. It's G.W. I'm worried about. He seems so out of sorts."

"But why?" Deborah looked for her brother and didn't find him.

"He can't get up on the ladders and help. He feels that he's not able to do his part. I told him it was nonsense, but . . . well, I'm wondering if you could speak to your uncle and maybe let him know what the problem is. He might have some idea for what G.W. could do to be useful."

Deborah nodded. "I'll mention it when I take the coffee. Don't you worry, Lizzie. My brother can be quite cantankerous at times, but he usually comes around." She smiled. "If not, I'll give him a good elbow to the ribs."

Lizzie laughed. "That's not exactly what I had in mind."

Pouring coffee as she went, Deborah greeted the workers and made comments about their progress. The men seemed pleased to hear her praise. A few of the single men tried to get her to stay and chat, but she made it clear that she had to be moving on so that everyone could have coffee while it was still hot.

She finally found Uncle Arjan and was happy to see he was just finishing. "I wonder if you could help me for a moment."

He looked at her oddly, but nodded. "What's the problem?"

She handed him the empty pitchers. "Follow me."

They went to where coffee was being poured into a large caldron to keep warm while more coffee was readied to perk in the pots. It had been like this all day, with Lizzie and a couple of other women focused on keeping coffee available to all the workers.

"Lizzie is worried about G.W. She says he's feeling rather useless. I was hoping you might have a special task for him." She took the pitcher from her uncle and handed it over to Lizzie, who nodded in agreement.

"His leg has been bothering him too much to get in there and really work," Lizzie admitted. "He doesn't like to favor it, but he can hardly do much else."

"I have the perfect solution," Uncle Arjan declared. "He can be in charge of positioning the interior walls. He knows exactly what we want. I'll tell him that since we've made such great progress, he can get the men to work inside while Rob and I get the upper floor finished and the roofing done."

Deborah smiled at Lizzie. "See—it's all resolved."

"I'll go find him and arrange things right now," her uncle said. "Thanks for a mighty fine dinner. A nap would suit me just fine, but I guess I'll get back to work."

ꕥ

The work continued until darkness made it impossible to see; the last of the shingles were put into place by lantern light. Those on the roof cheered loudly as Rob put in the final nail. He'd never been so tired in his life, but strangely, the action seemed to give him a second wind.

Climbing down from the roof, Rob immediately spied Mara Shattuck and made his way to where she stood. "Well, what do you think?" he asked her.

She smiled. "Looks like you won't have to worry when the rains come."

"If they come. Most of the state is sufferin' a horrible drought." He wiped sweat from his face with the back of his sleeve. The chilly evening air felt good. "So, do you plan to be around long?"

She looked at him and considered the question a moment. "I believe God brought me here, Mr. Vandermark. It seemed time to come and help my father with his ministry work."

"So is that a yes?" He gave her a broad grin.

She returned his smile. "I believe it is—at least for the time. I try very hard to go where God leads. What of you, Mr. Vandermark?"

"What do you mean?"

A coy look crossed her face. "Do you go where God leads?"

Rob felt a bit perplexed. He hadn't intended for the conversation to veer toward religion. "I reckon I try to. I don't suppose I've ever heard Him come right out and tell me exactly."

"Do you ask Him to speak to you?"

Her question took him off guard. "Am I supposed to?"

She gave a nod, her expression quite serious. "I believe we are. The Bible does admonish us to seek Him—to ask and it shall be given. It is of the utmost importance that we ask for His guidance. After all, surely we wouldn't want to go where He does not lead us."

"No, I reckon you're right on that." He grinned. "You know, for a pretty gal, you do a lot of deep thinkin'."

"Well, Mr. Vandermark, I am much more than my outward appearance." She turned to go, but stopped and gave him a smile. "Perhaps in time, you'll learn that for yourself."

Rob wanted to rush after her—to suggest he get started on his learning right away—but something held him in place. He was known in the community as something of a ladies' man. The family often joked that he had first spoken of marriage at the tender age of four when he spied a young neighbor girl at church and declared her just the kind of gal he'd like to get hitched with.

Since that time, there had been a great many young women who'd held his attention and his heart. Often when a new gal came to town, Rob would find himself convinced she was the one for him—at least until another young lady appeared to take his attention.

Now, however, he found himself feeling rather gut-punched. Mara Shattuck was unlike most of the other women he'd met. She seemed so sure of herself, and of course, she was easy on the eyes. But there was also something more. Something he couldn't quite explain. She had a way about her that left him feeling as though there was something more he needed to know—something that only she could tell him. Something that would complete him.

"She looks like Deborah," G.W. said as he joined Rob.

Rob looked at him and shook his head. "Who does?"

"Miss Shattuck. Don't you think she favors our sister?"

He shook his head, unable to imagine what G.W. was talking about. Sure, the beauty had dark hair and eyes, but she looked nothing like Deborah. "I think you need spectacles, brother of mine. Those two don't look a thing alike."

Chapter 7

March 1886

"Frankly, I can hardly believe the celebration is tomorrow," Rachel Perkins told Euphanel. "Seems like this year has already gone by so quickly."

"I have to agree. It started with so many sorrows," Euphanel replied.

"Indeed it did. Speaking of which, how is Sissy?" Putting down the curtain she'd been hemming, Rachel reached for her cup of tea.

"She's much better. She likes to sit for a little while now. Her head will start paining her, however, so she doesn't spend too much time up. Doc says it will be a while before she's herself again. She might always suffer headaches."

"That must be so hard for her. I've never known Sissy to sit for long."

Euphanel nodded and tied off her stitch. "She's never even been one for standing still. I know it's hard for her to just rest, but I remind her that it's the only way to heal."

Rachel smiled. "And what does she say?"

Laughing, Euphanel put the finished curtain panel aside and picked up the next one. "She tells me that the Lord can heal her with a single touch, just like He did folks in the Bible. I agreed, but told her that until He decided to do that, she had to rest."

"I do wish Zed could find out who was responsible. I know he had our boys go to Lufkin to ask around there about the White Hand of God, but he told me that no one seems to know anything—or if they do, they aren't talking."

"That doesn't surprise me. Folks seem steeped in their secrets when it comes to such underhanded events. I do wish we could do something to bring the people together, though. I hate that we sit separately at any gathering—that we have our separate churches. I want to sit with Sissy in church, but she's hardly welcome in ours."

"I heard Pastor Shattuck say that if skin color were the basis for acceptance, then Jesus probably wouldn't be welcome, either."

Euphanel put her hand to her mouth and suppressed a giggle. "I'm sure," she said, lowering her hand, "that didn't go over well."

"No," Rachel agreed, smiling, "but I thought it made a whole lot of sense."

Euphanel began working on the next hem and shook her head. "Funny how folks always think of Jesus as blond-haired and blue-eyed. I suppose it comforts them to see Him in their own way."

"I would imagine so, but then, Sissy probably thinks of Him with skin as dark as hers."

Looking up, Euphanel grew thoughtful. "Do you suppose folks all over the world think of God that way? Each in their own color and manner?"

"Seems reasonable," Rachel replied. "He is all things to all people."

"I'll have to ask Sissy sometime what color she sees our Savior."

Euphanel took careful stitches as she hemmed the heavy brocade fabric. Lizzie and she had found the dark gold and brown material at the commissary buried far beneath other more popular pieces. The price had been reduced because of a lack of interest, and Euphanel had taken the entire bolt. It seemed a nice heavy material to put up on the new bedroom windows.

"I just had a thought."

"About what?" Euphanel asked.

"You were talking about something to bring the people together. Pastor Shattuck suggested the black and white baseball game tomorrow, but what about the sacred-harp singing?"

Euphanel had once loved this community activity. Over the years, folks had gotten away from shape-note singing, or sacred harp, as others called it. "I think that's a wonderful idea. We could see if there was any interest at the celebration tomorrow—maybe in the evening, after the judging is announced. There are surely enough folks around here who've participated before that would want to do so now."

"We used to have quite a good group of singers," Rachel added. "Remember the old days when we would have gatherings on a Saturday after the mill shut down? We would sing all afternoon and into the night."

"Yes! I remember it well." Euphanel closed her eyes and could almost see the squared up formation. Altos facing the tenors, basses facing the trebles. "I enjoyed that so much."

"Then I think we should begin again. I don't know if the folks would feel comfortable asking the Negroes to join us, but it would be worth trying," Rachel said thoughtfully.

"Imagine using music to bring us all together."

ᘛᘚ

Deborah closed the Bible and looked at Sissy. "Are you ready to lie back down?"

"I reckon so, Miss Deborah. I'm feelin' a bit poorly."

Getting to her feet, Deborah put the Bible aside and went to help Sissy from the rocking chair. "Dr. Clayton said it would probably be some months before you felt completely whole again."

She helped Sissy to the bed and gently eased the woman onto the mattress. Deborah removed Sissy's slippers and carefully helped her lift her legs.

Sissy moaned softly. It wasn't like her to complain, and Deborah knew that the fact she'd made any noise at all signaled she was in pain.

"Would you like some more medicine?"

"No, I cain't think clear when I takes it."

Deborah nodded and drew her chair closer to the bed. "Would you like me to sit with you awhile longer?"

"It's always a pleasure to have you near, Miss Deborah. You's good company."

"I don't know about that, but I know I enjoy our talks."

"Ain't much to talk about these days," Sissy said, her voice thick with sorrow.

"Oh, there's plenty," Deborah countered. "It's just not the most pleasant of topics. Still, I can share the news from town. The Independence Day celebration is slated to begin bright and early in the morning. Rob and Uncle Arjan donated six feral hogs for roasting, and several of the men have been hard at work to ready them. Mother is quite excited to try out a new recipe on the canning committee. She has perfected her piccalilli."

"Weren't nuttin' wrong with her old recipe," Sissy said with a hint of a smile.

"Oh, and they got Pastor Shattuck to agree to judge the pies along with Mr. Perkins, and Dr. Clayton will make the final decision. Lizzie has made several pies to enter. I hope she'll win a ribbon, since this is her first time to try."

"Miss Lizzie's turned out to be a right-fine cook."

"Yes, she has." Deborah folded her hands. "I can't say the same for myself. At least not where pies are concerned. I'm better at other things."

"We all gots our gifts. You makes a mighty

good doctor." Sissy looked at Deborah. "I's been so proud of you."

"Thank you, Sissy. I'm very touched to hear you say so. It means a great deal."

"You's always been blessed by God."

Deborah considered that a moment. "Sissy," she began slowly, "have you remained close to God? I mean, in spite of what has happened, have you managed to keep your faith in Him?"

Sissy looked surprised. "What other choice we got, Miss Deborah?"

"Well, some turn away from God when things are bad. I can't say that I would blame you if your faith faltered. You've gone through more than anyone I know."

"I had a moment or two where I was hurtin' so that I couldn't hardly pray," Sissy admitted. "Your mama said that was the time when the Spirit hisself prays for me."

"Romans eight, verse twenty-six," Deborah said, nodding. " 'Likewise the Spirit also helpeth our infirmities: for we know not what we should pray for as we ought: but the Spirit itself maketh intercession for us with groanings which cannot be uttered.' "

"I shore 'nuf been groaning myself." Sissy smiled.

"It comforts me to remember that verse." Deborah reached out to grasp Sissy's hand.

"So many times I don't know how to pray. . . . It just seems too hard, too confusing. In times like these when our lives seem so scarred by hate, I can't help but wonder what to even say to God. I know He hurts for us. I know it grieves Him that we act as we do."

"We's weak and sinful. Ain't no amount of good doin's gonna change that. Onliest thing what changes our hearts is Jesus."

"So you don't feel that . . . well . . . that God abandoned you?"

Sissy looked at her oddly. "Abandoned me? I'd sooner say I could fly. God ain't abandoned me. Evil comed into this world, and the devil, he done worked his miseries on us all. God's more powerful and God has His plan. I ain't thinkin' He's left me alone. 'Stead, He alone is with me." She closed her eyes.

"That's a wonderful way to look at it." Deborah got to her feet. "Sometimes it's really hard to remember that." She covered Sissy with the blanket. "I think it's time I let you rest. I'll check on you in a little while. If you need anything, you just ring the bell."

"You's mighty good to me, Miss Deborah." Sissy's words were barely audible.

Deborah pulled the curtains, then tiptoed to the door. With one final glance over her shoulder, she stepped into the hall to find her mother making her way to the room.

"Sissy is tired, so I told her I'd check on her later."

"I was just wondering if she needed anything. I didn't realize you'd been with her the whole time," Mother replied.

"We got to talking," Deborah said. "I don't know that I would have her degree of faith, had I gone through what she did."

"God doesn't call you to have Sissy's faith. He calls you to put your faith in Him. He'll grow and develop it from there."

"I know, but sometimes I feel that my faith must be as shallow as a river in drought."

Mother smiled and put her arm around Deborah's shoulder. "The rains will come. Trust Him. Just when you think you can't go on, they always come. In the meanwhile, why don't you join Rachel and me? We're hemming the curtains."

"I need to check on G.W.," Deborah said, inclining her head toward the door. "He wanted to make sure he was handling the inventory ledgers the right way."

"Well, if you finish, feel free to join us. I'm sure we'll be sewing for at least another hour."

"Deborah's not going to come?" Rachel asked as Euphanel took her seat.

"She has to oversee something in the office.

G.W. is learning to take over the bookkeeping, but Deborah still has things to teach him."

"You should be proud of G.W., learning a new skill, despite his injury. I don't know if one of my boys endured the same kind of accident that they could make such drastic changes."

"It was God's hand that changed G.W.'s heart." Euphanel poured the last of the tea. "Would you like me to put on another pot?"

Rachel shook her head. "You don't need to for me. I'm fine."

Settling into her chair, Euphanel looked around the room. "I'll be so glad to get everything in the new addition completed. The boys have been working too hard. Arjan and Rob even took time away from logging. I know it makes Arjan feel rather out of sorts."

"Why do you say that?" Rachel questioned.

Euphanel shrugged. "He's always been more comfortable working outdoors. Rutger used to say that he was surprised Arjan would even live in a house." She chuckled. "He's a man of the land. I was really surprised when he stayed here after Rutger's death."

"Why should you be?" Rachel smiled and gave Euphanel a knowing look.

"What do you mean?" Euphanel shook her head.

"He stayed because of you."

Euphanel looked at Rachel to ascertain whether she was teasing. "You're serious? You think he feels responsible for me?"

"No, silly. I think he's in love with you."

Euphanel's mouth dropped open. She didn't even try to hide her surprise. "Rachel Perkins, that's ridiculous. He's an honorable man."

Rachel laughed. "Now, Euphanel, you know it's not ridiculous at all. Arjan cares for you. He always has. He acted quite noble, but now I believe he's just biding his time until you're done mourning."

The idea wasn't disagreeable to Euphanel, but it was totally unexpected. She tried to imagine Arjan declaring his love for her. What would she say? Could she allow herself to love again? What would the children think? This was their father's brother.

"I . . . well . . . I don't know what to say."

"You truly have never considered this before now?"

Euphanel picked up her tea and drank down the lukewarm liquid before returning the cup to the saucer. "I suppose I haven't. Rachel, please don't tease me." She leaned forward and replaced the china on the table. "Do you honestly believe that Arjan . . . that he . . . "

"Loves you? Yes I do. I've seen the way he looks at you, Euphanel. I believe he's been in love with you for as long as he's known you."

"But he's never said anything. He's never even hinted at having romantic notions."

"As you said, he's honorable."

Euphanel eased back against the chair and folded her hands. "What should I do?"

"Why do you have to do anything?" Rachel asked.

"I don't know, but I feel like I should do or say something."

Rachel leaned forward and patted Euphanel's knee. "Give it to God, as you do everything else. You once told me that God has perfect timing for everything. Allow God's timing for this."

Chapter 8

The day of the Texas Independence celebration dawned bright and clear and, despite needing more rain, the community was glad to have cloudless blue skies and low humidity. All of Perkinsville turned out for the event. Tables and booths were set up near the baseball diamond behind the church. Ladies assembled their canned goods, quilts, embroidery, and other fancy work on tables near the church, while the roasting pits and dinner tables had been positioned on the side of the clearing closest to Mr. Perkins's house.

The street had been roped off for horse racing, which would take place later in the day, as well as a parade of prized livestock that would be auctioned in the afternoon. It was unlike any other event the community held, and no one—regardless of skin color—would miss it.

Of course, Deborah thought, *there will be rules—for both the game and the social mingling.* Pastor Shattuck had convinced the town to have a black and white baseball game, but as was already in evidence, the people would still sit separately for the noon meal. And, in overhearing people talk, it wasn't just the whites who would want it that way. Many of the blacks wanted no part in comingling. Both sides displayed unspoken discomfort and evident tension.

Deborah moved among the people and exhibits looking for Christopher. They had agreed to meet at the festivities, and Deborah found herself anticipating the moment more than she'd expected. They would both be available to help should anyone get sick or injured, although Deborah knew there were few people who considered her an asset to the medical needs of Perkinsville. Folks in the area were more inclined to see her as fanciful, rather than useful. Thankfully, Christopher wasn't of the same mind. He appreciated her quick mind and desire to learn. The thought made her smile. She missed him more each time they were apart.

She'd just seen him at supper on Sunday, but his absences seemed more and more pronounced to her. Was that what it meant to fall in love? Many had been the night she'd lain awake, pondering the idea of marriage to Christopher Clayton. There were still so many mysteries about him, and she longed to know every one of them.

When she spied Christopher, he was standing beside Mara Shattuck. Dressed in his navy blue serge suit, Deborah thought the doctor cut a fine figure. The coat had been tailored to fit his broad shoulders and narrow waist, and the trousers were of the latest style. She couldn't help but believe him the handsomest man in attendance. Perhaps Mara thought so, too, for she leaned in closely and lifted her gloved hand to her mouth as if whispering a secret. The two seemed deep in discussion, and for a moment, Deborah experienced a twinge of jealousy.

The feeling took Deborah by surprise. Other women in the community spoke with Christopher on occasion, but something was different about this moment. Mara laughed and Christopher smiled. Deborah couldn't help but be drawn to them.

"Hello," she said, approaching the couple.

Christopher turned and extended his arm. "And here she is. We were just talking about you."

Deborah couldn't imagine what they'd said to elicit such laughter. "Oh, really?"

"Yes, from behind I mistook Miss Shattuck for you. I'm afraid I gave her a start."

All sorts of thoughts danced through Deborah's mind. Had he embraced her? Had he said something about her appearance that was much too personal?

"I told the good doctor that I had no idea what quinsy was, nor how to cure it," Mara added.

Deborah smiled. "He asked you that, did he?"

"He did indeed. When he learned I wasn't you, he was quite embarrassed."

Mara turned back to Christopher. "Now, if you'll excuse me, I need to see my father before he gets the baseball game started. However, if in the future one of you would like to explain the details of quinsy and the related healing methods, I promise to be most attentive."

She raised a pink parasol and swept gracefully across the grounds to join the pastor. Deborah shook her head. "I don't know how you could ever mistake her for me. She's far more elegant in her carriage and demeanor. I'll be brown as a berry in this sun—especially since I didn't see fit to bring an umbrella."

"Nonsense. You are just as elegant. I wasn't paying much attention when I approached her. I have to admit, your mother had just given me one of her orange spice doughnuts and I was deep in contemplation."

"Contemplation?" Deborah asked.

He laughed and leaned closer. "I was contemplating how to talk her out of another one."

She shook her head in mock disgust. Mother had always said that if she wanted to impress a man, it wouldn't be with how much knowledge she held but rather in examples of her cooking. Sadly, that had suffered over the years.

She feigned a pout. "I suppose you shan't want to court me unless I can make a doughnut as fine as my mother's."

"Don't be ridiculous," he said, taking hold of her arm. "I shall court you anyway. At least then I get to eat your mother's cooking."

She elbowed him just enough to get his attention and make him laugh. "I'm surprised you aren't more worried about the judging to come. I'm the one who will make the final decision on the pies. What if I'm swept off my feet by some wondrous creation?"

"What if I entered a pie?" she asked, brow raised slightly.

He looked at her and grinned. "Did you?"

Deborah shook her head. "No, but I might have."

"You'd be more inclined to enter your thoughts on curing quinsy." He stepped back a pace. "I must compliment you on your gown, Miss Vandermark."

She had hoped he might find the yellow crepe de Chine appealing. Her mother had worked hard to help her fashion it into a stylish gown that flattered her dark hair and eyes.

"I'm also quite glad you chose to leave off the elaborate bustles that so many find popular." He motioned his head toward the Perkins sisters, who happened to be strolling by.

"If you put them back to back, you could serve dinner atop their backsides," Christopher whispered against her ear.

Deborah shivered at the warmth of his breath on her neck. She giggled to conceal the effect, but found it impossible to speak. Christopher, however, seemed to have little trouble.

"Women and their contraptions shall always amaze me. I find a well-fitted corset to be advantageous to a woman's health, but bustles and the like are quite useless and sometimes downright dangerous."

"I find it rather amazing that we are standing here in broad daylight discussing women's undergarments," Deborah said, looking up at him.

Christopher's eyes twinkled mischievously. "Would you rather I wait until the dark of night?"

"Sir, you are positively scandalous."

He laughed. "Not at all. We are both interested in the medical well-being of women, are we not? Perhaps your delicate sensibilities are too fragile for a career in medicine."

She smiled. "Perhaps I shouldn't have agreed to court a physician. They seem to easily forget their manners." She started to walk away, but Christopher quickly pulled her in line with him.

"Oh no, you don't. I won't have you slip away from me that easily. Now come along. I want to watch the game."

He led her to one of the wooden benches that had been positioned for viewing the game. Deborah saw the pastor speaking to a collection of Negro players. The men were smiling and nodding at the minister. On the opposite side of the field, the white players stood with expressions that seemed mostly dubious. Deborah hoped her brother Rob would help keep the situation under control. He was to play second baseman, so he would be right in the middle of everything.

As the townsfolk assembled near the diamond, those of African ancestry took their place on the left side of the diamond toward third base, while the whites gathered more center and to the right. Pastor Shattuck climbed onto one of the benches and held up his hands. "Folks, it's time we got this game started. Let us have a word of prayer on this, our day of celebration."

A hush fell over the crowd. "Father, we commit this day to you. As we celebrate our independence, we recall that true liberty is found in Christ alone. May we, the people of Perkinsville, be mindful of your generosity to us and extend compassion and consideration to each person gathered here today. Amen."

He looked out across the flock of people, then turned to the players. "Let's commence the game!"

Cheers erupted from both sides, and Christopher settled in beside Deborah. "This should prove interesting."

"I was thinking much the same," Deborah replied.

The game started without conflict. Pastor Shattuck drew the two teams together. "For the sake of the day, we shall call this team the Perkinsville Razorbacks, as they have called themselves in the past." He nodded toward the captain of the white players. "And the other team will be called the Perkinsville Sawyers, since many of these men cut for a living."

"The Razorbacks will take their place in the field," Pastor Shattuck announced. "Sawyers—you're up to bat."

Deborah recognized the first player. "That's

Abraham Garby," she told Christopher. "He works for us."

One of the many Foster cousins stepped to the mound to pitch. He threw the first ball, which was immediately declared a strike by the officiating umpire Mr. Huebner. As the local schoolmaster, Curtis Huebner had called many a ball game in the past.

The next pitch split the air with a loud crack as Abraham sent the ball slicing out across the open field. He ran for first base, then rounded second for third before the ball was retrieved. Picking up speed, Abraham slid into third while those gathered nearby cheered.

Deborah clapped, as did several of the other people around her, but most of the white people remained silent. The next two players were quickly struck out, but the third man managed to drive the ball into right field, allowing Abraham to reach home plate. The Sawyers were on the board.

For the next six innings, things went well, but when the seventh found the score tied four to four, conflict began to stir. Name calling, at first jovial and teasing, became more meanspirited and derogatory. Pastor Shattuck asked the men to put aside such comments, but the truce didn't last for long. Then when the teams changed places in the bottom of the inning and the Razorbacks stepped to the plate, a disaster struck on the first pitch. The ball slammed into the shoulder of John Stevens and knocked him to the ground. Although John did not see it as a personal attack, others on the team were livid and rushed to the pitcher's mound to see their form of justice done.

In turn, many of the Sawyers players came forward to assist their comrade and soon fists were swinging. Deborah watched in horror as Pastor Shattuck tried in vain to calm the men. It wasn't until Zed Perkins fired a shotgun in the air that some semblance of order settled upon them once again. By then, no one felt much like continuing the game.

"It's very nearly time for the dinner bell," Mr. Perkins announced. "I'd suggest we call this game a tie and begin eatin'."

Murmurs coursed throughout the crowd and a general consensus of approval was evident. The men separated hesitantly, each going to their assigned team places.

"I think I should see to the Sawyers and their wounds," Christopher told her as he got to his feet. "A couple of those men look to have taken the worst of it to their faces."

"Can I be of any assistance?" she asked.

He looked at her sadly. "It wouldn't be acceptable, Deborah. Why don't you go save us a place to enjoy our meal?" He gave her a weak smile before heading off.

Deborah frowned and let out a heavy sigh. Would this town ever see it as acceptable for a young, single woman doctor to tend a man—even in the open company of others?

"Why am I bothering to learn how to heal folks if they'll never accept help from me?" she muttered under her breath. Thankfully no one seemed to notice. The last thing she wanted was to stir up yet another controversy for the day.

Chapter 9

"Don't need you," a bloodied black man told Christopher. "Ain't needin' no white man's he'p."

"I'm a doctor. Your lip looks like it could use a stitch or two."

The man wiped his mouth with the back of his hand. "Don' need your he'p—just like I said."

Another man nodded. "We got womenfolk what can fix us up."

Christopher looked around the group of injured men. "And that's how all of you feel?"

"Tha's the way it be for all of us."

The statement was matter-of-fact, and none of the other men so much as met Christopher's gaze. One by one, they turned and walked away until only Abraham Garby remained. He finally looked up and shook his head.

"Sorry, Doc. Iffen we ain't careful, there'll be more trouble than this. Best you go back to your folks and we go back to ours." He turned and walked to where he'd left his hat. Picking it up, he knocked it against his leg and kept moving.

Christopher wanted to go after the men, but he knew it would do no good. There was too much anger on both sides of this situation. He blew out a heavy breath and shrugged. If they didn't want his help, he couldn't win their trust by forcing it upon them.

The aroma of roasted meat filled the air and drew his attention. Christopher marveled at the long line of makeshift tables laden with food. This was his first time to celebrate Texas Independence Day.

"Doc, if you're lookin' for my sister, she's over yonder," Rob declared and pointed toward a stand of trees.

"Thanks." Christopher started to head in that direction, but Rob stopped him.

"Was anyone badly hurt?"

"I don't really know. No one would let me tend them."

Rob shook his head. "I don't rightly know

what got into folks. Seems to me it was just an accident."

"I think we can agree on that much," Christopher replied, "but apparently they can't. Sometimes I think people are just looking for an excuse to fight."

"Folks in these parts have plenty of excuses—leastwise, that's what it seems to me." Rob shrugged. "Guess it will always be that way."

"It shouldn't have to be." Christopher felt a heavy resignation wash over him. "But I suppose—at least for now—it will be."

"Ain't nothin' we can do by standin' here talkin' about it," Rob added. "If we don't get in line, we'll miss the white bread."

Christopher thought it ironic that even the color of the bread was of importance at this gathering. He understood that flour-based bread wasn't seen as often as corn bread, but another color-based preference was more than he wanted to face.

He found Deborah sitting alone and looking rather forlorn. This town wasn't interested in a woman doctor, but it was even less willing to accept an unmarried white woman working on the wounds of black men.

"Want some company?"

She looked up and studied him for a moment. "I didn't expect you to be back so soon."

"I know." He crouched down beside her.

"They didn't want my help any more than they would have taken yours."

"Truly? But why?"

"Because I'm white."

"But you've helped them before."

Christopher looked out toward the muddy creek. There was only a minimal amount of water within its banks. They could certainly use some rain. He felt Deborah reach out to touch his hand. He turned back to see her worried expression.

"Will it always be like this?"

"So long as good men allow this to be the acceptable manner of behavior." He shook his head. "But let's try to put it aside. Today's for celebrating, right?"

She nodded. "But it doesn't seem folks truly understand. Texas was different back then, Mama says. Before the war, they didn't seem half so worried about the color of a person's skin. Before Texas became its own country, the Mexican government respected men of all colors. Seems we've lost something in our liberty."

Christopher stood and helped Deborah to her feet. "Hopefully we'll get it back," he said, escorting her to the food.

"Come on, you two," Lizzie said as she and G.W. neared the food tables. "I can hardly wait to try a little of everything."

Deborah laughed. "You'd be hard-pressed to sample it all. Mother said there were over two hundred dishes."

"Oh my." Lizzie looked to G.W. "I don't suppose I can."

"Well, I sure intend to give it my best," G.W. said, giving her shoulder a squeeze.

"I'm glad you're feeling better," Deborah added. She looked to Christopher. "Lizzie's been a bit queasy of late."

"I thought it would be behind me by now, but in some ways it seems worse."

"For how long?" Christopher asked.

Lizzie considered the question for a moment. "Probably the better part of the last month. Seems to strike without warning at most any time of the day or night. I've always had trouble with nausea since I learned I was in a family way, but it seems that lately I have more trouble than ever."

Christopher thought for a moment. "Any other problems?"

Deborah looked at him oddly. "Do you think something's wrong?"

Now Lizzie and G.W. looked alarmed. Christopher put up his hand. "Don't make more out of this than needs to be. I'm just trying to be thorough."

"I'm tired all the time, but you told me I would be," she replied with a smile.

"I'd like to examine you tomorrow," Christopher said immediately, holding up his hands. "Not because I think anything is wrong. Come with Deborah to the office, and I'll see if I can't find something for the nausea."

Lizzie and G.W. seemed to calm and exchanged a smile. "She'll be there," G.W. told Christopher. "I'll bring them both myself."

Christopher nodded. "Then we'll discuss this more at that time."

As G.W. and Lizzie strolled toward the food, Deborah tugged on Christopher's arm. "Do you think there's a problem?"

He chuckled. "You are definitely one for speaking your mind—still, it would serve you well not to say the first thing that comes into your head. Especially when standing right in front of a patient."

"Well, there's no patient standing here now. What is it you suspect?"

He grinned. "Well, consider this. Your sister-in-law is only about four and a half months along, but in the last month she's grown considerably in size. The nausea has been more severe than most women and even now is extreme. I'm thinking she might be carrying twins."

Deborah's mouth dropped open and her eyes grew wide. "Twins?"

"Don't say anything just yet. We should have a better idea tomorrow."

"Oh, there's Mother with our dishes," Deborah said, pulling Christopher along. "We have a plate and silver for you, as well."

Christopher liked that he'd been included in the family. When he'd first arrived in the community, few wanted to associate with him, much less allow him to practice his medical skills on them. Now more folks openly allowed his care—and his friendship.

"Well, you two look like you could use a good meal," Mrs. Vandermark said, holding a plate out to Christopher.

"Thank you, ma'am. I'm quite happy to put a dent in the food." Christopher glanced at the vast arrangement of dishes on the food table. "Where are yours?"

Deborah's mother laughed. "Why, do you plan to avoid them?"

"On the contrary, I intend to start with the best."

She smiled. "In that case, I'll let Deborah point them out. She knows exactly what we brought. Be sure you get a piece of her butter cake before it's gone."

He looked at Deborah in surprise. "You baked?"

Her right brow arched slightly. "Indeed, I

did, and if you don't mind your manners, I won't tell you which cake is mine."

"Yes, ma'am," he said, nodding. "Thank you, ma'am."

Euphanel laughed and handed her daughter a plate. "You've got him well trained already."

Deborah rolled her eyes. "It's all just a show for you, Mother. Dr. Clayton has never listened to anything I've had to say. He thinks he already knows it all."

Christopher laughed and nudged Deborah forward. "What I really know is that I'm going to starve half to death if I stand around here waiting much longer. Come on."

Rob eyed Mara Shattuck trying to balance her plate and parasol and sauntered up to her as if he did this kind of thing every day.

"Can I be of service? Carry your plate?"

"Perhaps if you took the parasol," Mara said with a grateful expression.

Rob looked at the lacey pink thing and nodded reluctantly. No doubt he'd hear about this later if his brother caught sight of him toting the fancy umbrella around.

"Thank you." Mara handed him the parasol and focused on her choices of food. "Everything looks so good; it's hard not to take some of everything."

"I tried that once," Rob said, trying to decide if he should hold the parasol over Mara or just let it hang to the side. "It didn't work out so well. I got so stuffed, I was pert near sick."

"Gluttony is a sin, you know," she said sweetly.

"I suppose I do. Guess I'm just a regular old sinner."

"We all are sinners, Mr. Vandermark."

"Call me Rob. Mr. Vandermark is too uppity for me."

She looked at him, narrowing her eyes slightly. "It's a matter of etiquette and proper behavior, Mr. Vandermark. I am a single woman, and you are a single gentleman. We're only newly acquainted, and it would be unacceptable for us to pretend otherwise."

He looked at her and shook his head. "We might only be newly acquainted, but I'd like it well enough if we got to knowin' each other a whole lot better."

She stopped and turned. "To what outcome, Mr. Vandermark?"

Rob was momentarily stumped. "I . . . well . . . that is . . . I reckon I'd like for us to be . . . friends."

"I see." She shifted the plate from her left hand to her right. "I believe I'd like for us to be friends, Mr. Vandermark." She smiled.

"Would you care to sit with my father and me at dinner? We're set up just over there by the church."

Rob followed her gaze and could see that Pastor Shattuck was already busily eating. He grinned. "I'd be mighty glad to join you."

She reached out to take hold of the umbrella. "Wonderful. I shall see you there." She walked away, parasol blocking any view of her face.

Rob smiled to himself and quickly retrieved a plate for food. He was making progress with Mara Shattuck, and it wasn't turning out to be as difficult as he'd thought it might. Joining the Shattucks on their blanket, Rob plopped down and extended a hand. "Pastor. Good to see you again."

"Rob, I'm glad you could join us. Mara said you were quite helpful to her just now."

He flushed slightly. "I don't know how helpful I actually was, but I have to say it was my first time to hold a parasol."

Mara's father laughed. "Oh, the things we men do for women. I was just commenting to Mara that she shares a resemblance to your sister."

"Deborah?" Rob questioned, shaking his head. "G.W. mentioned some likeness, but they don't look alike to me."

"Well, of course they don't look alike, but

both have dark eyes and dark hair. They're even similar in size."

Rob glanced around as if looking for his sister, then settled his gaze back on Mara. "I reckon lots of folks can have some things in common. I think Miss Mara is much prettier than my sister, but don't tell Deborah." He grinned and picked up his fork. He quickly stuffed his mouth with some potato salad just in case someone wanted to ask him something else. This way he'd at least have a few moments to consider his answer.

"So tell me, Mr. Vandermark," Mara began, "where is God taking you on your life journey?"

Rob was momentarily mesmerized by the question. He finished chewing and swallowed before giving a shrug.

"I don't reckon I know for sure. I've been working in the family business since I was a small boy. My pa loved the forests, and logging became a way of life for our family."

"And now?" she asked, delicately picking at the food on her plate.

"Well, I guess there have been a few changes. My brother, G.W., got hurt last year. He took a fall out of a tree and injured his leg. Since then he's stayed at home to handle the office side of things. 'Course, he had to learn to read better. So my sister has been helpin' us both."

"So you're learning to read?"

He stiffened. "I could already read some; I'm just learnin' to do it better."

"But why?" she asked.

Her father saved him from having to answer. "Mara, I've never known you to be quite this inquisitive."

She shrugged. "People do not make changes without a good reason. I simply wondered what had prompted Mr. Vandermark to desire such skills."

Rob shrugged. "I don't rightly know. Strange as it sounds, I guess I just felt it was the right thing to do."

"God sometimes works like that," Pastor Shattuck said, nodding. "God will lay a matter on our heart, and we will find it impossible to rest until we act upon that urge."

Mara looked at Rob. "Was that how it was?"

He thought about it for a moment. "I suppose it was that way. Now I'm mostly readin' the Bible, and it's got me thinking more and more on God and what He wants from us."

"And have you learned what He wants from you?" she asked, her voice soft and appealing. "Did you try asking Him as I suggested?"

Rob contemplated the matter for a moment.

"I've asked, but I don't reckon I've figured it all out just yet."

"But you do believe God has a specific plan for you—for each person?"

"Of course. I reckon I've known that since I was knee-high to a grasshopper." He grinned and picked up a piece of white bread. "Doesn't mean I know what it is—but I know He's got a plan."

"That's a good start," the pastor told him. "Some folks don't even know that much."

"What are you doing to figure out what it is that God wants of you?" Mara asked. Both Rob and her father looked at her in surprise. She smiled. "I'm sorry. Have I made this conversation too personal?"

"No, I don't reckon you have," Rob said, giving her a lazy smile. "I just don't have an answer for you. I guess I'm not sure how a fella goes about figurin' out what God wants."

"There is always prayer and meditation on the Word," Pastor Shattuck told him. "Psalm 119:105 speaks to God's Word being a lamp unto my feet and a light unto my path. It's not that you have a light the size of the sun showing all the details of the journey. Sometimes just a portion of the path is revealed at a time."

"That's good to know, Pastor. I guess I hadn't thought about it that way before, but I can see where it would make a good amount of sense." Rob stuffed some more food in his mouth, hoping it would signal that he was done answering questions. He wanted to get Mara to talk about herself so he could get to know her better. He couldn't very well do that if they just kept talking about him and what God wanted him to do with his life.

"Pastor, could I have a word with you?"

It was Zed Perkins. He stood directly behind Rob and nodded when Rob looked up. "Good to see you, Rob. I was just speakin' to your mother. Miss Shattuck, I hope you won't mind me borrowin' your pa for a minute."

"Not at all, Mr. Perkins. I assure you, I am in good company."

Rob smiled at this and tried not to act too pleased. Hopefully with her father gone, Mara would be willing to share something about herself. At least he hoped.

"So, tell me about your life in New Orleans," he said just before popping a piece of pork into his mouth.

Mara put her fork down and seemed to think about the question for a moment. Rob was about to give up on getting an answer when she finally began to speak.

"My father thought it important that my brother and I be raised with a woman's influence after our mother died. He sent us to New Orleans to live with our grandmother."

"I forgot you had a brother. How old is he?"

"He's four years older than me," she replied.

Rob shook his head. "That doesn't help me much. I don't know how old you are."

She smiled. "I suppose that was rather remiss of me. He's twenty-eight. We were both very young when we went to live with Grandmother. She was quite strict with her religious beliefs and saw that we received a complete education in the Bible."

"Did you go to a university like my sister?" Rob asked.

Mara shook her head. "No, I was never that good at my studies, and frankly, I had little desire to further my learning. I've known for some time what God's plan was for me."

Now the conversation was finally headed somewhere that Rob wanted to go. "And what'd God tell you?"

"Well, one of the most important things is that He wants me to share His love with the people I come across, so that they might know who God really is."

Rob didn't mean to, but he gave a bit of a chuckle. "Don't you think most folks already know about God and His love?"

“I suppose most everyone knows about God, Mr. Vandermark. But I sometimes wonder if knowing about Him is the same as knowing Him personally.”

Rob considered her words. “I reckon there are folks who never really cared to know God.”

“I’ve certainly known that to be true,” she said softly.

“Well, what is it you think can be done?”

She appeared to consider this for a moment. “I think we should be a willing servant. Learn His Word—truly learn the Scriptures and what they mean. Know God in a more intimate way. As I do these things, I can better share His truth and love.”

“And what will you do when you learn all of this? Ain’t gonna work for a little gal like you to be a preacher. How can God use a woman, if you don’t mind my askin’?”

She smiled. “God can use anyone, Mr. Vandermark. Even so, that’s between Him and me for the time. When I feel He would have me share it with you, I assure you that I will.”

Her response left him rather confused. Why had she been insistent on knowing what God wanted him to do, but when it came to returning the same information, she took quiet and refused to speak? Women were such queer creatures. Who could know their minds—much less their hearts?

ꕥ

Lizzie waited rather nervously for Dr. Clayton to finish his exam. She'd been terribly worried about her condition ever since their conversation the day before. She had fervently hoped he would tell her that there was nothing to worry about.

Deborah didn't seem overly worried, but then again, she was quite capable of hiding her feelings if the situation merited.

"Well, I can't be completely certain," Dr. Clayton began as Deborah helped Lizzie to sit up, "but I think I have some interesting insight into your nausea."

Lizzie extended her hand to Deborah. If something was wrong, she wanted to at least have her friend close. She swallowed hard. What would G.W. do? He was so excited about the baby. At times, the pregnancy seemed to be the only thing that kept him pushing his recovery.

Deborah scooted closer and took hold of her hand. Lizzie looked to the doctor and nodded. "Is it bad news?"

He shook his head. "Not to my way of thinking. I believe you're going to have twins."

Lizzie felt the impact of his statement as the breath caught in her throat. "Twins?"

"We will know better as the weeks go by,

but I'm feeling rather confident that you carry two babies instead of just one. We'll watch you closely as time passes, and if you feel anything might be amiss, don't hesitate to let me know."

"Oh, this is so surprising." She put her hand to her stomach. "Twins."

Deborah patted her arm. "Let me fetch G.W. He will absolutely burst his buttons when he hears."

Lizzie shook her head. "Let's not tell him until Dr. Clayton is sure. I don't want to get him all excited and then disappoint him if it's not true." She looked to the doctor. "When do you suppose we can know for certain?"

"Probably in another month or so. Maybe less."

"That will be soon enough," Lizzie said, looking to Deborah. "We'll tell him only if we're certain. Agreed?"

Deborah smiled. "You're the patient. I will keep my mouth shut and wait for you to give me the word that it's all right to speak."

Lizzie nodded and let out a heavy sigh. Twins.

Chapter 10

Two weeks later, Rob found himself still considering his conversation with Mara. She made him look deep within his heart and mind. There were things about God that seemed simple and clear, while other issues were far more complex. Mara's comments challenged him in a way he'd never experienced before.

The evening was chilled, but not too humid. Rob found Deborah sitting on the porch quietly rocking. He hoped she wouldn't mind his intrusion. He thought with her being close to Mara's age, she might be able to help him understand the young woman's mind.

"Can I ask you some questions?"

Deborah looked up and stopped toying with her long thick braid. "Of course, you can. Have a seat and tell me what's bothering you."

"Did I say something was bothering me?" he asked as he plopped down on a three-legged stool. The seat rocked awkwardly as Rob worked to balance.

"You didn't have to. You only took two portions of Mother's lemon cornmeal cake and hardly poured any sweet cream atop."

He laughed. "That's only 'cause I'd already had three helpin's of her black-eyed peas and ate a whole fried chicken by myself."

Deborah nodded. "I suppose I should have taken that into account."

Rob sobered. "Still, fact is, I do have somethin' on my mind."

"Well, I hope talking about it might relieve your heart on the matter."

He thought for a moment. "Do you think God talks to each person?"

Deborah sat up and stopped rocking. "How do you mean?"

"Well, Mara Shattuck has asked me about where I figured God was directin' me to go. I don't think I've ever heard God talk out loud to me."

He watched his sister carefully. "I think God addresses each of us. Not always in the same way, but definitely with the same heart of love. He wants us to seek His will, but how can we if He doesn't speak to us? You grew up around folks who loved God—who revered His name. People in our family often talk about how God desires to guide us and have us walk with Him. A lot of folks in the world haven't the interest. A lot of people right here in Perkinsville probably think they know who God is but don't really have a clue."

"But have you heard God speak to you?"

Deborah eased back in her chair and started to rock again. "I believe I have. I think often when we get that nudge in our heart—when something keeps coming back to us in the Word or through the teachings the pastor gives or we hear wise counsel from someone who cares, those are the times God speaks to us. I think He can also speak to our hearts."

"And is that the way we can know Him better?" He couldn't hide the longing in his voice. He needed to know the truth.

"Some folks think just hearing about God means that they know Him. I think that really knowing Him requires we take an active role with Him."

"What do you mean?"

"As I said, we grew up with God-fearing parents. Our family has always talked about God and how we should respect and esteem Him. We were taught that the Bible is His infallible word to us—His inspired Word carefully written down by His faithful servants. There's never been a time in our lives when we didn't know who our parents believed God to be, and then to gradually learn who God was for ourselves."

"True enough."

A light breeze blew across the yard, rustling the trees and bringing hints of muscari on the air. Deborah pulled her shawl closer. "A great many people don't have it that way, Rob. I think having grown up as we did, it's easier to accept that God speaks to us. Some folks think God doesn't care—that He's just waiting to accuse us of our failings. I think God wants to talk to us like a Father—like our father used to talk to us. He offered us direction and encouragement. Why would God do any less?"

"I don't reckon He would."

She smiled. "I don't think He would, either. If you want to know what God is trying to say to you—ask Him to make it very clear. Ask Him to show you so there is no doubt the choice is right."

Rob nodded and mulled the matter in his mind. "Mara said a lot of folks know about God, but don't really know who He is. I guess if they never try to talk to Him or listen back, they won't get closer to Him."

"Exactly. They are just pretending so people

will believe them to be good. Sometimes they really want to impress folks, and they memorize all sorts of Scriptures so they can spout them off whenever it suits them. Unfortunately, they don't always understand what they're quoting, and they use God's Word to hurt other people."

"I don't reckon God approves of that," Rob replied.

"Even pastors can be guilty of this. They are wolves in sheep's clothing, pretending to be holy and knowledgeable of God, but they don't know Him at all."

"You mean they preach and know about God's Word, but ain't accepted Jesus as their Savior?" Rob shook his head, trying to fully understand exactly what Deborah was saying.

"Sometimes," Deborah admitted. "Sometimes they don't even know what the Bible says. They have a form of godliness, but they really don't know God at all."

Something deep within seemed to call out to Rob. He found himself longing to know more—to understand what this might have to do with him and the future God had for him. He started to ask Deborah how he might learn more, but as if she'd read his mind, the solution was in her next words.

"If you want to better understand, I'd talk

to Uncle Arjan or Pastor Shattuck. Either one is bound to offer you insight from a man's perspective—especially from that of a man who loves God and truly does understand, or at least seeks to understand, who God is."

"I'll do that," Rob declared. "Seems like a good thing." He got up and threw Deborah a wink. "Besides, if I go to talk to Pastor, then I'll get to see Mara."

Deborah smiled. "Somehow I doubt you'll have much trouble coming up with excuses to see Miss Shattuck."

ꙮ

Deborah finished reading the last of the books she'd borrowed from Christopher and looked rather sadly at the stack. Reading used to give her such joy, but the more she read about illnesses and cures, the more helpless she felt. How could she ever be of use in medicine if people wouldn't allow her to work with them?

A part of her could actually understand their fears and concerns. Women in medicine were usually relegated to working with other women or with children. Even Margaret Foster, the midwife and healer in Perkinsville, wasn't always allowed to treat the men. However, folks around here knew the ornery woman and most feared she'd put a curse on them if they didn't acquiesce.

"But she's a widow just turned fifty, and I'm young and unmarried." Deborah went to the dining room window and parted the curtains. The new dining room wasn't yet finished, so they were still using the old one. There were warm, comfortable memories in this room.

She thought of her father, sitting at the head of the table, reading the Bible to them. He had always helped each of them understand what the words meant and why they were important. Sometimes he'd share stories of when he'd been a boy and tell them something that reflected the same Bible lesson in real life. Mother called these his "walking the road" stories. It was all about applying the truth of God's Word to one's daily life. Deborah let the curtain fall back into place without really even seeing the outside. Her heart was turned inward, and that's where her vision remained.

"You seem awfully deep in thought," Mother said from the kitchen door.

Deborah looked up in surprise. "I thought you were with Sissy."

"I was for a spell. Then I went outside to work on a couple of the garden patches. I thought about putting some supper on to cook. You want to help me?"

She nodded. "I might as well. I don't seem to be of much use elsewhere."

Mother looked at her oddly. "Feeling sorry for yourself?"

Deborah laughed. Her mother knew her so well. "I suppose I was, in a way."

"Nothing to be gained from that." Mother motioned her to follow. "There's plenty of work to be done. It might not be exactly what you want to do, but it will be quite useful to me if you are of a mind to help." Mother took a large bowl of potatoes from the counter. "You can start by peeling these."

Deborah took up a paring knife and got comfortable. "Did you ever feel that God had somehow overlooked you, Mother?"

Pausing for a moment, the older woman cocked her head to one side. "Now your feeling of uselessness is about God forgetting you?"

"No. Not exactly. I just feel . . . well . . . confused. I always thought I was given the ability to easily learn from books because God wanted me to help with the business and keep the office. Now it seems really clear that G.W. is needed there. In fact, he and Lizzie often work together in the office, so he doesn't even need me to assist him."

Deborah paused as she began to cut away

the skin of a potato. "Then there's my interest in medicine. As a young, single woman, I'm not allowed to see and treat men—especially if those men have black skin. Not only that, but I'm not really even desired by the women. I thought because Mrs. Foster was so accepted by them that I would be, too. After all, I grew up with many of the folks in the area."

"Perhaps it's your familiarity that makes them uncomfortable," Mother suggested. "Still, you won't always be a young, single woman. The woman part you can't change." Her tone was teasing as she continued. "But the young and single will pass away before you know it. Believe me. I've watched my youth flee before my eyes."

"Nonsense, Mother. You're still quite young," Deborah countered. "You're young enough that you really should consider remarrying."

The crash of metal pots on the floor caused Deborah to jump. She turned to find her mother staring at her in stunned surprise. "What did you say?"

Deborah put the knife and potato aside and went to pick up the pans. "You heard me. I said you should consider marrying again. It's not good for you to be alone."

"Have you seen me be alone lately? I have people all around me," her mother said, taking the pieces from Deborah.

"That's not the same, and you know it."

Her mother turned to put the pots away. "I thought we were talking about you and how God had forgotten you."

Deborah touched her mother's shoulder. "I hope I haven't upset you. I know you loved Father dearly, but you are still very young, compared to some widows. You're not even forty-four."

"That's decades past the age a man would want a woman for marriage," her mother said with a nervous laugh. "Most men are looking for women to share a lifetime and start a family. I have my family in place, and who knows how long I'll be on this earth."

"Mother, you have no way of knowing where God will lead."

"And you think you do?" Her mother turned to face her. Her cheeks were flushed.

Deborah wasn't used to seeing her mother like this. She seemed almost embarrassed. "Mother, has something happened? Something to do with this matter?"

Mother's eyes widened and she opened her mouth as if to give a quick retort, but then closed it and lowered her gaze. "I . . . well . . . I . . . "

Deborah took hold of her mother's hands. "Please tell me what's wrong."

"Well, it's just that," Mother said, lifting her head, "Rachel Perkins said something to me, and I have to admit I've not had a decent night's sleep since."

"Come and tell me what she said." Deborah pulled her toward the table. Mother sat and folded her hands together. She seemed so upset by the matter that Deborah wondered if she should just let it go. Still, her own curiosity was great. What could Mrs. Perkins have possibly said that would cause such a stir?

Waiting for her mother to speak was difficult. Deborah wanted to urge her to explain but knew Mother would tell her when and if she decided to do so. Picking up the knife and potato once again, Deborah thought perhaps the normalcy of the action would ease some of the tension. She peeled quietly and waited.

Finally, without warning, her mother blurted out the matter. "Rachel believes your uncle is in love with me."

Deborah's head snapped up. She quickly forgot the potato. "Uncle Arjan?"

Her mother nodded and fixed her gaze on Deborah's face. "It never even occurred to me, but Rachel thinks he's loved me for a very long time. Of course, he's never said anything, if he does. And he's certainly never acted untoward."

Deborah knew her uncle cared deeply about Mother's well-being. He was always very attentive and considerate of her needs.

Goodness, why hadn't I considered that before? He's never married, and he's always remained close to Mother.

Deborah smiled at the thought of her uncle and mother marrying. "I think it would be a grand idea for you two to be together."

Mother leaned forward. "Truly?"

"Of course. You know Uncle Arjan better than anyone. He's a good man, and he obviously loves you or he wouldn't care for you so earnestly. Perhaps that love is more than merely a brother for his sister-in-law."

"I truly had never considered it," her mother confessed. The words flowed more easily now. "When Rachel mentioned the possibility, I felt so strange. I tried to think back and remember if I'd ever done anything to stir his feelings. I certainly loved your father and never meant to give false hopes."

"Mother, no one could accuse you of being anything but faithful to Father. I've never seen two people who loved each other more. Even when you two would argue, I could always see that spark between you."

"I don't know what to do."

Deborah smiled. "What would you like to do?"

Mother shook her head. "I've been praying about the matter ever since Rachel brought it up. But I've felt completely out of sorts and have avoided being alone with Arjan for even a moment. I'm sure he thinks he's done something wrong."

"Well, I think you should simply ask him how he feels," Deborah suggested. "I mean, what if his love is limited to just being your brother-in-law? You have a right to know, either way."

"I would feel so odd, asking him."

"Perhaps. But I think if you pray about it, God can surely give you a sign or arrange the situation so that you can learn the truth."

Her mother nodded and got to her feet. "I know He can, and maybe having Rachel say something was one of those ways. I just didn't expect such a thing at my age."

Deborah put the peeled potato aside and picked up the next. "Well, I think you're very deserving of love." She smiled and began to hum a tune often sung at weddings.

"Don't go marrying me off just yet." Her mother went back to the stack of pans and began organizing them. "I won't have you acting all silly about this."

Thinking of her mother and uncle together as husband and wife very nearly made Deborah giggle. There was no other man in the world she trusted more than her uncle. Perhaps God would even use her to help bring the couple together.

"Wouldn't that be something?"

"What?" her mother asked.

Deborah shook her head. "Oh, nothing. I was just thinking out loud."

Chapter 11

"You ladies have a nice time together," Pastor Shattuck bid as he headed for the front door of the parsonage. "I'm going to go visit the sick."

"We'll see you later, Father. I'll have a nice cake ready for your afternoon rest."

Pastor Shattuck smiled. "It's good to have a woman in the house again. My ministry has suffered without your mother."

After he was gone, Deborah couldn't help but question Mara. "I hope you won't mind my curiosity or find my words bold, but it seems odd to me that your father mentions his ministry suffering without your mother. I have asked on numerous occasions for him to clarify various things in the Bible, but he always directs me back to the men in my family. If the men in my family were knowledgeable, I would have asked them in the first place."

Mara smiled and poured Deborah a cup of tea. "It doesn't surprise me he should direct you in such a manner."

"So he doesn't believe women should study the Scriptures?"

Her new friend looked shocked. "Oh, it's not that at all. Father definitely believes women should study God's Word. He is of a heart that all people should."

"Then why wouldn't he be willing to speak to me? All I wanted to do was better understand, and oftentimes it had to do with his sermons."

Mara put the pot on the table and took her seat. "I will share something with you, because I believe I can trust you. However, I ask that this go no further than this room."

Deborah couldn't imagine what the young woman was about to say. Mara's tone was quite serious, and Deborah's imagination immediately conjured all sorts of thoughts. "I promise."

"Not long after my mother died, my father sent my brother and me to live with our grandmother. Father said it was because we needed a woman's hand, but I know that we reminded him of Mother, and he could hardly bear his sorrow.

"It was shortly after he sent us to live in New Orleans that a young widow in the church approached Father. Her family was quite wealthy. In fact, they pretty much owned the town. She told Father that she wanted to better understand God's Word. She opened her Bible and pointed to passages that were especially difficult. Father explained them to the woman and encouraged her to come to him anytime she felt confused."

"That would have been nice," Deborah said. She picked up the cup of tea. "He had no interest in doing the same for me."

"That's because as time went by, this woman came to him more and more. Soon she wasn't just coming to see him at the church; she was coming to the house. Then soon it wasn't just in broad daylight, but she began making evening calls, as well. Then without warning, she tried to seduce my father. She threw herself shamelessly at him and begged him to make her his wife. Father refused and forbid her to ever again come alone to the house."

"That must have been a very difficult situation."

Mara looked beyond Deborah at the fireplace where a small flame flickered. "It was devastating. The woman, like Pharaoh's wife with Joseph, told everyone she could that Father had taken indecent liberties. She had her family demand Father marry her."

"What did he do?" Deborah wondered how any woman could act in such a wonton, lying way. Why would she want to force a marriage that would surely leave her with a hateful husband?

"Father took his place in the pulpit on Sunday and announced quite clearly that nothing had happened. He told the people how he had done nothing untoward—he had in fact only answered the woman's questions about the Bible. He challenged them to seek the Lord to discern the truth of the matter. He further demanded that the woman stand before the church and God and tell the truth. She refused."

"What happened?"

"The woman's father came and offered Father a great deal of money to marry his daughter. He refused, of course, saying that his heart was still grieving for my mother and that he could not marry another. The man was furious. He felt his daughter's reputation had been damaged." Mara leaned toward Deborah. "Personally, we believe the man had endured such things from his daughter before this and merely wanted to make her someone else's responsibility."

"But why would any woman want a man who didn't love her? Wouldn't a man, in fact, be more inclined to despise her for forcing such a situation upon him?" Deborah asked.

"I cannot say. There are a great many women in this world who cannot bear to live without a man. For whatever reasons, she appeared to be one of those. Father eventually had to step down and give up the church and leave town. He felt it necessary to keep the church from dividing in two, but it broke his heart, nevertheless."

"So this is why he won't spend time teaching women?"

Mara smiled and nodded. "Exactly so. He truly wants women to learn all they can about God and the Bible, but he cannot risk his ministry for God to do so. He wants to be above reproach in all things."

Deborah considered this new information and felt a peace wash over her. She had a newfound respect for her pastor. He hadn't been disinterested in her learning—only that they should not be alone for the teaching. "If I need to ask questions in the future, I'll take someone with me."

"I'm sure that would be acceptable. Also if I'm around, it shouldn't be a problem."

Mara sampled a cookie, then quickly put it down. "Father is also very worried about our town and the tensions that have risen up between the blacks and whites," she said out of the blue. "That grieves him most sorely."

"As it does a great many folks," Deborah countered.

"I know that your family has been personally wounded. I am sorry for that," Mara said. "Father hopes to continue to encourage the congregation to make changes—to recognize the wrong in harming each other."

"That will take a miracle."

Mara laughed. "Good thing God is in the miracle business, then, yes?"

Deborah smiled, grateful for her new friend. Mara had a way of putting her at ease, even when her worries took front and center in Deborah's mind.

"So if I might change the subject, I wanted to ask you about your family. Father said your family had been in Texas for a long while—even before the war."

"Yes, my mother and father came here right after marrying. Mother was only sixteen years old. I believe it was in February of 1858. Father wanted to start a new life here, and his younger brother wanted to come, as well. "

"Your mother's people held slaves; is that not true?" Mara asked.

Deborah nodded. "Yes. Mother's family ran a large farm in Georgia. Sissy was her companion back then. When Mr. Lincoln set the slaves free, Sissy wanted to come west and be with Mother. Mother agreed, and Father hired Sissy to be our housekeeper and cook. Eventually, Sissy fell in love and married, but she continued to work for us."

"My grandmother owned slaves," Mara said rather thoughtfully. "For a long time she was convinced that it was her Christian duty to do so. She felt under her ownership she could guide them to a better spiritual walk. You must remember in New Orleans, there were a great many slaves who believed in superstitions and voodoo. It was quite frightening to see the effects of such beliefs. My grandmother was a strong woman of faith, however. She stood up to such things and, in doing so, taught me to make a stand, as well. She said that while she had no regrets in setting her slaves free, she had a great many fears for their well-being. Most couldn't read or write, and the animosity toward them made remaining in the South quite difficult. Your mother makes such a strong stand for better treatment of the former slaves, yet her own people were slaveholders. Was there anything in particular that caused her to believe slavery was wrong?"

"Mother once told me that she had never approved of slavery. She had seen too much cruelty. People often said, 'Oh, but the black man wouldn't even know how to dress himself without the white man to show him.' Mother thought it all hogwash."

Mara nodded. "I couldn't agree more."

"Now she still hears people making comments in regard to how the Negro will not understand the voting process or how to arrange for his own legal needs, and it causes her great frustration."

"Father says that the War Between the States ended only to have the War of Racial Antagonism begin. He believes this is something that will continue for decades, maybe even longer."

"I hate to think he's right, but I have little reason to doubt his judgment," Deborah replied.

"How is Sissy faring? Father said her injuries were terrible," Mara inquired.

"They were. She suffered a terrible head wound, but she is slowly improving. She's gaining strength every day, and while her full recovery is still some weeks away, we have hope that she will continue to do well." Deborah put aside her teacup. Mara offered her the plate of cookies, but Deborah shook her head. "Thank you, no. I shouldn't take much more of your day. I have some books to return to Dr. Clayton."

"Oh, might I come with you?" Mara asked. "I have a pie for him. It's cooling on the sill."

"Of course. That would be very nice," Deborah replied, though she had hoped for some time alone with Christopher. Yet she knew such privacy was frowned upon. They had, in fact, caused many raised eyebrows at the Independence Day celebration when Dr. Clayton had taken hold of her arm at an unexpected moment. Such things were usually reserved for married couples.

Mara got to her feet and collected the cups and saucers. Placing everything on the tea tray, she excused herself. "I shan't be more than a minute."

Deborah took the opportunity to study the small sitting room. She had been here before with her mother, but now it bore a decidedly more feminine touch. She couldn't help but smile at the doilies that now graced the back and arms of a rather large cushioned chair. Mara's influence had obviously taken hold.

There were other things, as well. On the fireplace mantel there was a lovely vase of flowers, and framed photos of family members sat on either side of the arrangement. Beside these were small porcelain figurines of birds.

Mara returned with her basket and hat in hand. She placed the basket on the chair she'd just vacated and secured her stylish bonnet. Her long black curls had been pinned carefully at the back of her head, and her bonnet was snug against the thick locks, leaving little ringlets to peek out at the bottom.

"There, now I'm presentable," Mara said, adding short crocheted gloves to her hands. She picked up the basket, and Deborah took the signal as one for them to depart.

"I was just admiring your decorating ideas. You have given this home a much-needed feminine touch." Deborah moved to the door. "Let me get that for you." She maneuvered past Mara and reached for the handle. Before stepping through the door herself, she picked up the books she'd deposited on the foyer table.

The two ladies made their way across the street, past the church, and around the corner to the doctor's house. Deborah commented on a variety of things from the weather to the thick smoky air that reeked of coal and sawdust before they finally climbed the few steps to Dr. Clayton's porch.

Deborah didn't bother to knock. She opened the waiting room door and called out. "Dr. Clayton, you have visitors."

No one was in the outer room, so perhaps Christopher had gone to make calls on the area people. Just then, however, she heard a child crying from beyond the inner office.

"Ah, he must have a patient." She smiled and motioned to Mara. "Might as well have a seat. This could take some time."

༄

Euphanel was surprised when Sissy announced she wanted to get up and walk a spell. The woman would simply not take no for an answer, so Euphanel helped her friend into a robe and steadied Sissy as she got to her feet.

"Feels good to be up," Sissy declared. "Me and that bed is gettin' to where we ain't such friends."

Euphanel smiled. "That's a good sign. Mother always said that when I was sick and tired of being sick and tired, I was on the mend."

"Dat be true." Sissy smiled and took an uneasy step. "Been lyin' there, feelin' sorry for myself, and the Lord done tol' me to stop. Said He got better things for me to do and so I's gonna do it."

"And did He tell you what it was you were supposed to do?"

Sissy smiled at Euphanel. "He just done told me to step out. So that's what I'm doin'. Jes' like Moses and the Israelites. I's bound for the promised land."

Euphanel put her arm around Sissy's waist

and noted that the older woman had lost a great deal of weight. "I should think that some of what the Lord has in mind is for you to have a good meal. You're as thin as an old barn cat after having kittens."

Sissy chuckled. "Ain't never been called thin, afore now. I'm bettin' it won't last long. Don' you be a worryin'."

Euphanel shook her head and helped Sissy to a chair. "You should rest a bit before we move on. I'm quite happy to have you sitting in the front room, but I don't want you collapsing in the hall on the way."

"I's stronger than you know," Sissy said, meeting Euphanel's expression.

Euphanel grew somber. "I know you are my dear, dear friend. That gift from God has brought you through so far."

Sissy drew a deep breath and eased back against the chair. "George used to tell me I was stronger than any man he knowed, 'ceptin' for hisself." She grinned. "He jes' didn't know I was stronger than him, too. Had to be. The Good Lord done knowed what I would be up against, married to such a man."

Euphanel laughed and nodded. "Truer words were never spoken."

"I'm shore thankful for this family," Sissy said, growing more serious.

"And we're thankful for you. I'm glad you've decided to stay with us."

"Ain't a whole lot of choices, what since the house done burned down."

Euphanel shook her head. "You know that isn't true. We would have happily rebuilt your house. I would just rather you live your days with us. I don't care if you ever do another thing but sit and sing."

"Speakin' of singin', what did you and Miz Perkins decide about the shape-note singin'?"

"We have our first gathering next Saturday evening. It will be interesting to see who actually turns up. We might only have a handful of folks at best."

"And you plan to invite colored folk, too?"

Smiling, Euphanel sat on the end of the bed. "I do. Rachel and I have already discussed it. We had thought to wait until people were used to getting together and then start asking the blacks to join us, but Rachel decided we might as well just go for it straightaway. I think she's probably right."

"Won't be to the likin' of some folks. Might cause some trouble."

"We'll put that in the Lord's hands," Euphanel declared. "He holds the future for all of us—black, white, red, or brown. I can't see worrying about it until it's time."

Sissy smiled. “Even then, ain’t no sense worryin’.”

“You’re right,” Euphanel replied. “Now, come on. Let’s get you up.”

Chapter 12

"Well, this is a pleasant and fortuitous surprise." Christopher smiled at Mara and then turned to Deborah. "I have a case I'd like you to see."

"And what might that be?"

Christopher motioned. "Come and see for yourself."

"What about Mara? She's brought you something."

Christopher motioned them to follow. "You can both come. I'm sure the patient won't mind—she's only five."

He led them back into the examination room. "Miz Pulaski brought little Mary in with a sore throat and difficulty swallowing."

Deborah nodded at the young mother. "I

remember speaking with you at the Independence Day celebration. You are opening a new dressmaking shop."

The blond-haired woman smiled. "Mighty kind of you to remember me."

Moving to where the child sat on the examination table, Deborah reached out her hand. "Miss Mary, I'm sorry to hear that you're feeling bad."

"My froat hurts," the girl replied.

Christopher brought a lamp closer. "Pick up that mirror and you'll be able to angle the light down her throat." He waited for Deborah to get into position. "Now, Mary, I want you to open your mouth and say 'ahhhhh.' Can you do that again?"

The little girl nodded. "Ahhhhh."

Deborah peered into her mouth while Christopher depressed the child's tongue. "Can you see the problem?"

"Her tonsils are quite swollen. It appears that an abscess is starting to form." Deborah straightened. "Quinsy?"

He nodded. She was smart to be sure. He had figured her to easily see the enlarged tonsils, but the abscess was in the very early stages and not fully formed.

"What will you do to treat this?" Deborah asked.

Christopher smiled and replaced the lamp

on the counter. "Well, I was just telling Miz Pulaski that since this is Mary's first time to have this trouble, we will treat it in the most widely accepted manner. Dover's Powder will help with the pain, warm apple cider vinegar gargles will hopefully eliminate any further development of the abscess, and plenty of fluids and rest will help with the rest of her miseries."

Deborah nodded. "I would have suggested the same thing. Maybe even a muellein poultice."

"I agree." He smiled and looked to where Mara had retreated to a chair across the room. "Remember when I asked you about quinsy that day at the celebration?"

"Indeed. I, however, could never have known what to do for such a matter. Miss Vandermark certainly has a mind for such things."

"Are you a doctor?" the child asked.

Deborah looked at Christopher and then at the girl. "Not exactly, but I'd like to be one day."

"Ain't never heard of no lady doctors," Mrs. Pulaski remarked. " 'Ceptin' for midwives."

"Yes, well, times are changing," Christopher said. "There are many fine physicians of the female gender. The world is starting to see that women are just as capable of learning as men, and women are being admitted into more and more fields. One day maybe Mary will be a doctor."

Mary's eyes widened. She shook her head. "Ain't gonna be a doctor. I wanna sew dresses like my mama."

Mrs. Pulaski smiled and came to the child's side. "That would seem far more fittin' than bein' a doctor."

Christopher shrugged. "I think Mary should be whatever she desires. First, however, we need to get her well." He went and retrieved the medicine. After instructing the mother on how to measure out the medicine and administer it, Christopher sent the Pulaskis on their way.

"I hope that's her last bout," he said, coming back to where Deborah stood, "but I doubt it will be. She's at the right age to start having these problems, and it wouldn't surprise me if she hadn't already had several bouts of tonsillitis before now. She probably never saw anyone unless it was Miz Foster."

"No, the Pulaski family is new to the area," Deborah said, shaking her head. "Mrs. Pulaski was mentioning that at the party. Her husband has been hired on at the mill with the expansion."

He nodded. "Just the same, I'm thinking it's possible the child has suffered this before.

Either way, only time will tell if the tonsils need to be removed."

"Have you done that surgery before?" Deborah asked.

"I have on many occasions." He grinned. "But you haven't, so that will be something of an experience."

Mrs. Foster entered the examination room door without so much as a knock. She seemed surprised to find Deborah there and lost little time in commenting. "Are you sick?"

Deborah shook her head. "Not at all. We were merely discussing a case."

"Ain't no reason for you to be talkin' about patients," the older woman countered. "Doc has my help, and that's all he needs."

"Now, Mrs. Foster, I told you that Deborah wanted to train to become a physician."

"Deborah, is it? Seems like you two have gotten mighty familiar. I heard you was a-courtin'. Seems to me that workin' together would be uncalled for. Ain't right for you two to be alone together." She looked to Christopher and waggled her finger. "Things get out of hand mighty easy."

"Well, they weren't exactly alone, Miz Foster," Mara Shattuck said, standing to join the group. Margaret Foster seemed surprised to find the young woman present but said nothing. "I baked Dr. Clayton a pie, and Deborah was kind enough to accompany me here for the delivery." She smiled up at Dr. Clayton. "I do hope you like pie."

"Absolutely," he replied. "Deborah . . . ah, Miss Vandermark, would you show her where to leave it on my desk?"

"Certainly." Deborah led Mara back the direction they'd come.

Christopher looked at the accusing face of Mrs. Foster and smiled. "You really needn't worry. Nothing is amiss here."

"Still ain't fittin'."

"I find that strange coming from you. Didn't you tell me you trained early on to learn healing?"

The older woman's face contorted into a scowl. "I was in a healin' family. My granny and mama were healers. It were only right that I take on the chore. Miss Deborah ain't from such a line. She's got no reason to be workin' in such things."

"I beg to differ," Deborah said, returning from the delivery of the pie. Mara was close on her heels. "I loved my science courses at the university and believe that I have a gift for such things. I've helped on many occasions with sickness and wounds and I want to serve others by increasing my knowledge and skill."

"Folks round here ain't never gonna accept you doctorin' them."

"And why is that, Miz Foster?" Mara asked.

Christopher almost felt sorry for the older woman. With Deborah and Mara standing up to her, surely Miz Foster had met her match. Of course, not many folks had the guts to face the woman who was known to put curses on a fellow without warning.

But Margaret Foster was not to be bested by the younger women. She gave a jerk of her chin in defiance. "Ain't proper for her to be treatin' folks. She ain't even married yet and shouldn't have any knowledge of a man's body. What man is gonna marry her, with her knowin' such things?"

"I don't believe that is an issue here," Christopher declared. He threw a wink at Deborah and found it most charming to see her blush.

"Papa says that men and women should do as God calls them," Mara countered. "Sometimes God calls us to tasks that seem unlikely, but He always has a reason. I think it's marvelous that Miss Vandermark would take on such an endeavor. I'd be pleased to have her for my physician. Seems a woman would better understand another woman's ailments."

"But it ain't needed here," Mrs. Foster declared. "I'm here to see to it."

"True for now, but that doesn't mean you will always be here. I think that anytime a person can increase their knowledge, it is good, don't you?" Mara questioned, looking to Christopher.

He crossed his arms and raised a brow. "I think that knowledge is always beneficial."

"I do, too," Mara replied, smiling as if the matter were completely solved. "I wonder, Miz Foster, if you wouldn't mind helping me with an herbal matter. I understand you have managed to grow butterbur. I think it's positively wonderful for headaches."

Margaret Foster seemed ready to speak on the earlier matter, then closed her mouth. She looked suspicious for a moment before finally nodding at the smiling young woman. "Come with me." She looked to Dr. Clayton and Deborah. "You two shouldn't be left alone. I'd get on home if I were you, Miss Deborah."

With that she marched to the door, Mara following quickly on her heels. Mara turned and gave a grin before following the older woman outside. Christopher let out a heavy breath and shook his head.

"That woman would try the patience of Job."

Deborah shook her head. "She makes me so mad sometimes. All I want is to do what I feel qualified and capable of doing. I don't mind studying until my eyes are blurry, but I have the right to be given a chance.

"How is it fair that she goes around turning people away from the idea of my becoming a doctor? It's not right." Deborah began to pace, waving her arms for effect. "It's pure jealousy. She's just out of sorts because she thinks I've taken something from her. But I haven't. And why is it not acceptable for a woman to treat an injured or dying soul, just as a man might do? I'm so intolerant when it comes to dealing with ignorance." She fisted her hands and let out a growl of frustration.

"Should I get the water pitcher?" Christopher asked casually.

"And another thing—" Deborah stopped and looked at him oddly. "What?"

"The water pitcher? Remember when you doused me to calm me down? I promised to keep it handy, and there it sits." He pointed to the table under the window. "I just wondered if I needed to retrieve it for the purpose of helping you to let go your anger."

"No. I'd rather not have to explain." She sighed. "I don't mean to be so volatile. It just crosses me wrong from time to time. I try so hard to do what's right, and then something like this happens. Maybe I should give up. Maybe it's not what God wants me to do. Maybe I just think it is."

Christopher heard her voice and figured a walloping dose of pity might be Deborah's prescription for dealing with the matter. Not that she didn't deserve to feel somewhat sorry for herself—but he couldn't allow it to steal her focus. "You might be right."

She looked at him oddly. "What do you mean?"

"Just what you said—you may not have understood God correctly. It might be best to stop what you're doing and go home to rethink and pray about the matter."

"But I have prayed. I pray about it all the time. I love learning how to help treat people. I've been so blessed to be able to help G.W. and Sissy. You said yourself that G.W. would have surely died had I not taken the measures I did when he was injured. I can't believe that God would give me such a desire and understanding if He didn't mean for me to use it."

"Then stop whining about what one backwoods woman thinks."

Deborah stopped and looked at him for a moment. She seemed to be considering his comment as if there were some great, hidden wisdom in the statement. Finally she nodded.

"You're right. I guess I lost sight of the truth for a minute."

"You are going to be fighting an uphill battle when it comes to your desires to train in medicine," he told her. Reaching out, he pushed back a wisp of her dark hair, then let his finger trail along her jaw. "You have to stop worrying about what other people say and think. Focus on what you know to be right. You are gifted when it comes to medicine. You've learned more in the short time since I've been here than many people learn in years of study. You devour the journals and books that I have to offer, and you retain most of the information without error."

He felt her body sway ever so slightly as Deborah leaned into his touch. He wanted to kiss her, but it would be a mistake, as this was a very public place. Using every last ounce of determination, Christopher stepped back.

"Now, if we've resolved this crisis, I need to go. I have some folks to call on."

For a moment, she said nothing. To Christopher, it almost seemed as if she was battling within herself to either go or say something more. Finally she turned.

"Don't forget your pie," she told him. "Also, I brought your books back. They're on the desk, as well."

"I'll be seeing patients at the mill all day tomorrow. How about you join me?"

She whirled on her heel and looked at him in surprise. "Truly?"

He grinned. "I wouldn't tease about such a thing. It's about time folks get used to seeing you in this role. You won't learn any other way than to see and experience the variety of ailments and injuries. None of these visits require anyone to disrobe, so there should be no hint of impropriety. If a man is truly uncomfortable with your presence, I will trust you to have the goodness of heart to excuse yourself."

She nodded. "I promise."

Christopher could see the excitement in her eyes. "Good. Be here at ten sharp."

ﬡ

Euphanel was busy in the garden when Rob appeared seemingly out of nowhere. "What are you doing here? I figured you'd be some hours yet in the log camp."

"Uncle Arjan said my mind wasn't on my work and I was dangerous." He plopped down on the ground just beyond where she knelt.

"You troubled about something?"

He nodded. "I guess that's what it is. I don't rightly know, exactly. I find myself thinkin' about two things all the time. They're consumin' my mind."

"Let me guess," his mother said with a smile. "One of them is Mara Shattuck."

"I reckon that's easy enough to figure out." He grinned. "The other might surprise you."

"And what would that be?" She straightened and felt the stiffness in her knees. Funny, she used to be able to kneel for hours on end. She supposed it was just another flaw of growing old, and another good reason that it was silly to consider remarrying at her age.

"Well, you know I accepted Jesus as Savior when I was just a young'un?"

"Of course. I was there, praying with you."

Rob plucked a weed from the side of the plot and toyed with it while he continued. "I've been thinkin' that maybe God wants more from me."

"In what way?" Euphanel asked.

"Like maybe I should become a preacher or somethin'."

She hadn't expected this train of thought. "A preacher?"

"I know it's a surprise to you. I've always been the wild one around these parts. Folks would probably laugh out loud iffen they knew what I was ponderin'. But . . . well . . . it just keeps comin' back to mind."

Euphanel carefully considered her words.

"You should always stand ready to answer God's call. If He is of a mind to make you a preacher—then that's what you should be."

"But what about the book learnin'? I ain't got a good education. That was never of interest to me. But now, what with Deborah teachin' me to read better, I guess I'm startin' to wish I'd gone to school more."

"It's never too late to learn, is it?"

He shrugged. "Can't hardly see myself sittin' in the Perkinsville School."

She smiled. "No, maybe not, but you could learn at home, and there are numerous schools elsewhere or tutors that could be hired."

"But what about the company and Pa's dream for us boys to share it?"

Euphanel could easily remember the times Rutger had talked of just such a thing over the dinner table or after devotions. His vision for Vandermark Logging had definitely included his boys. But she also knew her husband would not have wanted any of his children staying with a job they felt was wrong for them.

"I believe your father would have wanted you to do what you felt was right. If God is directing you into the ministry, your father would have been the last one to stand in your way."

"I kind of thought that, too, but I figured it might be wishful thinkin'." He smiled. "You know how I like to do that."

She started to get to her feet, and Rob jumped up quickly to assist her. "Thank you, Son." She dusted the dirt off her skirt and straightened. "Your father . . . and I . . . would be proud to have a preacher in the family. We'd be even prouder to know that our son was willing to put aside his own plans and desires and follow God's voice. Never think otherwise."

ꙮ

Saturday evening, Euphanel headed to the church to meet with those who wanted to sing. She'd been a little uncomfortable when Arjan announced he would drive her into town and join the ensemble, but since Deborah and Lizzie couldn't come, it was a reasonable alternative. Even if the girls had come, Euphanel was certain Arjan would have insisted on accompanying them. It would be dark by the time they concluded, and he would never hear of them journeying home alone.

So she swallowed her fears and made small talk as Arjan drove. Sissy joined them, although she sat in the back of the wagon and left Euphanel and Arjan to sit on the wagon seat together. Euphanel was startlingly aware of his presence—the warmth of his body next to hers, the scent of his cologne. Goodness, but she didn't even remember that he had cologne to wear.

"I'm lookin' forward to this evenin'," he told her. "I have the company of the best gals in the county, and while I won't promise to be all that good at singing, you'll have my undivided attention."

His words were still buzzing through her head as she stood in the center of the gathered singers. To her right were the sopranos or trebles, and opposite them were the basses. The altos were to their right and the tenors opposite them. This was the traditional setting, although Euphanel had, on rare occasion, seen it done otherwise. The trebles and altos were almost solely comprised of women, although a couple of young boys sat beside their mothers and would probably take on their part for the time being. These were the largest of the four groups, but Euphanel had been surprised to see at least twenty men show up to join them.

There were even a few blacks who'd felt brave enough to come, although they sat together and a bit apart from the others. Sissy sat in the alto section with some of her friends on either side. There were also two men who sat in the bass section with their gazes cast at the floor.

Euphanel raised her hand to quiet the

group. "I'm so glad we've had this wonderful turnout. I want to start by explaining a few things and telling you my thoughts. I think that sacred-harp music is one of the finest ways to draw a community together.

"I arranged to obtain some books for us to use. This will help a great deal for those of you who are unfamiliar with the shape-note singing that we'll do."

Euphanel went to the first of two wooden boxes. "If a couple of you gentlemen would do the honors of passing the books around, I'll continue to explain."

Arjan and Mr. Greeley got to their feet and began to hand out the hymnals, while Euphanel took up her own copy. Walking back to the center, she shifted her gaze now to the tenors.

"This is the traditional setting for shape-note singing. As some of you probably know, there is no real leader to this group. We take turns announcing what hymn we wish to sing and then leading that song with an open hand. The first time through, we will sing the fa-sol-la's instead of the words."

She opened to one of the pages in the book. "You can see, when you get your hymnals, that on page three, it shows you exactly what is meant by that. Now, I know that some of you can't read, but we'll help one another, and you'll soon be able to understand exactly why this type of music is perfect for you.

"In shape-note singing, we use the fa-sol-la-fa-sol-la-mi-fa scale. If you look at the notes on the page, you'll see where the term 'shape-note' comes from."

She waited until the last of the hymnals were given out before continuing. "Each of the notes is a stemmed eighth, quarter, or half note, as well as a whole note. But instead of the circle of the note being positioned on the staff, there are various shapes relevant to the fa-sol-la scale. You will see for example that the fa is a triangle, the sol is oval like a regular note, the la is a rectangle, and the mi is a diamond." She looked up and smiled. "Any questions?"

When no one asked anything, Euphanel glanced around the group. "Let's see a show of hands if you've done this before."

Most everyone raised their hand. A few scattered here and there, however, including the blacks, were unfamiliar. Euphanel smiled. "I'm so glad to have the experience of this group. However, bear with me. For those who are not familiar, we will endeavor to make this easy."

She refocused on the hymnal. "Shapes and notes are designations of scale rather than a particular note or pitch. The leader will set the fa, hopefully at a comfortable pitch for everyone, but once that is set, then you will just join in with your harmony note. As that is established, we will begin to sing through the song. This will familiarize everyone with the tune, and hopefully allow you to read the music quickly and easily."

"Now, turn to page six. We'll start with something we all know. The title here is 'New Britain,' but many of you know it as 'Amazing Grace.' I will begin by making this quite simple. I happen to sing treble, but for this purpose will give you the tenor's part right now, as it sounds familiar and is the main melody of the tune. I'll do the first few bars in shape-note—and then in the words."

She cleared her throat and started to sing. "Sol fa la fa la sol fa la sol, Sol fa la fa la sol la sol. Amazing grace, how sweet the sound, that saved a wretch like me." She stopped and looked up to see most of the people nodding. "It's that simple—really."

One of the women raised her hand. "Why not just sing the words? Why worry about all the shape-notes?"

Euphanel smiled. "It's a simple way of teaching folks to read music and harmonize. If you can read the shape-notes, you don't worry about stumbling around for the right key or even version of the song. You can see by the shape-notes where your scale is taking you. That's why we get the leader to give one note and the rest join in finding their particular notes. This is important for the harmony, because it's all done without any musical instruments."

The woman seemed to understand and nodded. She looked back to the book, and Euphanel could see she was trying hard to silently mouth her own part. She turned toward the basses and found Arjan beaming her a smile. Her knees trembled slightly.

"Let's get started."

Chapter 13

May 1886

"Lizzie, you are positively glowing," Euphanel declared. She bent to pull a ham from the oven, but continued talking to her daughter-in-law. "I suppose it's because that baby has grown to be such a big one."

"It's probably the heat," Deborah said with a grin.

"It has been unreasonably hot," Lizzie countered.

The temperatures were already making it necessary to use the summer kitchen, and there was no hope that things might cool off and give them an easier season.

Christopher was beyond doubt now that she was expecting twins, and today Lizzie planned to share the news with the family. First she would go and tell G.W. in private, and then she would announce it to the rest of the family at supper. That was, if her mother-in-law didn't guess that something was afoot.

"Why don't you go on back in the house and rest?" Euphanel told her. "We've nearly got supper ready. Deborah and I can bring this in. You go ahead and check on Sissy for me."

Lizzie nodded. It would give her a good excuse to see G.W. "I'll do that. Seems Sissy is doing so much better. Each day she's more like her old self."

Euphanel nodded. "Indeed. I know she's still bearing a great sorrow, but her heart seems renewed almost daily. She's a good example of taking life day by day."

"You'll send Deborah for me if you need my help, won't you?" she asked as she headed toward the brick archway that led outside.

"We'll be just fine. You go ahead," Euphanel replied.

Lizzie labored under the growing weight of the twins as she made her way back to the house. Dr. Clayton had told her it wasn't at all unusual for women to give birth early when carrying more than one baby. He also told her that he wanted her to rest in bed for the final weeks. That concerned her somewhat. There was a lot of work to do around the house, and while they were all situated now in their new rooms, Lizzie still had things she wanted to do before the babies came.

Inside the house was only moderately cooler. How she longed for the heat to quell and the rains to come. There had been some rumors of storms building off the coast, but they hadn't had so much as a drop of rain in what seemed forever, and everyone longed for relief.

Making her way to the office, Lizzie paused outside the door and put her hand to her mouth to suppress a smile. She had wanted to tell G.W. about Dr. Clayton's suspicions, but she knew it had been wise to wait. Lately G.W. had been rather cantankerous. He was still limping badly enough to use a cane, and it was evident that he'd never again be able to climb up the huge longleaf pines. Lizzie hoped this news might take his mind off his problems and give him something new to think about.

"May I come in?" she asked from the open door.

G.W. looked up and nodded. He scratched his closely trimmed bearded chin and leaned back in the chair. "I'd be glad for the company." He got to his feet and hobbled to where she stood. Offering her his arm, he led her to the chair opposite his. "So to what do I owe this pleasure?"

"I have something to tell you," she said matter-of-factly. Taking her seat rather awkwardly, Lizzie tried to find a comfortable position. It was a moot effort, however, and she finally gave up and grew still.

G.W. wore a rather curious expression. "You look tired," she said to divert his focus. "I think you've been working too hard."

"Hardly. This work is nothing compared to the real work I used to do," G.W. replied. He came to stand before her and sat on the edge of the desk. "Now tell me what you want me to know."

She grinned. "Perhaps I should make you guess."

He shook his head, but smiled. "When it comes to you ladies, I wouldn't even venture one. Are you feeling all right?"

Lizzie nodded. "I feel quite well. Overburdened with this added weight, but well."

"My boy giving you a difficult time, is he?"

She laughed and tried again to shift into a more comfortable position. "You're so sure it's a boy?"

"Absolutely. We need more men around here."

"Then why not add two instead of one?" she asked casually.

He nodded. "In time, I'd be happy with a dozen boys. I suppose we could have a daughter or two for you."

"What if we have two boys right away?"

He looked confused. "Whatever the Good Lord decides is fine by me."

Lizzie took pity on him. "G.W., we're going to have twins. Dr. Clayton has thought this for some time now, but today he told me for sure."

G.W. stared at her with a blank expression. She couldn't help but giggle. He was positively struck speechless—a rarity for her husband.

"Apparently twins often come early," she continued, trying to sound nonchalant. "Dr. Clayton has ordered me to spend the rest of my confinement time in bed. I'm afraid my useful days are at an end for a while."

Still he said nothing. Perhaps G.W. was not pleased. She'd never considered the fact that he might not be happy with twins. "I'm sorry if this is disturbing news."

He shook his head and got to his feet. Practically lifting her from the chair, G.W. engulfed her in his arms and held her as close as the pregnancy would allow. "I'm not disturbed," he whispered against her ear. "I'm beyond words."

For several minutes, all he did was hold her. Lizzie relished the moment and sighed as she put her head against his chest. It was an awkward position, to be sure, but she longed for the tenderness of his embrace and prayed that it might go on.

G.W. seemed to feel the same and continued to hold her until one, or perhaps both, of the twins gave a mighty kick. He pulled back rather startled. "Was that . . . ?"

"The babies," she replied, not waiting for him to finish. She gently took hold of his hand and drew it to her belly. The activity continued, as did G.W.'s awed smile. It wasn't the first time he'd felt them kick, but it was the first time he knew there were two of them.

He looked at her and shook his head. "I don't know what to say. I felt so blessed that we were going to have a child, and now to know there are two . . . well, I guess I feel doubly blessed."

"I know. Me too."

"Do the others know?"

She shook her head. "Only Deborah. She was with me at the doctor's the first time he suspected. I told him I didn't want to say anything to anyone until he felt confident of it being twins. I figured I would announce it this evening at supper. Better yet, maybe you should be the one to share the news."

"I think I'd like that," G.W. replied. "It'll be right fine to share something good."

*

Deborah waited for the dessert to come, knowing that Lizzie had planned to announce her news at that time. She could hardly sit still for all of her excitement. Twins had never been born in Perkinsville, and once the news was out, folks would be sure to come calling. Twins were usually seen as a good omen, and with so many superstitious people in the area, Deborah had no doubt they would want to touch Lizzie's belly for luck.

"I have something to tell everyone," G.W. began.

Quickly, Deborah turned her gaze to the plate, lest she give away the news. She was tickled to hear her brother make the announcement. It would do him good; lately he'd been rather distant and quiet.

"Well, do tell," Mother said, putting aside her fork. "What is it that you want to share?"

Deborah looked up and found all eyes turned to G.W. Lizzie looked as though she might burst into song at any moment.

"Lizzie found out today that she's gonna have to be in bed for a time."

Mother frowned. "Is there a problem?"

G.W. shook his head. "Not unless you

consider two grandbabies, instead of one, a problem."

Deborah clapped her hands at the stunned expressions around the table. "Isn't it grand news?"

Mother was the first to recover. "It's amazing news. Twins?"

Lizzie nodded. "Dr. Clayton has wondered for a time, but now he's sure. He said twins are likely to come early, so he wants me to spend these final weeks in bed."

Sissy, who sat beside Mother near the head of the table, leaned forward. "I was sure 'bout two babies a long time ago. Seems a doctor should'a knowed, too."

Deborah laughed. "I expected that you or Mother would figure it out before Lizzie made her announcement."

"We did discuss the possibilities," Mother admitted, "but I figured we'd know in time. Besides that, G.W. was a big baby, and I think I looked very nearly as large in my last months. Oh, this is grand news!"

G.W. smiled and put his arm around Lizzie's shoulder. "It's a double blessing from the Lord."

"To be sure," Uncle Arjan said, nodding. "Children are a gift from the Lord. The Good Book says so."

Rob nodded. "It does, at that. Guess you'll

get your quiver full a little faster, havin' two at a time." He smiled. "Leave it to you to do things in a big way."

"Well, the first thing we need to do is double our efforts at making baby clothes and diapers," Mother said. "Of course, once word gets around, I know the women in this community will be coming forward with gifts and any of their extras."

"And lying about in bed will provide me ample time to sew," Lizzie said. She looked to Sissy. "Maybe you can teach me how to do that lovely smocking you put on the baby gown you made."

"I shore 'nuf can. Be my pleasure. You and me ain't much help otherwise."

"You neither one need to worry," Mother declared. "Deborah and I can manage just fine."

"And if we need an extra hand," Rob added, "I'm sure Mara would be right here."

Mother nodded. "So you see, it's all worked out."

Deborah thought of the time she'd been spending with Christopher helping on his rounds. The men at the mill had been hostile to her presence the first few times, but now they seemed to take her in stride, and a few actually seemed to welcome her company. Of course, they weren't willing for her to actually do much in the way of tending them. Other times, the women in the area seemed to accept her help without too much protest. As long as Christopher was there, they appeared to tolerate her quite well.

She wondered, though, if this news would put an end to her work with the doctor. Mother would need her here to help with the house and garden. Sissy was only just getting to a place where she could do simple chores like shelling peas and peeling potatoes without tiring too quickly. She had trouble remembering things, and often garbled her words, but Christopher said that in time it would either straighten itself out or not. There wasn't really anything they could do.

Tomorrow, she decided, she would go and speak to Christopher and let him know the situation. He would understand, and perhaps even have some thoughts as to how she could continue to work with him. Maybe on days when the men were home or Mara came to help, Deborah would be able to slip away and attend patients with Christopher.

To her surprise, however, Deborah didn't have to wait until the next day. A knock at the door soon revealed the doctor himself. He'd come to see Deborah, but she knew once he saw her mother's cobbler, he'd happily postpone their courting.

"We've just heard the good news about the babies," Deborah announced.

"And the bad news about me going to bed," Lizzie added.

"Ain't bad news if it keeps you and the babies safe," G.W. added.

Mother nodded. "That's right. Dr. Clayton, you just sit yourself down. I'll get you a plate," she said, getting to her feet. "I know you have a particular fondness for rhubarb cobbler."

"Yes, ma'am," Christopher agreed, taking a seat beside Deborah.

He was quickly rewarded with a heaping portion and smiled with great satisfaction as Deborah passed him the cream.

"If you'd timed your visit a little more carefully, you could have had supper with us, as well," Mother told him.

"I'll try to remember that next time," he said, pouring thick cream on the cobbler.

"We were mighty happy about the news," Arjan joined in. "Our Lizzie is having twins."

Christopher nodded. "That she is." He looked to G.W. "Many congratulations."

"Thanks, Doc. I have to say, the news just about made my whole year."

"I'm pleased to hear it." Christopher dove into the cobbler and smiled with great satisfaction as he enjoyed the first mouthful.

"We will see to it that Lizzie spends her remaining confinement taking it very easy," Mother added. "I hope you'll give us any special instructions we need."

"The important thing is the rest, which will lessen the strain on the uterus." He looked around the table rather quickly. "Excuse me for being so blunt."

"It's not a problem," Mother insisted. "We are all quite capable of hearing the truth. Rest assured, we shall watch over Lizzie with great care."

"I've no doubt about that." Christopher refocused on the cobbler.

Deborah watched him enjoy the dessert and took joy in his pleasure. It seemed it took so little to make him happy. She supposed that if she were to take her courtship seriously, it might behoove her to hone her cooking skills. Maybe staying at home was just the right thing to get Christopher more serious about their marriage. After all, he'd really not spoken of such things in months. Maybe he'd changed his mind.

She frowned. Would he tell her if he had?

Soon enough, the coffeepot ran dry and everyone, including Christopher, had enjoyed their share of dessert. Mother smiled as she got to her feet and suggested Deborah and Christopher might like to take a walk.

"Now that the sun is starting to set, the air won't be so heavy," she told them.

Christopher nodded and helped Deborah to her feet. "I had just such a thing in mind."

Deborah didn't even bother with a shawl. The heat would still be too much to have need of it. She made her way outside with Christopher and waited for him to point the direction.

They walked slowly, as if heading to town. Overhead, the large pines swayed in the light breeze. The air wasn't nearly so humid, and Deborah breathed deep of the heavy pine scent. She had missed such things when she'd lived in Philadelphia.

"What are you grinning about?" Christopher asked, smiling.

"I was just thinking of how much I love it here," she replied. "I missed my home when I was in Philadelphia. It can be overbearingly hot here, but so can the city."

Christopher said nothing, and Deborah wondered if she'd somehow caused him to think of his own home. She moved the conversation on. "I suppose you realize I'll be needed at home more now that Lizzie will be confined?"

"Yes, I suppose I do."

They continued walking in the fading light. Deborah longed to take hold of his arm, but refrained. It seemed every time they touched, something stirred deep inside that left her with even greater longing.

"We shouldn't venture too far," Christopher said, turning back toward the house. "You never know what kind of trouble might lurk."

"It's true," Deborah replied and quickly matched her steps to his. "But we needn't rush."

He smiled. "Trying to keep me out here, all to yourself?"

She felt her cheeks grow hot, but returned the tease. "Of course. Isn't that what courting couples do?"

He gave a low chuckle. "Some do much more than that."

Now she really felt the heat on her face. "Dr. Clayton, what a bold thing to say. You have me blushing."

Stopping, he stunned her to silence by taking her in his arms. "Then this should positively turn you scarlet." He lowered his mouth to hers and kissed her. For a moment, Deborah forgot where and who she was. She felt as if her heart was aglow—growing brighter by the minute.

Pulling away, Christopher had to steady her before she lost her balance. Looking up at him, Deborah could only stare openmouthed.

She tried to speak, but the words seemed stuck in the back of her throat.

"I hope I haven't offended you," he said with a hint of a grin. "I'm not the least bit sorry I did that, but I would hate myself if I upset you."

"I . . . uh . . . I just thought our first kiss would . . . well . . . be . . ."

"Be what?" He frowned. "Wasn't it good? I mean, I liked it very much."

"It was wonderful," she managed. Touching her hands to her cheeks, she couldn't imagine anything more delightful. "I suppose I didn't expect it to be so . . . stimulating."

He roared with laughter and swung her around in a circle. "You never fail to amaze me, Miss Vandermark. I've wanted to kiss you for a very long time, and while I know it's completely inappropriate with the standards of proper etiquette, I want nothing more than to do it again."

He stopped and lowered her back to the ground. His expression suggested he was seeking permission. Deborah nodded and closed her eyes. "Me too."

Chapter 14

Christopher looked at the letter once again and felt the same sense of discouragement. His mother wrote to give him the news as she did every month, and it only seemed that things were worse than ever. Two of his brothers were in trouble for fighting. They'd been expelled from school with the suggestion that they were incapable of learning. The youngest two had caught the mumps, but were recovering. His father was his usual angry self, insisting his wife bring him liquor instead of food.

Daily he curses God, his mother wrote. *He says such hideous things that I cannot bear to listen. I spend less and less time with him, and I know he hates me for deserting him. God is all I have to cling to these days.*

Christopher could just imagine his father's tirades. The man had given up what faith he'd had in God after the accident that crippled him; Christopher could still hear his father bellow, *"God clearly doesn't care about the likes of me and mine."*

He glanced back at the letter, and this time, his mother's voice drowned out the bitterness of his father. *I know these things will never change. I used to have hope that they would, but it takes too much of my strength.* Christopher hoped the money he sent would be enough to ease her burden, but that was foolish. Some miseries couldn't be alleviated with money.

He pushed the letter away and stared at his empty coffee cup. Maybe it had been a mistake to come to Texas. Perhaps his mother would have fared better if he'd set up practice in Kansas City. Of course, that would have brought its own share of difficulties.

Pushing back his chair, Christopher stood. He reached for the letter and folded it carefully before replacing it in the envelope. He'd reply later tonight. It would give him time to consider what he wanted to say.

"Hello? Christopher?"

He smiled and cast the envelope on the table. "I'm back here in the kitchen."

Deborah wasted no time in joining him. "How are you? I haven't seen you for so long. Lizzie is doing well, but we've been so busy."

Christopher picked up his coffee cup. "I think there's still some coffee, if you want a cup."

She shook her head. "No, I was just hoping to go with you on your rounds. In some ways, I feel like Lizzie's confinement is my own."

"It won't be long. Besides, this is good practice for you. For you to tend an expectant mother is something that women will not balk at. Tending a woman who is to birth twins will be excellent to add to your list of experiences." He put the cup on the counter. "Now, if you'll give me just a moment to gather my things, we'll head out." She followed him from the kitchen and back into the exam room.

"Is there anything I can do?"

"No, most everything is ready." Christopher went to the cupboard and pulled out several small bottles to put in his bag.

"I saw you had a letter on the table. News from home?" she asked.

He turned and looked at her with a frown. "Yes, but not as good as I'd hoped."

"Oh, I am sorry. Can you speak of it?"

Deborah moved toward him, then stopped. Christopher thought she looked genuinely concerned. No doubt, she would ask him questions. He probably should have remained silent.

"It most likely wouldn't help anything if I did."

Her expression changed from concern to frustration. "You never talk about your family. You know everything about mine, and I know very little about yours. Don't you trust me to be discreet?"

He considered her question. Perhaps now was the time to tell her the truth. "It's not a matter of trust," he began. "I suppose there are things about my family of which I feel guarded—though not because of any flaw of yours."

Deborah moved a bit closer. "Christopher, we all have our secrets. I'm sorry if I made you feel bad for yours."

Smiling, he reached out to touch her cheek. "I appreciate your understanding. In time . . . well . . . I want you to know."

"Doc! Doc! Come quick."

"That sounds like . . . " Deborah jumped back just as G.W. limped into the room.

"It's Lizzie. She's having pain, and Ma says it may be time for the babies."

"Goodness, she was just fine when I left to come here."

G.W. looked at Deborah. "It started just

after you left. She thought at first she'd just turned wrong, but the pain continued."

Christopher grabbed his bag and motioned Deborah to the door. "Come on."

They raced to the wagon, with G.W. doing his best to keep up with them. Climbing into the wagon seat, Deborah moved to the far side to give her brother room as Christopher took his place in back. G.W. managed to take up the reins and release the brake very nearly at the same moment.

He quickly turned the wagon and headed the team down the road, ignoring the greetings of folks who walked along the way. Christopher took hold of the back of the seat, and Deborah glanced over her shoulder at him. She looked worried. Knowing the truth about medicine was that way. She would have to learn to conceal her fears, or her patients would suffer. If G.W. hadn't been there, he would have said as much, but the poor man was already a wreck.

The ride to the Vandermark place took less than half the time it would normally have taken. Despite the conditions of the road and other folks using the same path, G.W. managed to keep them moving. When they pulled up to the front of the house, he reined back the horses hard.

"Easy, G.W," Deborah said, climbing down

from the wagon. "Don't take it out on the team."

Christopher followed suit with G.W. beating him to the porch by inches. "She's right, G.W. Don't give in to worry just yet."

G.W.'s piercing blue eyes fixed Christopher with a hard stare. "You will take care of her." It was more a statement than a question.

Giving the poor father-to-be a brief slap on the back, Christopher smiled. "Absolutely."

ꕥ

Rob had just finished loading the last of the logs onto the train car when he noticed Zed Perkins in the camp. Handing the mule team over to one of the other men, Rob went to where Uncle Arjan stood talking to the mill owner.

"Howdy," Rob said, joining them. "Good to see you, Mr. Perkins."

"You may not think so when you hear what I've come to say. I was just telling Arjan that my situation has changed, and I felt it important we discuss the particulars."

Rob looked to his uncle. "In what respect?"

Mr. Perkins looked uncomfortable. "Well, the fact is I've been having a little difficulty with the banks. The money promised for the final steps of my expansion has been refused."

"I'm sorry to hear that. Would you like to sit and have a cup of coffee?" Uncle Arjan asked.

"Sittin' in the shade would be good," Perkins replied. He took off his straw hat and wiped his forehead with the back of his shirt sleeve. "Mighty warm today."

"That it is." Arjan led the way to where they'd had lunch earlier. The few campstools made a decent place to rest.

"I know this comes as a surprise to you," Mr. Perkins continued, repositioning his hat. "It came as an even bigger surprise to me. I went to Houston, thinking I was securing the revenue needed for my mill, and instead, I found myself facing a bunch of two-timers."

"How will this affect your plans?"

Tucking his hands deep in his coat pockets, Mr. Perkins looked even more distressed. "Well, the thing is, the situation has forced me to take on some investors."

"Investors?" Rob questioned.

"Partners, actually. Look, I wouldn't have done this if I didn't have to. I want you to understand that up front. If there had been another way to manage things, I would have."

"Zed, what's the problem here? We have no say over whether you take on partners."

Rob could tell the answer wasn't going to be good. Mr. Perkins was nervous about the situation. He wouldn't have taken all the trouble to come clear out here if the matter weren't critical.

"I . . . well . . . " Perkins fell silent, then drew a deep breath. "The fact is, I was approached by someone who had been here before—last year. Mr. Albright."

Rob wasn't sure he'd heard him correctly. "Stuart Albright? The fella that was supposed to marry Lizzie?"

"That's right. He came to me with his father-in-law while I was in Houston. I don't know how he knew about my troubles, but he did. They came to my hotel and presented their proposition."

Arjan looked to Rob and then back to Zed Perkins. "Which was what, if I may ask?"

"They would provide the capital I needed for the final stage of my expansion."

"No chance Albright was doing it out of the goodness of his heart. What do they get in return?" Rob asked.

Perkins looked at the ground. "I had to make them partners."

"Partners?" Arjan questioned. "You mentioned that before. Are you saying they now own half the sawmill?"

"Only until I can pay back the loan. We agreed it would be a short-term scenario." Mr. Perkins seemed desperate to ease their minds. "I had no other choice. Without the expansion, I can't hope to produce the promised lumber. I'm sorry if this is going to cause problems between us, but I'm hoping you'll understand."

Arjan put his hand on Mr. Perkins' shoulder. "You did what you thought was best. I'm sure it will all work out."

"That's my prayer," the older man said. "I never wanted to compromise our business dealings, however. That's why I came to you today."

"We appreciate your openness, Zed," Arjan told the man. "I always like it best when folks deal honestly with me. We'll let the family know what's going on. I can't imagine that we have anything to worry about. Seems to me that Albright fellow was all about making a dollar. If he's that way, then your benefit will be ours, I'm sure. We'll keep providing all the logs you need. Just let us know if anything changes."

Rob heard the hesitation in his uncle's voice, but he waited until Zed excused himself and headed back to town before asking about it.

"You're lookin' a mite concerned. Do you think there will be trouble?"

Arjan shrugged. "I'm not sure. Seems strange that Albright would even concern himself with this part of the country. Maybe he was intrigued by Perkins's situation, but it just smells a bit sour to me."

Rob nodded. "I agree. G.W. ain't gonna like hearin' about this. Not one little bit."

"No, I'm sure he won't, but we have to tell him nevertheless." The train whistle blew and Arjan jumped up. "Come on. Let's hitch a ride."

Rob thought about Mr. Perkins's announcement all the way back to the house. Perkins knew there had been bad blood between the Vandermarks and Mr. Albright. Seemed to lack consideration for his friends and neighbors that he would partner with the man, but Zed Perkins was obviously concerned for his own business.

They were back to the house before they knew it. The train slowed but didn't stop. "You boys take care," Jack said as Arjan and Rob jumped off. Jack gave the whistle two brief toots and was out of sight.

"Look there," Rob said, pointing. "It's G.W. What's he doin' just sittin' around?" As the men drew closer, Rob could see his brother's pale face and strained expression. He looked almost ill.

"Son, you all right?" Uncle Arjan asked.

G.W. looked up in surprise. "It's Lizzie."

Rob shook his head. "Is she sick?"

"It's the babies. Doc and Deborah are workin' with Ma to deliver 'em."

"Kind of early, ain't it?" Rob regretted the question the minute it was out of his mouth.

"It's normal for twins to come early," their uncle interjected. "I'm sure everything will be just fine. You need not fret. This is an occasion for celebration."

"I know," G.W. replied. "I'm tryin' to remember that. It's just that I . . . well, I can't help worryin'. She's my whole world."

A baby's cry could be heard coming from the house. Arjan grinned and slapped G.W. on the back. "That world of yours is about to get a whole lot bigger."

G.W. jumped to his feet, but Arjan took hold of his arm. "Remember, there are two of them to be delivered. We might as well sit here and wait."

Reluctantly, G.W. retook his chair while Rob pulled up two seats so they could join him. "I don't know what I'll do if something goes wrong," Rob heard his brother murmur.

"Then let me help you get your mind off matters for a few minutes," their uncle began. "You're no doubt wonderin' why we came home early."

G.W. nodded. "I guess so. I suppose I was thinkin' you knew about Lizzie, but of course you didn't." He rubbed at his leg and began to rock.

"We had a visitor at the camp. Zed Perkins rode all the way out on horseback to come talk to us."

Rob could see that this only slightly interested his older brother. "The news wasn't good," Rob interjected. "Fact is, it's givin' us a bit to consider."

G.W. held his brother's gaze for a moment, then turned to Uncle Arjan. "What's he talkin' about?"

"Seems Perkins had trouble securing the money he needed for the last of his expansion. Apparently he can't hope to fulfill the promises he's made without it, so he felt he had to take on some partners."

"Partners?" G.W. shrugged. "I don't suppose that should be so bad."

"You ain't heard who he took on," Rob said. He caught a look of reproof from his uncle just as a second baby began to cry.

"There, you see. It all sounds as though things are well," Arjan announced. "They'll be comin' for you soon, so I might as well get the rest of this tale told."

"Rob seems worried about who Mr. Perkins took on," G.W. said, glancing anxiously toward the door.

"Seems Stuart Albright and his father-in-law

are the new partners," their uncle said matter-of-factly. "Perkins thought we'd need to know right away. He doesn't expect it to change anything, but he knew we'd had some problems with the man."

G.W. frowned. "I'll say. What's Albright doing in Perkinsville, anyway?"

"He weren't here," Rob threw out. "Mr. Perkins said he was approached in Houston after the bank turned him down. He said he didn't know how they came by the knowledge that he needed help, but he felt he had to take it."

"Knowing Albright," G.W. commented, "he most likely arranged the matter. I wouldn't put it past him to do it, just out of spite. He knows we work with Perkins—probably wants to play boss man. Well, it ain't gonna work. He doesn't know how things are done down here. Albright won't have any say over Vandermark Logging. Ain't nothing he can do to change that."

Mother appeared at the porch door with a grin nearly as wide as her face. "G.W., come meet your children."

"Lizzie?" he asked, getting to his feet.

She nodded. "Doing just fine. So are your son and daughter."

"A boy and a girl?" Rob asked. "Now, how's that for fair and even?" He laughed and followed his brother toward the door.

Chapter 15

July 1886

The middle of the month arrived with no break in the heat. The twins were now clearly thriving, and in less than a week, they would be a month old and visitors would come to call on their presentation day. Deborah knew once that happened, the place would be pandemonium. She was thankful for the additions to the house, for the office was now slightly separated from the main living areas. It helped to keep the noise level at a minimum when she and G.W. were working together—although that happened less and less often.

Sissy was now fully recovered from her injuries and seemed to be regaining her old strength, doing the daily milking before heading to the garden. Mother was busy tending to her grandchildren and Lizzie; Deborah had never seen her happier.

Just after breakfast on the fifteenth, Christopher arrived to pay a visit to the new mother. Just the sight of his handsome form made Deborah's heart pound. She longed to find a moment of privacy where they might share another kiss. She giggled to think of how scandalous such a thing sounded, but couldn't help wishing for it just the same.

"There were rumors in town of storms off the coast," he told them. "Could be we'll have some rain soon."

"It would be most welcome if it ends this hot spell. There's been no relief from the heat! Let me take your coat. You know you don't have to stand on formalities here. You'll broil yourself to death if you stay in this," Deborah declared, taking the coat from him.

She herself had picked a lightweight cotton gown. It was an older dress and the once-vivid yellow was now a faded cream. The sleeves were unfashionably short, but Deborah didn't care. No one could survive Texas heat and worry overmuch about what the ladies were wearing in Paris.

"At least the air is clean here," Christopher said, wiping his brow with a handkerchief.

"The mill is putting out so much smoke and dust you can hardly see across the road."

"We'll have to pray for a good stiff breeze," G.W. said, joining them. He extended his hand to the doctor. "You come to see Lizzie and the babies?"

"I did," Christopher replied. "They're coming up close to a month old. I presume they're doing well, or I would have heard otherwise by now."

"They're growing quite fat," Deborah replied before her brother could answer. "And, of course, we are spoiling them with a great amount of attention."

Christopher grinned. "I've no doubt about that."

"Lizzie's feeding them just now," Deborah continued. "Would you like to have a cup of coffee and one of Mother's doughnuts?" She smiled sweetly knowing he would.

"Sounds good to me, but let's make it at least two. After all, I'm here to see twins."

Deborah laughed and led the way to the dining room. "Well, you're actually here to see Lizzie as well, so maybe we should make it three."

He nodded quite seriously. "I suppose that would only be right. It will be difficult, but I'll suffer through."

G.W. joined them but offered nothing to

their banter. Deborah met his serious gaze. "Can I get you a cup of coffee, as well?"

He nodded and took a seat opposite Christopher at the kitchen table. Deborah went to the cold stove and picked up a pot. "I just brought this in from the outdoor kitchen a few minutes ago. Should still be nice and hot."

"It's surprisingly cool in here," Christopher said. He took up the cup after she placed it in front of him. "My house isn't as comfortable. Especially if I go lightin' the stove to cook anything. I'm starting to think it's better to just eat everything raw."

Deborah shook her head. "Now, you know what Mama said—you can eat your meals here three times a day." She poured G.W.'s coffee and brought a plate of doughnuts to the table.

"I was hopin' I might ask you about something," G.W. said without so much as glancing at the food.

Deborah wondered if he'd prefer her to go. "I can leave, if you like."

G.W. shook his head. "No. What I have to say might well involve you."

Deborah took a seat and waited for him to speak while Christopher downed his first doughnut. She knew G.W. had something on his mind and would share it when he was ready. He was never one to keep a matter to himself if it was important, but sometimes he could be irritatingly slow to deliver. It reminded her somewhat of the way one of her college professors had lectured. He would begin speaking on the topic of the day, then halt in mid-sentence. Sometimes he would pace a few moments; other times he would stare at the students as if trying to remember what it was he wanted to say.

Finally, G.W. piped up. "I want to know what can be done to help me regain full use of my leg. I mean so that I can mount and ride a horse, walk without a cane—maybe even run. I have two children now, and I want to be able to keep up with them."

Keeping her gaze on the table, Deborah remained silent. She was never so happy to hear anything. G.W. had been moody and difficult to live with ever since the accident, but now he found hope for the future in the form of his two babies.

"There are a number of things we can do to strengthen the muscle," Christopher said thoughtfully. "It's not going to be easy, of course. A lot of tissue was damaged. You may always have a bit of a limp."

"I can live with a bit of one, but I don't want to be kept from doing things for and with my family. I know I'll probably never work in the camps again, and I can accept that."

Deborah was glad to hear him say as much. It was a long time coming.

Christopher took a slow sip of coffee and continued to hold the cup as he began to speak. "My father was injured in an accident. It left him unable to use his legs at all."

G.W. shook his head. "I couldn't live like that."

"Neither can he. At least, not well."

Deborah perked up at this. Christopher shared so little about his family that, even though the conversation was more for G.W.'s benefit than hers, she wanted to hear it all.

"My father was always a very strong man—a laborer who knew his own capabilities and wasn't afraid to learn new skills. He was admired by many, but also scorned. There will always be men who are unable to accept that someone has a stronger back or can work without rest for longer periods of time. Those men are partly to blame for my father's accident."

"What happened?"

Deborah was glad G.W. asked the question. She figured Christopher would be more willing to answer—especially since he'd brought up the topic.

"For a variety of reasons, there was a fight in the train yard. My father was the object of disdain—along with a couple of his friends. A group of men took it upon themselves to settle a score that wasn't really valid. They ambushed my father and his friends at the end of the work night."

Deborah noted the pain in his expression, and she couldn't help reaching over to place her hand atop his. Christopher looked at her for a moment and gave her the briefest of smiles before continuing.

"The beating they received was brutal. In fact, my father's friends were killed. My father was thrown from the back of an idle train car. His back hit the rail and broke. It damaged his spinal cord and left him unable to use his legs."

"That isn't an accident," Deborah protested. "It was murder and assault. No doubt they intended to kill your father, as well."

Christopher nodded. "But I don't tell the story to dwell on the wrong done my father, but rather to encourage you, G.W. My father allowed his life to change in a most negative fashion. My hope is that you'll continue to desire and fight to make yours better. The things you'll have to do to strengthen your leg won't be easy. The pain of your injury is still fresh in your memory, but this will hurt like nothing you've ever endured. But I believe there is hope that you'll recover most—if not all—of your use."

"That's what I want," G.W. told him. "I

don't want to give up, though I thought I did. I figured for a long while that my life was pretty much over. Deborah helped me to see that I could use my brain for something more than calculating board feet and where a pine was going to drop." He smiled. "She's a stubborn one, my sister."

"That she is," Christopher said before giving her a wink. "But I suppose we wouldn't want her any other way."

"So what does your pa do now?" G.W. asked.

"Mostly he makes life unbearable for my mother," Christopher replied without emotion. "He torments my brothers and sisters who are still at home, and he drinks. The latter is what he seems to do best. He says it's the only way he can deal with his miseries and pain."

"During really painful moments, I've considered it myself," G.W. admitted.

Deborah was surprised by her brother's words, but instead she addressed Christopher's comment. "Oh, your poor mother. How awful that must be."

"She gets by—barely," Christopher replied. "I suppose it's one of the reasons I've never been too anxious to talk about it."

"I can well understand," she answered, hoping her expression would convey her sympathy.

For several minutes, no one said a word. Christopher took up a second doughnut while G.W. nursed his coffee. Deborah had a million questions for Christopher, but she knew that now wasn't the time. There was no comfort in reliving such awfulness.

"Well, hello, Dr. Clayton. I didn't realize you were here," Mother said, coming into the kitchen. "Have you come to see my grand-babies?"

"I have," he said, getting to his feet. "And to eat your doughnuts."

She put her hands on her waist and eyed him quite seriously. "Did Deborah tell you that I was going to send her into town this morning with a batch for you?"

He looked at her as if he'd caught her walking out with another man. "She said nothing."

Deborah shook her head. "I would have gotten around to it. I figured you were more interested in eating than hearing about my plans for the day."

"If your plans involve bringing me your mother's doughnuts, it's only right that you share the news upon my arrival," he replied.

"Well, I'll certainly know better next time," Deborah said, then added with a teasing smile, "If there is a next time. One can never tell."

ꕥ

Deborah accompanied Christopher back to town, slowly driving the wagon while he let his horse amble alongside. She wanted to say something about what he'd shared earlier, but she didn't want to make him uncomfortable.

"Christopher, I'm sorry that things are so difficult for your mother. Is there nothing that can be done?"

He rode in silence for a moment, then looked at her. She had never seen such pain in his eyes. "She won't allow for anything to be done. My father is dying before her eyes, wasting away in a bottle of whiskey that, ironically, she supplies him. Yet, to refuse would be worse for her still. I can't imagine the dilemma she endures on a daily basis."

"I can see why you don't like to talk about your family, but I hope you know it does nothing to change how I feel about you."

He stopped the horse, forcing her to halt the wagon team. He drew up even with her and asked, "And how do you feel?"

She smiled. "I thought that was quite evident. I admire you greatly and enjoy spending time at your side."

"And that's all?"

Deborah grew a bit uncomfortable. "I try to guard my feelings as best I can."

His brow furrowed. "But why?"

"I suppose," she said, staring down the

road, "that it's because of the agreement between us. Given your obligations to your family, I know that you do not intend to marry anytime soon . . . and I find that I am easily given to thinking on just such things if I'm not careful."

"I thought young women liked to dream about their wedding day."

She fought to keep tears from her eyes. He couldn't possibly understand how it was for her. She had come to love him so completely that to know she couldn't yet count on their marriage was the most painful thing she had ever endured.

"Deborah?"

She looked at him and offered a smile she did not feel. "I like to dream on things that I know will come about."

"You doubt that we have a future?"

A hint of breeze brought a bit of relief from the heat, and Deborah took the opportunity to take off her wide-brimmed hat and let the air dry her sweat-dampened hair. "A future with you still seems too distant to spend any time in speculation and dreams," she finally answered. "I'm a practical woman—you've always known that. Daydreaming and pretending that I can make things happen any sooner isn't a good way to spend my time."

"And what is?" He sounded almost hurt.

Deborah fixed her hat back in place and picked the reins back up. "Exactly what I'm doing. Learning everything I can. Growing closer to God and getting to know you better. I'm not unhappy, Christopher, if that's your concern."

He narrowed his eyes just a bit. "You wouldn't lie to me, would you?"

"Certainly not." She smiled, hoping it might relieve his mind. "I agreed to court you, knowing that your family had to come first. I spent a lifetime feeling much the same way about mine, so I understand your position. Please don't think I've changed my mind."

He smiled and eased back in the saddle. "I'm glad. I thought there for a minute, I might have to give you another kiss to persuade you."

She laughed and slapped the reins. "I'm already persuaded, but it never hurts to reevaluate my stand." Despite his laughter, a part of her said there were still too many secrets between them. Too many obstacles to allow for true love to grow. She prayed it wasn't so, but doubt still lingered.

❧

Deborah had just finished her shopping at the commissary when she spied a young woman and older gentleman approaching from the boardinghouse. For a moment, she didn't trust her eyes. Perhaps she'd had too much heat for one day. She looked again, however, and could see that she'd been right.

She put the last of her packages into the wagon bed and hurried to greet the young woman. "Jael?"

"Deborah! How wonderful. I was just asking Father to find your house for me. He was going to check with the man at the store."

The two women embraced and drew apart once again to study each other. Deborah was amazed at how perfectly coiffed and gowned her college friend was. Of course, Jael had never been one for simplicity, but the pink-and-white bustled gown looked better suited for a party than a trip to a sawmill commissary.

"You look wonderful," Deborah declared.

"Are you terribly surprised to find me here?" Jael asked, laughing. "I can scarcely believe it."

"I am surprised, but I knew that your father and husband had become partners with Mr. Perkins. I dared to hope you might accompany them here one day, but hoping was as far as I got. I figured to mention it the next time you wrote."

"Which, I'm sorry to say, has been so infrequent," Jael replied. She looked at her father and smiled. "We've all been so very busy.

Father and Stuart decided to make a trip to Houston, and I insisted they bring me along. I actually threatened to come on my own once they departed, if they didn't bring me."

Deborah looked to Jael's father, who nodded. "It's true; she did. I knew better than to threaten her or encourage Stuart to do likewise. Once Jael sets her hat for something—that's the last of it."

Jael patted the old man's face with her gloved hand before turning back to Deborah. "You look so slender and lovely. I am so jealous. I could never hope to have a waist as small as yours."

Deborah laughed. "It comes from all the bending I do in the garden." She smiled at Jael's father. "Mr. Longstreet. It's been some time since I last saw you." Deborah started to comment that it had been upon the occasion of Lizzie's intended marriage to Stuart, but she caught herself just in time. "Will you be in the area for long?"

"It will depend on how our business shapes up," he replied. "I've come to finalize some matters with Mr. Perkins. Most likely, it will take us a week or more."

"Then you must come and stay with us. We live several miles north on the main road. We're the only house out that far. We added on earlier this year, and there is more than enough room."

"Oh, Father, might we?" Jael looked at him, hopeful. "The bed at the boardinghouse is ever so hard."

He looked at his daughter, then back at Deborah. "I need to be here to oversee business. Miles away from town will do me little good."

"Well, it would definitely let you sleep in better air," Deborah replied.

"I have no objection to Jael going to stay with you."

Jael beamed him a smile. "Thank you, Father. I shall be so happy to be occupied while you are busy. I'm sure Deborah and Lizzie will happily fill me in on all the news."

"Starting with the fact that Lizzie was delivered of twins last month," Deborah replied.

"Twins? How marvelous. Oh, but I can hardly wait to see them."

"Come with me now, then," Deborah told her. "I was just heading home. We can stop by the boardinghouse for your things."

Jael smiled and pushed back her dainty reddish blond curls. "That would suit me just fine. You don't mind do you, Father?"

"Not at all," he said, seeming almost relieved. "I will take myself on to the mill."

"Do join us for supper, Mr. Longstreet.

You can take this road and follow it north. You will come upon our place after several miles. As I mentioned, we're the only house that far out. Mr. Perkins can give you directions. The house is quite large with a huge porch, and there is a plain picket fence that skirts the roadside of the yard and across the front."

"What time should I come?" he asked.

"Six o'clock would be fine. We will most likely eat a little after that, and hopefully the temperature will have cooled some."

He nodded. "I would be quite happy to join you. Until then, ladies." He tipped his hat and turned to make his way to the mill.

Deborah looked at Jael and couldn't help but giggle. "It will be just like old times."

But Jael's face had sobered considerably with her father's departure. "I can't promise that, I'm afraid. My life is hardly the same."

Chapter 16

"We're fixin' to go to town. Are you sure you gals are gonna be all right?" G.W. questioned.

Deborah shooed him toward the door. "We'll be fine. Mother and Sissy need you much more than we will. We have to catch up on the past."

G.W. looked skeptical, but finally nodded and turned. "We'll be back before it gets too late."

"And be sure to remind Mama to have Mr. Longstreet come for supper," Deborah called after him, since business had kept him from joining them the night before.

Once G.W. was gone, Deborah turned back to Jael and Lizzie. Each held a baby and was happily engrossed in conversation. Now they could finally get down to hearing the details of why Jael had made the choices she'd made.

"So now that we're alone," Jael said without prompting, "I suppose you are both determined to know the reasons for my marriage to Stuart."

"Well, you have to admit, it was a rather shocking thing to spring on us," Lizzie said, putting baby Rutger to her shoulder.

"Yes, we were quite stunned," Deborah added. "You had tried to talk Lizzie out of marrying him, but we didn't think it was so you could catch him for yourself." She smiled to let Jael know she was just teasing.

Jael offered Deborah the baby girl before continuing. Deborah cuddled Emily close and took a seat near Lizzie. Jael smoothed the skirt of her stylish day dress and looked up to smile.

"Well, the story is not a very nice one. You know I had my heart set on Mr. Remington. And for a time I thought he, too, had his designs on me. Unfortunately, I gave of myself too freely and found myself in a family way."

Lizzie's eyes widened. "Oh, Jael, that must have been terrifying."

"It was. As you know, my oldest sister, Justine, found herself in the same situation, and Father dismissed her from the family for bringing them shame when the young man refused to marry her."

Lizzie and Deborah nodded. The story was indeed a sad one. When Mr. Longstreet had sent his daughter away in shame, Justine was unable to bear her grief and took not only her own life, but that of her unborn child.

"Well, I couldn't let that happen to me," Jael continued. "I knew Father would be livid, although I wondered if he might be more forgiving in order to avoid a repeat of what happened before. But I couldn't work up my courage, and so I went to Ernest and told him I was expecting. At first, he was all compassion and agreed we would marry immediately. He said we would travel abroad and have the child there so no one would know exactly when the baby had been born. I thought it a perfect solution. Then the next thing I knew, he sent me a letter telling me he was on his way to England—alone—and was sorry that he couldn't bid me good-bye in person. There was never any mention of an engagement, because we never had formally announced such a thing. He merely escaped his fate and left me to mine."

"How hard that must have been," Lizzie said, shaking her head.

"Oh, Jael, you should have known you

could have come to me—to us here in Texas," Deborah declared.

"I thought about that, believe me. I was preparing to consider just such a thing when Stuart returned from having seen you here. He stopped by to do business with Father, and when Father was called away for nearly an hour, I was left to entertain him. We talked about what had happened when you left him at the altar, Lizzie. I hadn't realized that his inheritance was tied up in marrying, but he was in great despair over what might happen. I took that moment to tell him that I, too, bore a great burden."

Jael let out a heavy sigh. "I told him about Ernest and the baby. He was livid that the man was such a cad. I told him his problem and mine were very similar, for once Father learned of my condition, he would disinherit me. Stuart was the one who suggested we help each other. Please understand—he was kind and gentle with me. He didn't pretend that he loved me, and neither did he expect me to pretend that I loved him. At least not privately. He asked that I be an attentive and loving wife in public, and that seemed easy enough. After all, he was coming to my rescue."

"Oh, but, Jael, to live in a loveless marriage . . . " Lizzie said with tears in her eyes.

Deborah could see that Jael wanted badly

for them to understand, and she knew how that felt. Sometimes a person's choice never seemed justified until it received the approval of those around you—those you loved.

"Many people marry as if it were business, Lizzie. We cannot condemn our friend for her decision."

"But what now?" Lizzie asked. "What of the baby?"

Jael bit her lower lip for a moment. Deborah thought it looked like she might cry and reached over to pat her arm. Jael raised her head. "I lost it. After two months, I miscarried. Few people knew about it, and those that did thought it was Stuart's. You see, when Father returned that day, we told him our plans to elope. He was surprised, but not upset. He thought it very fine that I should marry into such a good family—especially to a young man with whom he did business and could trust implicitly."

"What happened between you and Stuart after you lost the baby?" Deborah asked.

"Really, he did nothing. He consoled me, told me how sorry he was that I should be inconvenienced, but added that we could one day have our own children." She looked at Lizzie and Deborah. "He was neither overly kind nor meanspirited about any of it. That, in fact, has been our marriage. We both needed each other in order to keep our reputations and social standing in place. I'm not sorry for my choice, but I am sorry that I did not consider how difficult it would be to live without love."

Tears ran down Lizzie's cheeks, and Rutger began to fuss as though he knew his mother was upset. Emily didn't like that her brother was unhappy and joined him. Deborah soothed her while Lizzie began to rock Rutger in her arms.

"I'm sorry. I didn't mean to be all weepy," Lizzie said, regaining control. "I feel that you have suffered—not only in marrying a man you did not love, but with the loss of your child. I would never have wished it on you, Jael, and yet I feel by rejecting Stuart, I have had a part in . . . well . . . "

"You had no part," Jael said firmly. "I made my choice based upon my need. If Stuart hadn't been agreeable and available, I still don't know what I might have done. Besides him, you two are the only ones who know the truth, and I'd like for it to stay that way."

"Of course." Deborah looked to Lizzie and then back to their friend. "It is your secret, and we shall keep it."

"I just wanted to explain my decision. I figured you both thought me quite out of my senses." She smiled. "I suppose there for a while, I was."

Lizzie relaxed, and so did Rutger. She seemed to choose her next words with great care. "So what . . . does the future hold . . . for you?"

Jael picked at the lace on her sleeve and refused to meet their gazes. "I'm not sure how to answer that."

"You mentioned that Stuart talked of having children together," Deborah threw out. "How do you feel about that?"

Jael finally looked up. "I want to have children. I'm hoping that somewhere along the way, Stuart and I actually might come to care for each other. Perhaps children would help that matter."

"Oh, Jael, do be cautious," Lizzie warned. "It's not a good idea to expect that a third person can spark affection between two people. Children often get used by their parents—look at what happened with me. My mother and father held no affection for each other and very little for me. Well, I suppose that's not fair. Father loved me, but he was unavailable to me. Mother loved her cause. Don't suffer a child to bring together a bad marriage."

"The marriage isn't so very bad," Jael replied. "It's more . . . well, it's rather boring. Stuart spends little time in my company, and I certainly haven't a mind for the things that hold his interest. I spend my days doing mostly as I please, and on occasion, Stuart comes to my bed." She blushed and added, "Although those occasions are infrequent, and always for his benefit."

Deborah could see that Lizzie was trying hard to hide her feelings. Likely they were both feeling the same emotions—sorrow . . . despair . . . grief—for their friend. The idea of being married to someone who so rarely shared one's company appalled Deborah. It only served to remind her of how much she wished she could be with Christopher. She thought of their conversation some time back when she'd assured him she was fine in waiting until the day he was free to marry her. That had been true at the moment, but sometimes it wasn't.

"As for the future," Jael said, seeming to lighten up a bit, "Father and Stuart are actually talking of moving to Houston. Business transactions here in the West have profited them greatly, and they are anxious to be near their investments."

"Houston isn't so terribly far," Deborah said. She couldn't begin to imagine what G.W. would have to say about it, but then again, perhaps Stuart and G.W. could now get along. Especially since losing Lizzie hadn't cost Stuart his inheritance.

Lizzie seemed to be on a different thought. "I am surprised you were allowed to accompany them."

Jael nodded. "I insisted. It was really the first time Stuart had seen me assert myself. I told them that since they were planning to be gone for a great many weeks, I should accompany them.

"Then I added that if they were serious about moving to Houston, it was only right I see the place that had so enthralled them. I also pointed out that I should have a say in the house we might purchase. After all, I would spend most of my time there."

"And so they were in agreement?" Lizzie asked.

"At first not so much, but when I threatened to follow the day after they left, they changed their minds."

"And what did Stuart say about your . . . uh, determination?" Deborah braved the question that she knew was on both her and Lizzie's mind. Stuart was not one to graciously consider challenges to his authority.

Jael eased back in the chair. "He came to me that night and told me he didn't like being forced into anything. I told him neither did I. I reminded him I had friends not far from Houston, and that frankly, I would enjoy a visit. He brought up that you were his enemies, but I told him that was nonsense—that just because Lizzie found someone to marry for love didn't mean he should condemn her for such an action. Not everyone was stuck in our situation."

She paused and shook her head ever so slightly. "I was actually surprised Stuart was taken aback by my comment. He actually asked me if I was unhappy."

"That is surprising," Lizzie replied. "Stuart never used to care whether I was happy or not."

"It's true," Deborah said. "Maybe Stuart has feelings for you, after all."

"I think he's grateful to me. He knows I helped him out of a difficult situation. I told him it wasn't so much a matter of true unhappiness, but rather discontentment—a sort of displacement. I felt a sense of loss from the baby and from ideals and dreams I had once believed in—a loss of innocence, if you would."

Deborah could hear something else in Jael's tone. Was it longing? Regret?

"But I mostly wanted to make sure my presence wouldn't make you uneasy, Lizzie," Jael said, changing the subject. "If it does, I'll go. My desire to see you both and enjoy your company is not nearly as strong as my need to make certain we remain friends. If distance is the only way to accomplish that, then I will regretfully go."

"No!" Lizzie declared, startling Rutger. He had just nodded off to sleep and for a moment stared up at his mother before closing his eyes once again. Lowering her voice, Lizzie continued in a calmer tone. "Our friendship is far more important than what's between me and Stuart. In time, perhaps we can meet socially and he will not be ill at ease, but even so, it would never have anything to do with you."

Deborah agreed. "She's right. We are more than friends—we are like sisters, and that bond will not be easily severed."

ꕥ

Despite G.W.'s misgivings, Euphanel and Sissy made their way to meet Zed Perkins at the sawmill. Euphanel assured her son she was going, either with him as an escort or without.

"Miz Vandermark, I must say this is a surprise," Zed said, coming from his office. "Won't you step in here? It's marginally cleaner and a little quieter."

Euphanel followed him into the office with Sissy and G.W. behind her. She took the seat Zed offered and smiled. "Thank you so much."

"It's a hot one today, and I had Miz Greeley

bring me over some sweet tea and ice. Would you care for a glass?"

"That sounds wonderful," she admitted. Looking to Sissy, she asked, "What about you?"

Sissy glanced up to where Mr. Perkins stood. It was clear to Euphanel that she feared his reaction to the invitation. White women were offered refreshments, but black women were ignored. To ease the woman's concern, Euphanel spoke. "I'm sorry. Where are my manners? I presumed you would have enough for all of us."

"Of course," Zed said, not acting the least bit put out. "The invitation was extended to each of you."

Sissy seemed to breathe a sigh of relief. She nodded. "I'd be mighty grateful."

"Me too," G.W. said, limping over to his mother, "but I need to head on over to see the doc. Mr. Perkins, could I impose upon you to escort my mother and Sissy to the commissary after they conclude their business here?"

"Certainly," Zed replied. "It would be my honor."

G.W. excused himself, closing the office door behind him, while Zed went to get the ice and tea. Euphanel waited until he'd returned and she'd taken a sip of the tea before picking up the conversation. "This is quite good. Thank you so much. Now, I suppose you're wondering as to why we've come."

"I was rather curious," the older man admitted.

"It's been over five months since we lost George and David. In that time, no one has come forward to speak on the matter or offer any witness or hearsay on who the culprits might be. In my deep frustration over this matter, I've decided to offer a reward for information."

"Now, Miz Vandermark, I don't know as that's a good idea."

"Zed Perkins, you have had this matter in hand for all this time. I see no other ideas being shared or suggested." Euphanel's temper began to flare. "If this had been the murder of white men, the man or men would have been caught and hanged by now."

"Look, I know the unfairness of it all," Zed began. He hooked his thumbs in his vest pockets, which only served to draw attention to his pudgy midsection. "We have sought the murderers. We've asked questions of the law officials in the surrounding counties. Every county has had some sort of trouble from the White Hand of God, but no one seems to know who the men are or what they're planning next."

"Then our community is truly at the mercy of killers? This happened just after the war, and good men refused to sit still for it. It's a sin, and you know it. If we don't take a stand again, it will only continue. Money always loosens tongues with these sorts. I'll stake a twenty-dollar reward for information that leads to the capture of these men."

Zed frowned. He paced back and forth a moment, then finally took a seat behind his desk. "Miz Vandermark, I wish you wouldn't. I fear it will only stir up problems."

"Problems?"

He nodded and continued. "You go wavin' around that kind of money—especially in a company town—and there's going to be trouble. Folks will be inclined to lie about what they know."

"That's why the money is contingent upon the men being caught. If the information doesn't lead to such an arrest, the informant will not be paid."

"That's all well and good, Miz Vandermark, but the men who call themselves the White Hand of God are smart. They ain't been caught yet, and they've been practicin' their misdeeds for some time."

"And that is a good reason for moving forward instead of doing nothing," she insisted.

Zed scratched his cheek. "I think it will only bring more danger to our community."

Euphanel looked at him oddly. "How so?"

"Well, like I said, those fellas appear to be smart. What's to stop one of them from bearin' false witness—setting up a situation so it looks like an innocent man is to blame?"

That possibility had never occurred to Euphanel. "Well, there would have to be evidence."

"But don't you see? Who better to give evidence—or worse still, hide evidence—to support their claim? It would be simple enough for the White Hand of God to do something that underhanded and then the wrong person will hang."

"Ain't no white man gonna hang for killin' a black man, anyhow," Sissy muttered. "Miz Euphanel, this were a mistake."

Turning to Sissy, Euphanel shook her head. "It's not a mistake—or a lost cause. There has to be something we can do."

Zed got up and came back around. "We are keepin' our ears and eyes open to the matter, but frankly, I think you need to accept that we most likely won't ever know the truth of who killed those men."

A knock sounded from behind them. Euphanel turned to see a well-dressed man standing at the open door. "Pardon me if I'm interrupting."

"Mr. Longstreet, we were just concluding our discussion," Zed replied, looking quite relieved.

Euphanel got to her feet and Sissy did likewise. "Mr. Longstreet, you must be Jael's father."

He smiled and gave a bow. "I am indeed, but you have me at a disadvantage."

"I'm Euphanel Vandermark. Deborah's mother."

"Mrs. Vandermark, it is a pleasure." He once again bowed. When he glanced back up, Euphanel felt as though he were assessing her from head to toe. His study caused her cheeks to grow hot.

"I hope you will do us the honor of joining us for dinner this evening. Zed, you and Rachel are invited to come, as well."

"It's a rarity when I pass up one of your meals, Miz Vandermark," Zed replied. "We'll be happy to join you and will bring Mr. Longstreet. If that agrees with him."

Mr. Longstreet gave his hat a twist. "I'd be honored to share the company of such a beautiful woman."

Euphanel didn't know quite how to respond. She looked at Sissy and then Zed. "Well, I will expect all of you this evening around seven.

Hopefully the house will have cooled somewhat by then."

"We'll be there," Zed told her.

Longstreet's grin danced all the way up to his cocoa brown eyes. "I will count the hours until then," he said in a husky voice.

Although the office was roasting in the July heat, Euphanel actually felt a chill climb her spine. The man was dashing and charming, unlike most anyone she'd ever met. She felt like a silly schoolgirl again.

"Let's be on our way, then, Sissy," she said, fighting her feelings of confusion.

"I'll walk you to the commissary as I promised." Zed motioned to Mr. Longstreet. "Please have a seat, and I'll be right with you."

As they crossed the street to the commissary, Euphanel dismissed Zed and took Sissy's arm. "Goodness, but it's a hot day."

"Ain't jes' the day what got heat in it," Sissy replied. "That Mr. Longstreet done put off his own sparks."

Euphanel looked at her friend in surprise. "I thought I was imagining that."

"No, ma'am. It were like the devil hisself offering Eve the apple." She smiled. "Best be warned—we know what done happened to Eve."

"We certainly do."

Chapter 17

Mother's announcement that their supper would include Christopher gave Deborah a reason to give special attention to her appearance. She decided to dress carefully in a beautiful gown lent her by Jael. Garner's extra fine sateen flowed in a regal waterfall over the small collapsible bustle Deborah had chosen.

"It's really designed for the larger bustles," Jael had told her, "but I think this looks just fine—it lays surprisingly well."

Giving a turn, Deborah praised the moderately low-cut gown. "I haven't worn anything this grand since Philadelphia." She gently fingered one of the lavender ruffles that had been trimmed in peacock blue. All of this had been set atop a white sateen foundation. "I'm also glad it has the shorter sleeves. I would surely have fainted from the heat if they were long."

Jael laughed. "I suppose the heat is something I shall have to get used to if we move to Texas. Of course, Philadelphia can be quite stifling. Father always had us go to Newport during the heat of the summer. I don't suppose he'll do likewise if we move here."

"That would be quite an expensive venture," Deborah said, still studying her profile in the mirror. "This makes me look so thin. I hope Mother won't be worried."

"And that's without having to even cinch up your corset very tightly." Jael assessed her friend. "You look beautiful, Deborah. Now come here so I can put the final pins in your hair. The curls we gave you are going to look lovely once we get them arranged."

Half an hour later Deborah walked into the front parlor. The men got to their feet, and Christopher gazed at her as if seeing her for the first time.

"Got yourself all gussied up, I see," Rob declared.

"You're gonna make the rest of us feel a bit shoddy," G.W. said, then noted his wife's transformation and nodded toward her. " 'Cept for Lizzie, of course, and Miss . . . Mrs. Albright."

The name came slowly, but nevertheless was acknowledged.

"Jael and Lizzie never look shoddy," Deborah declared. "Jael let me borrow this gown, and I must say, it feels quite wondrous. The material isn't as heavy as I thought it might be."

"It's the height of fashion," Jael commented. "I had it made not long before coming to Texas."

"It's quite grand," G.W. replied, "but probably a bit too formal for pickin' beans."

Jael seemed to think about this for a moment, then nodded. "But perhaps not too out of place for tomatoes."

The men chuckled just as Mother entered the room. "Supper is ready. If we are all assembled, I suggest we make our way to the dining room." She glanced at Deborah. "Goodness, but you girls look exquisite this evening. If I'd known, I would have gussied up a bit." She put a hand to her hair. The long braided coil suited her well.

"You are always beautiful, Mother," Deborah said, leaning over to give her a kiss on the cheek. "It is we three who aspire to reflect your gracious beauty."

Mother shook her head. "Flattery is the mouthpiece of the devil." She smiled and gave Deborah a kiss in return. "Now come along before everything gets cold."

"That'll be the day," Rob said with a hint of humor in his tone. "It's been hot enough to melt metal; I doubt the food will cool off even hours from now."

Mr. Longstreet hurried to Mother's side and offered his arm. "If I might be so fortunate, may I escort you?"

Mother looked rather shocked, but nodded. Deborah quickly caught sight of Uncle Arjan's frown. G.W. escorted Lizzie, while Mr. Perkins brought in his wife. Rob graciously offered his arm to Jael. Deborah stood, waiting for Christopher to offer to do the same for her, but he seemed strangely distant—almost disinterested.

"You'd better grab that little gal's arm before I do," Arjan told him.

Christopher seemed to snap out of his fog at this. "I do apologize. My mind was clearly elsewhere."

Arjan passed by him and spoke in a whisper loud enough for Deborah to hear. "Hard to believe with a gal lookin' that fetchin' that your mind would be anywhere but on her." He threw Deborah a wink, then made his way out of the room.

"You are quite lovely. I was completely taken aback. I've never seen you gowned quite this grand."

Deborah smiled. "I wanted to show you that I clean up good."

"That you do, Miss Vandermark." He came closer and offered her his arm. "Please allow me to escort you to supper."

She grasped the crook of his elbow and nodded. "I would like that very much, Dr. Clayton."

Deborah took her seat and suppressed a frown. Mr. Longstreet only had eyes for her mother, and it didn't bode well with Deborah. She had long been thinking on seeing her uncle and mother married. Now Mr. Longstreet's arrival was disturbing her plans.

Throughout the meal, Deborah could see that Uncle Arjan was also quite unhappy with Mr. Longstreet's focused attention. By the time dessert arrived and praises were sung for her mother's pecan pies, Uncle Arjan looked like he'd been sucking on a sour persimmon. Frankly, it made Deborah want to giggle. Her uncle must be in love to act in such a manner. Perhaps the arrival of another potential suitor would stimulate him to action.

"I am astonished to hear you say that you made this supper yourself," Mr. Longstreet told Mother. "At home, I have a staff of five in my kitchen who do not manage to turn out such delicious food."

"I had help. I have such a wondrous group

of women in this house, and each is equally talented. We all had a hand in the creation of this meal."

"Well, not so much me," Lizzie added. "I was busy most of the time with the babies."

"I'm amazed that you don't have a full-time cook . . . and a nanny," Longstreet replied. "Such lovely ladies deserve to have help." He looked at Arjan and added, "Wouldn't you agree?"

"Euphanel's always had whatever she wanted—or needed," Uncle Arjan stated firmly.

"That's right," Mother agreed. "I've always wanted to tend my own home. And Sissy has been here to help. We hired her on long ago and since she's such a dear friend, she's now come to live with us after the death of her husband and son."

"I understand you're a widow, Mrs. Vandermark. I myself am a widower. Jael's mother passed on many years ago."

"And you never remarried?" G.W. asked.

He gave Mother a devilish grin. "I haven't yet found the right woman. Perhaps all of that will change with my move to Texas. I am coming to greatly appreciate Southern ladies."

"So you're for sure movin' here?" G.W. asked.

Deborah wondered if everyone could feel

the tension as much as she did. She pretended to focus on the pie, but found it nearly impossible. She had a very quiet and distant Christopher on one side and her blushing mother on the other. At the head of the table, her uncle sat scowling, and beside him, the ever-flirtatious Mr. Longstreet. It hardly mattered where anyone else sat. At the moment, there was a sense of foreboding that things might not turn out well—especially for the latter three.

"I wonder if I might impose upon you for a tour of your property?" Jael's father asked Mother. "I realize it's growing dusky, so we could limit it to the area here around the house. I would love to hear why you chose this land to settle on."

"The boys and I would be happy to walk you around and tell you everything," Arjan said, getting to his feet. "Wouldn't we?" He looked to G.W. and Rob, who nodded in agreement.

"There you are," Mother said as she, too, pushed away from the table. "That will give me time to put things here in order. Deborah, I suggest you and Dr. Clayton enjoy the evening air, as well."

"I'm happy to change my gown and help you, Mother."

"Nonsense," Jael said quickly. "I will help

your mother. Now go." She smiled knowingly at Deborah.

Deborah looked to Christopher. "Would you care to take a stroll with me?"

"I would," he said, helping her from the chair.

They made their way outside, pausing on the porch to enjoy the cool of the evening. It was still warm enough that Deborah had no need of a wrap. "Do you suppose we could just sit on the porch swing? I'd hate to get the hem of this gown dirty."

"Suits me," he said. "I rather like sitting beside you. I could detect your lovely perfume throughout the meal. It was intriguing."

"It belongs to Jael," she said, strolling across the porch. "Perfume seems like a senseless novelty for my life. Sateen gowns are much the same. I'm only put together tonight because of her help and mercy."

He helped her to sit on the porch swing, but looked at her oddly. "That bustle is a wonder."

She giggled. "Christopher, you are the most outspoken man. It collapses—if you were wondering. Now come join me."

He did as she commanded, but Deborah couldn't help but feel there was something pressing on his heart. "You've been very quiet all evening. Please tell me what's wrong."

"I didn't say anything was wrong." Bull-frogs and cicadas began a natural symphony of sounds.

"Maybe not in so many words." Deborah eyed him. "But I see it in your expression and feel it in your absence."

"Absence? I've been beside you all evening."

"Maybe in body, but not in mind." She took hold of his hand. "Christopher, what is it? More family trouble?"

He let go a sigh. "One of my brothers. I'm not yet sure what the trouble is, but my mother is worried. I suppose I shall know in due time."

"I am sorry. I know how hard it is when your loved ones are struggling."

Christopher put his hand atop hers and smiled. "You are always quite understanding. I like that about you, Miss Vandermark."

"Why, Dr. Clayton, are you paying me a compliment?"

He looked surprised. "I do so all the time, and well you know it. Do I not admire your ease in learning and retaining medical information? Haven't I spoken of how much I enjoy your company?" He paused. "Not to mention how beautiful you are. Though I might have a few criticisms on a profession level, of course."

"Of course," she said with a hint of laughter.

Across the yard, she could see her brothers and uncle showing Mr. Longstreet the chicken coop. "It would appear Mr. Longstreet is rather captivated by my mother."

"I think it goes without saying."

"I thought Uncle Arjan might well get up and punch the man square in the nose. But maybe it's good that Mr. Longstreet has arrived. After all, if my uncle loves my mother and wants to marry her, it's about time he spoke up."

"What?" Christopher looked at her as if she'd suggested someone commit murder.

Deborah put her hand to her mouth almost immediately. She hadn't meant to speak the latter part aloud. She shook her head and lowered her hands. "Oh, goodness gracious, I shouldn't have said anything."

"Well, you have now, so you might as well come clean. What's this about your uncle and your mother?" he whispered.

"Mother believes he's in love with her—at least that's what others have suggested to her."

"And why would anyone make that presumption?"

Deborah looked over her shoulder and lowered her voice even more. "Mother said that it was because Uncle Arjan has never married and yet has always stayed close to take care of her. Then it also has to do with the way he looks at her."

"But he's said nothing?"

"Not yet," Deborah replied. "But after tonight, it may come sooner than later." She smiled. "It would be wonderful to see my mother happily married again. Then I'd know she had someone to take care of her no matter what—someone to love her."

Christopher said nothing for several minutes, causing Deborah to look at him. "Did I say something wrong?"

He shook his head. "I was just thinking about how much I'd like that for my mother. I keep thinking my other siblings will come to her aid, and yet they don't. My sisters obviously have little say—the ones who are married must do as their husbands wish, the others are too young. My brothers who are old enough and making their own way in the world know how bad the situation is, yet they do nothing but cause grief." He blew out a heavy breath. "I just don't know where it's all headed."

"But God does, Christopher. He is faithful, and He won't leave you or your family. I'm going to be praying for you—that you will have peace of heart and mind. I'll pray, too, for your family." She paused for a moment. "I know it's not generally acceptable to speak of such things, but I have some money saved . . . "

He put his finger to her lips and shook his head. "No. I won't take your money."

She wanted to protest but held her tongue. Christopher got to his feet. "I should head back before it gets too dark."

"I thought you were going to follow the Perkinses' carriage." She stood. "I can't imagine they'll be much longer. Mr. Perkins said he wanted to head back to town early. Why don't I go and check on their plans." She started for the front door but came up short when someone called her name.

"Why, Miss Deborah Vandermark, if you ain't the purdiest gal in all of Texas."

She turned and found a familiar face gazing up at her. "Mr. Wythe. Whatever in the world are you doing here?"

※

Arjan was never so glad to see anyone leave as he was Mr. Dwight Longstreet. The man was annoying and definitely inappropriate in his conduct. He had flirted all evening with Euphanel and, even as he left, asked if he might come again to check on Jael's comfort. Euphanel didn't even realize his real intention was seeing her again.

The man had nerve, that was for sure. He would also have the freedom to visit while Arjan would be busy in the forest.

"What's eatin' you?" Rob asked as they checked on the mules before calling it a day.

"Oh, I didn't care for the way that Longstreet fella acted with your ma. He wasn't at all respectful."

Rob shrugged. "She didn't seem to mind the attention."

This further irritated Arjan. "She's a lady. Of course she didn't act as if she minded. He was a guest in her house, and she didn't want to make a scene."

"I ain't never known Ma to keep from puttin' a fella or lady in their place, if needed." Rob put the last of the mule harnesses on the wall.

This was the last thing Arjan wanted to hear—mainly because it didn't alleviate his concerns. Rob was right, and Arjan knew it as well as anyone. He'd seen Euphanel over the years stand up to any number of folks. If she had been annoyed by the attention and flattery given her by Mr. Longstreet, she would have made that clear. She'd have done it with grace and eloquence, but she'd have done it.

But she hadn't.

When he realized Rob was watching him, he grew embarrassed. "It's gettin' late."

"Wait a minute, Uncle Arjan. I . . . well, something ain't quite right."

"What do you mean?"

Rob stuffed his hands deep into his pockets. "I don't know. I just feel like something ain't right. I know you care about Ma. You've proven that over and over. Do you think something is wrong with this Mr. Longstreet fella? Are you worried that he might mean Ma harm?"

"Could be," Arjan said, then regretted the words. "I don't know. Maybe I'm just tuckered out."

"Why don't you stay home tomorrow? We're well ahead on our quotas, and I can oversee what has to be done. That way, someone will be here for Ma, just in case. I mean, G.W. is here, but he ain't strong enough to fight off a fella, unless he did it with a gun."

Arjan felt torn. He wanted to do just as Rob suggested, but at the same time, he knew it would look odd. Rob, however, was already assuming he would do as suggested.

"I know I'll feel a whole lot better if you're here, and you can finally have time to put in those shutters you promised Ma."

"Not another house in all of Angelina County has shutters, but if that's what your ma wants—then I figure that's what she should have."

Rob grinned. "It's always best to give Ma what she wants."

And without saying another word, the matter was resolved for him. He would stay home and do odd jobs and keep an eye on the person he cared about most of all.

Chapter 18

The sun wasn't even up when the Vandermark family sat down to breakfast. Arjan offered a prayer, then opened the morning's conversation by inquiring after Jacob Wythe.

"Seems you're a ways from home, Son. What brought you down here?"

Jake grinned and his expression grew mischievous. "Well, sir, I knew the purdiest gals in all the world lived here in this area."

Arjan laughed. "That they do, but ain't it gettin' kind of late in the summer for you to be gone from the ranch?"

The young man's expression quickly sobered, causing Deborah to take note. She'd never thought that something might be wrong. She'd just presumed that Jake had traveled south to secure cattle or do some other piece of business for his family.

"Fact is, my pa sold out. The drought killed off half the herd. There just wasn't water to go around. Grass ain't growin' and the cost of feed was gettin' so high, Pa said he'd had enough."

Deborah felt horrible for him. His mother and father had been born in Texas, and the ranch had been in the family since 1840.

"I'm surely sorry to hear that. What're your folks gonna do?" Arjan asked.

"They sold the land and the last of the cattle for what little they could get and headed to California. I didn't want to leave Texas, and so I'm trying to find a job. I remembered that you folks were running a logging operation and wondered if you might need an extra hand."

"It's mighty dangerous work," G.W. put in.

Wythe smiled. "So's ranchin'."

"He's got a point," Arjan replied. "Still, it will be different from anything you were doing on the ranch."

Deborah felt sorry for Jake and looked to her mother. "I'm sure he's a fast learner. And if you don't need him in the logging camp, then maybe we could put a good word in for him at the sawmill."

"That's a good idea," her mother answered. She turned to Jake. "We are good friends with the owner of the Perkinsville Sawmill. You might want to consider that before taking on logging."

"Pardon my sayin' so, ma'am, but I'd rather work outside. I've spent all my life either in the saddle or on the ground. I don't reckon I'd do so well inside a building."

"Well, I can definitely understand that," Mother replied. "What of it, Arjan? Surely we have need of another worker."

Arjan looked to Rob and G.W., who both nodded. "Seein's as how he's saved Deborah from harm more than once, I figure we owe him at least that much. Rob can show you around the camp today and discuss the various jobs. You may change your mind once you see how much work is really involved."

Mother passed a bowl of grits, and Jake smiled as he took them. "Thank ya, ma'am, and thanks to all y'all for givin' me a chance." He spooned grits onto his plate and passed them to G.W.

Sissy appeared with a huge platter of fried ham steaks and eggs. "Reckon these will fill you boys up." She put the food on the table, then took her seat near Lizzie.

Jake looked rather surprised at this move. He glanced at Deborah with his brows raised.

"This is Sissy. She's a part of our family. Sissy, this is Jacob Wythe."

"Most folks call me Jake or Slim." His words were stilted—almost awkward.

"Any friend of Miss Deborah's is surely my friend," Sissy said, taking the grits from Lizzie.

Mother started the platter around and followed this with a plate of biscuits. Deborah quickly picked up the bowl of gravy and offered it to Jake. "Mother's biscuits and gravy are quite delicious." He nodded and helped himself to a healthy portion.

"Mr. Wythe," Jael began, "Deborah tells me you attended university."

"That's true. But it wasn't for me. Like I said, I don't care to be fenced in. Sitting in classes day after day isn't very satisfying."

"I don't know about that," Deborah interjected. "It may not have been satisfying to you, but many of us quite enjoyed it."

He swallowed the big mouthful of grits he'd just spooned in and nodded. "I apologize if I made that sound as if nobody enjoys school. I forgot that you were quite fond of book learnin'."

"Deborah's definitely supportive of education," her mother said, "although many of our neighbors see no need for such things. We have a good school in town, but there are times when the older children are removed from class to work. Mr. Huebner is a dear friend and the schoolmaster in Perkinsville. He's often left with just a handful of the young girls to teach. We all think it's sad that the boys aren't encouraged to stay in school, but it's the way things are around here."

Mother smiled at Deborah. "However, Deborah has helped her brothers improve their reading skills. They are doing quite well at it, as I hear tell."

Jake looked at Deborah. "Well, if my teachers had been that purdy, I probably would have stayed in school."

Deborah felt her cheeks grow hot and focused on her plate. Much to her further embarrassment, however, Rob had to offer his thoughts.

"She may look decent, but she's a hard taskmaster. In fact, she can be downright mean if she thinks she won't get her own way."

Chuckling, Jake looked at Deborah. "I've seen her riled up a bit, so I don't doubt your words."

"I will not allow you to malign my dear friend," Jael declared. "Deborah is the most giving and compassionate person I know. She's training to be a doctor."

Lizzie leaned forward to look down the table at Jake. "That's right, and while we are quite grateful for the help you extended us in Houston last year, we certainly aren't going to allow you to hurt her."

He leaned toward Deborah and winked. "I had no intention of hurting you."

Deborah didn't want his attention and quickly dismissed him. "Apology accepted. Now, if you don't mind, I'd like to change the subject." She looked past Jake to her mother. "How is the sacred-harp singing coming along?"

Her mother dabbed the napkin to her mouth. "Well, so far it's going quite well. We have quite a few singers who have done this before, so that helps."

"I've even come to enjoy it myself," Arjan announced, looking at Mother.

She returned his gaze for a moment. "And he's been very quick to pick up the particulars."

Deborah wondered if she were the only one who saw the exchange. She glanced around the table, but no one else seemed to have noticed. Or, if they did, they didn't seem to think anything of it.

"I used to sing in the choir at church," Jake threw in.

Mother offered Jake another round of biscuits, but he declined. "Though we do sing hymns for the most part, this is mainly a social event. We get together and sing for the pleasure of it all. In the old days, we would sometimes sing for hours on end, with occasional pauses for food or fellowship. It's a wonderful way to draw a community together."

"We had quite a few square dances up around our place. Folks seemed to prefer dancin' for their entertainment," Jake replied.

"Well, if we know what's good for us," Arjan interrupted, getting to his feet, "we'd best get a move on."

"I thought you were going to stick around here today," Mother said, sounding slightly upset.

"I am," he said with a smile, "but I need to get to work. I know you want those shutters put in place before the next storm threatens to bust up the windows."

Deborah thought she heard a sigh of relief from her mother. The matchmaker within her begged to be given a chance to encourage the feelings brewing between the two.

"Mother," Deborah said, pushing back from the table. "Why don't you assist Uncle with the shutters? Jael and I can help Sissy with the kitchen and Lizzie with the babies. The sooner we get those shutters in place, the better you'll feel."

Arjan spoke up before Mother could respond. "I could use a hand, Euphanel."

G.W. looked at Deborah. She could tell by the look on his face that he was about to volunteer himself. She shook her head and jumped up. "G.W., I wonder if I might speak to you in the office before I get to work here."

His expression showed confusion, but he nodded as Mother agreed to help Uncle Arjan. Rob tossed down the last of his coffee and went to grab his hat. "Come on, Jake. We need to get up to the camp—the mules will be gettin' mean."

Deborah lost no time in heading out of the room. G.W. followed her into the office and closed the door. "What was that all about?"

She wasn't sure what to say. "Ah, I hoped to see Christopher this morning and wondered how your leg is feeling. I'll let him know so that he can evaluate the situation and decide if the exercises are working or if you're overdoing."

G.W. narrowed his gaze. "Deborah?"

"What?" She could see that her innocent tone didn't fool him. He fixed her with a look and crossed his arms, much as their father used to do when waiting for an answer.

Crossing to where he stood, Deborah lowered her voice until it was barely audible. "Mother and Uncle Arjan are in love."

"What?" His voice boomed across the sparsely decorated room.

"Shh." She put her hand to his mouth. "You heard me. Don't shout about it."

He lowered his voice as she took her hand away. "Where did you get that idea?"

"It's quite clear. Just the way they look at each other. Not only that, but haven't you ever wondered why Uncle Arjan never married? He is in love with Mother."

G.W. shook his head. "I can't believe we're having this conversation."

"Then let's not," Deborah replied. "But don't interfere. I think with just a little help, we might see a wedding before summer's end."

Rolling his eyes, G.W. shook his head again. "You need to stay out of it. If they are . . . " He paused and looked over his shoulder at the closed door. "If they are in love," he whispered, "they will figure it out."

"So you don't mind?" she asked, smiling. "Personally, I think it would be marvelous."

He laughed. "I do, too—if it's their idea and not yours."

ꕥ

With Jake close on his heels carrying a double-bitted ax, Rob led the way to the trees they would consider for cutting. The introductions had gone all around to the boys, except for the ones clearing brush near the cutting.

"It's the bull, look sharp!" one man called out to the others.

Jake looked at Rob. "The bull?"

Rob looked back and nodded. "The 'bull of the woods.' That's what they sometimes call the woods boss. I'm the boss today, since Arjan stayed home. 'Course, I'm often the boss for the likes of these fellas, even when he's here."

Jake nodded and Rob pointed the way with his measuring stick. "I like the looks of that big one over there. Let's get to it, boys."

Heading to a tall longleaf pine, Rob gave a look skyward and Jake did likewise. "I'm checkin' to see what the crown is like and what kind of toppin' we might have to be doin'. See, it's my job to figure out exactly where to make the undercut and such so that we can drop that tree down within inches of mark."

"Sounds hard."

"It takes practice," Rob admitted.

"Yeah, but he's the best there is . . . 'ceptin' for G.W.," another man announced.

"Jake, this is Warren Crandel. He's a sawyer. Practically can operate a two-man crosscut by himself."

Warren extended his hand. "You must be the new man."

"Name's Jake," he replied.

"Good to have you," Warren replied. "Days are long, usually ten to twelve hours. Iffen you git home afore dark, it's just 'cause you cheated the bull out of hours."

Jake grinned. "Since I'm temporarily living with 'the bull,' I won't have much of a chance to cheat him out of anything."

Rob shook his head. "We're gonna drop this one, Warren. Get Wolcott to top it off for me while I figure out the wedge cut."

"Will do, Bull."

Rob waited until the men were helping Ashton Wolcott with his gear before squatting down at the base of the tree to evaluate. Jake got down beside him, only to pop back up when Rob moved to the side of the tree and repeated the action. He gazed upward again, trying to tell the list of the trunk. This particular tree was just about as straight as a chopper could want.

Next he stood and walked several paces out from the tree. He glanced around gauging the other trees in the area and the lay of the land.

"We try to spare the seedlings and young trees," he explained. "Unlike some, we want to keep growin' this forest, so we are mighty particular about which trees we cut."

"But most aren't?"

Rob shook his head. "Most have what we call the 'cut-out-and-get-out' way of thinkin'. They are only tryin' to harvest the most wood in the fastest way possible; then they move on to another location, leaving a field of stumps behind. We clear the stumps—that's the reason I brought out the kerosene from the house. Once a tree is felled, we drill a hole as deep as possible and pour kerosene down it to kill the roots. After a while the thing just rots and we can pull out the stumps, easy-like."

He walked around the tree several times, then marked the trunk and walked out through several tall pines to pound a stake in the ground.

"What are you doing now?" Jake asked.

Rob grinned up at him. "I'm markin' where I want the tree to fall. The boys sometimes wager as to whether they can drive that stake into the ground. Mostly they do it, but sometimes they miss."

"Looks like an awful narrow place to put it down. You got trees all around it."

Rob straightened and handed him the mallet. "If they do it right, it won't be a problem at all. Once Wolcott gets the upper section of the tree cut off, you'll get to see firsthand how it works. I'm gonna let Warren show you how things are done."

Jake nodded. "Sounds good to me." He pulled on well-worn leather gloves and squared his shoulders. "I'm ready."

By the time the afternoon light was starting to fade, some ten longleafs had been cut and prepared. In all but one instance, the choppers were able to pound the stake into the ground, so Rob rewarded them with a short day.

"I feel like celebratin', boys. It's Friday and we're well ahead of schedule. I'm callin' it a week. Once we finish loading out the logs, you can head into town. We won't work tomorrow."

A rousing cheer went up from the men, who quickly stepped up the process of skidding the logs to the train car. In another two hours they were done, anxious to clean up and get to town.

Rob himself was spruced up and standing at the door of the parsonage a short time later. He couldn't help but be unnerved by the beauty of the young lady who greeted him.

"Evenin', Miss Shattuck. I was wonderin' if you cared to take a walk with me, but I see it's gettin' pretty dark." Rob fought to keep his voice steady.

"I have a better idea," she said. "Why don't you come inside and have some cake and coffee. I just poured Father a cup and was getting ready to cut the cake."

He followed her into the house. "Thank you. Thank you, kindly. I reckon that would just about hit the spot."

"Father, look who's come to call," she said, leading Rob into the kitchen. The parsonage was much too small for a separate dining room, but Mara had made a lovely setting in the kitchen. The small table and chairs could manage up to four people and perfectly suited their needs.

"Welcome, Rob. Good to see you. What brings you around?"

To their surprise, Rob didn't reply as they expected. "I had a question about finding God's will."

Mara gave her father a brief glance before heading to the counter. "I'll get your coffee."

"Have a seat, Rob," the pastor directed. "I'll do what I can to help you in this matter."

Rob did as he was told but lost little time in expressing his thoughts. "I've been thinkin' a lot on it, and figure God is after me to do somethin'. I'm just not exactly sure what that is. I think I have an idea, but I want to know without any doubt that it's God's will."

Pastor Shattuck nodded. "I can appreciate that. It's only a fool who doesn't seek the Lord on such matters."

Mara came to the table with the steaming mug. "Would you care for sugar and cream?"

Rob shook his head. "I drink it black. The stronger the better."

She smiled. "I think you'll find this to your liking, then." She walked back to the cupboard and took down some small plates.

Rob turned back to the pastor. "My uncle

told me—well, Ma and Deborah told me the same thing—that a fella ought to pray and read up on the Bible. I've been doing that quite a bit, and I'm still not sure."

"Some things take time, but you can rest assured that the Lord has thoughts on what He wants for you." He took hold of his Bible and opened it. "Here in Jeremiah, chapter twenty-nine, verse eleven, it says, 'For I know the thoughts that I think toward you, saith the Lord, thoughts of peace, and not of evil, to give you an expected end.' " Pastor Shattuck looked up. "Do you understand that passage?"

"I reckon so," Rob said. "Seems to me it means that God wants to make us hopeful about our days. He's tellin' us that He doesn't want evil for us—and that He has an expected way for things to turn out."

Pastor nodded as Mara put down plates of cake in front of them. "This is your mother's lemon cornmeal cake recipe," she told Rob.

"Thank you. It's one of my favorites."

She went back for forks and napkins, then joined them at the table. "Would you mind if I share this conversation?"

Rob shook his head and got to his feet to help her with the chair. "Not at all."

"If he doesn't mind, I surely don't," her father replied.

Mara situated herself and smiled. "One of my favorite verses is in the first chapter of James. 'If any of you lack wisdom, let him ask of God, that giveth to all men liberally, and upbraideth not; and it shall be given him.' He goes on to caution that we should ask in faith, believing that God will answer and that we not be wavering."

Rob considered the words. "I've been askin', that's for sure."

"And what is God telling you?" Pastor Shattuck asked.

"Well, that's the thing," Rob began. "I felt like He wanted me to learn to read better—maybe learn more than I already knew. So my sister has been helpin' me with such things. I've mostly been readin' on the Bible, and because of that, I feel sort of like maybe God wants me to do somethin' more than loggin'."

"Such as?"

Mara remained silent, but Rob could sense a quiet intensity in the way she listened. He shrugged. "Well, that's the problem. I'm not entirely sure. Sometimes I think maybe He wants me to become a preacher like you."

Mara gave a sharp intake of breath, but when Rob turned she looked perfectly at ease. She smiled and asked, "More coffee?"

Rob shook his head and rubbed his jaw. "I don't know how a fella tells what's God sayin' somethin' to his heart and what's just his own self wantin' such a thing."

"And have you long thought of becoming a pastor?" the older man questioned.

"No. Not a'tall. I figured to be loggin' all my life. My pa figured both of us boys would take over for him and Uncle Arjan. Now I don't feel at all certain about that. Ma says she'd be right proud to have a preacher in the family and that I should do what God's callin' me to do. I just want to be sure it's God doin' the callin'."

"And why would Satan benefit by having you study the Word of God and teach it to others? Seems to me the devil would rather put people away from such notions."

"Well, that's what I figured, too," Rob said. He took a long drink of the coffee.

"I find that fasting and prayer often help me to resolve matters," Mara said. "I will happily fast and pray for you, Mr. Vandermark."

He looked at her in disbelief. "You would? But why?"

She smiled. "Because you want an answer, and I care about you getting that answer."

"Mara's good about that," Pastor Shattuck said, patting her arm. "She's prayed and fasted many a time for me. She's a good woman."

Rob couldn't deny that—not that he wanted to. They finished their cake and coffee, and by the time Rob was headed to the door, Pastor Shattuck excused himself to head over to the church and followed Rob outside.

"Trust the Lord, Son. He will guide your steps," the pastor told him. "Mara, I'll be home in an hour."

Mara stood in the doorway to bid Rob good evening. The soft glow of lantern light cast elusive shadows around them, but Rob felt a nearly uncontainable urge to kiss her. He held back, though, and instead simply studied her for a moment. He had never met another woman like her. She made him feel . . . well, whole.

"I appreciate you bein' willin' to fast and pray for me. It's a kind and generous offer. I still don't understand why you would take on such a task."

Mara smiled and backed up to take hold of the door. "It's what we are to do for one another, Mr. Vandermark. And I have a vested interest. When God gets through showing you what all you need to do for Him, then I will benefit, as well."

"How's that?"

She began to close the door, but murmured, "Because then He will see us become man and wife."

Chapter 19

August 1886

On Sunday, the first of August, Deborah waited outside the church to speak with Christopher. She'd not seen much of him in the past few days, and though she had been free to assist him in his rounds, he had refused or simply not been available to explain.

"Are you avoiding me?" she asked as he started to head toward his house.

He looked at her, his expression rather pinched. "I'm sorry. I've just been dealing with several matters." He paused and shook his head. "Look, I can't explain just now, but I won't be able to use your help in the next few weeks."

"But why?" She crossed the short distance. "Have I done something wrong?"

He shook his head. "No. Certainly not." He glanced up and Deborah could tell someone was approaching. "I can't talk about it right now." With that he departed just as Jael came up to join her.

"What was that all about?" her friend asked.

"I honestly don't know." Deborah watched Christopher disappear from view. "But hopefully I'll soon find out."

She was still pondering Christopher's words the following Saturday. Deciding that enough was enough, Deborah told her mother she was going to take Jake into town to meet Mr. Perkins and also so that she could speak with Dr. Clayton about making rounds next week.

"Jake went to get the carriage ready," she told her mother in the summer kitchen. Sissy bent over a big mixing bowl and threw her a smile.

"Goin' a-courtin'?"

"Not exactly," Deborah replied. "I do plan to see Dr. Clayton, but it may not be all that pleasant."

"Well, if you're going to see Dr. Clayton, be sure to take him these corn cakes. Remind him they're awfully good with molasses. That should sweeten the matter."

Deborah took the cloth-wrapped bundle from her mother. "I doubt I'll have to remind him." She made her way to the barnyard and found that Jake was still harnessing the horses. The growing heat made Deborah irritable, and that, coupled with Christopher's strange actions and Jake's increasing attentions, made her want to run and hide in the forest.

Spotting her uncle inside the barn, Deborah climbed up on the carriage to set down the corn cakes. "I need to speak with Uncle Arjan for a minute. I'll be right back."

"I'll be fixin' to go when you are," Jake replied.

Deborah entered the barn and felt the temperature drop only slightly. Her uncle was forking hay into the stall of one of the milk cows. They had just sold her latest calf, and the animal was rather forlorn.

"Poor Dottie," Deborah said, stroking the cow's face. The mother cow gave a mournful call for a calf that was long gone. "She sure misses her baby."

Uncle Arjan stopped what he was doing. "I see Jake's gonna drive you into town."

"Yes. He asked me to show him around. He wanted to see the sawmill, and Mr. Perkins said today would be best."

Uncle Arjan leaned on the pitchfork handle

and smiled. "I suppose you'll be seein' that young man of yours."

"Well, I hardly know if he's mine," she snapped. Feeling rather embarrassed by her comment, Deborah smiled. "Sorry. I feel out of sorts today."

He nodded. "I can understand that. I feel that way a great deal of the time."

Deborah looked at him for a moment. For the life of her, she couldn't remember what she'd come to talk to him about. Frowning, she started to explain, but her uncle was already speaking again.

"I think each person has someone out there that the Good Lord intends to see them spend their life with. When the time isn't yet come and those folks are separated, I think there's a powerful longin' to set things right."

Deborah cocked her head and without thinking said, "Like you and Mother?"

Arjan straightened and looked at her as if he hadn't heard right.

"Uncle Arjan, I . . . well, most all of us can see that you love Mother. The thing is, I believe she loves you, as well. I do wish you two would stop being so respectful of each other and just get the words said."

"I . . . well, I guess I didn't expect . . . " He stopped and fixed Deborah with a narrowing gaze. "Do you really think she feels that way?"

Deborah laughed. "I do. Now, look—you did not hear that from me." She stepped forward and kissed her uncle on the cheek. "You've always been a part of my life, like a second father. Why not make it official? If you don't, it seems that Mr. Longstreet may well try to join our family."

She didn't wait for him to comment but hurried back to the carriage where Jake stood to assist her. Taking her seat, Deborah couldn't keep from grinning. She was rather glad her uncle's own words had opened the door for her to say what she did.

"You look like the cat what swallowed the bird," Jake said, taking up the reins.

"I'm just happy, is all."

"And is part of that happiness on account of your spending the day with me?" he asked hopefully.

Deborah could see that she needed to set yet another matter straight. "Jake, I'm courting Dr. Clayton. He's my beau."

"But you ain't engaged."

"No, we aren't, but our courtship is with marriage in mind."

Jake laughed. "Most are, aren't they?"

"Well, I just don't want you getting the wrong idea."

"I think until there's a ring on your finger, I have just as good a chance as he does in winning you over."

"That's a very bold thing to say. I think—" She fell silent at the sight of another buggy coming in from the road. "Oh my."

"What's wrong?" Jake looked at the well-dressed driver.

"Mr. Albright," Deborah said.

"I've come for my wife," he replied curtly. "Would you be so good as to get her?"

Deborah nodded, and Jake tied off the reins and helped her down. She heard Jake introduce himself to Stuart as she hurried toward the house. Jael wasn't going to be overly happy at this news. She had only said that morning what a peaceful blessing it had been to be with the Vandermarks and how she wished to remain here forever.

"Jael, you need to come quickly," Deborah called.

Her friend scurried into the foyer from the front sitting room. "What's wrong? I thought you were headed to town."

"I was, but Stuart's here. He said he's come for you."

Jael sobered and stiffened. "Very well. I knew it was only a matter of time. Tell him he may come get my trunk. I have it nearly ready. Father had already told me to expect him."

"Why did you not say anything to me?"

"I didn't want to spoil our time together. I was afraid you would fret and fuss over me." Jael took hold of Deborah's arm. "I'll be all right. In time, I truly believe love will grow and that Stuart will be an attentive husband." With that, she turned and headed up the stairs.

Deborah had no choice but to return outside and give Stuart his instructions. "She asked that you come and retrieve her trunk. She's just now finishing her packing."

Stuart nodded, his icy blue eyes narrowing slightly. "I understand Elizabeth has given birth to twins."

"Yes. Last June. They arrived early, as twins usually do, but they are quite plump and healthy now."

He said nothing for a moment, then secured the brake and climbed down from the carriage. "If you'll direct me."

Deborah led the way into the house but found it unnecessary to go any farther. Jael was tying on her bonnet as she descended the stairs. "Hello, Stuart. My things are ready and waiting in the room just to the top right of the stairs."

She stepped into the hallway to give him access to the stairs. Without a word, Stuart left the women to their good-byes.

"I will come to call on you in town," Deborah

promised. "Please feel free to send word if you need me for anything." She embraced Jael. "If you leave the area, please let me know."

"I promise I will." She smiled as they pulled apart. "Please tell Lizzie and your family good-bye for me and thank them. I have so enjoyed my stay and the hospitality. Hopefully I will be able to visit you from time to time. I know my father would certainly like to see your mother again." Deborah said nothing, and Jael continued. "If nothing else, I will see you in church tomorrow. I might have a better idea of what to expect after I have time alone with Stuart."

Just then Stuart came back down the stairs, a small trunk on one shoulder and a suitcase in the other. "Is this everything?"

Jael moved away from Deborah. "Yes. That's all I brought. The rest is with my father at the boardinghouse."

Stuart exited the house without asking for assistance. He had already secured the luggage and was back waiting to hand Jael up into the carriage when the ladies appeared on the porch. With another quick hug, Deborah let her friend go.

"I will see you tomorrow," she called after Jael.

Stuart turned the horses and headed back out of the yard almost before Deborah could descend the porch steps. The entire matter had taken less than ten minutes.

"You ready to go to town now?" Jake asked, drawing the buggy closer to the house.

Deborah nodded. "Yes, I suppose I am."

They followed Jael and Stuart to Perkinsville, taking care to keep far enough back so the dust could settle. The deeply rutted road was miserably dry, and it seemed all of the earth cried out for rain. Glancing upward, Deborah could barely see the skies through the thickness of pines, but it was clearly void of clouds.

"If you're thinkin' it might rain, I wouldn't get your hopes up. We spent much of the last year doin' that heavenward gawk. Didn't do us any good."

"I haven't had a chance to tell you how sorry I am about your ranch. I can't imagine how you must feel."

"Mostly angry," Jake said matter-of-factly. "Angry that I couldn't do anything to make it right. Angry that God didn't seem to hear our prayers."

"We can't always understand why things happen the way they do, that's for sure," Deborah replied. "Still, we have to have faith that God will keep us in His care—that no matter what happens, He is still in control."

"Sometimes I think that's askin' a lot."

Deborah didn't know what to say, and so she moved the conversation in a different direction. "I do wish it would rain. Uncle Arjan is very concerned about fires. One spark from the train or a carelessly tended fire, and we could have a disaster on our hands."

"That would surely trouble a great many folks."

"It's the dichotomy of living in the Big Piney. You want things damp and moist to keep the fire chances down, but you don't want the storms that bring the rain. If lightning comes with the rain, there's always the possibility that it will strike a forest fire."

"But you seem to really like livin' here," he said, keeping his gaze on the road.

"I do love it here. Texas is my home, and I know most every path and turn in these woods—where the rivers run and where the creeks twist off. When I was gone from here, it was all I could think on."

"I can see why. The forest has an appeal, just like the range. I miss it."

She looked at him in sympathy. "Goodness, but I don't know what I'd do if we had to give up our place."

"It ain't ever easy to lose what you love."

His words made Deborah uncomfortable, and so she settled back into the seat and said nothing more, pretending instead to be completely transfixed by nature. By the time they reached town, Deborah felt pretty certain that Jake's feelings for her ran deep. At one time she might have welcomed his attention. He was a very nice man—quite the gentleman for being raised on a ranch.

"Just stop over there by the commissary," she instructed. "I'll walk you over to the mill."

Once she had Jake tended to, Deborah made a straight path to Christopher's office. Entering the side examination room after knocking, she was surprised to find the room empty. She checked his office and the front waiting room, but there was no sign of him.

"Christopher? Are you here?"

Something drew her attention to the kitchen. It was just a hint of noise that sounded something like the fluttering of paper. Before she could go see what it was, however, Christopher emerged. He looked awful—as if he hadn't slept all night. There were dark circles under his eyes, and his face was pale.

"Are you ill?" she asked, crossing the room.

"Why are you here, Deborah?" His question was curt and to the point.

She stopped and crossed her arms. "Well, that's a fine way to greet someone—especially someone you supposedly care about."

He sighed. "It would be better if you go."

This made her angry. "So we're finished with the courtship? You've given up and are releasing me?"

"I didn't say that." He tossed the letter onto the exam table.

"No, you didn't. You don't say much of anything. I can't read your mind, and you won't share it."

He pointed to the letter. "Read that and then tell me how much you want me to share with you."

Deborah went to the letter and lifted it. "You could just explain what's in here."

"Better you read it for yourself."

Scanning the contents of the letter, Deborah could barely read the script. Apparently it was from someone in Indianola. The letter was brief and to the point.

> *You have been requested to support your brother Calvin Kelleher at his murder trial on the nineteenth of the month of August. He stands accused of killing a man in a saloon fight. Seemed to some to be a case of self-defense, but others are accusing him of provoking the attack. He says you are the only one who can come to his aid.*

She looked up and found Christopher watching her intently. She wanted to ask why

Calvin's last name was different than his own but knew that now was hardly the time.

"So do you still see yourself in a courtship with a murderer's brother?"

"Your brother isn't you. You have no reason to bear his shame," she protested.

"You marry a man's family as well as the man," he countered. "My family has murderers and thieves, apparently. My mother tells me in another missive that two of my other brothers are in jail in Springfield for attempting to rob a bank there." He began to pace and mutter inaudible things to himself.

"Christopher, you cannot let the misdeeds of your family cause you this grief. We must pray for them and do what the Lord would call us to do, but we needn't take it on our shoulders."

"He wants me to come to Indianola. No doubt he wants me to pay for him to have a lawyer and a fair chance. Maybe he even hopes for a character witness. Who can say? I've not seen Calvin in ten years. I went away to study when he was young and when I returned, he had left home with Benjamin and Andrew—the two in jail in Springfield."

Deborah moved toward him, but Christopher held up his hands. "Don't. Don't try to console me. I don't deserve it. If I'd been the man my family needed, I would have been there to see that they had a better time of it."

"You did what you could. They weren't your responsibility—that belonged to your father and mother." Deborah inched closer. "Christopher, you aren't to blame for this. Fact is, it really wouldn't matter who was in error of their upbringing; they are grown men. They make their own choices."

He seemed to calm a bit at this. "I know you're right, but it angers me to see the waste. They were good boys—they were smart. They had a future."

"They still do," she told him. "Maybe Benjamin and Andrew will use this time in jail to straighten out their lives."

"And what of Calvin? He's just twenty. His life has barely begun, and already he may lose it."

Deborah gently touched his arm. "Then you should go to him."

"This will kill our mother. She doesn't even know." His voice broke.

Taking him in her arms, Deborah pulled him close. Christopher buried his face against her straw bonnet and wept silently.

"I'm so sorry, Christopher, but we will see this through together. No matter what, I will be at your side in prayer, even when I can't be with you physically."

For several minutes, she simply held him. She remembered a similar scene many years ago when her father's mother had passed on. It was the only time she'd seen her father cry, and it frightened her. Christopher's tears didn't frighten her; they made her love him all the more. She longed to promise him that the world would right itself, that tomorrow he would awaken to find it all a bad dream. But, of course, that wasn't going to happen.

Deborah barely heard the door open behind her. When she glanced up, she found Maybelle and Annabeth Perkins staring at her with their mouths open. Christopher pulled away from Deborah and exited the room to compose himself. Deborah turned in greeting, as if nothing were amiss.

"Are one or both of you ladies ill?"

Maybelle shook her head, but it was Annabeth, the elder of the two, who spoke. "That was hardly appropriate for us to witness. You were in the doctor's arms."

"Actually," Deborah replied, "he was in mine. He received tragic news regarding family. I was merely offering consolation."

Maybelle giggled and Annabeth shot her a reproving glance. "No matter what his problems might be, it's totally unacceptable for you, a single woman, to be embracing a single man. Especially one whom everyone knows you are courting."

Deborah shook her head. "I'm sorry you feel that social rules should cancel God's. The Bible tells us to bear one another's burdens and offer comfort. I did no more or less, and for you to judge otherwise is wrong."

"We will see what Pastor Shattuck has to say about that."

Knowing the Perkins sisters, half the town would know what she'd done before the sun even crossed the sky. Deborah felt a pang of regret. She wasn't so worried about her own reputation, but Christopher had fought hard to win these people over. Her actions would put him in an unfavorable light, as everyone would assume he was the one to take liberties with her.

Shaking her head, Deborah tried hard not to show her irritation. "You will say whatever you see fit. I have done nothing wrong."

But what bothered her most was that she knew that was a lie. As far as she'd been taught, it was wrong for her to have been embracing Christopher—even in a moment of great sorrow. They weren't even to hold hands in public.

Christopher reappeared, his eyes still red-rimmed, but he'd managed to compose himself. "May I be of assistance to you ladies?"

Maybelle giggled again. “Mother wished for us to extend to you an invitation for dinner,” Annabeth told him.

“I must go.” Deborah felt more ill by the minute. The consequences of that one moment of oversight would no doubt haunt her for weeks to come. Reputations were easily lost in gossiping communities.

Christopher looked at her, but only nodded. Deborah hurried outside, the voices of the Perkins sisters prattling on about how their parents were entertaining the new partners and wanted Dr. Clayton to meet them over supper.

To her surprise, Jake was waiting for her at the carriage. “Did you have a nice visit?”

“Get in the buggy,” she ordered, climbing up without assistance. She took up the reins. “Pull the brake.”

He did as she instructed without questioning her actions. Turning the horses, Deborah caught sight of Maybelle and Annabeth standing just outside the doctor’s office. Christopher stood behind them, his gaze fixed on Deborah.

“Are you all right? Is somethin’ wrong?” Jake asked.

Deborah shook her head and urged the team to pick up speed. “Nothing I want to discuss. Nothing I think you’d understand.”

Chapter 20

Rob couldn't shake the memory of the dream—or was it a nightmare?—that he'd awakened to that morning. In the haze of his sleep, he'd seen himself saying good-bye to his family, to Mara. Mother was crying, but he felt that he had her approval for whatever it was he was about to do. That was what bothered him the most. What was it he was doing? Why was he telling them good-bye?

He headed to church with the family. No one seemed to notice his silence, or if they did, they said nothing. He was grateful not to have to explain. How could he tell them when he couldn't figure out what bothered him so much? He'd had bad dreams in the past, but this one seemed different. This one seemed so real that he could almost recall the scent of the air—the feel of Mara's hair as she handed him a ribbon-tied memento.

Seeing her at church only stirred up the memory. He thought of the words she'd said to him—that they would one day marry. He wanted to know how she could just say something like that. They hadn't known each other long at all, yet there was something so unexpected about their relationship. He'd been the wild one—the guy who made himself available to all the girls. He'd had his share of stolen kisses and flowery words. Those kinds of things used to make for pleasant memories. Now, however, they didn't matter. He could think only of Mara.

Once they were back home and lunch had concluded, Rob decided to walk in the woods. Jasper and Lula followed after him. Lula was heavy with pups again but managed to keep up with Jasper just fine.

The day felt more humid than it had in the past months, and he could feel the perspiration form on his neck. A scant few clouds dotted the sky. Rob prayed it was a sign of rain. He hated working with the logs when they were slippery and wet, but the water was much needed. Besides, they were well ahead on their cuts. It wouldn't hurt to take a day or two for other chores. There were always axes and saws to sharpen, equipment to check, and a bevy of other menial tasks to see to that slowed them down when not tended to properly.

He breathed in deeply of the heady pine aroma. He was at home here, yet something seemed to be pulling him away. But where? Shaking his head, Rob studied the road ahead. The paths he walked were well-worn. His mother was always using them to gather herbs or bring the cows home.

Pausing, Rob caught sight of a rabbit scurrying amid the ramble ahead. Jasper and Lula raised a ruckus and took off after it. The rabbit hardly looked big enough to worry after, but that didn't stop the dogs from giving chase. Rob sat down beside a young pine and waited for their return. He had no real destination in mind, anyway. Resting here was just as good as walking deeper into the woods. He leaned back against the tree and gazed skyward. Up through the pine boughs he could see spots of blue with wisps of white.

Rob closed his eyes. *God, I don't know where you're taking me. I don't know for sure what I'm supposed to do, but I have some ideas. You're gonna have to show me, though, iffen for real it's your plan and not just my own.*

Of course the idea of becoming a preacher had never been one of Rob's dreams. Rob remembered breaking out in a cold sweat the first time it had come to mind, in fact. How could he, an unlearned man, share the Word of God?

"Saw you head out this way and figured to catch up to you," Arjan said as he came upon Rob.

Rob opened his eyes with a start. "Somethin' wrong?"

Arjan sat down beside him. "I was about to ask you the same thing. You ain't seemed like yourself for days, but today was particularly bad. I figure there's somethin' on your mind."

"I had a dream last night—kind of a vision," Rob admitted. "I was fixin' to head out—to leave the area. I was telling all y'all good-bye. Ma was cryin' and . . . well, I don't know where I was headed. And it really bothers me."

"Why?"

" 'Cause it felt like the Lord was showin' me somethin' I needed to know. I can't explain it, but when I woke up . . . well, now I think I'm supposed to do somethin'."

Arjan pushed back his hat and scratched his neck. "You've been thinkin' a lot lately."

"True enough. Seems like God's givin' me a lot to ponder." He turned and fixed his uncle with a questioning stare. "Do you believe God speaks to fellas like me? I mean, really talks to them?"

"I reckon so. Bible says that God doesn't change. He talked to men in the Bible, so why wouldn't He talk to us now?"

For several minutes, Rob said nothing. Then he leaned forward. "Mara Shattuck told me that God had plans for her and me to be man and wife."

Arjan grinned. "Well, I'll be. She said that, did she?"

"Yup. Then she closed the door on me and left me to figure it out for myself. Problem is, it just made matters more confusin'."

"So you came out here to sort your love life. I reckon I came out to do the same."

"Ma?"

The single word hung between them. Arjan nodded slowly. "I guess I can't deny my love for her."

"Why would you want to?"

Arjan laughed. "I don't. I guess I just want to ask your permission to ask your ma to marry me."

Rob grinned and raised a brow. "You promise to take good care of her?"

"You know I do—haven't I shown you that by now?"

"Of course you have." Rob got to his feet, and Arjan did likewise. "I'd be right proud to have you marry my ma."

"Think G.W. will feel the same way?"

Rob gave a whistle for the dogs. Arjan stepped in pace with him as Jasper and Lula came bounding out of the woods. "I reckon G.W. will want Ma to be happy, and I know Deborah does."

"Your sister has already given me her blessing," Arjan replied. "She's the one who really made me feel hope about the possibilities."

"When do you plan to talk to Ma?"

Arjan looked up. "I guess there's no time like now."

Rob caught the reason for his words. Ma was coming toward them just now—herb basket in hand, broad-brimmed straw hat on her head. She smiled and waved.

"What are you two doing out here?" The dogs rushed forward to greet her, then tore off in another direction when something caught their attention.

"Came out here to think and jaw," Arjan replied. "How about you?"

"I'm after herbs."

Rob nudged his uncle. Arjan looked at him for a moment, then turned back to Euphanel. "Would you care for some company?"

She smiled and lowered her gaze. "I'm always happy for a friend."

"I need to get back to the house," Rob said. He went to his mother's side and kissed her on the cheek. "Love you, Ma."

She smiled and patted his cheek. "I love you, too."

Euphanel looked after her son for a moment. "I wonder what he's up to?"

"Why does he have to be up to anything?" Arjan asked with a smile. He reached out and took the basket from her gloved hands.

"He's been acting strange. Ever since he started wondering about becoming a preacher. Seems like he's worried about leaving the logging business and home. I told him not to fret over it. Why is it so hard for my children to understand that I'd be proud of them no matter what they decide to do?"

"I suppose because Rutger made it clear to them that he had plans for them to take over the business."

"But he never intended for them to go against their calling," she countered. "If God wants Rob for a minister, then I want it for him, as well."

They continued down the path and Arjan fell silent. Euphanel wondered if she'd somehow upset him. Perhaps he, like Rutger, wanted the boys to stay focused on working for the logging company.

"I'm sorry if you think that's wrong. I know the company is something you two had a vision for." She smiled and looked down the canopied trail. "I always figured they would follow in Rutger's footsteps, but I won't force it. I hope you won't insist on it, either."

"I had no mind to."

"I'm glad." She rubbed her hands together. "You just seemed a bit put off by what I said."

He stopped. "Not at all."

When he didn't pick up walking with her again, Euphanel turned back. "Is something wrong?" She could see the uncertainty in his expression.

Arjan stepped forward. "Nell, I've long wanted to say somethin', but I haven't had the nerve."

Euphanel began to tremble. This was the moment she'd hoped would come—the moment she could speak of her heart and he would speak of his. Her knees quaked beneath her petticoat and skirt. She hoped he wouldn't notice the rustling of her dress. She met his eyes and knew that all she wanted was to spend her life enjoying his company. Why had she been so blind to this before now? Rutger had been gone for over four years now—it was time to move forward.

"I've had something to say to you, as well," she said in a quiet voice. "Something that I never thought I'd ever say."

He took a hesitant step, but kept his gaze

fixed on her face. "Maybe you should speak first."

"I hardly know where to begin." She hadn't felt this nervous in ages. She tried to remember what she wanted to say—tried to remember what she'd said to Rutger when he'd declared his love for her. It was funny, but she couldn't bring any of it to mind. Looking into Arjan's eyes, she couldn't think of anything but him.

"Arjan . . . " She let the name linger on the air.

Without saying anything, he dropped the basket and stepped forward. Taking a hold of her, he whispered her name. "Nell."

She let him draw her into his embrace. Slowly she lifted her face to meet his. He hesitated only a moment, then lightly touched his lips to hers. Time seemed to stand still and Euphanel lost herself in the kiss. For so long, she had believed herself beyond love. When Rutger had died, she was sure that she had buried her heart in the grave with him. That her days of loving and being loved were over.

She'd been wrong, and she was glad.

The idea of giving her heart to a stranger was something she couldn't fathom, but loving Arjan was easy. She trusted him more than anyone. They shared the same history—they knew each other's likes and dislikes, fears and hopes.

He trailed kisses along her mouth and jaw. "Oh, Euphanel, you don't know how long I've wanted to do that."

She pulled back slightly. Her heart threatened to beat out of her chest. Putting her hand up to touch his cheek, she shook her head. "I don't know what to say—to do. This is unexpected to me . . . well, not completely. Seems like folks of late have been telling me how you cared for me. I guess I was the last to know."

A strange look crossed Arjan's face. "I never wanted you to know while Rutger was living. I never wanted him to know. It wasn't right to be in love with my brother's wife. I used to pray that God would take that feeling from my heart and for a long time I was able to keep my mind on my work. I wouldn't have ever done anything to dishonor you or him. I loved you both too much for that."

"I know. I never even suspected," Euphanel said. "I don't think Rutger knew, either."

"I only wanted to do right by both of you. I want to do right by you now." He covered her hand with his own. "Marry me, Nell."

She nodded. "I want to marry you."

He grinned. "Truly?"

Euphanel pulled away and reached down

for the basket. She hadn't felt this good in a long, long while. Straightening, she smiled. "Truly. I might tease about a great many things, but falling in love for a second time isn't one of them."

ꕥ

"Well, look at that," G.W. said, nudging Rob. His brother had already told him what Arjan had planned. "Looks like he wasted no time." The brothers exchanged a grin at the sight of their uncle and mother walking hand in hand.

"What are you two prattling on about?" Deborah asked, coming to stand beside them on the porch. She looked around G.W.'s shoulder. "Oh, I see."

G.W. turned to her. "I guess there will be no livin' with you now."

"Why do you say that?" Deborah looked at him oddly.

"Well, you were the one who told me this was comin' our way. Rob said that Uncle Arjan meant to propose to Ma."

She gave a clap and giggle. "Oh, this is a wonderful day. What a grand celebration we'll have!"

Mother and Arjan approached and looked at the threesome on the porch. Arjan broke into a smile. "She said yes, if that's what you're wonderin'."

Deborah hurried down the porch steps. She went to embrace her mother. "I'm so happy." She reached out to hug Arjan, as well. "We should celebrate."

"I'm glad you're pleased," Mother said, looking rather sheepish. "I don't suppose it will take long for everyone to hear the news."

"Not around here." G.W. gave Mother a kiss on the cheek and smiled back at Arjan. "Rob said you asked for our blessin', and you surely have it."

"I told your mother I wanted to give you and Lizzie my cabin. You don't have to take it, as there is plenty of room here, but I thought you might like the privacy."

"That's generous," G.W. replied. "I think we'd like that very much."

"When is the wedding to be?" Deborah asked. "We have to make you a dress and bake a cake and—"

"Now, hold on," Mother said. "There needn't be a lot of fuss. Arjan and I just plan to make it a quiet affair. We prefer it that way and hope you will understand."

G.W. took hold of Deborah's shoulders. "She understands and so do we. We'll do it your way."

"But we could—"

"Deborah, your ma wants it this way, and whatever makes her happy makes me happy." Uncle Arjan looked to G.W. and then to Rob. "I'm sure you boys understand, since you have gals you've come to care for."

G.W. saw a joy in his mother's eyes that he'd not seen since Father died. The pain he'd felt in his father's death—the way he'd blamed himself for the accident—seemed to fade a bit more. He felt a sense of peace in knowing that she would love again and be cared for.

He thought of Lizzie and the children. Life was good, and this only served to make it better.

Chapter 21

I'm so glad you could both come," Jael told Lizzie and Deborah. "I wasn't sure you could get away from the babies, and I knew Stuart would never approve of my driving out to see you."

"Mother is watching the twins," Deborah offered. "What's wrong?"

Jael motioned for them to have a seat and lowered her voice. "Shh." They were in the front parlor of the boardinghouse, and Mrs. O'Neal, the housekeeper, had a penchant for gossip. "I don't wish for us to be overheard. I told Mrs. O'Neal that we were going to have tea and discuss old times. Do you remember when we were in Philadelphia?"

Deborah looked to Lizzie and then back to Jael. "Of course. What about it?"

"We were happy and innocent then," Jael said rather sadly. "Life was different and we were different."

"That's true enough," Lizzie replied. "It seems like a million years ago."

Jael nodded. "There. That should suffice. I didn't wish to be a liar. We have discussed old times. Now we need to talk about the current state of our lives."

"Are you all right? Has something happened?" Deborah asked in a whisper.

"I'm not sure. I overheard Stuart and Father talking. I had hoped that Stuart was past his jealousy and anger toward your family, Deborah. He never speaks of it to me, so I presumed it had passed. I was wrong, however. I believe Stuart has underhanded plans when it comes to your family's well-being."

"But how could he possibly harm my family?" Deborah asked, looking to Lizzie. "Can you imagine anything he might do?"

"I can imagine a great deal," Lizzie replied. "I wouldn't put anything past him."

Jael moved closer to her friends. "I don't know what he has planned, but he was speaking to Father about some of their business dealings and how he never took on a project without a purpose. When Father asked him what his purpose was in coming to Texas,

Stuart said he couldn't explain in full because a good part of it was personal."

Deborah felt her brows knit closer. "Personal? Did he say more?"

"Part of it I couldn't make out. They weren't exactly speaking freely. I pretended to be busy with something else on the far side of the room, hoping they would continue."

"And did they?" Lizzie questioned.

Jael looked rather worried and glanced around the parlor, as if the walls themselves had ears. She motioned for the girls to come closer. "I think Stuart means to exact revenge on your family. I don't yet know how, but the last thing I heard him mutter was something about how when he needed to teach someone a lesson, he very well knew how."

Deborah straightened. "That could mean almost anything. It certainly needn't be about us."

"Still, Jael is right. It could be, and for that reason we should warn the men," Lizzie replied.

There was wisdom in what Lizzie said. And Deborah worried about her as much as the rest of the family. Lizzie was the one who had rejected Stuart. If he was in the business of holding grudges, then Lizzie's name was no doubt at the top of his list.

A couple of men came into the parlor, deep

in conversation. They didn't seem to notice the women at all as they headed toward the open French doors that led to the smoking porch.

"Seems to me that if the Negroes do not know how to mind their place in society, they deserve whatever punishment is meted out," the taller of the two men declared.

"I agree, Horace, but liquor was involved and that always serves to muddle men's minds."

"Where the black man is concerned, I agree. There is no call for the Negro to be drinking. He hasn't the constitution for it. Think of giving whiskey to a small child and there's little difference."

They exited the house, oblivious to the women. Deborah shook her head. "What was that about?"

Jael eased back in her chair. "Apparently some of the blacks were involved in an altercation at the white saloon. There was quite the fight, as I hear. The blacks were beaten severely and thrown unconscious onto the train tracks. Had someone not come along to find them, they might have been killed."

Deborah could hardly believe her ears. "That's hideous. How can good Christian people act in such a manner?"

"Perhaps they weren't good Christian people—after all, they were, as I heard it told, quite drunk."

"That's still no excuse to take a man's life," Lizzie said. "And just because they didn't die this time doesn't mean the next time won't prove fatal."

"I wonder if Christopher knows about this," Deborah said, getting to her feet. "I think I'll go check in with him and see what the extent of the injuries were. I'm sure if anyone knows, it will be the company doctor."

"I'll stay here and visit with Jael," Lizzie told her. She glanced at the grandfather clock in the corner. "G.W. will be back for us in less than an hour. Don't forget."

"I won't."

Deborah hurried from the room, nearly running Mrs. O'Neal over as she scurried to get away from the open pocket doors. "Good day, Mrs. O'Neal," Deborah called loudly. She hoped that would be enough to let Jael and Lizzie know the old woman was trying to overhear their conversation.

Crossing the dusty street toward the commissary, Deborah found several black women standing at the bottom of the stairs. The blacks were given certain hours when they could shop in the commissary, and the women were waiting for their turn. Deborah thought it all nonsense. Why should the color of one's skin dictate the ability to shop?

She maneuvered past a group of children who were busy chasing after a cat and approached the doctor's house. A strange feeling came over her as Deborah approached the front door. Something didn't feel right, but she couldn't put her finger on it.

"Hello? Christopher?"

She heard some shuffling and scuffing from the examination room. Mrs. Foster came through the door into the waiting room. "He ain't here."

"Oh," Deborah said, nodding. "I can wait."

"He ain't here. He's gone."

"On rounds?"

Margaret Foster shook her head. "He's gone to be with his brother. He left a letter for you. It's on his desk. I'll be handlin' the sick now."

Deborah quickly moved past Mrs. Foster and picked up the letter from his desk.

"When did he leave?" she asked, frustrated he hadn't said good-bye.

"Yesterday. Took the afternoon train out. Said he had business somewhere near Victoria."

"Indianola," Deborah murmured, opening the sealed envelope.

She moved away from the older woman

and went to the window for better light. Christopher's neat and orderly script spilled out across the pages.

My dearest Deborah, I never intended to hurt you, the letter began. Deborah braced herself and continued to read.

> *There is never an easy way to tell someone good-bye, but I feel I must—at least for now. I am going to Indianola to see Calvin and offer whatever assistance I can. The situation does not look hopeful. If they hang him, I will need to go to my mother and give her the news. She will never be able to bear this alone.*

Deborah could feel a lump rising in her throat.

> *I have never cared for anyone as I have cared for you. It's because of my feelings that I know now that I must release you from any attachment or loyalty you may feel you owe me. You deserve so much better, and I long for you to be happy.*

She slumped against the wall. Glancing up, she could see Mrs. Foster watching her. She quickly folded the letter and composed herself. "I need to go. My brother will be waiting to take me home."

Hurrying from the office, she found her

vision blurred by tears. She wiped the dampness from her cheeks and went to where the family carriage awaited. G.W. was nowhere in sight, but she climbed into the back and opened the letter once again.

" 'There are so many things I wish I could have told you,' " she whispered, reading more of his words. " 'So many things I should have said. I know this will be difficult to understand, but in my mind I was protecting you from the truth. Now, however, I see that selfishly I was protecting myself.' "

Tears fell onto the page, causing the ink to run. Deborah held the letter away from her so that the wetness couldn't destroy the words. Once her tears abated, she continued.

> *I pray this letter will allow you to know that this decision was not easily made. I cannot hope that you will understand, but choices and decisions I've made make it impossible to continue our courtship. I don't know if I will return to Perkinsville or not. A great deal will depend on my brother's trial, but if I do not return, I want you to know that none of this was your fault. I accept full responsibility.*

She turned to the second page, feeling a sense of desperation that would not be stifled.

When I saw the reaction of the Perkins sisters, I knew there would be trouble. Pastor Shattuck came to visit me shortly afterwards and told me that your reputation was threatened. I couldn't bear that.

Deborah felt livid. "Gossips. They had no right."

I never wanted this for you. I cannot be the cause of seeing your name smeared in gossip. I hope you will continue your studies in medicine. You have a gift that should not be discarded.

No matter what, please always know that my feelings for you will never change. I will never love another as I have loved you.

Christopher

She stared at the page shaking her head. He'd never uttered words of love before. She'd felt the passion of his kiss, had known his concern and tenderness—but he'd always held something back. Folding the letter, Deborah fell back against the leather carriage seat and closed her eyes.

This wasn't happening. It couldn't be. She'd known Christopher was troubled over the matter of his brother's incarceration—knew too that his mother's suffering was of constant concern to him. Still, she'd never expected him to just pack up and go without seeing her first—without explaining in person.

"Ah, I see you're here already," G.W. said, climbing up to the seat. "I heard something in the hardware store about the doc leavin'. You know anything about it?"

Deborah was grateful that he didn't bother to look around and study her face. "I just found out myself."

"Seems strange he would just up and leave. I was talkin' to some of the boys, and they said there was some kind of problem. Said the preacher was known to have gone and talked to him about some issue. You wouldn't know about that, would you?"

"I can imagine a lot of reasons the pastor would seek out Dr. Clayton." She said it in such a way that she hoped he wouldn't ask any more questions. She knew that Christopher didn't want anyone else to know about his family and their problems. "Oh, Lizzie is still at the boardinghouse."

"We'll pick her up on our way out." G.W. took up the reins, then released the brake. "Walk on," he called to the horses. "So what do you suppose the doc is up to?"

Deborah tried to maintain a hold on her emotions. "He told me he needed to help his brother. He got into some trouble down in Indianola. I'm not really at liberty to say more."

"He's a good man to go to the aid of his family."

Deborah did her best to wipe her tears and arrange her appearance. She hid the letter inside her blouse. There was no sense in having to explain it right then and there. Lizzie would suspect that something was wrong, but knowing her friend, she would wait to question her later or presume that Jael's worries were the reason for her concern.

G.W. brought the carriage to a stop at the boardinghouse walkway. Jael and Lizzie stepped from the porch and approached.

"Did you have a good visit?" G.W. questioned, hopping down to help his wife into the carriage.

"We did, but there is something we need to discuss," Lizzie said. She turned to Jael and kissed her cheek. "Thank you for letting us know. We'll talk soon—you must come for a visit."

"If I can get away," Jael said. She came to the carriage and looked up at Deborah. "Thank you for your visit."

Deborah nodded, not quite trusting herself to speak without giving away her pain. Lizzie took the seat beside G.W. Once she was settled, G.W. took his place. "Afternoon." He tipped his hat.

They were barely out of town when G.W. turned to Lizzie. "So what do we need to talk about?"

ꕥ

At home everyone gathered around the dining room table to discuss the news about Jael's father and Stuart Albright. Deborah knew her brother's mood was dark. Lizzie had explained the situation to him on the way home. G.W. was livid.

"I should have known he'd try to do us harm," G.W. said, bringing his fist down on the table.

"There's no sense in letting anger lead your thinking." Arjan turned to Rob. "We've met all of our quotas on time, haven't we?"

"Yes, sir. We're ahead of schedule, in fact."

Arjan nodded. "That's what I thought. G.W., are the books in order? Are our debts being paid in a timely manner?"

"They are. Albright and Longstreet can't say otherwise."

"Then there really isn't any problem," Mother threw out.

"No, except that Albright wants to cause us harm. It ain't good for a man to have enemies, especially when those enemies can affect his livelihood," G.W. said, shaking his head.

"Maybe we could speak in private to Mr. Perkins and see if he's privy to anything that might explain what Stuart has planned," Deborah suggested.

Mother looked to Arjan. "That's a good idea," he replied. "Your mother and I had planned to speak to the preacher tomorrow after church. Maybe we could also have a talk with Zed."

"It certainly couldn't hurt. Zed would never do anything to cause us harm," Mother said. "If we explain our concerns, I'm sure he'll be willing to talk to us."

G.W. seemed to calm a bit, and Lizzie put her hand atop his fist. "I'm so sorry about this. I feel that it's all my fault. Stuart is taking his anger out on your family because of me."

"You had nothing to do with it," Mother interjected. "If Mr. Albright is hateful and vindictive because a better man won your heart, that's something he'll have to deal with. We don't hold you responsible."

The babies began to fuss from the other room. No doubt, Sissy would soon pop out to say that they were hungry. Lizzie got to her feet. "I'd best see to them."

"I'll come and help you," Mother said, pushing back her chair.

Deborah looked at her brothers and uncle. "If you don't mind, I have some things I'd like to tend to." She got to her feet and hurried from the room. She'd not yet been able to think clearly about Christopher and longed for some time alone. Her hopes were dashed, however, when Rob followed her out the kitchen door.

"Wait up there a minute, Sis."

She turned at the door. "What is it?"

"That's what I want to know. Does this have somethin' to do with Dr. Clayton leavin' town, all quick-like?"

Deborah met his eyes and fought to control her emotions. She'd had a lifetime of teasing and joshing from her brothers, but she'd also known their protective attention. "I can't talk about it just yet—I promised Christopher. You understand, don't you?"

He gently touched her shoulder. "Just wanted you to know that I'm happy to listen."

She smiled, touched by his kindness. "Thank you, Rob. You've quite changed since I've returned home. I suppose it has something to do with growing up, but maybe also a bit with a certain preacher's daughter."

He laughed and backed away with his hands in the air. "If you ain't talkin', then neither am I."

Chapter 22

Deborah avoided going into town for the next week. The last thing she wanted was to face questions about where Christopher had gone and what she knew about it. Except for the understanding that Christopher's brother was in trouble, Deborah knew little else, and she couldn't admit to even knowing that much. She had no desire to share the news that the doctor had ended their courtship. She would never be able to escape the questions and suppositions should that information get out.

She tried to put the matter aside, telling herself that he hadn't really meant to end their courtship—that he had acted without thinking. He would come back. He had to. But just as she found the tiniest comfort in such an idea, reality would pour over her in waves.

Why did he do this? Why didn't he just come to me and tell me what was happening?

None of it made sense. She drew a deep breath and forced the truth to the front of her mind. Of course it made sense. There were far too many secrets between them. Christopher was never all that forthcoming with information regarding his life. He was a very private person, he had once told her.

"So private, in fact, that I haven't a clue who he really is," she muttered, attacking the hard ground with a hoe. She'd offered to weed the garden, and the task had at least kept her body busy.

Rob arrived home and, seeing his sister, headed her way. "I see you're out in the heat of the day," he said as he strolled up. "Good thing you're covered up. That sun's mighty fierce today."

Mother liked the weeding to be done in the heat of the day to ensure the deaths of the unwanted intruders. Deborah wore one of her father's old long-sleeved shirts over her lightweight cotton gown. On her head she'd secured a sunbonnet in the old-fashioned style her mother had once worn as a young woman.

"You're home early." She looked at the sky. "What time is it?"

"Only four. Uncle Arjan said it was too hot

to keep workin'. He told the men to stay in camp but to quit for the day. Nobody argued with him. In fact, last I saw, several of the men were headed to the river to cool down. Not that they'll find an abundance of water there."

Deborah leaned against the hoe and prayed for a breeze. "So what are your plans for the rest of the day?"

"Well, I kind of figured to talk to you for a spell." He pushed back hair from his face. "Then I'm gonna see if Ma or Sissy can give me a haircut."

She knew her brother would probably want to talk about Christopher, but to her surprise, Rob began to speak on something else entirely.

"I know this is gonna sound abrupt-like, but I've given it a lot of prayer and thought," he began. "I believe God has a change planned out for my life."

Deborah straightened. "What kind of change?"

"Well, that's what I figured to talk to you about. See, I'm kind of worried that it's gonna upset Ma. Maybe Uncle Arjan and G.W., too."

"I can't imagine what that would be."

Rob hooked his thumb in his suspenders. "I'm gonna be leavin' this area."

His announcement took her totally by surprise. "I figured you were going to tell me that you'd asked Mara to marry you. I certainly didn't think you'd talk about leaving. Where did you have in mind to go?"

"Houston. There's a seminary there that I want to attend. I think my readin' and cipherin' has improved enough, not to mention that I've pert near read the Bible cover to cover. I don't figure it'll be easy, but I think God wants me to be a preacher."

"You seem quite certain."

"I am." He went over to the fence rail and climbed atop to sit. "I've been prayin' for God to show me, and He keeps bringin' me back to the same place."

"Have you talked to Ma about it?"

"Only the bit about thinkin' I might be called to be a preacher. She gave me her blessin'. She knows it would mean me leavin' the logging business, but she said she didn't want anything to stop me from my callin'. I haven't really talked much with anyone else. I wanted to talk to you, because I figured you'd understand. Sometimes the choices we make aren't that popular with other folk."

"To be sure," Deborah answered.

"I know Doc had something important to tend, but it seems to me he could'a come and said good-bye."

Deborah's gaze snapped up to meet Rob's. "He left me a letter." She knew her tone sounded defensive, so she added, "But I would have rather talked face-to-face. Christopher wanted privacy on the matter, but I need advice. He went to help his brother."

"What kind of trouble did his brother get into?"

She glanced around. "Please don't tell anyone else—promise? This town is so full of gossips."

"Of course I'll keep quiet."

"His brother Calvin has been arrested in Indianola for killing a man." Deborah stared at the garden patch and began to hoe again. "Some say it was self-defense, but others say it wasn't. If his brother hangs, Christopher said he would be obligated to return to his family in Kansas City."

"And what about you?" His tone wasn't accusing or otherwise harsh.

Deborah continued working, unwilling to meet his gaze. "He didn't want me to feel that I had to wait for him. He wasn't even sure he'd return to Perkinsville."

"Why not?"

She stopped and leaned the hoe against the fence. Pushing back her sunbonnet, Deborah wiped perspiration from her forehead. "His mother may need him to stay in Kansas City.

His father is pretty useless. He's taken to drinking because he can't bear being an invalid. Christopher's mother suffers greatly."

"I see. Well, I reckon I can't fault a fella for somethin' like that."

"No." She gazed past him to the railroad tracks. She thought of Christopher leaving the town by means of the train. She couldn't help but wonder where he was now. Maybe he was sitting at his brother's side in some trial. Maybe he was pleading for his brother's life.

"I'm sorry he's gone," Rob said, drawing her attention back to him. "I reckon that must be powerful hard for you."

She nodded. "It is, but I'm trying to just put those feelings aside and focus on the work that needs to be done. Garden can't hoe itself and the clothes can't wash themselves."

"If it's any help," he said with a smile, "I feel pretty certain the doc will come back. You two are intended to be together."

"And how would you know about such matters?" she asked with a teasing smile.

"That's part of God's blessing on me, I guess," he said, his tone becoming serious. "I think on a matter long enough, and pretty soon, I'm not just thinkin' about ideas for fixin' the problem, but I'm seeing the problem already done in my head. It's like a vision or something."

"That sounds amazing." Deborah put her hand on Rob's knee. "You've picked up your reading so quickly, and just look at the gift you have for memorizing Scriptures. I think God has a definite path for you."

Rob nodded. "I do, too. Will you come see me in Houston?"

"Absolutely," Deborah promised. "However, I may well go off to get some training myself."

He looked at her oddly. "Like what?"

"Medicine. I'd like to continue my studies and become a real doctor. Since Christopher may not return for some time, I'll probably need to find another doctor to train me."

"I don't know that I like the idea. I hope you'll be givin' it a lot of prayer and thought."

"I will," she promised. "There might even be a doctor in Lufkin who would take me on once he knows about the details of my previous training." She gave a shrug as if it were all of no consequence. "We will just have to wait and see."

"Seems like you should give this a whole lot more thought."

"But don't you worry. I'll make sure the business won't suffer. G.W. now handles the office and business affairs quite capably. The exercises he's been doing to strengthen his leg have really improved his usage of the limb. It won't be long at all before he's fully capable of doing just about anything he wants. Uncle Arjan knows the logging business, and even with you off training to be a preacher, he'll hire the workers needed. Vandermark Logging will go on as it always has."

"Still, I'd hate to see you goin' away again. I know Ma would, too."

"I know. It's not ideally what I want," Deborah admitted. "I had planned that Christopher . . . Dr. Clayton would continue to train me. I suppose those who didn't feel it appropriate are happy now."

Rob studied her for a moment. "Just make sure your choices aren't about running away."

His comment took her off guard. "Why would you say that?"

"Seems to me you were quite content to be here until the doc up and left. I'd hate to see you change all your plans just because you feel out of sorts with him."

The conversation was taking a turn she'd rather not travel. She took the hoe back in hand. "But what about you? Have you thought to talk to Pastor Shattuck about being a preacher?"

"Yes. He's the one who told me about the seminary. We talked and prayed about it."

"What about Mara?" She knew her brother

was more than a little sweet on the preacher's daughter.

"Well, she knew God had a plan for me before I did. Fact is, she told me that once I get done what God has for me to do, we'll get married."

Deborah laughed. "She did? Well, that's quite a proposal. I would never have expected Mara to speak so boldly."

"She's full of surprises," Rob admitted with a grin. "I can't say that I mind, though. I like a woman knowing her own mind and heart. I'm even happier that she looks to know God's, as well."

Deborah considered the young woman for a moment. "And have you asked her to wait for you?"

"Didn't have to," Rob replied. "She told me she'd be here waiting when I got back."

"Well, it sounds like you've truly considered all of this. I have to admit, I used to wonder if you'd ever settle down." She grinned. "I never figured you'd do it in such a big way."

He hopped down from the fence and gave her a hug. "I guess it's time I go talk to Ma and the others." He started to go, then stopped. "Say, you ought to know that Jake's pretty sweet on you. He's always askin' about you."

Deborah shook her head. "I know. I've made it clear to him that I have a beau." She frowned, thinking of Christopher's letter releasing her from their courtship. "But I guess that's changed."

"You think the doc will forget all about you?"

"Could be. He didn't ask me to wait for him. In fact, it was just the opposite." She moved back to the garden row.

"I'm sorry," Rob said. "Don't give up on him. You don't know yet what God has planned, but you two worked real well together. I can't believe God would just send you off in different directions. Findin' another person who understands your heart . . . well, it isn't easy."

"No, it certainly isn't," Deborah agreed. She looked at her brother. "Please don't speak to others about it. I'm not really ready to discuss it. Please just pray for me to know exactly what God has in mind."

ꕥ

"You were mighty quiet at supper," Jake said, finding Deborah alone on the front porch.

The last person she wanted to deal with was Jake, but she didn't want to hurt his feelings. Lifting her closed fan, she waved it from left to right. "It's so much cooler out here than inside—don't you think?"

He took the chair beside her and turned it around. Straddling it, he leaned forward against the back of the chair. "I suppose you ain't exactly wantin' to jaw with me."

She smiled. "It certainly isn't personal. I don't feel like speaking with anyone. I'm not good company tonight."

"I find that hard to believe," he said with a smile. "My granddaddy used to say that sometimes when a fella felt like he couldn't find the words, it was 'cause he needed someone to help him."

"And you're offering to direct me? Is that it?"

His smile broadened. "Sure, why not? You and me, we've been talkin' on and off for some time now. You know you can trust me. I'm the honorable sort."

Deborah couldn't help but laugh. "Yes, I suppose you are."

"So why not share your worries with me?"

She looked at him and had to admit she found his expression endearing. He tried so hard to impress. "It's not so much worries. I'm really not sitting here fretting as much as thinking. It seems my life is changing once again, and I just want to be sure I know where God wants me to be."

"Seems to me what with Him bein' God, He's able to put you where He wants you to be without you havin' to think overmuch on it." He sobered. " 'Course, my ma used to say that God didn't force us, so I suppose a fella could make a bad choice and go somewhere God didn't want him . . . or her."

"It's true," Deborah admitted. "My mother used to tell me that God has a perfect way for each person, but sometimes we don't care to know what that is. I honestly want to know, but it seems that just when I start to figure it out, everything changes."

"Like courtin' Dr. Clayton?"

Deborah stiffened. "I'd rather not talk about Dr. Clayton."

"Why is that?"

"Because it's a private matter. I wouldn't feel comfortable talking to you about it."

Jake grinned again. "Why, 'cause you know I'm wantin' to court you myself?"

Deborah looked at him and lowered her fan. "That's one very good reason for us to change the topic of our conversation."

"I think you're afraid to step out with me."

"I am not." Deborah hadn't meant to sound so indignant. She softened her tone. "So how are you enjoying your new job?"

He looked for a moment as if he wouldn't allow for the conversation to change course, then shrugged. "It's hard work. But I surely appreciate your family takin' me on."

"I wish things had gone better for your folks," Deborah said, thinking how sad it all was that Jake should have to leave the only home he'd known. "I know you must miss them."

"I do," he admitted. He got off the chair and walked to the end of the porch. "I always figured to take over the ranch when my pa passed on; instead, it's gone to strangers."

"Who bought your family's land?"

Jake shook his head. "I don't know. Some fella from up Chicago way. He was buying up a bunch of ranches. Told my pa the drought wouldn't last forever and when the rains finally came, he'd own a good piece of Texas."

"So he has the luxury of waiting for the rains, but your father didn't."

Frowning, Jake turned away. "No."

"I'm sorry, Jake. I really am. I can't imagine how I'd feel if we suddenly lost our land. For all the years I was away from here, I always knew I'd come home one day." She got up and walked to where Jake stood staring off across the yard. "Still, you did say that you believed God was able to put you where He wanted you. Maybe that's here. Maybe there's another kind of life God wants you to experience."

Jake turned and Deborah was more than a little aware of how close he stood. "Could be He sent me here because of you. Ever think about that? Maybe I lost one family—one home—because I'm gonna have another." He winked. "And maybe you're gonna be a part of it."

On Saturday the fourteenth, Euphanel and Rachel decided to host a sacred-harp gathering for the community. They posted notices around town at the commissary, mill, and new dress shop encouraging everyone to attend, whether they could sing or not. The ladies felt that the heat of summer, coupled with the worry over drought was enough of an excuse to have a party.

Zed thought it was a good idea, as well. He talked of tempers running high at the mill and even some conflicts with his new partners. He donated scrap wood to build temporary tables and moved the benches from the ball diamond. By the time things were set in place in the grassy park area beside the church, it looked like the party might rival the Texas Independence Day celebration.

Most folks seemed happy to break their routine, as well, and by the time the singing began in the early evening, Euphanel was convinced that most everyone in the community was present. She was pleased to see that while some folks were surprised by the blacks joining in the sacred-harp choir, no one said anything to suggest it was inappropriate.

"My, you look lovely," Mr. Longstreet told her. He took hold of her hand and raised it to his lips. "I do hope there will be a chance to share a private moment." He kissed her hand, leaving the onlooking Rachel to gasp at his boldness.

"Euphanel, I need to see you about something," she told her friend.

Mr. Longstreet looked perturbed but said nothing as Rachel led Euphanel away from his company. Euphanel was more than grateful for her friend's attentive action.

"Thank you. I swear, the man has gone out of his way to charm me."

"Maybe he doesn't realize you've already been charmed elsewhere," Rachel smirked.

"How could he not know? This is a small town and gossip travels fast."

"I'm so excited that you and Arjan will be

married tomorrow," Rachel gushed. "It's going to be a beautiful ceremony; I just know it."

Euphanel nodded. "It's definitely a new start for the both of us." Seeing that everyone was pretty much assembled, Euphanel motioned to Rachel that it was time to take their places.

After directing the first song, Euphanel took her seat and Rachel led the next. Folks seemed to settle in and enjoy the music, even if they didn't sing along. With an ever-watchful eye, Euphanel prayed the celebration would ease the racial conflicts they'd known throughout the year. She was especially prayerful that the folks of Perkinsville would begin to see that skin color was not a barrier to friendships.

One of the tenors led them in a moving rendition of "How Long, Dear Savior." It only served to cause Euphanel to remember Sissy's husband. This was one of his favorite songs.

How long, indeed, she thought. *Dear Lord, how long must we suffer each other to such miseries and oppressions?* The war was years behind them, but the consequences seemed certain to carry on for generations.

Texas was different, she had to admit. Texas was mainly interested in what was best for Texas. It was a country unto itself, and Euphanel often wondered if it would go back to being a Republic instead of a state after the War of Northern Aggression. There had been talk in the early years following the war, when Texas was waiting to be officially readmitted to the Union. Many folks didn't want to be a part of the Union—not just because of slave issues, but because of Texas issues. They were quite happy to govern themselves and quite proud to stand on their own.

They sang another seven songs without a break before Zed Perkins stepped to the center and held his hands up to draw everyone's attention.

"I'm not gonna volunteer to lead you in a song," he said with a chuckle. "Instead, I've come to make an important announcement that has to do with a couple of special folks—folks most of you know quite well." He turned to Arjan and then to Euphanel. "You two might as well step up here, too."

Euphanel hadn't realized Zed was going to make their engagement a public announcement, but she didn't really mind. If it helped with the community spirit of things, she was more than happy to do her part.

She made her way to the center and stood beside Arjan as Zed continued. "Most of you know that we lost Rutger Vandermark many years ago to a logging accident. He and Euphanel had been married a good number of years and had three children together. Rutger and his brother, Arjan, started the Vandermark

Logging Company, and some of you work for them."

He put his hand on Arjan's shoulder. "I just learned that Arjan and Euphanel plan to marry, and I felt this should be a time of celebration for our town. I know the ladies planned this to be nothing more than a summer gathering, but I hope you'll join me in extending your best wishes to the happy couple. They're plannin' to tie the knot tomorrow after church."

"Why not tonight!" someone called out from the crowd.

Zed looked to Arjan. "Indeed. Why not tonight? Why don't we make this a weddin' celebration?"

Euphanel did her best not to appear nonplussed, but she'd never been so stunned. The idea of turning the casual get-together into a wedding party had never once entered her mind. Why, she'd even made it clear to Deborah that she and Arjan planned a simple, quiet ceremony. She wasn't even going to make a special dress for the occasion. In fact, she'd probably wear exactly what she had on tonight. Her simple mauve gown with the cream lace edging was more than stylish enough for a second wedding.

Arjan looked at her with a devilish grin. "I'm ready for it—how about you?"

She felt a flutter in her stomach. She was really going to do this—remarry and have a husband—after all these years alone?

Is this all madness? Am I doing the right thing?

"Well, what do you say, Miz Vandermark? It's not like you have to change your name or anything," Zed teased.

Euphanel gazed about to find her children. Rob and G.W. were sitting with the basses. They nodded with big smiles, letting her know they approved. Deborah was off to one side with Lizzie and the babies. She, too, offered an encouraging smile.

"It seems everyone approves," she said. She hoped no one noticed the tremor in her voice. She licked her dry lips. "I suppose we might as well have ourselves a wedding."

Cheers went up from the crowd. Suddenly Euphanel felt like a young girl again. A moment of shy hesitation washed over her.

"Where's the pastor? Let's commence this joining here and now," Zed declared.

Arjan took Euphanel by the arm and whispered, "You're as white as a sheet. You sure you wanna do this?"

"I do," she said, nodding.

He grinned. "That part comes later."

She smiled. "I don't mind . . . truly. It's just a surprise. I had thought we'd have a very private ceremony. Now here we are, with the biggest wedding possible."

"But what better way to join our community together," he replied. "You can have Sissy stand up with you, and I'll have Zed. It'll be the first wedding in these parts to have both blacks and whites."

What he said was true. Euphanel had no better example to share with her friends and neighbors than to bring Sissy alongside as her witness. And if there was any question as to Sissy's legal ability to bear witness to the arrangement, well, nearly another hundred people could sign their names in her place.

Euphanel left Arjan's side to where her friend sat. "Sissy, will you stand up with me?" she asked.

The woman beamed a smile and got to her feet. "I'd be mighty proud."

They made their way back to the center of the gathering where Pastor Shattuck waited with Zed and Arjan. The two women took their place on the preacher's right, while Arjan and Zed stood to the left.

"Let us as one community—as one heart in the Lord—offer up our prayer of blessing for this couple." He bowed his head and Euphanel did likewise. She found herself praying privately as Pastor Shattuck prayed aloud.

Father, I know you've brought me to this place where I can love and be loved by a good man. I never thought it would happen again—I figured myself lucky to have found Rutger, but now you've given me Arjan, as well. I pray you will guide me—show me the way to be a good and godly wife.

"And give them your peace and blessing, Lord, we pray. Amen." The preacher looked at Euphanel and grinned. "Usually I add in a prayer for a healthy number of children to bless the union, but I wasn't sure you and Arjan would want me to do that."

The congregation roared with laughter, while Euphanel felt her face flush hot. Looking up, Arjan threw her a wink. Goodness, but was everyone determined to fluster her?

The ceremony itself was rather short and without pomp. Pastor Shattuck spoke the words Euphanel had heard at a hundred weddings before. Within a matter of minutes, he was offering a prayer of benediction.

Euphanel was so overwhelmed she didn't even think to close her eyes. Most folks looked happy for them. There would be many congratulations and even some teasing. Oh, but she hoped no one was of a mind to shivaree them. Nothing would be worse than to have the men hauling Arjan off or sneaking back to the house to put pinecones in their bed.

The thought of sharing her bed that night with Arjan was almost Euphanel's undoing. They had planned to stay in his cabin for a week or two, then move back to the main house. She'd been nervous about being alone with her brother-in-law husband before, but now it felt overwhelming. What if Arjan didn't love her as much as he thought he did? What if marriage proved to be a disappointment? She hated to think of their relationship turning sour. She'd depended on Arjan for comfort and help after Rutger's death. She certainly didn't want to lose that now.

" . . . and we commit this to your hands, Lord. Amen. You may kiss your bride," Pastor Shattuck announced.

For a moment, Euphanel couldn't even think of what she was supposed to do. Her knees began to wobble. Arjan took hold of her and steadied her.

"You all right?" he asked, looking deep into her eyes.

She swallowed hard. Her heart picked up speed. "Well . . . I thought I was." She gave an unexpected giggle. "Goodness, I feel just like a girl again."

He grinned and lowered his mouth to hers. The kiss wasn't long, but it definitely left

Euphanel breathless. She vaguely heard the cheers and clapping of her friends and family, but otherwise, there was only Arjan.

Deborah felt both a sense of loss and joy at the marriage of her mother and Uncle Arjan. She had never thought to see her mother married again, much less before she herself had a chance to marry once. She knew it was a good thing—knew her mother would be well cared for and loved, but there remained that nagging reminder that love had once again passed her by.

"You must be pretty happy for your ma," Jake said, coming up from behind her.

She whirled around, nearly tripping on her dress. In a flash, Jake reached out to take hold of her arm.

"I am," she managed to say as she regained her footing. Jake dropped his hold. "Thank you for keeping me from falling on my face."

"My pleasure." His expression turned serious. "There's quite a bit of talk going around about Dr. Clayton . . . and some about you."

"I've no doubt about that," Deborah replied. "Folks are such gossips."

As if proof were needed, Mrs. Greeley and Mrs. Pulaski came up to speak to Deborah. "My dear," Mrs. Greeley began, "I'm so relieved that Dr. Clayton is gone. Your reputation was suffering greatly, and I feared for you."

"I did as well," Mrs. Pulaski added. "I heard it said that Dr. Clayton was the sort to take liberties with you."

Deborah shook her head. "Then you heard wrong, I'm afraid. Dr. Clayton was quite the gentleman—very conscious of proper etiquette."

"Well, I heard it said that you two were seen embracing in his examination room," Mrs. Greeley accused.

No doubt the Perkins sisters had been busy. Deborah nodded. "Indeed. Dr. Clayton had received bad news about a loved one. The embrace, however, was my misjudgment, not his. I saw his sorrow and couldn't help but desire to comfort him. Now if you'll excuse me, Mr. Wythe was just about to escort me to the refreshment table."

That was all the encouragement Jake needed. He smiled at the ladies and nodded as he and Deborah moved away.

"Thank you," she said, keeping her voice soft. "I'm sorry to have involved you. No doubt, you'll be the next to suffer their scrutiny and gossip."

"I can't say that I'd mind, so long as it includes you."

She looked at him and shook her head. "Believe me, you do not want to be the topic of the gossip this town is capable of delivering. They can cut deep when they want to, and the wounds are sometimes long to heal."

"Then I might need comforting," he said with a sly grin. "You could offer me the same sort of comfort you gave the doc."

Deborah stopped and fixed him with a hard stare. "That, Mr. Wythe, is totally inappropriate."

He laughed. "Don't worry. I'll mind myself. I wouldn't want the doc to come back and feel the need to teach me a lesson."

"I wouldn't worry overmuch about that. There's no telling if he is coming back," Deborah said, moving away from Jake. She hadn't meant to speak aloud—the words had just come and now she regretted them.

"What are you saying?" he asked, catching up to her with ease.

"Nothing that matters." She'd reached the refreshment table and glanced at the selections of cookies and cakes, pies and breads. She wasn't at all hungry, but figured occupying herself with food might hide her inner turmoil.

"You and the doc end your courtship?" he asked.

Deborah selected a cookie and started to walk away. Jake followed, much to her displeasure. She walked to the far edge of the gathering and waited for him to question her again, even while she prayed that he might simply drop the matter.

"You gonna answer my question?"

"It's hardly any of your business," she said a bit harsher than she'd intended.

"It is if I have my say about it. I'd like to court you myself."

Deborah had to think fast. "I have no intention of courting anyone else. I am . . . well, actually, I'm considering heading back East—to Philadelphia."

"Why?"

She drew a deep breath. "I feel that I should continue my training in medicine. The college I attended there will allow for that. It is highly progressive and believes women should be allowed to be doctors in their own right."

"And you'd just up and leave?" he asked. "You wouldn't give me any consideration at all?"

"I must do what I feel called to do," Deborah told him. If only she knew exactly what that was.

ꕤ

"I was hopin' to talk to you for a minute," Rob told Mara. He'd never seen her more beautiful. She'd pinned her dark hair high atop her head, and he longed to pull out the pins and watch it cascade down her back. Though completely improper, he couldn't deny the thought was there.

She smiled and moved closer. "I would be happy to hear what you have to say."

"I don't reckon I know quite how you'll feel about this, but I figure it's best iffen I just say the words and then we can talk about 'em."

"Seems reasonable to me," she replied.

He noticed the necklace she wore. It was a small gold cross—a reminder of her faith and the sacrifice that was made by Jesus. It reminded Rob, too, of what he'd come to say.

"I'm gonna be leavin' in two days. I feel that God wants me to go to Houston—to the seminary there. I reckon it may seem strange, but I believe God wants me to be a preacher."

She smiled. "It doesn't seem strange at all, Mr. Vandermark."

He looked at her with great curiosity. "It don't?"

Mara shook her head. "In my prayers for you, I felt certain this was the decision you would make. Later, I cornered my father and spoke with him. He told me that he'd shared with you about the seminary his friend runs in Houston. It seems a very good place for you."

"And you aren't upset with me? I mean, what with . . . well, what you said . . . and . . . " Rob felt helpless to put it all in words. He wanted to challenge her comment—to ask her how she was so certain he was the one she would marry when now he was planning to up and leave.

"How could I fault a man for following after God's heart?" She glanced up, and Rob did likewise. Overhead the night skies were nearly as bright as day, lit by the full moon. "God has a plan and purpose for each of us. I would want only that you follow His direction for you."

"But what about us?"

She turned her gaze to his face. "It all works quite perfectly. You see, I always knew I would marry a preacher. The fact that you've only now come to this decision may seem surprising to you, but not to me."

"How is it that you knew these things?" he asked. "I reckon I'm hearin' God more than ever. I see things in my mind that reflect things He's showin' me through His Word. But you've acted like you've known about us since before you even got here."

She laughed lightly. "I suppose I have—at least, in part. I knew since I was young that God wanted me to be a preacher's wife. I have done everything in my power to work toward that day. I've studied the Word of God and obtained my education in a school run by the church. Everything about my life has revolved around learning to be a helpful mate to a pastor. When I felt the time was right to come and help my father for the purpose of furthering my training, God laid it on my heart that I would meet my husband here—that he might not seem at first like the man God was bringing into my life, but that I should trust and wait upon the Lord."

Rob shook his head. "That's mighty amazin'. I can't help but feel the hair on my neck give rise."

She nodded. "I felt the same way when I first met you. I knew that we would one day be together. I suppose that sounds very presumptuous, but it's the truth. I'm not prideful in this—merely firm in my faith. If God wants this marriage to take place, it will."

He reached out and put his hand on her cheek. "I will come back to you a better man. I promise that. Will you promise to wait for me?"

She surprised him by touching her hand to his cheek. "I will wait, just as I've been waiting. I am yours, Robrecht Vandermark. I will always belong to you."

Chapter 24

Rob had been gone only three days when word came that a terrible storm had hit the Gulf Coast. There was no way of telling exactly how powerful the hurricane was, but the information given the town of Perkinsville suggested it might well bring rain and wind their way.

"Arjan said the depot master said the telegram was brief but to the point. The storm looks to be heading this direction and it is still quite powerful. They're to get the trains north and out of harm's way," Mother declared.

"Did they say where the storm hit land?" Deborah asked. She couldn't help but think of Christopher and his brother in Indianola.

"No. Just that it hit and was moving fast. I'll feel better if we take precautions," Mother told Deborah. "I know Arjan thought me silly for wanting those shutters. I can still hear him saying that there wasn't another house in all of Perkinsville with such luxuries."

"He ought to be glad for them now," Deborah replied. "I remember once before when we had to replace nearly every window on the south side after a hail and windstorm."

"Oh, I know he's glad for them now."

Deborah helped her mother begin the task of closing the shutters. Uncle Arjan caught the train to the logging camp, and G.W. was busy securing the livestock and outbuildings. Lizzie and Sissy went to work preparing lunch.

The waiting was always the hardest part. The storm would never give them as much grief here as it did on the coast, but they could still experience tornadoes and wind damage, harming areas that weren't in the path of the original storm.

"Let's put Lula and her pups on the back porch," Mother told G.W. "That should keep them safe enough." G.W. nodded and headed back outside.

"I'll get the last of the second-floor shutters," Deborah told her mother. She hurried upstairs and went to the far end bedrooms first. The windows, being new, opened easily and Deborah was able to lean out and draw the shutters together without any trouble. As she progressed to the windows in the older part of the house, however, Deborah encountered more difficulty. She soaped a couple of the window's tracks to ease the tension; growing humidity had swelled the wood a bit and made for a tighter fit. At last she finished up in her own bedroom, grateful to have the task completed. The coming storm filled her with a sense of dread.

Christopher was in Indianola on the Matagorda Bay. While Deborah had no way of knowing exactly what the storm would do, she knew Christopher was at risk, simply because he was now on the coast. What if there had been no warning for him?

"Are you all right?" Lizzie asked from the doorway.

Deborah turned and met her friend's worried expression. "I'm afraid for Christopher. He's in Indianola, or I presume he's still there. Perhaps the trial has already taken place and he's long gone. I have no hope of knowing."

"I'm sorry. I know that must grieve you."

"It's the waiting and the not knowing," Deborah replied. She moved across the room and opened a blanket chest. "I know I must give it over to the Lord, but it's so hard."

"Out of your control, eh?"

Lizzie's comment didn't offend her; Deborah knew her friend was right. Taking a stack of blankets from the chest, Deborah straightened. "I suppose I always feel better when I have some hand in the solution." She shook her head. "All of my life I've been like that."

"Taking charge isn't always a bad thing, Deborah, but sometimes it's best to let others handle their messes. God will guide Christopher."

"I know He will." She let out a heavy sigh and shifted the bedding. "I just wish I could know what has happened. It's a terrible thing to be here safe and sound, knowing that Christopher and his brother might well be injured or even dead."

"Don't borrow trouble," Lizzie reminded her. "Give it over to God. He has a plan in all of this, and like you used to tell me, His plan is always better than those we have for ourselves."

Deborah tried to let the words calm her spirit. "I shall continue to pray and hope for the best."

"Do you need help with the blankets?"

"No," Deborah replied. "Mother wants them in the extra bedrooms. The loggers will come and stay here until the storm passes. It wouldn't do for them to live in the tents during such a time."

"No, I can't imagine staying there in good weather, much less bad." Lizzie came to Deborah and smiled. "God is in control of everything. Here . . . in Indianola . . . in the middle of the storm, itself. He will see you through this. Dr. Clayton, too."

Deborah tried to take solace in Lizzie's words. "I know you're right. I know there is nothing I can do, but oh, how I wish it could be otherwise."

By noon the skies darkened and the air hung heavy, but so far there were no other signs of the storm. Deborah hugged herself and rubbed her arms as if chilled. She felt so anxious, and yet nothing had changed. The storm was not here—perhaps would never come—but she could sense the possibility of it, and that proved enough to make her uncomfortable.

Her life felt the same way right now. She could see the threat of turmoil on the horizon—feel the tension that came with the uncertainty—yet she was perfectly safe. Why couldn't she just rest in that?

"Would you help me make corn bread?" Mother asked.

Deborah put away the last of the dinner dishes before answering. "Of course. Are we making extra, in case the weather turns destructive?"

"Yes. I thought it would be a good idea. Arjan is concerned that we may lose a number of trees if the winds pick up. The turpentine harvest always weakens them, you know. If that happens, they'll have to strike camp where they're working now and head farther away to harvest any fallen pines. He wants to have plenty of provisions to take with them if that happens."

Sissy had already been hard at work on baking corn bread, but she happily relinquished the task to Euphanel and Deborah in order to help Lizzie with the children. By late afternoon, enough corn bread sat cooling that the men could easily be gone a week without needing additional provisions. "We have plenty of hams they can take with them, too," Mother said, bringing in a wooden crate. "Let's put the bread into the cloth sacks we saved and load it all in this crate to keep it from crumbling too bad. Don't bother to cut it into squares; the fellas can take care of that themselves."

The sweltering temperatures of the summer kitchen left Deborah damp with sweat. She assembled the sacks of corn bread while her mother checked the stew she'd prepared for supper. The first drops of rain began pelting the window as Deborah loaded the last of the bread.

"I guess it's starting," Mother said, looking out the door.

Joining her mother, Deborah watched the

storm move in with thick and swirling clouds. The wind picked up, driving the rain down a little harder. Still, there was no real relief from the heat. "I guess we'd best get things into the house."

Lizzie came out the side door about that time. "Do you need help?"

Mother motioned her over to them. "You and Deborah take the bread in, and I'll get the stew for our supper. G.W. has already seen to bringing in some of the hams from the smokehouse."

Lizzie and Deborah each took an end of the crate and lifted. "Who knew corn bread could be so heavy," Lizzie said with a grunt.

By the time they had secured everything in the main house, the rain was beating down in earnest. Mother paced the floor until Arjan showed up with the loggers.

"I feel better knowing we'll all be under one roof," she said as the men started to file in, dripping wet.

Deborah handed out towels and couldn't help but smile at her mother's comment. *That must have been how Noah felt as he gathered his family in the ark.* The idea gave her a moment of amusement as she imagined their house turning into a large ship and sailing away.

"I ain't seen you smile since Dr. Clayton went away," G.W. said, coming alongside her.

"There hasn't been a whole lot to smile about. Still isn't, what with the uncertainty of this storm."

"Can't do anythin' more about the storm. As for the doc, I can't imagine he'll stay away long—not when I remember how he looked at you. He's just as gone over you as you are with him."

Deborah shrugged. "I thought so, too. Now I'm not so sure." She looked at her brother. "I can understand better than anyone the need to help your family. He knows that. But there were still so many secrets between us. I always felt like he was hiding parts of himself from me."

"Why do you reckon he would do that?" G.W. asked.

"I think . . . perhaps Christopher has fears."

G.W. looked at her oddly. "Fears of what?"

"Girls, would you set the table for supper?" Mother asked as she passed by. "Put out ten extra places."

"Of course, Mother." Giving her brother a shrug, Deborah followed Lizzie into the dining room and took out the plates and silver from the sideboard.

"What were you and G.W. talking about?" Lizzie questioned.

"He asked me about Christopher. The

talk led to why I felt Christopher remained so guarded with me."

"And what conclusion did you arrive at?" Lizzie asked, arranging silver at each place setting.

"I think he was afraid of my reaction to the truth. Maybe he's afraid that if I know the details about him or his family, I'll want nothing more to do with him. After he told me about his brother's murder trial and the fact that two other brothers were in jail for robbery, he looked at me as if expecting me to flee any second."

Deborah paused for a moment to count the place settings. She needed two more and went to the sideboard for additional plates. "I haven't told anyone this, but when I read the letter asking him to come and help his brother, there was something that was most curious. His brother didn't have the same last name. Instead of Clayton, his given name was Kelleher."

"That is strange. Do you suppose his mother was married to someone else when she bore Christopher?"

"I thought of that possibility. He's never said anything, though. I suppose it's part of the mystery." Deborah stopped at the table and grew thoughtful. "That would make a lot of sense. If Christopher was the son of, say, someone disreputable—then he wouldn't want anyone to know about it. He might have never even known the man. Mr. Clayton could have married his mother later on and become a father to him."

"And it would be even worse if his mother and father divorced," Lizzie said in a hushed voice. "Think of the scandal."

Deborah nodded. "I'd never really thought of the possibility until now. It does make sense, however. He is the eldest."

Somehow, such thoughts served to comfort Deborah. Not because she wanted Christopher to have endured such a life, but if it were true, it would explain a great deal.

She pondered her discussion with Lizzie throughout supper and said very little. Deborah was so absorbed in her thoughts that even Jake gave up trying to talk to her. By the time supper had concluded, it had been raining for over an hour, the winds howling and the house nearly shaking at times.

"Guess this breaks the drought," Jake said, shaking his head. "A little too late to help my family, but hopefully it'll be a blessin' to someone."

"It's a blessing here, for sure," Mother said. "The moisture will keep down the fire hazards with the trees, and we can definitely use it for crops and the animals."

"It'll make working tough," G.W. said. "The roads and paths are difficult enough, but when they turn to mud, it's nigh on impossible to travel 'em."

Arjan nodded. "Givin' a listen to that wind, I'm figurin' we'll have enough downed trees to keep us busy for a spell. We'll need to take all the mules with us when we head out. No doubt we'll have to skid logs back aways to reach the railroad siding."

"We can probably do some loads on the wagons—iffen the roads ain't too bad," Warren offered. " 'Course, G.W. may be right. They might be nothin' but mud by the time we get there."

"The storm should pass in the night, and tomorrow we'll be ready to face whatever comes," Arjan said. "Until then, no sense borrowin' trouble."

ꕥ

After the men headed out in the morning, Euphanel and Lizzie stood on the front porch with Deborah and surveyed the yard. There were a few downed branches, some shingles that had been torn off the barn roof, and a few outdoor articles that had been tossed around by the wind.

"It could have been much worse," Euphanel said, grateful that none of her windows had suffered damage. The cost of glass was nearly unreasonable, and she had no desire to go replacing windows after just a few months of use.

"Was Uncle Arjan going to send word back to let us know how bad the damage in the camp might be?" Deborah asked.

"He said he would try."

"I want to head into town and see how they are faring there. I'll bet Jael will be glad they all headed back to Philadelphia last Monday when she hears of the storm. She said they were planning to return in another month or so and stay in Houston permanently, but maybe after this, they'll change their minds. After all, Houston could have been hit quite hard," Deborah said, unfastening her apron.

"I pray not." Euphanel tried to conceal her concern.

"G.W. mentioned that Mr. Perkins is to have a house for Stuart and Mr. Longstreet in town so that when they come on business, they will have a place to stay," Lizzie added.

"They seem intent on becoming active partners in the sawmill." Euphanel didn't want to worry about the implications of such an arrangement. Arjan had told her that Zed was worried about some of the changes the two Easterners wanted to make. Apparently they each had equal votes on how things would be done, and with Mr. Longstreet and Mr. Albright agreeing on most things, Euphanel could only guess what might happen.

"Do you want to come to town with me, Mother?"

She looked at Deborah a moment, then nodded. "I believe I will. It would be good to check on folks and see how they fared. Good to let them know how we are, as well." She held her hand out. "I'll take your apron if you want to go hitch up the carriage. The boys took our wagon."

Deborah gave her the apron and headed down the steps. "Lizzie," she called over her shoulder, "if you need anything from town, just make us a list."

Euphanel smiled at her daughter-in-law. "Yes, we can pick up whatever you need—if the store is still standing."

On their drive, Euphanel could see that Deborah was fretful.

"I wish you wouldn't worry so," she told her daughter. "Worry won't change a thing."

"I know," Deborah said focusing on the road. "It's hard though. I have no way of knowing if Christopher is safe."

"But God knows, and He's with Christopher, just as He is with us."

"Do you suppose I could send a telegram to Indianola?" Deborah asked suddenly. "I mean, I could just send it to the sheriff there and ask that it be forwarded to Christopher. Since his brother is in jail, surely the law officials would know where Christopher was staying. It can't be that big of a town."

Euphanel could hear desperation in her daughter's voice. She put her hand on Deborah's arm. "I think that would be a good idea."

"Thank you for understanding. I can hardly stand not knowing."

"I do understand," Euphanel assured. "I've been wondering about Rob and whether Houston sustained damage."

Deborah pulled back on the reins. "I'm so sorry, Mother. I've been quite selfish in my concern. It never came to mind that Rob might be in danger, even when I mentioned Jael."

"We shall pray for both of them, Deborah. God has them in His hands, and I refuse to give in to the seeds of doubt the devil sows. In time, we shall know the truth, and when our answers come, we must know where our faith is fixed. Otherwise, we'll be tossed about, just like the tree branches in the wind."

Chapter 25

The air near town smelled of smoke, and while it was generally stale with dust and the scent of woodsmoke, this was different. A stiff breeze from the southwest moved most of the haze off to the northeast, but it was still evident that something was terribly wrong.

A great many people stood in the roadway near the boardinghouse, so Deborah turned the carriage down one of the side streets. She figured she could bring the horses around past the church and park alongside the doctor's office, avoiding the crowd. Doing even this, however, took some creative thought. Tree limbs littered the road, and she couldn't imagine why folks hadn't cleared them away. Studying the area around her, it seemed that no one had even bothered to begin their cleanup.

"You don't suppose the train jumped the tracks, do you?" Euphanel asked.

Deborah looked at her mother and shrugged. "Anything's possible. It's certainly notorious for that kind of thing, and the bulk of the people seemed to be standing near the depot office at the commissary. Still, I thought all of the trains were driven north yesterday."

Her mother nodded as Deborah maneuvered the horses onto Main Street. She gasped at the sight of flames that rose up from where the sawmill was positioned. "Oh no!" She pointed in the direction of the fire. "The mill!"

Her mother stared in disbelief. "It can't be."

Deborah hurried to park the carriage in front of the doctor's house. She climbed down from the wagon, then reached up to help Mother do the same. Many of the town's women and children were gathered by the commissary. The gathering spilled out, blocking First Street.

The two women hurried to join the others and learn what had happened. Deborah saw several women gathered around Rachel Perkins and moved that direction, with Mother on her heels.

"Rachel," her mother called.

Mrs. Perkins looked up. Her face was smudged from the ash in the air and streaked with tears. "Oh, Euphanel," she sobbed. "It's so awful."

"What happened?"

The women who had been standing with Mrs. Perkins moved away a bit to make room for Deborah and her mother. Rachel fell into Euphanel's arms. Deborah looked to Mrs. Greeley, who stood just to their left.

"We figure it must have been lightning," Mrs. Greeley whispered. "Fire started sometime during the storm. They've been trying to fight it all night—even in the fiercest winds."

"That must have been difficult," Deborah murmured.

Her mother pulled away from Rachel and lifted her friend's face. "Tell me, has anyone been hurt?"

"I don't know. The men have been gone for most of the night. Zed and my boys are all over there fighting the fire with the others. They are desperate to keep it from spreading. The women and children did what they could to water down the buildings nearby, as well as the stacks of lumber."

Deborah moved to get a little closer to the front of the crowd. To her surprise, Mother and Mrs. Perkins followed. She fixed her gaze on the front of the mill but could see very little through the smoke billowing out the open doors. Flames licked the already charred walls on the north side, however. Given the amount of smoke that clouded the sky, it was obvious that the fire had burned out a good portion of the roof.

Others in the crowd were crying. The children seemed uncommonly quiet and still. Perhaps, Deborah thought, they were thinking of what might be happening to their fathers and brothers. She felt sickened by the thought that some of the men might lose their lives fighting the flames. She wondered if she should volunteer to open the doctor's office, but realized Margaret Foster had probably already done so.

"I do wish Zed would come here and tell me what's happening," Mrs. Perkins said, taking the handkerchief that Mother offered her.

"No doubt he's much too busy, Rachel. Don't fret. I'm sure that with all the men helping, the fire will soon be out. Is there anything we can do to aid them?"

"No. Like I said, we were putting water on everything we could, but the heat got so intense, the men told us to wait over here. Zed got the bucket brigade going just after the pump was in position. The men are drawing water from the millpond. The pump can't put out a great deal, but it's better than nothing."

Mother nodded and looked at Deborah.

"Why don't you go ahead and see about sending your telegram. The wires run along the other side of the tracks and shouldn't be burned."

Deborah hadn't even considered that possibility. She left her mother and the others and hurried to the depot office, hoping someone might be there to help her. Old Mr. Parsons sat at his post, ever faithful. She watched him as he wrote down a message to the clicking of the telegraph. He didn't so much as glance her way until the final words were given. Only then did he put down his pencil. Shaking his head, he looked up.

"Mornin', Miss Vandermark. Surely is a sad day."

She nodded. "It is indeed, Mr. Parsons. Mother and I just arrived and could scarcely believe that the mill was a-fire."

The smoke wasn't too bad, but the August heat warmed the room, making it quite stuffy. Deborah could see that the windows had been shut to keep out the ash and fumes. It was a wonder the old man could endure it.

"Ain't just the mill, neither," he replied. "Bad news comin' in from the storm. Seems it were a mighty strong hurricane. I've had word about damage in Houston."

She immediately thought of her brother. "How bad was it?"

"Well, it caused some destruction, but ain't near as bad as down the coast to the south. There's reports of towns bein' all torn up."

Deborah swallowed hard. "Can we send telegrams south?"

"Only for a ways. Some of the lines are still workin' and some ain't. Couldn't get word through to Victoria. Mrs. Greeley wanted me to send a wire to her ma to see if she was all right, but the lines are down. Seems the storm came right up the coast from that area. Galveston got through for a time. My daughter's family is down that way. I heard from the operator that the town took damage, but he didn't say how bad. Told me word came in that a lot of the towns on the Gulf are just gone—underwater. Wires are down and even the mail has stopped."

Deborah felt her stomach churn. Indianola was only about thirty miles from Victoria. If they had seen destruction that far inland, Indianola was bound to have met with a worse fate. It sat right on the water and rivaled Galveston for the busiest port in Texas.

"Have you heard . . . has there been word . . . " She stammered and looked to the older man for some kind of hope. "I wondered if there was word on Indianola?"

He shook his head. "Ain't heard a thing. I reckon once things settle down, the wires will get back in place and then we'll hear it all. 'Course, the newspaper folks down Houston and Galveston way will probably be gettin' any information they can, but it will most likely be weeks before we know for sure what's happened."

She couldn't help but detect the hopelessness in his words. Deborah fought back tears. "Thank you, Mr. Parsons." She started to leave, but remembered her brother. "I need to send a wire to my brother Rob."

"He's in Houston, ain't he? Gone off to be a preacher." The old man picked up his pencil. "We'll give her a go and see if it goes through. Never can tell."

Deborah arranged for Mr. Parsons to send a wire to Rob inquiring if he was all right and if he needed anything. The old man also promised to try and get a message through to Christopher, but he didn't hold out much hope. Deborah felt pretty deprived of it herself. Surely if Christopher were alive and well, he would have let her know. Wouldn't he? Of course, as Mr. Parsons told her, lines were down and the mail wasn't even getting through. How could he possibly hope to send word?

She rejoined her mother and was surprised to find a large gathering of black women crossing the tracks to join them.

Mother looked up to see them and smiled. Miriam, the wife of a one-time Vandermark Logging employee, came forward and Mother reached out to greet her. She took hold of her hand and squeezed it briefly. "It's good to see you."

"We comed to pray. Our men are over there fightin', too."

Deborah saw her mother nod and turn to Mrs. Perkins. "It seems," Mother said, "that the storm has done what we couldn't. Our men are all working together—side by side—no one caring what the color of the other man's skin might be."

Mrs. Perkins looked at Miriam and gave a weak smile. "You are very welcome to pray with us."

ꕥ

Hours later, the fire was finally out and the destruction evident. The mill was nearly consumed. Patches here and there were unharmed—stacks of lumber watered down enough that the sparks didn't catch it on fire. But little was untouched.

The men staggered back, blackened from head to toe with soot and ash. Their eyes were red-rimmed and watery from the acrid smoke, and most were gasping and coughing. Mr. Perkins and his sons came to join them. The

Perkins boys looked for their wives in the gathering and quickly found them, while the elder Mr. Perkins pushed blackened red hair back from his face and fixed his gaze on Mrs. Perkins. They said nothing, but Deborah could see the unspoken relief between them.

"Is there anything we can do, Zed?" Mother asked.

He shook his head. "We kept it from burnin' down the town, at least. Saved some of the equipment, but not much. Some was just too big to get moved in time."

"What will we do?" Mrs. Perkins asked.

"I don't guess I have an answer for that just now," Mr. Perkins replied. "If you don't mind, I just wanna bath."

She put her arm around his waist and nodded. "Come on. I'll see that you have what you need."

In similar fashion, other men appeared and rejoined their families. Very little was said as the couples moved off and headed home. Deborah watched as the crowd thinned until only she and Mother remained.

"This is surely a great tragedy," Mother said.

"It's only the start," Deborah replied. "Mr. Parsons said there are rumors of destruction all along the coast—some towns are underwater. He tried to send a wire to Victoria, but the lines are down. Galveston and Houston have both suffered damage."

"Houston?" her mother asked, her tone taking on an anxious edge.

Deborah squeezed her hands. "I sent a wire to Rob asking if he was all right and whether he needed anything. The wire went through, so hopefully we'll get a reply."

Mother's eyes filled with tears as she looked about. "Oh, this is such a nightmare. How could anything good come from it?"

Staring past her mother to the still smoldering remains of the mill, she shook her head. "I don't know. I honestly don't know."

ꙮ

That night the Vandermarks gathered around the dining room table and prayed. Word had come during the day that the turpentine harvesting area had been greatly damaged. Numerous trees had fallen in the wind, and Arjan figured they would be out restoring the area for some time. He would need for the women to keep an ample supply of food readied for them.

G.W. had seen to cleaning up the debris in the immediate yard, while Sissy and Lizzie had tried to right the damage to the garden. Everything had taken such a beating, it was unclear as to whether any of the vegetables would revive.

"We thank you Lord that we are alive and safe—that no loss of life was had in the fire," Mother prayed. "Guide us now and teach us what to do."

When she said nothing more, G.W. began to speak. "Father, we are troubled by what's happened. Ain't hardly words to explain."

He went on to ask God's mercy, but Deborah couldn't focus on his prayer. Instead she silently pleaded with God to bring her word from Christopher, to bring him home safely. She knew it was a selfish prayer, given all of the people who had been devastated by the storm. Word had come that the storm hadn't played out until it'd nearly reached the northern counties. It would, no doubt, go down in history as the worst Texas had seen.

Even that solemn thought didn't sway Deborah from her desperate longing to know of Christopher's safety. The entire state could lie in shambles, and she would still only have thought of the man she loved. And she did love him—loved him more than life itself. Nothing had made it more evident to her than the last twenty-four hours.

God, my heart is overwhelmed, she prayed. *I want so much to know that Christopher is alive and well. Rob, too, Father*, she added, remembering her brother. *Please, Lord, don't leave us without word. I can't bear the thought that I might never know. I can't bear that Christopher might be hurt and need me.*

She wiped away tears that spilled from her closed eyes. It was all she could do to keep from crying aloud. Lizzie seemed to understand her misery and reached over to squeeze her hand. Her touch was like a lifeline to Deborah—the only thread of support she could feel at the moment. Mother was worried about the men, about Rob. The others had, no doubt, forgotten all about Christopher.

Lizzie leaned close and whispered, "I've prayed for him, too, Deborah. God will surely hear our prayers."

She opened her eyes and met Lizzie's gaze. Nodding, Deborah tried to find strength in her sister-in-law's statement. Only God could intervene on Christopher's behalf.

Chapter 26

Weeks slipped by without much news. September brought relief to the heat, but not to Deborah's heart. She had tried unsuccessfully to get a wire to Christopher, and the rumors were more and more troublesome in regard to the damage done by the hurricane. Houston papers suggested that much of the coast between Galveston and Corpus Christi had been devastated by high winds and tidal waves. She couldn't bear the thought that Christopher might never have had a chance to escape. He wouldn't have left his brother, and since Calvin was jailed, she doubted he could have gotten away from the storm, either. Would they have moved prisoners inland? Had there been any warning? The questions tormented her.

She found no comfort in her routine chores. While helping her mother gather plums, Deborah prayed and prayed, but peace seemed far out of reach. How could there be no word? Surely Christopher would have known her worry, and even if he didn't plan to return to her, he would have let her know of his safety. Wouldn't he?

"I know you're fretting over the doctor," Mother said, pouring a basket of plums into a larger crate. "Your worry won't bring him back."

"It could be nothing will bring him back." She didn't want to believe that, but as the weeks passed, Deborah found hope a fleeting comfort. "But I can't help believing he'd at least let us know if he was all right. He knows folks here care about him."

"That's true enough. Still, he may not yet be able to get word out. If the devastation is as bad as some say, he may have no recourse."

"He also might be injured," Deborah said, unable to consider the extent to which this might be true.

"Who could that be?" Mother questioned, putting her hand up to shield her eyes.

Deborah heard the unmistakable sound of a horse approaching and ran to the edge of the road. She prayed it was Christopher but was further disappointed when the rider proved to be Zed Perkins.

"What brings you out our way?" Mother joined Deborah by the road.

Zed dismounted and walked with his horse to where the women stood. "I needed to talk with you and Arjan."

"He's still out working the fallen trees. Why don't you come on up to the house and have a cup a coffee? G.W.'s in the office and he can join us. Oh, we had word from Rob. He's safe and the damage was minimal in his area."

He nodded and they started up the road, toward the south side of the house. "That's mighty good news. I know Miz Greeley's news wasn't near as good. Seems Victoria bore a heavy blow from the storm." He turned and tipped his hat. "Miss Deborah—it's good to see you. You haven't been in town of late."

"Hasn't been much reason," she replied. "Margaret Foster made it clear she didn't want my help with the sick."

"Have you heard anything from the doc?" he asked.

She shook her head. "I had hoped maybe you had."

"No, there's been no word. 'Course, if Victoria was damaged, then Indianola must have been, too. Could be the doc is busy helping the hurt folks there."

Deborah could only hope that he was doing that, instead of being tended himself. She said nothing more, choosing instead to focus on the ground as they walked. There was nothing there of interest, but she didn't want her mother or Mr. Perkins to see her face and know how hard this was on her.

"I heard that a good number of people were packing up and leaving Perkinsville," Mother said. "Sissy was speaking to some friends of hers, and it seems this was the talk going around."

"Well, I reckon, what with the mill shut down, there are a lot of folks movin' on to other places. I'm offerin' what help I can, but there's very little I can do. All of my money was in the mill and the stores."

"What about the mill?" Mother asked. "Can it not be rebuilt? A good portion of lumber was saved, as I understand."

"It was and has now been sold. I've ordered some parts to start up small again, but I'm not sure where it's gonna take us. That's why I came out here today."

Mother waited for him to tether his horse before they headed together to the house. Deborah followed after. "I'll fetch G.W.," she told her mother and hurried to the office.

She found her brother deep in thought, ledger before him and a stack of papers beside him. "Mr. Perkins is here. He says he needs to speak to us about the business."

G.W. looked up. "I kind of figured he'd come callin' soon." G.W. closed the ledger and got up. The exercises Christopher had given him had done wonders to strengthen his leg. He still walked with a limp, but he was much faster now and had more endurance than even a few months back.

Deborah and G.W. joined Mother and Mr. Perkins in the front room while Sissy brought coffee and cookies. Deborah wanted neither and took a seat across from Mr. Perkins while he accepted a cup of black coffee.

"How's it going for your family, Mr. Perkins?" G.W. asked.

"It's been hard. I've got to say, there isn't a lot of happiness at my house these days. None of us is sure what to do. The boys all counted on the mill for their livelihood. They have families to feed and clothe so they'll need to do something—and soon."

"We'd be happy to help any way we can," Mother told him. "We've got plenty of smoked pork we could share."

"That's mighty good of you," Mr. Perkins replied. "I guess the worst of it is my girls. They want to leave right away and go stay with their grandparents back East. I can't say as I blame them, but that, too, will cost money."

"Perhaps they can be encouraged to bide their time here and be useful to your recovery."

"I'd like to see that happen, but I didn't do right by those gals. They're spoiled and used to havin' their own way. Not like your Deborah." He gave her a smile. "I'd be mighty proud if my girls were half as industrious as you."

Deborah was surprised by the praise and felt uneasy. "Tell us what's happening with the mill," she encouraged.

Mr. Perkins shrugged. "Nothing, unfortunately. Like I said, I've ordered a few parts in order to start back up on a small level. Mostly I need to cut lumber to rebuild. I have the logs in the millpond and figure to at least get a frame up in order to start over."

"Sounds wise," G.W. said. "What can we do to help? Do you want another load of logs right away?"

"That's why I've come out here, actually." He put the coffee aside. "I can't pay to bring in more logs just yet. I wanted to let you know that straightaway so you could sell your harvest to one of the other sawmills. I'm sure they'll take them in Lufkin."

G.W. nodded. "Probably will. I'll talk it over with Uncle Arjan."

"I hate doing this to you. I know you're counting on the income, just as I was counting on the mill to provide for me." Mr. Perkins sat back and shook his head. "My partners are set to arrive tomorrow. I suppose they will help me to assess the matter. I'm hoping they'll be willing to pour more capital into the business to see it rebuilt quickly. That would be to their benefit as much as mine."

Deborah frowned as she thought of Stuart Albright having any say in the welfare of Perkinsville.

"They certainly got word quickly," Mother commented.

"They don't actually know about the fire just yet. They'd already wired prior to the storm to say they were headin' back to Perkinsville."

"I reckon they'll be surprised to hear the news," G.W. said. "Especially since they were countin' on the mill to help them make their fortune."

"I'm deeply concerned. I'm trying to get as much accomplished as I can before they arrive, but the cleanup is still in progress. What few men I could afford to keep on are doin' their best to clear out the debris so we can get to rebuildin' right away."

"Do you know yet what started the fire?" G.W. asked. "Mother said it was rumored to be lightnin'."

Mr. Perkins looked up with a frown. "It wasn't lightning. I saw no sign of a strike. Fire started inside. Someone had to set it."

"Set it?" Mother asked in horror. "Surely not!"

"Some say the blacks set it as a means of avenging the deaths and beatings they've had in their number. Others say it was whites who done it—unhappy with me because I hired blacks instead of them. I can't say who exactly is to blame, but someone did it on purpose."

Mother shook her head in disbelief. "But no one benefits from such a tragedy. The entire town was dependent upon the mill for its existence."

"Well, someone figured to benefit somehow," Mr. Perkins replied. "Ain't never known a man to do much of anything without there bein' a benefit to it."

"We need to let Arjan know the situation as soon as possible." Mother looked to G.W. "I know it's nearly evening, but he should be here."

"I'll ride out to the camp where he's working," G.W. told them. "I'll bring some more food for them and let Arjan know what's happened." He got to his feet. "Do you want us to travel to town tomorrow?"

Mr. Perkins considered this for a moment. "I suppose it would be best. Albright and Longstreet should be here."

Deborah hoped that Jael would also travel

with them. She couldn't imagine her friend allowing them to leave her behind—especially once they became aware of the hurricane and storms. She would want to see Deborah and Lizzie and hear all the news. Besides, Mr. Perkins said they'd settled their affairs. That surely meant they were making the move to Houston as planned.

"Mother, I'll bring Uncle Arjan back as soon as possible. It's late though, so we might just stay in camp tonight."

"I think that would be wise," Mother replied. "I don't want you pushing yourself too hard. You've done a wonderful job of keeping the supplies going to the camp, but I know your leg still gives you problems from time to time. There are also the hogs to contend with."

He bent down and kissed her head. "I'll be fine. Don't look for us until mornin'. Now, if you'll excuse me, I reckon I'd better let Lizzie know what's happening."

Deborah waited until he'd gone to voice her opinion. "It seems to me that the sooner the mill is back up and operating, the better for everyone. You mentioned folks were moving out—heading elsewhere for work."

Mr. Perkins nodded. "Some were leaving to be with family members who were hurt by the storm. Others were just needin' to keep wages comin' in to provide for their family. I hate to see them go; trained men are so much more valuable to me than greenhorns. When I do get the mill up and running, I'll be delayed as I train the new fellas."

"Well, hopefully we can work together," Mother said. "I'm sure God will provide."

Mr. Perkins picked up his coffee cup. "That's my prayer." He finished the contents and put the cup back down. Getting to his feet, he squared his shoulders. "I don't mind telling you, though, I'm pretty discouraged. I can't figure out why anyone would do a thing like this. I've tried to be a fair employer—always generous with my workers. I didn't figure I had any trouble with them."

Mother stood and Deborah did likewise. "It probably wasn't one of the workers," her mother told him. "A worker wouldn't risk losing his job. I'm confident this must have come from someone outside the company. Perhaps it's even the work of the White Hand of God. After all, you employ former slaves. Someone may be trying to prove a point."

"Yeah, but they're usually good about leavin' notes around after their deeds. This just doesn't add up."

"Let me get your hat for you," Mother said, moving into the foyer.

"I know this is gonna be hard on your family, as well," Mr. Perkins said as they stood by the front door. "I only hope Arjan and G.W. won't have trouble gettin' somebody to take their logs."

Mother smiled. "I'm sure they won't. Especially now with Texans working to rebuild the damaged areas, lumber will be in demand. Don't you fret about us, Zed. We'll be just fine. Please tell Rachel that if she needs anything—anything at all—she only has to call on me."

Deborah and her mother followed him outside and watched from the porch as he mounted and rode away. For a moment, neither said a word. Then Deborah voiced what had been on her mind the entire time.

"What if Stuart had something to do with this?"

Mother's concerned expression seemed to offer an unspoken question. Deborah hurried to explain. "You remember that Jael was certain he meant us harm."

"But why burn down your own investment—especially since it won't really hurt us at all? We'll simply load out the logs and send them elsewhere."

"I don't know," Deborah said, shaking her head. "It just seems like the kind of hateful thing he might do. I know it doesn't make any sense, but I can't help feeling there is something to this that involves him."

"I can't imagine it, but I suppose we shall

know in due time." Mother looked toward the plum trees. "We'd best get the fruit into the kitchen. I don't want to lose any more to the birds."

ჲ

Night fell and it seemed particularly quiet without the men. Deborah and Lizzie put the babies to bed and found their way out to the front room, where Mother and Sissy mended shirts.

"Emmy and Rutger sleeping?" Mother asked as the girls joined them.

"They were quite worn out from their adventurous day," Lizzie told her. "I had them on a blanket in the middle of the floor while I worked on some new clothes for them. They seemed quite captivated with the new location."

Mother smiled and refocused on her work. "Hard to believe they are nearly three months old. Time goes by so quickly when they're small. Seems like just yesterday, Deborah was a baby."

"Shore do," Sissy said, nodding and rocking. Deborah could see that she'd been busy fixing a tear in one of Arjan's shirts.

"It's getting late," Deborah said suppressing a yawn. "I suppose I'll head up to bed."

"We should all get some sleep," Mother

said, tying off her thread. "I've a feeling when the men get back, we'll have a busy day."

Deborah couldn't help thinking it wouldn't be busy as much as troublesome. "I'll see you in the morning."

"Good night, sweetheart." Mother got to her feet. "Come on, Sissy. We need to call it a night. I'll take this lamp, and you get the other."

The black woman put her mending in the basket at her feet and slowly rose. Deborah looked to Lizzie. "If you need help in the night, come get me."

Lizzie nodded. "I should be all right. G.W.'s never that helpful in the wee hours, anyway. He sleeps like a log whether the twins are fussing or cooing."

Mother laughed. "Rutger was the same way. Never did see a man who could sleep through such noise. The whole house could have fallen down around him, and he would have slept on."

Deborah readied for bed and slipped between the sheets, thinking of her father and days gone by. Her father would often take her on rides through the forest. She'd sit in front of him on his favorite horse and listen to him talk about the land.

"Land is good," he told her, *"but family is*

better. God gave us the earth to tend, but our families to love. Never forget that."

"I won't," Deborah whispered to the air. "I won't forget any of the things you taught me, Papa."

An image of Christopher came to mind, and she couldn't seem to push it aside. He was all she wanted in a husband—everything except here and willing. He'd broken the courtship without even speaking to her. That served to anger as much as grieve her. She could never marry a man who refused to listen to her heart on matters.

"Of course, marriage isn't something I need worry about now," she muttered. Deborah snuggled beneath her covers and sighed. "Maybe I'll just always remain a spinster." She imagined herself earning her medical degree and spending the rest of her life alone. It was a daunting thought.

Deborah tossed and turned, unable to find rest. She was about to give up and light a lamp to read by when the dogs began to raise a fuss. She crossed to the window to see what the trouble might be—probably nothing more than an old coon or hog.

By the time she gazed out, the dogs had quieted. *That isn't typical,* she thought. Usually once they were riled, they continued to bark until someone demanded they stop. The blackness below her revealed little, though, and Deborah turned to go back to her bed just as the sound of broken glass came from somewhere on the main floor.

She pulled on her robe and got into her slippers. Making her way down the stairs, she saw that her mother was in the hallway. Lamplight revealed nothing immediately out of place.

"What was that?" Deborah asked.

Mother shook her head. "I don't know."

Sissy and Lizzie were soon at her heel. "Did you hear glass break?" Lizzie asked.

"I heard the dogs raise a ruckus and then the glass," Deborah replied.

Mother went to the door and opened it. She placed the lamp on a table behind the door, then tightened the belt on her robe. Peering outside for a moment, she stepped hesitantly onto the porch. The others followed suit.

"I don't hear anything," she said, turning to Deborah. "Do you?"

Deborah looked around and walked to the end of the porch. "Nothing."

"What's that? Is someone in the barn?" Lizzie questioned. "I see a . . . " She gasped. "Fire!"

Mother turned to follow her gaze. "Deborah, come help me." They rushed across the yard to the open barn door.

Inside, Deborah could see where someone had ignited straw in the corner of the empty front stall. She hurried to where a bucket of water sat. The fire had barely started, and she hoped to douse it before the flames could spread.

Mother followed right behind with a horse blanket. Together, they contained the fire with minimal damage to the area. Lizzie had come to the door with a lantern. With its soft glow, they surveyed the barn. Everything appeared normal.

The smell of burned straw was enough to drive them all back out into the fresh air. Deborah looked at her mother through smoke-blurred eyes. She spoke the words they were all, no doubt, thinking. "Someone means to harm us."

"Someone," Mother replied. "But who?"

Deborah looked around for Jasper and Lula. She called for them, but they didn't come. "You don't suppose they ran off after whoever it was?"

Mother glanced around the yard. "I don't think they would have gone. You know how protective they are—especially at night."

Deborah motioned Lizzie to bring the lamp. "Maybe they're hiding in the barn. Could be they were frightened by the fire." They walked back into the haze and began to search the stalls. Fortunately, Dottie and Dorothy had been turned out to graze in the fenced pen to the north of the house. Since G.W. had taken the remaining horses, the barn was empty of life.

Moving to the far end of the barn, Deborah could see the carriage door was open. She hurried forward and Lizzie followed on her heels.

"Oh no," she moaned and fell to her knees. She touched Jasper's lifeless body. Lula lay just a few feet away, a pitchfork planted through her body. From the pooled blood around their heads, it was clear that someone had slit their throats.

"They killed them," Deborah said, a sob catching in her throat. "Someone has killed them both."

Chapter 27

In the humid dampness of the morning, Deborah wept and dug graves for the family dogs. She had heard the commotion that signaled her brother's return to the homestead, but continued to focus on the task at hand. She wanted to be alone with her grief, but it wasn't to be. In silence, Jake Wythe appeared. To her surprise he said nothing, but came up and took the shovel from her hands and began to make much faster progress.

Deborah carefully wrapped each of the dogs in an old bed sheet and squatted down beside their bodies. She buried her face against her knees and let out all the pent-up pain she held. She'd cried through much of the night and knew she looked a sight, but she didn't care. Someone's heartless ugliness had ripped away another piece of her comfort and security.

It wasn't long before Jake put the shovel aside and came to get the dogs. Deborah tried her best to regain control of her emotions. She stood and watched in silence as the graves were filled first with the bodies of the animals and then dirt. It was only after the burial was complete that Jake turned to look at her.

"I'm sorry we weren't here to stop this, but I promise you I'll find out who's responsible and see they pay."

She shook her head. "I wouldn't want you to get hurt. There's no way of telling who did this—it was dark and we didn't see anyone."

"There are always ways to learn the truth," he told her.

"Why should I expect to learn who killed my dogs, when we can't even figure out who murdered George and David?" Her anger seemed to boil over. "I can't believe how backward this part of the world can be. Folks will probably rise up in arms over the death of two hounds. I can just picture it now: Someone will probably form a posse to hunt the monsters down."

Coming to where she stood, Jake shook his head. "I'm so sorry, Deborah."

The gentle way he spoke her name caused Deborah to calm and dissolve in tears once again. She didn't try to hide her grief from him, nor did she push him away when he took her in his arms. He did nothing untoward; he simply let her cry. Yet despite his tenderness, Deborah wished it was Christopher's arms around her. She couldn't help but remember how she'd held Christopher and let him mourn the sorrow of his family's troubles not so long ago.

And then he left me.

"You'll make yourself sick if you keep goin' on like this," Jake said softly.

Deborah pulled away. "I am sick. Sick at heart. I don't understand why this happened. I cannot comprehend the heart of a man who acts in such a way—to kill people and animals." She wiped at her tears with the back of her sleeve before continuing.

"I don't understand why God has allowed this to happen." She knew she spoke of far more than just the deaths of Jasper and Lula. Why had God allowed her to lose her heart to Christopher and then taken him away from her? Why had the hurricane been allowed to wreak havoc all along the coast? Why had the mill burned down?

"I want answers." She looked at Jake, knowing he would have no solutions. Deborah turned to leave, but Jake took hold of her arm.

"Sometimes we don't get answers," he told her. "Leastwise we don't understand the answers."

Deborah knew his words were true, but they offered no solace. She looked at him hard for a moment, then relaxed. "I know you're right, but it hurts just the same."

She headed back to the house, aware that Jake followed just a few steps behind. Once she reached the back door, she opened it and stood to one side and glanced at the ground. "Thank you for your help with the dogs."

He paused and reached out to lift her chin to meet his gaze. "There ain't nothin' I wouldn't do for you, Miss Deborah. I know you love another, but maybe someday—if that love fades—you'll remember that someone else cares for you, too." He dropped his hand and stepped into the house.

Deborah stared after him for a moment. "That love will never fade, Jake. I have no hope of loving another," she barely whispered, knowing he couldn't hear.

❧

In town, Arjan and Euphanel met with Zed

Perkins at his house. Deborah had come along at her mother's insistence. Euphanel had been firm. She knew her daughter needed to put her attention on something other than her pain.

"You know Mr. Albright and Mr. Longstreet, of course," Zed said as he escorted them into his formal parlor.

Albright and Longstreet got to their feet at the sight of the ladies. They gave a brief bow of greeting but appeared otherwise disinterested. Euphanel thought Mr. Longstreet almost avoided her gaze altogether. Perhaps he was embarrassed now at the forward way he'd acted prior to her marriage to Arjan.

"I'm glad you could be here," Zed began. "I just wanted to make sure we could discuss any concerns or problems that needed to be addressed. Like I told Euphanel last evenin', I know this situation greatly affects Vandermark Logging, since you were under contract to us to provide logs." He motioned them to take their seats, then waited until everyone was settled before continuing. "I've no idea how long before we're able to produce lumber."

"Euphanel says that you're already working to get the mill back up and running," Arjan said. "We'd like to help anyway we can."

Zed nodded. "I appreciate that. I'll be usin'

the logs I have in the millpond to begin the reconstruction. There ain't funds available just yet, but in due time, I hope to be able to receive your logs. I'm positive you'll have no trouble selling your cuttings to another mill in the meanwhile."

"No, I don't imagine so," Arjan replied.

"If I might interrupt," Stuart Albright said, leaning forward in his chair. "Selling to another company is not an option at this time."

Zed's puzzled look suggested he'd not expected this comment. Euphanel could see that Longstreet, however, was not surprised. He simply nodded and stroked his mustache a time or two.

"Then you'll need us to continue delivery?" Arjan questioned.

Albright's face took on a most menacing expression. "No. I have no interest in taking on additional wood at this time."

"Then what are you saying?" Zed asked before Arjan could get the words out.

"I'm saying that you will simply have to stockpile your logs until we decide what is to be done with the mill," Albright replied.

"Stockpile? But there's no reason for that," Zed interjected. "It'll be some time before we can start up production in earnest. They might as well make their livin' elsewhere. They have employees and debts to pay as much as anyone else."

Euphanel saw Stuart give Mr. Longstreet a quick sidelong glance before continuing. "It would seem that you have forgotten the terms of the contract. Let me bring to mind the paragraph that states Vandermark Logging will sell their cut pine logs exclusively to Perkins Sawmill."

"Yes, but that was before the fire," Zed countered. "They can hardly be expected to wait until the mill is once again running before they sell their wood. It could be months."

Mr. Longstreet spoke for the first time. "If not longer."

Euphanel looked to Arjan and then back to Zed. "What is this about?"

Zed shook his head. "I don't rightly know. What are you saying, gentlemen?"

"Simply this," Albright began. "We haven't yet decided if we will rebuild."

"You can't be serious," Arjan interjected. "It would be pure waste not to rebuild."

"Not at all, Mr. Vandermark, and I assure you I am very serious. My partner and I own two-thirds of the mill. There are a great number of debts to be paid, and our debtors will not care that the place lies in charred remains—they will expect their money. We will have to consider the most advantageous plan for seeing our obligations fulfilled."

"Well, surely that includes having the mill up and running. You can hardly make money to pay your debts if the mill sits idle," Deborah said, looking to her mother. "I've read that contract. You are under obligation to us, as well. You have pledged to take a certain number of logs and are required to pay us in a timely manner whether the market suffers or not."

"Ah, but this has nothing to do with the market," Stuart countered. "The mill is unable to manufacture lumber. We have not yet come to terms on the costs or ability to rebuild the mill. Until that decision is agreed upon, Vandermark Logging will be forced to stockpile their logs. I've already checked with a lawyer on this matter—a judge, as well. You may feel free to contact one or both. I can give you the information on how to locate them when we conclude this meeting."

"Just how long before you are able to decide about fixin' up the mill?" Arjan asked.

Euphanel could tell by the tone of his voice that he was barely containing his anger. She started to reach out to take hold of his hand, then thought better of it. Rutger never liked to be touched when he was mad. It was probably the same for his brother.

Albright and Longstreet looked at each other and shrugged before turning back to the others. "It is difficult to say. I intend to thoroughly establish the cause for the fire before rebuilding. You see, there is the matter of insurance coverage. The inspectors will want to take a full account of the situation."

"Insurance?" Zed asked. "But I don't have any fire insurance."

"No, you don't, but Mr. Longstreet and I took out our own policy. We had to protect our interests, you understand."

"So you have insurance that will provide for you to rebuild?" Arjan asked.

Again Stuart shrugged as though he were discussing nothing more important than what would be served for supper. "The insurance inspectors will have to decide that matter. They will be delayed, no doubt, due to the storm. A great many fires have arisen in areas damaged by the hurricane. When the inspectors are able to come to Perkinsville and see for themselves what happened, then and only then can we consider rebuilding."

Arjan leaned back in his chair and crossed his arms. "So you want us to sit and do nothing while you wait for your inspection."

"Not at all, Mr. Vandermark. As I said, I expect for you to stockpile your logs for future use."

"But that means we will have to continue paying wages and keeping men employed, even though we won't be bringing in any money."

Albright looked at his fingernails as if something had magically appeared there. "The day-to-day running of your company is hardly my concern." He lifted his gaze to Deborah. "Wouldn't you agree, Miss Vandermark?"

Euphanel saw her daughter stiffen. Deborah returned the man's gaze without difficulty. She opened her mouth to speak, but Euphanel decided it might serve them better to remain silent. She jumped to her feet and held up her hand.

"I'm sorry, but I must put an end to this meeting. I'm afraid we need to see the constable before heading back to the house. We found ourselves vandalized last evening, and it is important we contact the law officials in order to see if they can figure out who might be responsible." She looked to Deborah, hoping she would remain silent. She did.

Stuart and Mr. Longstreet got to their feet, and with this, the others followed suit. Deborah took hold of Euphanel's arm and gave her a light squeeze as if to reassure her.

Arjan looked to Albright and Longstreet. "I reckon the best thing for me is to have a lawyer of our own look into matters." He turned to Zed. "I'll be in touch. You let me know if you need anything."

Zed seemed overwhelmed by the turn the discussion had taken. "I'm sure sorry about this Arjan—Euphanel. I'll do what I can to get the matter straightened out."

Euphanel reached out with her free hand and patted Zed's arm. "I know you will. You've always been a good friend to my family. I know we can trust you to do what's right."

ꕥ

Once they'd spoken to the constable about the attack on their home, the Vandermarks climbed into the wagon and headed out of town. Deborah was furious with the actions of Stuart Albright.

"He's only doing this to punish G.W. and Lizzie. He's punishing me, as well, because he knows that I encouraged Lizzie to leave him at the altar. I suppose this is really all my fault."

"Nonsense," Arjan said. "Ain't nobody's fault but Mr. Albright's and Mr. Longstreet's.

Zed isn't a part of this. You saw how upset he was."

"Poor man." Mother met Uncle Arjan's gaze. "I feel so bad for him—for Rachel, too. They are going to suffer tremendously from this."

"I should have known Stuart would try something like this," Deborah muttered. "He said he would punish Lizzie, and now he has."

"I suppose we must tell Lizzie and G.W. what's happened. This certainly will be upsetting to them."

"Now, Nell, you can't hardly keep this from 'em. G.W. is handling the books, and Lizzie knows the kind of man Albright is. They may both expect somethin' like this."

Deborah eased back in the leather carriage seat and frowned. "What if Stuart also had something to do with the attack last night?" The question hung in the air for several moments before her mother turned.

"We can't know that for sure. Like Ralph said—if we didn't see anyone, there's little hope of figuring out who was responsible."

"I can't help but think this is all related," Deborah replied. "Stuart hates us and would stop at nothing to see us pay for what he perceives as our wrongdoings."

"But he wasn't even in town until this morning," Mother reminded.

"She's right," Uncle Arjan threw out. "Can't say he did it when he wasn't even here."

"He didn't have to be here to pay others to do his dirty work. Same with the mill."

"Now be careful what you say, little gal," Arjan replied with a glance over his shoulder. "You can't go accusin' a man without proof."

"Why not? Folks around here weren't at all shy about accusing me of inappropriate behavior. They gossiped and told stories each time Christopher and I worked together. They didn't think it was proper for me to be a doctor; then they didn't feel it was proper for us to court if I was going to insist on being a doctor. It's not right that townfolk can accuse me in such a way, then refuse to listen when we know that Stuart only wishes us ill for what happened with G.W. and Lizzie."

Arjan seemed to understand her anger and gave her a sympathetic nod. "I can see what you mean, but Albright and Longstreet would have no reason to burn their own mill down. They're sufferin' in this, too."

"Not if they have insurance," Deborah replied. "The policy is between the two of them. They will make money whether Mr. Perkins does or not. They can easily take their profits from the insurance and never look back."

"Oh, Arjan, you don't suppose she's right?"

Deborah could see her uncle's face darken. "If she is right," he said, fixing his gaze on the road ahead, "then we're dealin' with men of much worse character than I figured."

"I can't speak for Jael's father," Deborah said, shaking her head, "but Stuart is a demanding man who would have forced a woman into marriage purely to keep from losing his inheritance. He's the very kind of man who would cut his nose off to spite his face . . . or burn his mill in order to make us pay."

Chapter 28

Deborah pored over the contract once again. She chided herself for not having been more thorough in her examination. Especially since she was the one to encourage her family to accept it. Had she been less prideful—less focused on what she perceived as her intelligence in business dealings—then perhaps she would have suggested they go to a lawyer.

"This contract is vague enough that I suppose they can manipulate it however they want," Deborah said, pushing away from the desk.

"It's not like we were used to havin' a contract," Arjan said. "I never wanted one in the first place, but Zed needed it for the bank." Her uncle shook his head. "That wood can't sit on the ground forever—it'll rot. Which may be exactly what Albright wants."

Deborah looked at the office door. "Where are G.W. and Lizzie now?"

"They're helping Sissy bring in the laundry," Mother replied. "Why?"

She drew a deep breath. "I think we need to tell them the truth now. Stuart isn't the kind of man who will keep this a secret. I say we call them in here and simply explain the situation for what it is. But it will be hard on Lizzie. She'll blame herself."

"I don't want her to feel responsible," Mother said.

"Then we need to tell 'em the truth, Euphanel."

Deborah was surprised by her uncle's declaration. Mother looked at him oddly and he continued. "If we try to hide it, they're goin' to feel that we were lyin' to them—even if it was to protect them. To my way of thinkin', that would only serve to make them feel it was their fault."

"How so?" Mother asked.

"Well, I'd figure that if I had nothin' to do with it, folks wouldn't be afraid to discuss it with me."

"He's right, Mother. You know that G.W. would rather be dealt with openly."

Mother nodded. "I'll go get them." She

rose slowly and hesitated. "I know that God will give us direction. I'm not going to let Mr. Albright's underhanded actions take my sight from God's faithfulness."

With that, she walked from the office. Deborah looked to her uncle. "She's right, you know." She smiled ever so slightly. "I'm sure the devil uses these kinds of matters to steal our hope. Perhaps we just need to look at this in a different way."

"What do you mean?" her uncle asked.

Deborah picked up the ledger. "First, we need to cut our costs."

"My first suggestion would be to get rid of the workers, but I can't very well produce logs without loggers."

"What if we speak to the employees? If we explain the situation, maybe some sort of arrangement can be made."

"Possibly," Arjan agreed.

Mother returned with G.W. and Lizzie. Their expressions told Deborah that they knew the news wasn't going to be good. Deborah got up from behind the desk and motioned G.W. to take his regular place. She moved quietly to the side of the room and remained standing. Lizzie crossed to stand beside her.

"What is this about?" she whispered.

"Trouble with the business."

Lizzie frowned but said nothing more as Uncle Arjan began. "We called you here to let you know what we learned in the meeting with Mr. Perkins." He paused and seemed to think about what to say next. "Mr. Albright and Mr. Longstreet have returned."

"I should have come with you," G.W. said, looking apprehensive. "I can tell this isn't going to be what I want to hear."

"Well, it's not exactly what any of us wanted, but facts being what they are—it can't be helped. The mill may not rebuild for a time. There was some sort of insurance policy held by Longstreet and Albright, and until the company can come out and assess the details of the fire, apparently nothing can be done."

"So we cease production or find another buyer—is that it?" G.W. asked.

Arjan glanced at Mother and then to Deborah before he answered. "It's not that simple. Apparently our contract requires that we stay in production, and that we can only sell to the Perkinsville mill. Since that mill is temporarily out of operation, we must stockpile our logs."

"For how long?" G.W. asked.

"For as long as it takes them to make a decision," Uncle Arjan answered.

"I don't understand." G.W. fixed his gaze

on Deborah. "There's something you aren't telling us."

"Not at all," Mother said. "That's why you're here. The business arrangements have been complicated not only by the fire, but by the arrival of Mr. Albright and Mr. Longstreet."

He frowned. "What have they got to do with this?"

Deborah took hold of Lizzie's hand. "They now own the majority of the company. They have say over whether the mill gets rebuilt. They have the only insurance on the property and will obviously be the ones who hold the responsibility of paying the debts against the mill."

"And Stuart warned us that he would get back at us," Lizzie murmured.

For a moment, the room went silent. G.W.'s expression changed to one of anger. He looked to his uncle. "This is Albright's idea?"

Arjan nodded. "He says they've had a lawyer look into it—a judge, too. They can force us to continue working in order to have the log quota available if and when they need them. We can't sell to anyone else."

"That's hardly fair," Lizzie said, shaking her head. "If they can't take the logs, then they are breaking their part of the contract."

"That's what I presumed," Deborah declared, "but apparently the wording leaves it open to question."

"We can't keep paying our workers if we aren't getting paid," G.W. said. "How are we supposed to run a business if we don't have money coming in?"

Lizzie was growing more upset by the minute. Deborah turned to her sister-in-law and smiled. "We have some ideas. Why don't you go sit beside Mother?"

Lizzie hesitated only a moment, then did exactly as Deborah suggested. Mother took hold of her hand and patted it reassuringly. "Please don't fret."

"This is outrageous. I'm gonna go give Albright a piece of my mind," G.W. said, getting to his feet.

Deborah stepped forward. "Not until you hear me out."

Everyone looked at her in surprise. Deborah looked to Uncle Arjan, who nodded.

Reluctantly, G.W. took his seat. "All right. Get to it."

"Look, we know that Stuart Albright holds this family a grudge." She gave careful thought to her words. "But that problem won't help us accomplish what we need to do. God will avenge any wrongs done to us, and we need to look to Him to direct our steps."

"Deborah's right," Arjan said. "We've started thinkin' of some ways to handle the situation. First, I think we can all agree that we need to hold on to as much of our money as possible."

"That will mean letting our workers go," G.W. said. "How are we supposed to produce without workers?"

"We talked briefly about that," Deborah said, hoping her words wouldn't make G.W. feel they had planned things out behind his back. "That's why we needed you here. What if we ask the men to work mainly for room and board with the promise that we will pay them in full within a certain time?"

"How can we be sure to meet that time frame?" G.W. asked.

Deborah gave a slight shrug. "The question of the mill can't remain unanswered forever. We can get our own lawyer to help us."

"That's gonna take money we don't have to spare." G.W. practically growled the words.

"My father!" Lizzie declared. "Father would help us with the contract issues, and he wouldn't expect pay. He said when he left that if there was anything at all he could do to help, he would, because it would give him a good excuse to come see us." She fixed her husband with a smile. "He hasn't yet seen the twins."

"That's true," G.W. said, sounding a little more hopeful.

"We can also step up the turpentine production. They've been after us for months to give them more trees," Arjan said. "I think if we double their acreage, we can meet our loan payments and have a little money left for other needs—maybe even a bit of pay for the men."

"But the best of the summer is over and spring is months away." G.W. shook his head. "They can do the fall and winter scraping, but I don't know if it will do us much good."

"All we can do is try," Arjan declared. "We can speak to the turpentiners and get their opinion on the matter. Let's call the boys in and have a meeting here at the house tomorrow. It'll be Saturday, and we can give those who stay the rest of the day off and reconcile with those who want to go."

"I think that's a good idea," Mother said. "Will you go and bring them in?"

Arjan nodded. "I will. That way I can secure the camp before I head back."

G.W. reached for the ledger. "I'll see if I can find ways to save us more money."

Deborah went to his side. "I'll help you. If we put our heads together, we can come up with something that will help."

ꕥ

The loggers listened as Arjan detailed the problems at hand. Mother and Sissy had put together a magnificent dinner, and now everyone remained at the table, trying to figure out their futures.

"Look, I know some of you have families, so stayin' on with us probably isn't possible. There will be no hard feelings if you have to quit. The rest of you will have a place to sleep and three meals a day. We'll see to your injuries and keep a detailed record of the pay owed you.

"If possible, we'll have a little money each week for you. It might only be script, but it will be something. We won't work to exceed our planned production, either. We'll just do what's necessary and nothing more. We've been performing at the level designated by Mr. Perkins for when the mill expansion was complete. As G.W. pointed out to me, we can cut production down to what was required for this phase."

"Mr. Vandermark?"

"Yes, Jake?"

Jake pushed back his chair a bit. "I have what may sound like a strange question, but I hope you'll hear me out."

Arjan raised a brow. "All right."

"Well, I'm just wonderin'—Vandermark Loggin' owns a lot of land that's already been harvested. Now, I know you have young trees growin' as replacements, but that will be some time—if ever—before they're ready to cut."

"Go on," Arjan encouraged.

"Is there any chance you might consider sellin' off some of that land for farmin' and ranchin'? I, for one, wouldn't mind takin' some of my pay in acreage."

G.W. got to his feet, and Deborah was afraid for a moment that he would be wholly against the idea. "That's something we overlooked," he said, quite enthused. "I think it would be a great idea. We could sell or trade off pieces of the unproductive acres and bank the money for our future needs, as well as maybe trade some acreage for wages."

"Who of you here would be of a mind to take acreage?" Arjan asked.

"I wouldn't be able to live without some money," Warren replied, "but I'd sure be interested. I always wanted to have a few acres—nothin' big."

"It wouldn't be large pieces," G.W. countered. "Probably more like ten- or twenty-acre parcels, at the most."

"I like the sound of that," Warren said, looking to Jake. "That was a good suggestion, whistle punk. You'll be fellin' trees before you know it."

"We will continue to work out the details of how we can make this situation work," Arjan continued, "and let you fellas know what's expected. However, if you need to quit us, I'd like for you to come talk to me in the office."

He sat down and motioned to Mother. "Now, if you don't mind, I'll have another slice of pie."

Chapter 29

October 1886

With October's arrival came the devastating news that Deborah had feared. Indianola, Texas, had not only suffered the brunt of the hurricane's forces, but it had been, for all purposes, destroyed. First, the storm itself had sent tidal floods and heavy winds. The newspaper account Uncle Arjan brought her reported that many people had tried to gather in the Signal Station, which was thought to be the strongest of buildings. However, as the water rose, the building began to rock. People, fearing for their lives, abandoned the place and hurried in the rising water to find shelter. The Signal Officer, a

Mr. Reed, was charting the weather changes and remained behind to set the anemometer. The act proved to be fatal. A signal lamp set fire to the building and burned not only him, but an unidentified doctor. The fire didn't kill them, however. They drowned as the water swept through the town and engulfed everything.

Deborah felt numb as she lowered the paper to her lap. Her mother and uncle sat beside her, waiting for her to say something. She looked at them, shaking her head. No words would come. Surely the unidentified doctor wasn't Christopher.

"We heard the news in town," her mother began. "Then I read it for myself in the paper. They say that over twenty-five people were lost in the Indianola area. Victoria sustained incredible damage, as well. We came home as quickly as we could to give you the news."

"But that doesn't mean the doc was there," her uncle began. "It could be he was able to get out of Indianola before the storm hit."

"And go where?" Deborah murmured. She looked at them both. "I need to be alone." She got to her feet, the paper fluttering to the floor of the porch.

Without another word, she walked deep into the woods that she had always loved, her place of refuge. Even as a young girl she had come here to pray and seek God's comfort when things were difficult. But there was no comfort to be had today. She could hardly form words of prayer.

"Oh, God," she prayed, "Oh, God, please . . . please let Christopher be all right. I cannot bear the thought that he might be dead."

Speaking the words aloud seemed to drain her of any pretense of strength. Deborah fell to her knees sobbing. "I cannot bear this, Lord. It's too much." She buried her face in her hands. All of her life, she had relied upon her intelligence to reason away complications and sorrows. She'd always found a way to make sense of things, in some capacity or another. To find some measure of solace.

But there was no solace to be had in this.

She remained on the damp forest ground for a long while. Easing back against one of the longleaf pines, she pulled her knees to her chest and hugged them close. She felt empty inside. Maybe this was a sign that Christopher truly was dead.

Deborah couldn't get the words "unidentified doctor" out of her head. Surely, if the newspaper reporter had been able to learn the identity of the signal officer, the townsfolk could have told him the name of the doctor, as well. Unless, of course, that doctor had arrived in town only the week before.

A gentle breeze filtered through the trees and touched her damp face. Deborah lifted her gaze skyward, watching the gentle sway of the pines. Their lofty branches made a green canopy, allowing just enough light through to cast streams of illumination here and there.

"Are you with me, Father? I feel so alone." A rustling in the brush nearby caused Deborah to take note, but she didn't move.

A feral sow with her piglets came onto the path. The hog froze in step and stared at her as if trying to ascertain the threat. Deborah did nothing but return the stare. If the tusked animal charged her, Deborah would most likely suffer a fatal injury. Maybe that would be God's mercy. Maybe Christopher was dead, and God knew the pain would be too much for her to endure. The hog snorted and the piglets came running to her side.

Deborah closed her eyes as if accepting her fate. There was no need to be afraid or to prepare for a fight for which she had no strength. If this truly was to be the end of her life, she wanted to face it without fear. She drew a deep breath.

I give my life to you, God. I have nothing left—no strength of my own.

When she opened her eyes again, the sow had moved on. Deborah could only see the hind ends of the piglets as they headed deeper into the woods with their mother. There was neither relief nor regret in the moment. It simply was as it was—nothing more, nothing less.

Deborah got to her feet and began to walk once again. She pushed into the heavier stand of pines, into areas where the trails narrowed and the brush had not been burned away. The drought had kept them from doing all of their normal winter burns the year before and only minimal work had been accomplished. This left them with a higher threat of fire, but the longleafs were strong. Fire actually stimulated their growth, so long as the temperatures of the flames weren't too intense.

If I were a longleaf pine, Deborah thought, *I could surely withstand this fire.*

But even the pines would be reduced to stubble if the fire burned hot enough. There was always a point at which any living thing could be killed.

She knew she should be aware of her surroundings—snakes and other Piney Woods rooters could harm her. Deborah tried to focus on the ground and the path ahead, but her mind imagined horrific scenes—collapsed, burned rubble and flooded streets. Images of the dead laid out side by side, waiting in their eternal rest for someone to take them home.

Tears anew blurred her eyes. *I feel no hope. No hope.*

The words seemed to pace themselves to the beat of her steps. *No hope. No hope. No hope.* Despair poured over Deborah, leaving her breathless. She spied a stand of trees where the forest grass was not too deep and moved across the opening. Without being mindful of the ground, she collapsed and closed her eyes.

No hope. Oh, God, do not leave me without hope.

ಬಂ

Deborah awoke some hours later. She had no idea of the time, but the light was greatly diminished and an uneasy silence hung over the woods. Getting to her feet, Deborah brushed off pine needles and dried grass.

For a moment, she couldn't remember why she'd come here, and then the memories came rushing back. Christopher might be lost to her forever. He might be dead or injured . . . or if he was alive, not even care that she suffered.

No, surely he could never be that cruel. Not the Christopher she knew.

Deborah looked around to get her bearings, then spied the path that would lead back to the house. Her mother would be worried by now. They might even be looking for her. Deborah had never intended to be gone for so long. Despite her sorrow and confusion, she didn't want to add to her family's worries.

She lifted her skirt to avoid tripping over it as she maneuvered through an area of fallen branches. Once back on the path, Deborah let out a long sigh. "I feel so weak now, but maybe that's the point," she murmured. As a human being—especially a woman—her strength was quite limited. These were the times, she could very nearly hear her mother say, when God's strength was sufficient to carry her through.

"But how, when I don't know what to do? How foolish to think myself so full of wisdom and knowledge that I would never make the same mistakes—endure the same hardships—that others might face."

Perhaps the best thing to do would be to go back East and live with Aunt Wilhelmina. It would be getting cold up north, but she could be there before the first snows set in. Aunt Wilhelmina would happily welcome her back—she had said as much on many occasions. Perhaps her aunt could also help Deborah find a doctor who might be willing to train her. Philadelphia was a very progressive town. Surely there were equally progressive physicians.

The robust scent of the earth and pine wafted on the air, reminding Deborah of how much she loved this area. It wouldn't be easy to leave again. It wouldn't be easy to say goodbye to her family.

"And this time I won't have Lizzie and Jael with me in Philadelphia." The thought momentarily gave her pause. Could she live happily without her friends and family? Aunt Wilhelmina was a dear, to be sure, but she was aging and quite self-focused. She had spent much of her life on her own, after being widowed at a young age. Because her husband had left her a small fortune, her aunt had lived quite comfortably, doing exactly what pleased her. She had no children, offering instead her love and kindness to her sisters' children. That was how Deborah had come to benefit and, hopefully, would be blessed again.

If I return to Philadelphia and offer to work, she will, no doubt, tell me it isn't necessary. However, if I work, I can afford to send money back to Mother and Uncle Arjan.

She frowned. Mother would never allow for her to tell Aunt Wilhelmina of their problems. Money issues were simply not spoken of in such a manner. It was one thing for an aunt to offer her riches to spoil a much-beloved niece, but entirely another for that niece to bring the intimate details of the family's struggles to her aunt's attention.

Staring ahead as the trail widened once again to the main road, Deborah felt defeat threatening her meager plans. Her mother would want to keep her from leaving—G.W. and Uncle Arjan, too. Lizzie would never understand and would certainly beg her to stay. And then there were the twins. They were so precious, and Deborah couldn't imagine living so far away. "If I can't convince myself—how can I hope to convince my family?"

The light was fading fast. Quickening her pace, Deborah put aside her concerns. She would figure out the details of her trip and what she would tell her aunt after she announced the matter to her family. She needed for them to believe that this was something she was doing out of a desire to complete her medical training. And in truth, that was part of her reasoning. They didn't need to know that she also wanted to go to escape her memories and relieve the burden of an extra mouth to feed.

But what of Christopher? How could she ever know for sure what had happened to him? Could she perhaps write to his mother in Kansas City? Did Mr. Perkins have the address there? She would check with him tomorrow—or better still, she'd go to the doctor's office and look through Christopher's papers. Having a plan in mind gave her a moment of courage.

As the house came in sight, Deborah wasn't surprised to see her mother standing on the porch with a lantern in hand.

"I'm here," Deborah called as she stepped into the clearing. "I'm all right."

"Oh, Deborah. I was so worried. We all were. Where have you been?" Mother declared, putting the lantern on the post. She hurried down the steps.

"I am sorry. The news about Indianola was just so overwhelming," she admitted. "I tried to pray and I guess I fell asleep."

"Oh, child, did you not think of the dangers?" Mother embraced her, and for a moment Deborah found comfort there. It was easy to imagine she was a child again—safe and secure. Her father would round the corner of the house any moment to announce that it was time for supper and evening devotions.

She pulled back, fighting tears. "I never meant to grieve you," Deborah told her mother.

"I know, just as I never wanted to grieve you with the news from Indianola. I realize you're very worried for Dr. Clayton. We mustn't give up hope, however."

Deborah shook her head. "I've searched deep inside myself and found that place empty."

"Oh, darling, your hope doesn't come from within—not in the sense of self, anyway. It comes from God alone. If not, then it will crumble and blow as dust to the wind. You have only to fix your sights on Jesus. Remember the words of the psalmist.: 'Why art thou cast down, O my soul? and why art thou disquieted in me? Hope thou in God: for I shall yet praise him for the help of his countenance.' You will find your strength in Him, Deborah."

She nodded, knowing her mother's words were true. "It just seems that He is so far away."

Her mother cupped Deborah's chin. "He isn't. He promised He'd never leave you. Perhaps you are simply afraid to trust—afraid to hope."

Deborah nodded. "Does that make me an

awful person? I love God with all my heart, but I feel so weak—so tired."

"You aren't awful at all," Mother said, smiling. "Everyone is afraid at one time or another. If not afraid, then perhaps nagged with doubt. But God will take away your fear and doubt. When you look for Him, you will find Him there waiting, as He has always been."

"And I can count on Him to direct my path," she murmured.

"Of course," her mother said. "The Bible even tells us we can make our plans, but that we need to put our faith in God to direct our ways. You have trusted Him far too long to let doubt control your heart."

Her mother was right, but God still seemed distant—not really gone, just standing afar. Maybe He was just waiting for Deborah to catch up or ask for help—like Father used to do when they would go for walks and she would tire. If the trek was too exhausting, she would beg her father to come and carry her. He always did. She wondered if her heavenly Father would carry her now.

"I've been thinking I'd like to complete my medical training. I want to go back East to live with Aunt Wilhelmina and attend classes. I've saved some money and can purchase my own train ticket."

"Oh, Deborah . . . please don't go. I missed you so much when you were gone before."

"But it would be a good thing, and when I complete my studies, I could come back here or to Lufkin. I wouldn't live far away. I love this land. I am at home here."

"Then why leave it?"

In the muted light of the lantern, Deborah could see her mother's worried expression. This wasn't how she'd wanted things to go. "We can talk about this later. I'm starved. Can I help with supper?"

"It's all ready, but we delayed eating to wait for you; we figured to send out the men soon to look for you. Everyone will be so glad to see you've returned."

Making their way up the steps, Mother put her arm around Deborah's shoulders. "I'll be praying God will give you peace and help you through this difficult time. I love you, and I only want the best for you. He wants the best for you, too. Never forget that."

They joined the others in the house. Most of the men were assembled in the front room and Uncle Arjan seemed to be instructing them.

"She's back!" G.W. said, leaping to his feet. He hardly limped at all as he crossed the room to take hold of her. "Where have you been? We've been worried about you."

"I . . . fell asleep."

"What were you thinking?" G.W.'s tone was quite stern.

"I obviously wasn't keeping a clear mind," Deborah said. "Now stop fretting, big brother. I'm fine." She forced herself to take strength in the moment. So long as she put her mind on the worry she'd caused others, perhaps she could keep her own concerns at bay.

"Oh, Deborah!" Lizzie exclaimed, coming into the room.

Turning just as Lizzie embraced her, Deborah felt guilt drive away her fears for Christopher. "I'm so sorry to have worried all of you." She hugged Lizzie and pulled away to face the others. "Please forgive me."

"We're just glad you're unharmed," Uncle Arjan said. His smile assured her that all was forgiven.

"Let's go eat," Mother said, putting her arm around Lizzie. "If I recall, Sissy has made us a wonderful dessert. She wouldn't tell me what it was, but said it was something new and quite delicious. But first, we must get through the main meal."

"That won't be a problem, Miz Vandermark," Warren declared. Several of the other loggers agreed and followed her and Lizzie toward the dining room.

Arjan gave G.W. a slap on the shoulder

and grinned. "Maybe we should harness that little sister of yours. That might keep her out of trouble." He winked at Deborah.

Deborah heard someone laugh from behind her and turned to find Jake. "So you think this is funny?" She narrowed her eyes and feigned anger. "I'm going to tell Sissy not to give you any dessert."

"You wouldn't," he said, grinning impishly. "I thought I was your favorite punk."

She rolled her eyes. "I have no favorites."

"Well, that's not . . . " Jake's eyes widened and the words seemed to stick in his throat. Deborah thought he looked as if he'd seen a ghost.

"What's wrong with you?" she asked.

Deborah heard her uncle give a whistle. She couldn't imagine what had stirred such a reaction. Whirling on her heel, she felt as if the wind had been knocked from her. Standing in the doorway was Christopher.

"Deborah." He spoke her name like a prayer.

It was all Deborah heard. The room closed in and went dark as she felt strong arms wrap around her from behind. After that she knew nothing more.

Jake lifted the unconscious Deborah in

his arms and shook his head at the man who rushed forward. "I've got her."

The doctor's gaze narrowed. "Not if I have anything to say about it."

Arjan stepped between them and took Deborah from Jake's arms. Jake immediately missed the scent of her hair and the softness of her in his arms. He stepped back, but his gaze never left Dr. Clayton's face. There was an unspoken challenge between them, but Jake had a feeling that wasn't enough. Deborah thought she was in love with this man, but Jake had a plan to change all of that.

He couldn't let the doc just come back from the dead and steal the woman he planned to marry.

Chapter 30

Deborah opened her eyes to find Christopher sitting beside her. He looked pounds thinner and far more careworn. Was that a scar along his left eye? She shook her head, not quite trusting her eyes. Reaching up, she touched his beard-stubbled face.

"Are you really here?"

"Yes." He pulled her up into his arms and crushed her against him.

Deborah could scarcely draw a breath, but she didn't care. She clung to Christopher as if he were the only thing that would save her from certain death. There were no words—no other thoughts. They were the only two people in the universe, and this moment was all they had.

She didn't want him to ever let go of her.

If this were merely a dream, Deborah never wanted to wake up. The warmth of his embrace left little doubt that it was all real. Christopher had returned to her.

Reluctantly, Deborah pulled away to look deeply into Christopher's eyes. "I thought you were dead."

"I very nearly was," he replied. He touched her cheek and trailed his finger along her jaw.

Tears formed in her eyes, blurring her vision. Deborah closed her eyes and felt the tears trail down her cheeks.

"Don't cry, sweetheart. It's all over—it's behind us."

She opened her eyes. "When you left, I understood that your brother needed you. But I needed you, too, and I didn't understand how you could so easily cast me aside."

"There was nothing easy in leaving you. You were all I could think of—even at the worst of the storm. I wanted only to live in order to get back to you. I will always love you." He lowered his mouth to hers and kissed her gently.

Deborah wanted the moment to go on forever. She didn't care about the propriety of the situation or that she was sitting on her mother's bed, embracing the man she loved. None of that mattered.

He took hold of her face as he pulled away. "I thought so often of doing that."

"Where have you been?" she asked in a whisper. "Why didn't you let me know you were all right?"

"I wanted to, believe me. I was hurt for a time—my brother, too. They took me south to Corpus, and I couldn't send word to you."

"I read just today that the signal man in Indianola died. He drowned with an unidentified doctor. I was so afraid it was you. I didn't even want to go on living."

"I'm so sorry. I came as soon as I could." He smoothed back her hair. "My brother was much worse off than I was. After I started to heal, I worked to help him. Calvin gradually recovered."

"Were there many injuries?" she asked. "Were you in Indianola when the storm hit?"

He nodded. "Yes to both questions. We had no real warning. We knew a storm was moving in, but some of the old-timers didn't think it would be all that bad. They mostly sat around, telling stories of the hurricane that had wreaked havoc in the seventies. We had figured to leave, but the sheriff told me it wasn't a good idea to try and travel with a hurricane bearing down, so we decided to take shelter and wait it out."

"I read about the floodwaters and the fire."

"The water came in so quickly—it was like nothing I'd ever seen before. The winds were so fierce, you couldn't hear the words of the person standing next to you." He shook his head. "Then the fire spread, destroying everything it touched. We were forced from the building. Into the flooded streets. Into the heart of the storm." He shuddered.

Deborah hugged him close. "I'm so very sorry."

"I nearly lost my hold on Calvin," he continued as if he hadn't heard her. Deborah released him while he went on. "We were being swept into a fierce current. It had a terrible pull that we tried hard to fight. I managed to get hold of a post of some sort. I held fast to it and to Calvin while the water kept rising. It was a nightmare."

"But you're safe now," she said, gently stroking his arm. "You're safe."

He looked at her blankly for a moment, then drew a deep breath. "I'm here with you. I should never have gone."

"Your brother needed you. I understood."

"I'm sorry that I handled things so badly." He hung his head. "There have been far too many secrets between us, and I have to be honest with you now. It might cost me—it might take you from me—but I cannot lie to you anymore."

"I have my secrets, too," she replied. "You may well not want me after you hear them."

He looked at her in disbelief. "There is nothing you could say that would ever make that possible."

She cocked her head slightly and smiled for the first time since she'd awakened. "And yet you think it possible for me to stop wanting you?"

This made him drop his hold and lower his head. "You don't know the truth of my past. It's not something I've borne very well."

Deborah took hold of his hands. "Let me bear it with you, then. Start with your brother. You said he was injured, but you didn't speak of the charges against him. What was the outcome of his trial?"

"He was acquitted. A witness came forward and defended Calvin's actions. He made it clear my brother had no choice in the matter. It was kill or be killed."

"And where is Calvin now?"

"I sent him back to Kansas City," Christopher replied matter-of-factly, pulling his hands from hers. "He had a broken wrist and badly injured leg. Even so, he's promised to seek employment and help our mother. He seems to be a changed man."

"Perhaps this ordeal opened his eyes."

Christopher lifted his gaze. "Perhaps. I suppose only time will tell."

"And what else must I know?" she asked.

He drew a deep breath. "My name."

"But I already know that."

He shook his head. "No. You know what I changed it to."

She looked at him oddly. She had imagined that he would tell her his mother had been married before—that he didn't share the same father as his brothers and sisters. "What are you saying?"

"I wasn't born with the last name of Clayton. It's actually my middle name. My mother named me Christopher Clayton . . . Kelleher. I dropped the Kelleher to keep people from realizing that I am Irish."

Confusion swirled through her thoughts. "But why?"

"Why? Because the Irish are hated in many places. My father and mother worked hard to disassociate themselves from the prejudices and conflicts, but it followed them no matter where they went. The accident that nearly took my father's life was a fight between the Irish workers and the non-Irish. The attitudes and actions against those of Irish ancestry were not so different as what we've seen here in the South with the blacks."

"I'm truly sorry, Christopher. I had no idea."

"When I went east to study medicine, I decided that I would go by Clayton. That was still my name, and it could be associated with the English if questions arose. After all, I also shared some English ancestry."

"And did it work?" she asked.

"It did. I felt like a liar, but it worked. I never figured it would matter much in the long run. I didn't have an Irish brogue, so I believed I could forever bury the truth. I told my mother and siblings that I was going to call myself Christopher Clayton and that any correspondence should be addressed accordingly. My father was livid. He disowned me and told me to never again darken his doorstep. Then he was injured in the fight that killed some of his friends. It killed his spirit and left him without hope."

She reached up to touch his face. "I don't care if you're Irish or Indian or anything else. I love you. I never knew how dearly until you left me."

Deborah's mother came into the room with a basin. "How is she?"

Christopher eased away from Deborah. "She's much better. I shouldn't have shocked her with my return that way."

"Do you feel up to some supper, Deborah?"

Mother put the basin on the dresser. "If not, I could bring you something here."

"I can come to the table. In fact, I feel quite well—almost as if the world has suddenly righted itself." She paused and looked past Christopher to where her mother stood. "Mother, how do you feel about Irish people?"

"Irish? Why do you ask a question like that? The Irish are fine folks. We've had dear friends who were Irish."

Deborah grinned. "It's not important right now. I just wondered."

ꕥ

The special dessert turned out to be a most amazing chocolate cake that Sissy said was made entirely without flour or cornmeal. The cake was then drenched in a buttery brown sugar sauce and topped with whipped cream. There wasn't so much as a crumb left after everyone pushed back from the table.

"That was a mighty fine meal," Uncle Arjan said, giving Sissy a nod. "Especially that cake. Mighty fine."

Sissy laughed and got to her feet. "I's glad you enjoyed it. Much more pickin' at the plate, and I won't even have to wash it."

Mother began gathering the dishes, and Deborah started to do likewise. "Oh no," she told Deborah. "You go spend time with Dr. Clayton."

"Thank you very much for having me to supper," Christopher replied. "And thank you for freeing Deborah from her chores." He turned and smiled at her. "Would you care to take a walk?"

"It's already dark and gettin' a bit chilled out there," Uncle Arjan declared. "Maybe you'd prefer to sit on the porch? I'm sure we can find something to do elsewhere—can't we, boys?"

The rest of the men chuckled and got up from the table. All but Jake. He didn't seem at all happy about this new arrangement. Deborah allowed Christopher to help her from her chair while the others shuffled out of the room.

Deborah looked to Christopher and smiled. "Let me get my wrap."

They made their way to the front porch swing. Deborah enjoyed Christopher's arm around her and leaned closer.

"When I thought I might never see you again," he said, "I came to realize how important you were to me. I had always dreamed of the kind of woman who could share my life—my desire to help people. When I came here and met you, it seemed that you fulfilled all of my hopes for a wife. I didn't ask you to court me without giving it great consideration."

Deborah straightened and looked at him. "And I didn't accept without great consideration."

He laughed. "You said yes before the words were hardly out of my mouth."

"That's not true, Christopher Clayton Kelleher." She stopped and smiled. "I like the sound of that. Anyway, you are completely mistaken. As I recall, we discussed your family and your age before I ever agreed to court you. Oh, and we talked about your willingness to marry a female doctor."

He shrugged. "I'm still pondering that one."

She elbowed him and got to her feet. "Well, I suppose you can ponder that alone, because I plan to go back East and finish my medical training." She gave him a coy smile. "Unless, of course, you know some other way to remedy the matter."

"I might have some ideas," he said in a low, husky voice.

His tone caused Deborah to feel weak in the knees. Goodness, but this man could set her all a-flutter. He held out his hand, and she again sat beside him.

"The past doesn't matter," she said, looking into his eyes. "I'd much rather think about where we go from here."

"Where would you like to go?"

She smiled. "Well, I'd like our courtship to be reinstated, for one."

He shook his head. "I've no interest in that." He took hold of her hand. "I'd rather we begin our engagement."

Deborah felt her breath catch. Had he really just proposed? "Say that again," she whispered.

He smiled. "Would you marry me, Miss Vandermark?"

"I know you two wanted some privacy," Jake Wythe said, coming up the porch steps, "but I figure this is important enough to interrupt."

Frustrated, Deborah pulled back from Christopher's hold. "What is it, Jake?"

"I heard the doc propose to you."

"What business is that of yours?" Christopher asked.

"I want to propose, as well."

Deborah looked at him in surprise. "I beg your pardon?"

Jake smiled. "You heard me. I want to marry you, Miss Deborah. I know you care for me—maybe not exactly the same way you do the doc, but I figure we deserve a chance to explore your feelings for me before you go runnin' off to marry him."

"I think you've misjudged me, Jake. I do

care about you, but . . ." She fell silent, unsure of what to say. She could feel Christopher tense. The last thing she wanted was a fight.

"Doc left you, without even speakin' to ya face-to-face. Just because he finally figured out what he wants doesn't mean you should just fall into his lap. He was unkind to you, and you deserve better."

Deborah got to her feet and Christopher was quick to follow. "He had his reasons for leaving me," she said, putting herself between the two men. "I don't need to explain them to you. I've never led you on or given you reason to think that I held more affection for you than I do. Please don't ruin this happy occasion for me."

Jake's expression fell. "I don't want you to ever be unhappy. Especially not on account of me."

"I'm sorry to hurt you, but I cannot accept your proposal. I've already accepted Christopher's. I accepted the night he asked me to court him. He held my heart then—just as he does now."

The younger man's shoulders slumped, and he shook his head. "Ain't hardly fair. I just figure out that I'm in love with you, and you go and agree to marry someone else. You ought to at least give me a chance."

Deborah felt saddened by the obvious pain

she'd inflicted. She wanted to tell Jake she thought some young woman would be lucky to have him as a husband, but she knew it wouldn't ease his hurt.

She was grateful that Christopher remained silent. "I'm sorry, Jake. I'm going to marry Christopher." Her statement was firm, yet she tried hard to keep the timbre of her voice gentle.

"I reckon I can't change your mind right now," Jake said, lifting his head. "But that don't mean I can't try to change it between now and the weddin'."

Christopher put his hands on Deborah's arms in a most possessive manner. "I believe you've out-stayed your welcome, Mr. Wythe. The lady has made it quite clear what her intentions are."

Jake fixed his gaze on Christopher for a moment, then returned it to Deborah. "I guess only time will tell that for certain."

He walked back down the porch steps and disappeared around the corner of the house. Fearing that Christopher would want to follow him and teach him a lesson or two, Deborah decided to distract him the only way she knew how. Turning in his arms, she smiled.

"Now, where were we? Oh yes—you had proposed marriage. I accept. Now I think it would be quite appropriate for us to share a kiss."

Christopher's anger seemed to fade. He pulled her close. "I think I can manage that."

She grinned. "Indeed, I believe you can."

His lips on hers left her heart aglow in a blaze of passion and the promise of what tomorrow would yet bring.

Turn the page to enjoy
some of Tracie's family recipes,
featured in this book!

Lemon Cornmeal Cake

1 cup yellow cornmeal
1 ¾ cups sugar
2 cups all-purpose flour
 (can substitute Splenda)
2 teaspoons baking powder
1 Tablespoon grated lemon zest
½ teaspoon baking soda
¼ cup lemon juice
¼ teaspoon salt
4 eggs
1 cup butter, softened
1 cup buttermilk

Glaze
1 cup sugar
 (can substitute Splenda)
⅓ cup lemon juice

Heat oven to 325°F. Grease and flour a 9 x 13 or Bundt cake pan.

Sift together flour, cornmeal, baking powder, soda, and salt. Set aside. In a separate bowl, beat butter and sugar until creamy. Add lemon zest and juice mix. Beat four eggs together, then add to mixture. Blend in flour mixture and buttermilk until batter is smooth. Pour into pan. Bake 1 hour.

For glaze, mix sugar and lemon juice and brush onto warm cake. Let cool and serve.

Rhubarb Cobbler

Filling

1 ½ cups sugar
1 ½ cups water
½ teaspoon cinnamon
2 Tablespoons butter
4 cups rhubarb, chopped

Topping

1 cup flour
¼ cup butter
½ cup sugar
6 Tablespoons milk
1 ½ teaspoons baking powder
⅓ cup chopped pecans
¼ teaspoon salt

In a saucepan combine 1½ cups sugar and cinnamon. Add rhubarb and water. Cook and stir until mixture boils; reduce heat and cook 5 minutes. Stir in 2 Tbsp. butter. Pour into a greased baking dish.

For topping, mix flour, ½ cup sugar, baking powder, and salt. Cut in ¼ cup butter; stir in milk and pecans. Spoon dollops onto hot filling.

Bake at 400 degrees for 25–30 min.